"YOU'RE BEAUTIFUL, CAMILLE. SO BEAUTIFUL, YOU MAKE ME ACHE."

Alex spoke in a low tone, kissing her softly. Against the curve of her lips, his murmur filled her ears. "But if I don't do this"—he began to slip a button back into place—"you'll have to fire me. And then I'll miss your telling me I stink as a ballplayer." Then he slowly put the front of her dress back together while she sat in stunned silence.

When she was in order, he kissed her once more. Just a peck that said he was sorry, or so he hoped she'd take it. Damn but if her eyes didn't begin to moisten.

He didn't carry a handkerchief, so he grabbed an embroidered white napkin from the counter. She took it. "I think you're all cried out for tonight, honey. But for what it's worth, if I were that Lady Prussia woman, I would have voted for you."

She dabbed the corners of her eyes with the tea towel, its edge colorfully embroidered with songbirds. "Lady Prussia is a white cake."

"Yeah, well." He meant to brush the comment off, but then he paused and said, "It is?"

"Yes." Then out of left field, she asked, "Would you like a piece?"

Alex stood motionless, Camille still sitting on the counter in front of him, her hair a river of gold about her shoulders. His chest hurt as if he'd been slugged in the ribs. *Would he like a piece?*

He reached up and caught her beneath her arms and lowered her gently onto her feet. "Sure."

Books by Stef Ann Holm

Honey
Hooked
Harmony
Forget Me Not
Portraits
Crossings
Weeping Angel
Snowbird
King of the Pirates
Liberty Rose
Seasons of Gold

Published by POCKET BOOKS

STEF ANN HOLM

Honey

SONNET BOOKS

New York London Toronto Sydney Singapore

This book is a work of fiction. Names, characters, places and incidents
are products of the author's imagination or are used fictitiously. Any
resemblance to actual events or locales or persons, living or dead, is
entirely coincidental.

An *Original* Publication of POCKET BOOKS

A Sonnet Book published by
POCKET BOOKS, a division of Simon & Schuster Inc.
1230 Avenue of the Americas, New York, NY 10020

Copyright © 2000 by Stef Ann Holm

ISBN: 0-671-01942-2

First Sonnet Books printing February 2000

10   9   8   7   6   5   4   3   2   1

SONNET BOOKS and colophon are registered trademarks of
Simon & Schuster Inc.

Cover photo © Robert Holmes/Corbis

Printed in the U.S.A.

To Caroline Tolley, an editor I've had the pleasure of working with for nearly a decade now. You still get my Editor of the Year Award sans the torched marshmallow trophy and taped applause.

To Lauren McKenna, Paolo Pepe, and Amy Pierpont, for their efforts on my behalf.

And to everyone at Pocket Books who has helped get my books on the shelves for the past ten years.

I am most grateful.

Honey

❧Prologue❧

Baltimore Park
Baltimore, Maryland

The day was hot. Sweltering.

But the fans didn't seem to mind. They crowded the grandstands that surrounded the playing field. Men in shirtsleeves, women in white blouses tucked into long broadcloth skirts, their voices a low buzz of excitement as Alex Cordova considered his next pitch.

Most people thought he was the greatest player in baseball. Definitely the best pitcher the Baltimore Orioles had ever had.

He was elevated on the pitcher's mound, his broad shoulders blocking a portion of blinding summer sun. His hard-muscled chest gave way to lean hips and legs that were long and as strong as steel. Built of sheer brute strength, his body could stop a solid punch.

Men looked on with grudging admiration and dreams of glory. Women dreamed of more than that—a glance their way, a look or a kiss. But Alex stood silently, concentrating, his dark eyes narrowed on the batter.

Everyone was sure it would be a hard slider. Even

Joe McGill, the Giants' catcher, as he waited at the plate, his bat held in ready tenseness.

Alex glanced over his left shoulder, then turned to Joe and exploded with a pitch that was up and in. Quick thinking made Joe drop to his belly. Dust choked the inside of his nose as he lifted his head. That son of a bitch could have clipped him if he hadn't moved fast.

Vaulting from the ground in a cloud of dirt and curses, he hurled his bat and charged Alex, who was already coming at him.

Joe was blindly aware both dugouts emptied in his wake and took the field in a hot-blooded dukeout. His fight with Cordova had to be broken up by the umpire, who threatened fines and ejections to get both sides to return to their benches. The game continued as Joe resumed the batter's box.

His chest heaving, his mouth tight, he glared at the pitcher with a hostility that was returned.

Alex wound up for the next pitch, his eyes hooded beneath the bill of his cap as he nodded, shook his head, then released the ball. Joe chased it and lobbed a fly right at the Orioles' center fielder to end the inning.

The side retired and Alex was first at bat for Baltimore.

Joe McGill crouched behind him from his place as catcher. His thighs burned from the beating his body had taken in the brawl. It was a hell of a thing to have his joints ache and quiver. He was twenty-five but he felt fifty-five.

From last week's game against the Cincinnati Reds, he sported black and blue marks imprinted by seventeen foul tips, a bruise on his hip the size of a melon where a thrown bat had struck, and two spike marks on his shins. Yet he considered himself lucky.

But he would have been luckier if Cordova hadn't slammed a fist in his gut. Because of that throbbing pain, he leaned forward to irritate Cordova, his knee brushing against the jersey covering the back of Cordova's calf. Joe rode him, just the way Cordova hated it, while the man took a few practice swings.

"It was a fair pitch, McGill, not a beanball," Alex said with a cold edge. "You went down because you couldn't hit it and you didn't want a strike called."

"That's a load of clams," Joe bit out, adjusting the headband on his catcher's mask. The cheek pads settled tightly against his sweat-slicked face. He socked his fist into the pocket of his mitt, looking at the Giants' pitcher, Amos Rusie.

Rusie had the face of a mortician. You could never read the guy. But Joe was the best. *He* could read him. It was his job to decipher what the man was thinking, how he was feeling on any given day out at the pitcher's box.

Today Rusie was feeling like fastballs. The trouble was, Cordova liked to hit fastballs. But he couldn't find leather on a spitter. So Joe gave Rusie the signs for a spitball, down and out.

Rusie nodded.

Alex took his stance, gripping the bat with his large hands apart.

Through the wire cage of his catcher's mask, Joe taunted, "Try and hit this one, busher."

Calling a player busher was about as insulting as telling him his mama was ugly.

A low grunt came from Alex.

Joe spit. The brown tobacco juice landed on Alex's shoe heel. But before Alex could slam him, he prompted, "Heads up, busher, the ball's coming at you."

Rusie grooved one right down the middle of the

strike zone. He threw so hard, Joe had to line his mitt with lead to lessen the impact. Behind him, the umpire made the call.

"Sttttttttttrike one!"

Joe rocked back on his heels and threw a bullet, knee high, right over the base and back to Rusie. "I'm having a picnic at the plate, busher. You aren't even making me work."

"You throw like an old woman," Alex responded.

The next pitch came in, and Alex missed it.

"Sttttttttttrike two!"

Joe caught the lopsided ball; he coiled his arm and delivered it back to Rusie. "One more to go, busher, and your ass will be back warming the bench." He moved closer, kneeing in hard and tight against Alex's right leg.

Gazing down, Alex said, "You'll see me when I cross home plate." His confident smile opened the crack on his lower lip, and he winced. Joe took satisfaction from it; he'd belted him one on the mouth.

"You won't make it to home plate. I'll mow you off, just like shooting a blackbird off a bush—*busher.*"

Bunching his muscles, Alex swung. The bat crashed against the ball for a foul tip. The ball made a hard hop and shot into Joe's knee with the force of a hammer. Red-hot arrows darted up his leg, and he violently swore as he staggered on his feet.

He wanted a piece of Cordova, but he couldn't come to blows over a foul tipped ball. Any catcher who couldn't shake it off had no right to be in the game.

So he limped back to the plate, adjusted his mask, and squatted back down. He had to refocus. Remind himself he was the best catcher the New York Giants had ever signed. He was batting .320, had the highest earned run average in the league, and had perfected double steals. Women chased him, and he got free drinks in saloons. Everybody liked him.

As for Alex Cordova . . .

Some of *his* teammates and most of the league resented him because he was so damn good. With that greatness came arrogance. For the past two years, the *Sporting News* had rarely written about him in a flattering light—even when he was pitching flawless games and hitting home runs.

And all this "Grizz" crap. What was that about? Cordova had spent the '95 winter out West somewhere and had come back telling reporters he was a grizzly bear, fearless and untouchable. Now he called himself Alex "the Grizz" Cordova. Joe didn't need a handle to play ball. Just plain Joe McGill got the job done.

Rousing cheers from the fans brought him out of his reverie, reminding him that not everyone resented the Orioles' pitcher. Perspiration blurred his vision. He squeezed his eyes closed, and when he opened them, he could have sworn he saw a white butterfly wavering on the motionless air. He blinked, then squinted. It was gone.

A chill gripped him. He was superstitious. Most every ballplayer was. A white butterfly meant calamity. A yellow or red one would have been a lot friendlier sight.

"Boo." Heavy sarcasm weighted Alex's voice.

The ribbing drove Joe's fury, making him ride Alex. He pushed in close, too close, but he wanted to make Cordova sweat. Needed the umpire to call him out. Then Joe was going to tackle Alex and ram his knuckles into his smug jaw. He didn't give a good night if he got bounced out of the game.

Joe gave Rusie the signal to throw another spitball, down and out.

Rusie nodded, but the ball that came Joe's way was hard and fast.

He began to straighten his legs, shoving his shoulder against Alex to glove the ball. It was an outside pitch Alex shouldn't have gone after. But he did, putting his body into the motion of the bat as he swung.

Then Joe's world went black.

Chapter
❧ 1 ❧

Three years later
Harmony, Montana

Men were drawn to Camille Kennison like bees were to honeysuckle blossoms.

While she walked to her father's hardware store, gentlemen doffed their hats and wished her a pleasant day. She always gave them a smile. But where most women would be flattered by the attention, for Camille it became a chore to say "Good afternoon" so often.

She liked men, of course. But she noticed the way they looked at her. They were more interested in her appearance than in what she had to say. As her father so often reminded her, pretty women were never thought of as smart conversationalists. And throughout her life, Camille had been told she was a regal beauty.

Men saw only that she was a statuesque woman with honey-blond hair, had a gracefully curved figure, and an oval face with skin like fine ivory. Dozens of times, she'd been told her mouth was lush and kissable, its color a deep blush like that of dew-washed

7

roses. And if she were honest with herself, she'd have to admit that she'd been kissed by dozens of men. Chastely. Demurely. Certainly not passionately. No man had ever ignited that in her, so she didn't believe sexual delirium existed except in fiction tomes and poetry.

However ... Alex Cordova sorely tested her theory. With his shoulder-length black hair and full, sensual lips, he could look at her as if she were brainless and she probably wouldn't care.

Alex Cordova was deliciously appealing.

The man was an enigma. Nobody knew much of anything about him now that he didn't play baseball, and that made people curious. Women couldn't keep their eyes off him when he came into town. Herself included.

Shifting a lunch pail from one hand to the other, she opened the store's door and walked across the sawdust floor. A smoky kerosene odor hovered in the air. The interior was poorly lit, but James Kennison kept things neat and tidy. She skirted three stacks of zinc washtubs. Piled on big tables were slop jars, cuspidors, dishpans, sadirons, washbasins, coffee grinders, and household necessities.

Camille's father stood at the counter in conversation with Dr. Teeter, who could talk up a week's worth of Sundays all in one day. The dentist had an ingrained need to show off his mouthful of white teeth. He never missed an opportunity to talk and grin and laugh. She didn't know why he felt he had to use himself as an advertisement. Being the only drill-and-fill man in town, he wouldn't have lacked for customers even if his teeth had been less than perfect.

Her father interjected "Is that so?" in the appropriate places while Dr. Teeter droned on, but Camille suspected he listened only out of obligation to his customer. Wearing a cashmere suit, and with string apron tied around his slim waist, her father dressed the part of a successful businessman. And he was. He worked hard to turn a profit while establishing his good name in the community.

"I brought you lunch, Daddy." A trace of Camille's Louisiana accent always came out when she addressed her father. The slight emphasis she put on the last syllable of *da-Dee* made it sound faintly Southern.

He barely noticed her, saying without a word of thanks, "Put it over there, Camille."

She slipped behind the counter and set the lunch pail next to the cash register. The clasp of her pocketbook easily opened beneath her gloved fingers. She took out the tiny notepad and flipped the cover over. On the pristine paper, she'd written everything she needed to get her garden started this year.

Early May had been unseasonably wet, so she hadn't been able to plant her beds. But she could console herself with the fact that everyone else would have a late start, too. She'd still have the opportunity to cultivate the best flower and vegetable beds in Harmony. It was imperative that she did so, because this was the year she planned to run for president of the Harmony Garden Club.

She had a fairly good shot at it, too. Last year, Mrs. Calhoon held the esteemed position. The year before, Mrs. Plunkett—for a record three terms. Both ladies had made competent leaders, but they weren't willing to try new things. During the past few years, younger women had started to join the club, and it was time for a younger woman to run it. Camille had a host of ideas that were a bit unconventional. Modern fertilizers and up-to-date pruning methods. She planned to show the club ladies exactly what open-minded thinking could do for one's garden.

Camille had barely taken a step toward the Burpee seed display when Dr. Teeter's comment stopped her short.

"It's a shame about yesterday's game," he said, lounging next to the counter's edge. "If it weren't for bad fielding, we could have won."

Her gaze darted to her father, and she held her breath. These days, there were two subjects you didn't bring up with him: baseball and Ned Butler.

Daddy's hardware store owned and had sponsored the local baseball team for ten years. Kennison's Keystones had never caused any fanfare on the field. But since they'd been accepted for membership into the American League this year, her father had high hopes for the officially renamed Harmony Keystones.

Only those hopes had been diagnosed with a bad case of eczema. Dr. Porter said that Ned Butler, the manager of the Keystones, had a condition brought about by exhaustion of the nervous system. It had gone haywire dealing with James Kennison day in and day out.

Ned had begun to itch during spring training. Then, three weeks ago on opening day after the Keystones had been trounced by the Detroit Tigers 9–0, he collapsed with a skin rash the likes of which the townspeople of Harmony had never seen. Per doctor's orders, Ned wasn't supposed to become excited, be exposed to undue or sudden transitions from heat to cold, exercise excessively, breathe impure air, or wear improper clothing.

In short, he was confined indefinitely to a sickroom while Mrs. Butler painted glycerine on him to alleviate his itching.

Ned Butler was the tenth manager the Keystones had had in as many years. Her father had been in Ned's way from the moment Ned stepped off the train to the moment he dropped flat on his keister after that Detroit game. Daddy could be a tad anxious when things didn't go well. And they weren't. The Keystones had lost twelve of the last twelve games they'd played this season.

Her father existed in a constant state of irritation that was getting harder and harder to live with. Camille had considered growing and selling potted plants, decorating flower containers to go with them. She would earn only a modest amount, but it would be enough to allow her to pay for a room at the boardinghouse and to gain a bit of independence. Not to mention distance from her father's volatile moods.

"Bad fielding!" Contempt sparked her father's words as he wielded a feather duster. "It was a lot more than bad fielding. Charlie Delahanty and Specs Ryan slammed into each other chasing a fly ball in the fifth inning." He vigorously brushed off the case beside him, then took out the dangerous-looking knives it housed and swished the duster over the shelves. "Doc Nash overthrowing to first base in the seventh." White feathers scattered in the air as if chickens were taking a dust bath. "And that bonehead play at home plate with Cub LaRoque and the wild pitch in the ninth."

Camille had watched the game from the stands. And no matter her father's reasoning, all the fielding in the world wouldn't have allowed the Keystones to catch up to the Cleveland Blue's six *un*earned runs. Because the Keystones couldn't hit worth a darn, either.

"Well, the season's still young," Dr. Teeter remarked, teeth filling his optimistic grin. "The Keystones could be in the pennant race."

Her father continued to dust an area that hadn't needed dusting in the first place. "I promised Harmony a winning team this year. And I'm a man of my word. We'll get there if I have to manage the team for the entire season myself."

Camille fervently hoped that wasn't going to happen. She'd brought him his lunch today because he had to close the store an hour early to get to Municipal Field on time for this afternoon's game. There, she knew he would alternately stand and sit and pace and yell and throw down his hat and pick it up, only to throw it down again. On a good day, her father had a short fuse. On a bad day—which had been all the days since Ned had been confined to his bed—he was as sour as a crabapple.

Thinking the touchy subject had been dropped, she took another step. She hadn't put her shoe heel down when Dr. Teeter added, "Although it would have been a lot surer bet"—she froze and braced herself for what would come—"if we'd been able to keep Will White."

"Will White!" Her father's temper exploded like a blast from the lumbermill's lunch whistle. The feather duster came to an abrupt halt and his face grew ruddy. "When I find that young no-account, he'll be sorry he ever ran out on his contract."

Between paying Will White a bonus—just before the man skipped town, paying Ned Butler a partial salary the manager hadn't earned, and building a new clubhouse this year, James Kennison couldn't invest much more money into his team without its becoming a financial burden.

The Keystones had had a chance of seeing a pennant when her father signed the quick-delivery pitcher this past February. He'd cost a handsome price, but Will brought the most hope to Harmony's baseball fans they'd had in years. But he left in the middle of spring training, taking off with his contract pay before ever pitching a scheduled game.

If Will hadn't gone to the Elm Street theater to watch a performance of *Antony and Cleopatra,* he wouldn't have seen Pearl Chaussee. Or her legs in a pair of opaque tights and her ample bosom in a low-necked silk tunic. The Women's League had drawn the curtain on the "scandalous" production after two nights. If they'd shut it down after the first performance, Will wouldn't have become lovesick over Pearl and left the Keystones high and dry.

Dr. Teeter, realizing he'd struck a nerve—which didn't bode well for his dental skills, focused on Camille. "How's that third molar of yours you had me check in January?"

"It's still rooted to the spot," she replied.

The dentist guffawed, all teeth. "That's a good one. I'll bet next to my wife, you were the smartest girl in your finishing-school class."

Johannah Treber Teeter and Camille had both graduated from Mrs. Wolcott's Finishing School this spring.

"She doesn't need to be smart," her father informed the dentist, laying the duster back on the shelf. "She's pretty. With her looks, she could have any man for a husband." He scowled at her. "She's just picky."

Camille did her best to hide her embarrassment. Her father had been saying things like that since she turned thirteen. She only wished he wouldn't say them in public. It made people look at her differently. As if she were stuck up. She had never considered her appearance an attribute. In fact, she thought it a nuisance.

"I suppose I should be on my way," Dr. Teeter said, adjusting the angle of his hat. "Nice talking with you, James."

"See you again," her father said in farewell as the

dentist retreated out the door. As soon as the man was gone, her father whined, "Doesn't he have any patients to occupy his time? Make another appointment with him, Camille."

"I don't need to." She squinted in an effort to read the items on her list, then glanced at the light flickering above her head. "When are you going to tap into the city's electrical lighting instead of using kerosene lamps?"

"Never. I don't want my store so bright that anyone standing clear over on Hackberry Way can see inside. If the place were lit up like a Roman candle, I couldn't see what Bertram Nops was up to without him knowing I was watching him."

James Kennison and Bertram Nops had been having a hardware feud since back in '89 when Camille's family arrived in town. Nops Hardware Emporium was located directly opposite of Kennison's. Hackberry Way and Sycamore Drive separated the two businesses, the town square sandwiched in the middle. If the two men spent less energy trying to outdo each other with sale prices, giveaways, and dastardly tricks, they'd have more time to actually enjoy doing business.

Camille sighed in frustration. "I just think electric lights would improve things, is all."

"You leave the thinking to me, Camille sugar. All you need to worry about is what hat to wear and who you're going to marry."

How could he not see she had interests other than hats? She was twenty-one. She *did* have a brain in her head, and she used it quite a lot—only he never gave her a chance to use it on things that mattered. She would have liked to push up her sleeves and reorganize his store, but he'd scoffed when she'd asked him. If he hadn't, she could have brought Kennison's

Hardware into the new century. She didn't need a hat or a husband to figure out that washtubs displayed near wash soap would sell more of both.

But he wouldn't take her seriously. Not once had he told her she'd done a good job on anything. Even when she'd won an essay-writing contest on why education was important when she was nine, composed a poem about the Mississippi River that was printed in *American* magazine when she was eleven, and came up with the winning entry in the Armour's Beef recipe-writing competition when she was twelve. None of those accomplishments had bowled him over, so she gave up entering contests.

Because she could never please him, she'd spent her whole life trying to be perfect at what she did. With her bid for the Garden Club presidency, she'd prove to him she could accomplish something. And in the process, prove to herself how successful *she* could be. She'd make such a splash with her gardening innovations, her father would have to take notice and be . . . proud.

At the idea, tears burned her eyes. Her throat tightened. She dashed away the sudden, foolish tears.

Her attention was diverted when the door opened and a tall, dark-haired man entered. She doubted he was older than thirty, his body solid and strong, yet he had a simple mind. She'd spoken to him a few times. He worked doing odd jobs at Plunkett's mercantile. A relative newcomer to Harmony, he was named Captain. Alex Cordova fiercely looked after him. Talk in the small community said they were related somehow.

James Kennison saw Captain, and his face lit up over the prospect that Alex wasn't far behind.

"Alex sent me in for something," Captain said with a good-natured smile. "He's making a chesty bride."

Both Camille's and her father's eyes went wide.

Captain frowned deeply in thought. "Or was that a bride's chest?"

"Ah. A wedding chest," her father said in clarification.

Alex Cordova owned a modest woodworker's shop at the end of Elm Street, where he kept mostly to himself. On several occasions, Camille had seen some of his pieces displayed in the homes of her friends. He favored soft colors in his woods and finishes, and to say he had talent was a gross understatement. He was a classic craftsman.

"So . . ."—her father looked beyond Captain's wide shoulders—"where *is* Cordova?"

"He's not coming in."

Her father's hopeful expression fell. "Why not?"

"He says he's tired of you pestering him to play baseball."

For seven months, James Kennison had tried every persuasive tactic he'd known to lure and snare Alex "the Grizz" Cordova into playing baseball for the Harmony Keystones—to no avail.

"Then tell him to say yes and I'll stop," her father proposed.

Camille held on to a smile. Inasmuch as she wanted the Keystones to win this year, she thought it admirable that Alex had such staying power.

When he'd come to Harmony, he hadn't made any attempt at hiding his identity. But neither had he boasted of the fact that he'd been the one to bring the Orioles the pennant in '96 and '97. And because of that, he'd been the most sought after player in the National League before he quit the game and dropped out of sight in 1898.

Captain only shrugged at her father's suggestion, then drew up next to the counter. He was a head taller than her daddy and had a black beard. "Now what was it that Alex said he wanted?" He slipped his hand into his pants pocket and produced a penny. Staring at it, he grew contemplative.

Camille watched him struggling with his thoughts, a fierce look of concentration on his face. She could feel his discouragement. What he was trying to recollect wasn't coming to him. Her sympathy went out to him, but from the pride set in his shoulders, she doubted he wanted it.

"I didn't get a headache today." Captain put the penny back in his pocket.

"Headaches aren't pleasant," Camille said.

"One time, I had a headache and I didn't know how much medicine to pour in the glass and I slept for a really long time. Now Alex keeps it locked up. I have to take medicine every day. I don't like it, but Alex says it's good for me."

Her father's handlebar mustache wilted at the constant mention of Alex and the apparentness that he wouldn't be making a visit. "Is Cordova all out of finish nails?"

Captain shook his head. "I don't think that was it. If I had asked Alex to spell what it was, I would have remembered. When I have the spelling of a word, it sticks with me."

"Does he need something for his wood shop?" Camille questioned. It would help if she knew what tools a woodworker used. As it was, her query wasn't much help. There were too many possible answers.

"Could be that." Troublesome lines settled on his forehead as he apparently weighed out his choices. "I hate when I can't remember things."

Her father began to put the knives back in their glass case. "Maybe he needs a new saw blade?" He held up a knife; the blade shimmered under the flickering lamp light. "Something like this?"

Camille could literally hear the breath sucked into Captain's chest as he paled. "That's not a razor, is it?"

"No—" Her father was cut off.

"R-a-z-o-r. Razor. No shave."

"It's not a razor," Camille quickly assured him.

She watched in growing concern as Captain's gaze fixed on the knife, panic rioting in his eyes. "A-A-Alex," he stammered, raising a hand to his temple. "Where's Alex? My head's starting to hurt."

He began stepping backward, as if he were afraid to turn his back on the knife.

"My father isn't going to harm you," Camille said in a rush.

Captain bumped into the stack of small washtubs and they tipped over with a loud crash onto the floor. In spite of the noise, he didn't look down. "A-Alex! Where's Alex? N-no shave today. No shave. No shave. No shave." His hand fumbled with the doorknob.

"Captain," she called after him, but he'd already stumbled outside onto the boardwalk.

She quickly followed and found him slumped on the bench in front of the store. He was trembling so badly, he couldn't keep his knees from knocking into one another.

"No shave," he pleaded. "No shave."

Hesitantly, she laid her hand on his arm and tried to calm him. "You don't have to shave if you don't want to."

"No shave. R-a-z-o-r."

He needed help, but she was unsure what to do for him. Her eyes met her father's. James Kennison stood in the doorway with an anxious look. "I'll get Dr. Porter," he said, then took off across the town square and headed for the physician's office.

Alone with Captain, she tried to console him. "Everything will be fine."

He looked at her, but she could tell he didn't see her. His brown eyes glittered. "No shave."

Distraught, she looked across the town square, searching for a glimpse of her father and the doctor, and found Alex Cordova instead.

He stopped at the end of the boardwalk, then quickened to a sprint. Black hair blew from under his worn Stetson. Each boot heel that landed hard on the planks sent reverberations to where she knelt. A determined hardness set the features of his face, defined the flare of his nostrils and his well-cut mouth. His dark eyes never left Captain. If he saw her at all, it had been for only a brief moment.

Reaching them, Alex dropped down beside Captain. "Cap, what is it?"

Captain wouldn't speak. His cheeks had turned the color of ash as he stared blankly ahead.

A lock of hair fell over Alex's brow as he lowered his chin. He didn't turn toward her when he asked in a tight and composed voice, "What did you do to him?"

If only she had a tangible explanation. "Nothing."

Slowly, he lifted his head and looked directly into her eyes. Her focus fluttered. "It was the knife," she heard herself saying. "My father was putting them away and the light caught on a blade. That's when he got upset—"

"A knife?"

Alex turned his attention to Captain, gripped his shoulders, and gave him a soft shake. A quiet tenderness filled Alex's expression. There was an almost imperceptible note of pleading in his voice when next he spoke—as if he willed Captain to come around, he would. "Cap, it's *all right.*"

"Alex? Is that you?"

"Yes, Cap. It's me."

"No shave." The despair in Captain's voice squeezed Camille's heart.

And yet, with those two words, the situation changed. Comprehension fell across Alex's face. His eyes welled with understanding; he clenched his jaw to keep himself under control. Visible sorrow bent his broad shoulders as his hand grazed Captain's with a compassion Camille could feel through her bones.

"Ah, Cap," Alex whispered on a soft exhale. "You don't have to take a shave. Never again."

Hope lit Captain's eyes. "Really?"

"Really."

Silent understanding passed between the two of them. Camille felt like an outsider. An intruder who had no business witnessing something understood only by those involved.

So, quietly, she slipped back into the store unnoticed.

Chapter
2

"I thought Matthew Gage had quit his muckraking!" James Kennison bellowed his indignance from behind the black-and-white pages of the *Harmony Advocate*. His huff and bluster had become a regular part of breakfast. "And he says he's a journalist!" The china practically rattled in the sunny dining room, but neither Camille or her mother batted an eye. "What in the blue blazes do you call this jaded journalism Gage has printed in this morning's edition of the *Advocate*?"

Her mother, Grayce, took it all in stride as she sipped her coffee. "The same jaded journalism you said Mr. Gage printed about your baseball team in yesterday morning's edition, dear." With her blond hair stylishly high on top of her head and her filigreed earrings dangling delicately from her lobes, she was the epitome of refinement. Even in the most extreme of circumstances, Camille had never seen her mother use less than perfect judgment. She was, after all, one of the Jeffries from Vidalia.

Placing a napkin on her lap, Camille suggested, "I think you should quit reading the newspaper, Daddy. All it does is upset you."

He lowered the crisp sheet and stared over its headline to address his wife and daughter. "I'll tell you what upsets me. Opinionated reporting. Now *that* upsets me!"

If he didn't have the newspaper, he wouldn't have to read the reporter's opinions. But Camille made no further comment. There was no reasoning with him when he was hot and bothered. Besides, her attention wasn't fully on his diatribe anyway. The thoughts that took up her mind were of Alex Cordova.

Yesterday had been the first time she'd seen him up close. The sight of him from a distance hadn't prepared her for the effect he would have on her. With just that brief meeting of their eyes, she'd felt strangely aware of herself as a woman. The dainty batiste of her corset had suddenly seemed too tight to allow her to breathe.

And when he'd looked at her, for the first time ever, she'd been glad she was thought of as pretty.

His eyes were a deep brown; the color of richly tilled earth, and were framed by thick black lashes that weren't too long. She'd unconsciously fought against leaning toward him, his face, his eyes . . . his mouth.

Her father's raised voice broke into her daydreams. The next thing she knew, she'd be imagining what it would be like to be kissed by the famous ballplayer.

"Just because Gage owns the paper doesn't give him license to print nonsense." He snorted his displeasure. "Listen to this: 'In this first year of the American League's history, Harmony's Keystones have created their own record book by losing their thirteenth consecutive game in their first thirteen games of the season, the worst start ever for any team since baseball's inception.' "

Camille and her mother exchanged a glance, then Camille sighed and buttered her toast as her father continued to read the newspaper in a tone that made Camille think of Mrs. Kirby's hymn singing at the General Assembly Church from last week as soothing to the ears.

" 'The rope the Keystones have tied around their necks in the three weeks of the new season is getting tighter. It gripped some more last night when six of Cleveland's seven walks came in the bottom of the eighth inning as the Blues scored six runs, sending Harmony's team to a 12–0 defeat before hometown fans at Municipal Field.' "

He slammed a tight fist on the table. "And as if that weren't enough, Gage goes on: 'Kennison's pitchers couldn't hit water if they fell out of a boat—much less deliver the ball in the strike zone. But that seems to be the least of James Kennison's problems. The manager of the Keystones, Ned Butler, is laid up and could be out for the season.' " His face went as red as strawberry preserves, and he bunched the newspaper into a tight ball before tossing it to the floor.

"James, you're not doing your health any good by getting this excited," Camille's mother reminded him, lightly touching his hand.

"What would do my health a world of good would be to have a piece of Will White's hide for running off with Pearl Chaussee." He frowned. "As soon as my investigator finds him, I'm going to sue White within an inch of his life."

Pouring her father more coffee, her mother asked, "Any word from Mr. Hogwood?"

"Not a one in over a week." His brows rose. "Grayce, I believe that detective likes spending my money. He's taking his sweet time about looking. I got a bill from the Excelsior Hotel in Denver. Now I ask you, what would Will White be doing in a thirty dollar room at the Excelsior Hotel?"

"I wouldn't care to speculate, James."

Annoyance marked her father's tone when he said, "It chafes my hide to pay for a luxury room that I can't enjoy—much less afford."

"Are we that bad off?" Concern worried the corners of her mother's mouth. "I could cut back on the household spending and—"

He bristled "We aren't starving. I have money. Just not as much as we once had."

"Still no replies on your advertisement for a manager?"

"None," he grumbled.

And it had been two weeks. Camille didn't think there was a man left in the country who'd be willing to manage the Keystones. No one was fool enough.

Right now, the players were fending for themselves, with her father as temporary manager. But the thirteen games he'd overseen had taken their toll on him. Considerably more hotheaded than normal, he couldn't run a business and a baseball team at the same time—not to mention going on road trips without hiring help for the store. He adamantly refused to let his wife or daughter behind the counter. Bertram Nops would think he was a powder puff, needing a woman to help him get along.

"I don't know why an able-bodied manager hasn't stepped forward," he continued. "I ask you, what man could turn down a salary of twelve hundred dollars for the season?" He tossed a cube of sugar into his coffee, messily splashed in some cream, then stirred the brew with a spoon—over and over and over. *K-clink, k-clink, k-clink.* "Do I give a man grief? Do I cause aggravation? Am I a hard person to get along with? Did I not tell the then Miss Huntington that Tom Wolcott had bought that red paint himself?" *K-clink, k-clink, k-clink.* "And for my honesty, did I not forfeit that much desired rubber froggy lure I'd been wanting? I think that makes me a likable fellow." *K-clink, k-clink, k-clink.* "I never get under anyone's skin."

"Never under *my* skin, dear," her mother replied.

"Then why does Ned Butler think I cause him stress?" he shot back, a slosh of murky coffee jumping out of the cup. "I've got to get things turned around. And soon."

Camille grew pensive. If Alex's skill as a pitcher was even half of what had been written about him, he could turn things around. Then it popped into her head: What about his reputation off the playing field? She had heard he was a notorious womanizer. A lady's man. But she hadn't seen him keeping company with women since he'd been in Harmony. Maybe he visited them late at night. . . . Maybe—

"I don't suppose you could convince Alex Cordova to play for you," her mother said.

At the name, Camille jumped. Thank goodness her mother couldn't read her mind. Even so, her wayward thoughts put guilty heat on her cheeks. She locked her gaze on her father's face, waiting for his reaction.

The clinking motion of spoon and cup ceased. "Grayce, now I ask you, how many times have I tried to get Cordova?"

"I haven't been counting."

He exploded. "Well, you should have been!" Her mother didn't flinch a bit. "I've done everything but grease his palm with pure gold oil. The man is iron-clad. Built of a steely resistance stronger than that of a string of locomotives. If I could, Grayce, I'd sign him."

Camille ate her toast in silence.

The conversation on the boardwalk had been the only one she'd had with Alex since he'd moved to town. Now, she couldn't quit wondering how she could meet him again.

The front bell cranked and her father quickly pushed away from the table, his coffee untouched. "That'll be Duke and Jimmy. They said they would check on Ned's condition and report to me. With any luck, his skin has cleared up and he's all set for tonight's game."

He'd barely rounded the table when Leda, the housemaid, showed the two players into the room. Both men removed their hats and nodded to Camille and her mother.

Duke Boyle had broken his nose in a fight, which had left it angled. Jimmy Shugart flashed his teeth, the uppers as crooked as an old picket fence.

"Mr. Kennison," Leda announced, "Mr. Duke and Mr. Jimmy are here to see you."

"Yes, yes," he said impatiently.

She gave him a frown, her currant-black eyes silently chastising him for his shortness with her. Leda and James Kennison got along about as well as the Wolcotts' dog and cat.

As he gazed at the left fielder and first baseman, his expression filled with optimism. "Well? What's the word?"

Jimmy held his hat out in front of him and nervously turned the brim in his hands. "The word is, he's still scratching."

"We saw for ourselves," Duke added. "As soon as we mentioned your name, he started itching again. His wife made us leave."

"Thunderation!" Her father ran his hand through his hair and through the pomade he'd earlier combed through it. For a moment, he put his palm over his mouth, forefinger on his nose, tapping in thought. Apparently he didn't come up with anything brilliant, because he merely said, "All right. We'll play this one on our own again. We won't give up. We'll get a manager. Eventually." Absently, he fussed with his tie and let out a long sigh.

"Maybe Alex Cordova would manage us," Duke suggested.

James's fingers stilled.

Duke made an apologetic face and took a step backward. "Never mind."

"I tell you what, Duke," James countered, "if you can get me Cordova, I'll make *you* the manager. How's that?" The knot in James's tie was now crooked, a match for his uneven mood. "In fact, whoever gets me Cordova can be the manager."

Jimmy grinned. "No kidding?"

"I most certainly am not. As you well know, I'm a man of my word," he said, clearly enunciating his oft-repeated maxim. "All right, boys. I'll see you later today."

Duke and Jimmy showed themselves to the door.

Camille's father bussed her mother on the cheek. "I'm going to the store."

"Daddy, let me see if I can change Alex Cordova's mind." The words were uttered before Camille could thoroughly think the idea through.

"What was that?" He must have been too startled to immediately object.

In those seconds, she had enough time to gather her wits. As her father didn't possess the best of temperaments and the situation was desperate, somebody who kept a level head should approach Alex. And she was the perfect candidate. "I'd like to try to persuade him to sign on."

"You most certainly will not," he fired back. "I won't have my daughter gadding about Elm Street. It isn't respectable." He glared at her with a critical squint. "And besides, Camille sugar, I've given up on him. Nobody can persuade Alex Cordova—not even if it were to sign on with the Lord, with the Devil right there reaching for his passport to hell."

"James!" her mother admonished.

Camille opened her mouth, but her father plowed ahead. "Grayce, I won't have you telling me she's capable of convincing that man. She's too soft. She doesn't have it in her. He'd chew her up and spit her out before she knew what happened. Cordova is iron-clad. *Ironclad*, I tell you." With a flick of his thumb next to his watch's face, the case snapped open and he noted the hour. "I really have to get to the store or I'll be late."

When he talked about her as if she weren't in the room, Camille wanted to scream.

"Will you be home for dinner before tonight's game?" her mother asked, trying to keep the peace and change the subject. "What would you like Leda to fix for you?"

"A bicarbonate," he replied glumly, slipping his timepiece into the slash of his vest pocket. "Game three against the Blues should be a real lollapalooza. No doubt Gage will be happy to report the grim results in tomorrow morning's newspaper."

On that, he quit the dining room with a grimace.

His bay rum aftershave had barely drifted away when Camille said, "If he weren't my father, I would have thrown my toast at him."

"If it's any consolation, you threw up on him when you were a baby."

Camille's mouth curved into a smile.

Grayce rested her hand on Camille's. "He's too set

28

in his ways to change his thinking, Camille. Try not to let him bother you." Then, letting out an airy sigh, she asked, "Well, what are you going to do today?"

"The same thing I did yesterday." With a snap of her wrist, she tossed her napkin onto her plate. "Make mad passionate love to men all afternoon."

Her mother laughed.

Camille and her mother didn't mince words for the sake of "delicacy." Grayce Kennison had always encouraged her daughter to freely express her emotions and thoughts, be they in jest or in sincerity.

"I'm going to meet with the ladies this morning," Grayce announced as she stood. "We're still just so tickled by Mrs. Wolcott's news that she's going to have a baby. Mrs. Brooks has suggested we begin planning a cradle party for her even though the blessed event isn't going to be here for another seven months."

Camille politely listened, but her heartbeat still raced.

She's too soft. She doesn't have it in her.

"Would you like to come, Camille? We're meeting at Mrs. Wolcott's house."

He'd chew her up and spit her out before she knew what happened.

"Meg Gage will be there. So will Crescencia Dufresne and Johannah Teeter."

Focusing now on her mother, Camille debated seeing her former schoolmates from Mrs. Wolcott's Finishing School. Meg Brooks, Crescencia Stykem, and Johannah Treber. Properly tutored and well mannered from their education. All three were now married.

And Lucille Calhoon had gotten engaged at last Friday's Elks dance to Julius Addison, her childhood sweetheart. Her friends were getting married fast and

Camille was the only one to hold out. But somehow she felt there had to be more. But what?

Cordova is ironclad.

"No, Mama. I'm going to stay home." Did her casual tone sound too forced?

"Well, if you change your mind . . ."

"I won't. I'm going to work on my garden plans."

She lingered a moment after her mother left, then stood and went directly to the parlor window. Looking out, she watched the bob of plumes on her mother's hat as Grayce headed toward town.

Camille really had planned on drafting a layout for her garden. How she sowed the seeds and bulbs would determine how the next six months would color and blossom. The apple tree needed pruning and dusting for codling moths as soon as two thirds of the petals had fallen. And then there was . . .

Camille sugar, nobody can persuade Alex Cordova . . .

. . . the snail bait to be spread.

She's too soft. She doesn't have it in her.

The Garden Club meeting was Friday night and she wanted to make a good impression. She had to make preparations and plan.

I won't have you telling me she's capable of convincing that man.

But those plans had now changed.

As soon as her mother disappeared from view, Camille's heart skipped a beat. Before she could think better of it, she snatched a straw hat she kept hanging on the hat rack and pinned it over her hair. She buttoned her gloves, exited the door, and went down the steps.

So much for respectability.

Miss Camille Kennison was going to take a walk down Elm Street.

*   *   *

Alex had an appreciation for wood.

Most of his life, he'd earned his living from it. In his early youth, by carving scythe handles for cutting tobacco in Cuban fields. At nineteen, by swinging a bat at baseballs, a professional career that had lasted six years. And now, at twenty-eight by designing and creating furniture.

To Alex, wood defined who he'd become, where he'd been.

He skimmed a jack plane across the hinged top of the bride's chest he was finishing for Grant Calhoon's daughter. The tool seemed dwarfed by his grasp and, to an observer, would look ineffectually held by his large hand. But Alex was always in control, passing the blade with a fluid motion over the wood's surface.

The wood felt warm and smooth beneath his touch. He caressed it like he would a woman, slowly sliding his hand over the grained surface, feeling every sensation in his fingertips. Sometimes he'd leave a slight dimple on the finished surface—much like that of a barely discernible mole on a woman's inner thigh. Small blemishes lent certain furniture character.

Inside the wood shop, the mellow scent of old wax and boiled linseed oil hung in the air. They mingled with the woodsy distinction of ash. He'd left the barn-size doors open so the fresh smell of that particular wood wouldn't trigger memories. But it did.

It stirred in him the overwhelming desire to once more become a part of the American pastime: baseball. To go home. Home to the sport he'd loved because of its speed and grace, failure and hope, and the defining moment that overrode every other feeling ever known: winning the game.

That surging emotion, that passion to play that came with the arrival of spring and ended with onset of autumn, could still grip him three years after he'd quit. But now, they were merely two seasons in a calendar of four. He no longer allowed himself to anticipate either, because he'd sworn to never again pitch another ball or swing another bat.

Thoughts clouded his gaze, and he set the jack plane down. He left the bride's chest and went to his workbench, where he placed both hands on the side rest and leaned forward. A suffocating feeling pulled the air from his lungs.

He couldn't afford to let baseball haunt him now. Only the present mattered.

Alex reached for the door handle on one of the wall cabinets above the bench. Hidden behind the boxes of cut nails and cans of varnish was an envelope. He slid it from its niche and held on to it as if it were thin glass. He read the typeface in the left corner.

Silas Denton Sanatorium for Nervous Diseases
209 Niagra St., cor. Main
Buffalo, N.Y.

Holy Christ—a big problem weighed on him.
Money.
He needed a lot of it. Close to four thousand.

Alex didn't know why he felt he had to look at the envelope. By memory, he knew what was typed on the outside and printed on the inside.

Silas Denton was renowned for his treatment of brain disorders. His sanatorium had pioneered innovative ways to deal with patients. Alex had no intentions of abandoning Captain to their care. He would go with him and make sure nothing went wrong. Because none of those blood-letting docs who'd put Cap through hell for years in the Baltimore Hospital for the Public had made any progress. They'd scared him senseless.

Within a week, Alex had moved him to the State Orthopaedic Hospital and Infirmary, hoping they'd be able to help. During the day, Alex worked as a carpenter so he could pay for the bed and treatments Cap needed. The nights, he spent with Captain, reteaching him everyday things like how to tie his shoe, use silverware, and recognize the letters of the alphabet.

Although Cap lived in relative peace, his outbursts of paranoia, terror, and desperation made Alex fear Cap would lose what was left of his mind if he left him in the infirmary. So he made the decision to have him released into his care. The physicians told him he was making a severe mistake, but they gave him Cap's medicines and told him to keep him on a specified dose and to mail them for more when he ran out.

It had been with unshakable belief that Cap could recover that Alex had put Cap and himself on the first train out of Baltimore to Montana. Montana held a special meaning for Alex, and he hoped that the spirit that had touched him years ago would touch Cap and make him better. Only Cap wasn't getting better. In fact, he seemed to be getting worse.

He had his good days and his bad days. Sometimes a spark of memory from the hospital would ignite in his head and he'd become petrified. It was growing more and more difficult for Alex to reassure Cap that things would turn around. What had happened yesterday at Kennison's Hardware had been the deciding factor for Alex.

He couldn't always be with Cap. If that woman hadn't been there—he hated to think of what could have happened.

Alex drew a deep breath. He didn't know her name. He'd been aware of the vague scent of her perfume, but he hadn't really looked at her. Their eyes had briefly met, hers brimming with genuine concern. For a moment, he tried to remember their color. Light. Blue? Like summer skies? It really didn't matter. He wouldn't be sticking around in Harmony. So he put the image of her face out of his head.

It was clear Captain had to see the best doctor there was. And that was Silas Denton. But for that to happen, Alex had to come into a large sum of money.

Tucking the letter in its place, he closed the cupboard and went back to the bride's chest. As he smoothed the jack plane across the wood, he went through his options.

He could sell the wood shop. But he'd barely make squat. Whoever bought it would have to know what to do with it. The tools were of no value to somebody who didn't understand wood.

He could advertise his skills in nearby Waverly or Alder. But it would take a hell of a long time to accumulate extra income. The bride's chest he was finishing sold for twenty-eight dollars. He'd have to make a couple hundred of them to come even close to the four thousand.

So how to come up with it? Of course he knew the answer. In truth, he understood what he would have to do—a sad irony that only Captain would understand—if only he could.

"Mr. Cordova?"

Alex swung around, his body tight, his thoughts evaporating into the thin summer air. He hadn't heard anyone approach the shop.

A woman stood in the double-wide doorway, sunlight spilling over her. She looked like an angel—blond, tall. She wore pale colors, the light fabric of her skirt doing a soft dance around her ankles.

Christ. It's her.

Alex slowly relaxed his stance. "Who wants to know?"

She took a few steps forward, her walk assured. He liked the way she held herself, the way her hair looked soft tucked beneath her hat.

Then she did something that surprised him. She extended her hand.

He didn't readily take it. Merely stared at the white silk of her gloves. The slenderness of her fingers. The tiny pearl buttons that ran up the inside of her wrist. He swore he could almost see her pulse point, that muted beat of her heart beneath her delicate skin and glove.

The awkward moment dragged on until he grasped her outstretched hand. A jolt of heat shot up his arm from her touch.

"Mr. Cordova, I'm Camille Kennison. And I've got a proposition for you."

Chapter

3

Alex arched a brow that had as much suggestion in it as his smile did. "I'm always interested in a proposition from a beautiful woman."

The forthrightness in her handshake weakened, but her confidence didn't diminish as she slid her hand from his fingers. "Not that kind of proposition. You see, my father owns the hardware store—"

"I guessed as much. You have the same last name."

Turning away, Alex began to work on the chest again. He sat on the overturned crate and ignored her as best as he could. He had no trouble guessing the nature of her proposal. What got his back up was that he hadn't though Kennison would stoop so low as to have his daughter do his bidding.

"Mr. Cordova." She moved closer to him. The sheer layer of lace on her skirt nearly brushed his elbow. "I'm sorry about yesterday."

"Forget about it."

"Is Captain feeling better?" When he didn't reply, she went on. "He felt very strongly about not having his beard shaved."

36

Alex never talked about Captain's confusion. It was a private matter between him and Cap. "Go home, Miss Kennison."

"I can't. Not until you hear me out." She laced her fingers in front of her. *Dammit.* Even knowing what she'd say before she said it, a cold sweat broke out on his brow. "The Harmony Keystones would like to contract you to play baseball."

"Not interested."

"I know my father's asked you before, but this is different. *I'm* asking now, and I—"

"Not interested." His glare warned her not to push him.

Her pale blue eyes didn't flicker in alarm. Or fear. Or show any other kind of emotion but set determination. Because it came at the expense of wearing him down, he grudgingly admired her fortitude.

"I can understand your reluctance to talk with me, but I can assure you that I don't have my father's temperament. Or that I don't use his tactics to make my point."

A light draft of air stirred the fine curls of wood shavings littered over the dirt floor. He watched them as they tumbled over one another, skittering across the tips of Camille's tan shoes. The fragrance of her perfume intruded into his male sanctuary. Lavender. Sweet lavender.

"There is no point to make." Alex quit using the jack plane and rubbed his thumb over a small nub in the grain. He liked it. He'd leave it.

"Oh, but you're wrong," she said.

The conviction in her voice had him looking at her once more. A skein of golden blond hair touched her ear, and he grew mesmerized by it as she spoke.

"I have a substantial offer for you to consider. One I'm sure my father has never brought you."

Snapping out of the fog that held him, Alex gave her a hard stare. "I don't play baseball."

"So you've said. But as you know, the Keystones have lost their first thirteen games this season—"

"No, I don't know. I don't follow the game anymore."

"Then you aren't aware of the American League."

He said nothing.

"They're newly formed this year. Clean ball is their main platform. No profanity on the playing field, and the umpires are legitimate agents of the league. Even your old club, the Orioles, are now in the American League. Things are quite different from the National League. The motto is 'a fair game and a good time.' "

"I don't give a bag of peanuts, honey."

That got her. She seemed to stand a little taller—as if to show him she wasn't weak. The soft-spoken Camille Kennison might not raise her voice, but she had a thread of stubbornness that lay hidden beneath the cool white surface.

"I *do* think you'll *give a bag of peanuts* when you hear the details." The edginess vanished, replaced by calm. "We're prepared to pay you two thousand five hundred for this season. We can't legally offer any more. The American League has imposed a salary cap."

The amount didn't stick in his brain because he didn't want to remotely consider it. But he did slant his gaze over her shapely breasts and curvy hips. He'd never run across a woman who had the body of Venus and could walk and pin her hat on at the same time. "How do you know so much about it?"

"My father eats baseball, breathes baseball, thinks baseball, dreams baseball, and incorporates baseball into every meal in our house." She gave him a glib look. "I'd have to be deaf *not* to know."

Well, hell. So maybe there was more to her pretty head than just a place to put her hat.

"We may not be able to pay more than twenty-five hundred," she repeated. She was wasting her breath. He couldn't play baseball. Not for her father. Not for anyone. "But we can give you a bonus of three thousand five hundred for the exclusive use of your photograph and signature."

He went still, his throat tightening. Swallowing, he asked, "What was that?"

"A bonus of three thousand five hundred dollars."

The computation in his head was lightning quick. Six thousand. Two thousand more than he needed.

She had to be screwing with him. He pinned her with a dark frown, but those rosebud lips of hers didn't twitch. They remained as lush and full as when she spoke those his-problem-was-solved figures.

"Let me assure you," she continued, "this is on the up-and-up."

For an instant, he let himself think about getting all that money. Then his mind flashed on what he'd have to do for it. He couldn't. Not for six thousand. Not for sixty thousand.

"Did you know Cy Young has only given up two home runs so far this season? Pitch against him and you could shake up the statistics, Mr. Cordova."

Trying to sweeten the deal by appealing to his ego wouldn't work. But his pulse picked up a notch. Cy Young. The last time Alex had pitched against the right-hander, Young had been playing for the Cleveland Spiders. And beat him and the Orioles.

Six grand. Hell.

He rose from the crate. "Young's in the National League—I couldn't very well play against him now, could I?"

"He left the National League for a better offer,"

she quickly replied. She kept her distance, but she was close enough for her perfume to encompass his senses like a lover's embrace. "This year, Mr. Young is with the Boston Somersets. American League."

Conflict raged in Alex, twisted in his belly. It would be fun to go after Cy, but that's not what this was about. She'd put the offer on the table. Big money. But how could he take it without going back on a promise he'd made to himself?

She waited, expectantly. She showed no signs of relenting. He cursed. She'd hit him up on a day where he couldn't say no. He needed the money. He had no choice.

Straight white teeth snagged her bottom lip. She hastily added, "I can also offer you your own hotel room on road games and—"

"You had me with the six thou, Miss Kennison." It was with a clenched jaw that he said, "I'll do it."

"You will?"

He quipped, "You want me to change my mind?"

"No!"

"Then you'd better close your mouth and get that contract written up before I do."

He'd only play out the season. A bonus for advertising rights was usually paid up front but covered a long period of time. The extra money now would give him living expenses while he had to cut back on carpentry jobs. And as soon as September was a page off the calendar, he'd be on a train to Buffalo with Captain.

"Oh . . . oh, well!" She extended her hand for him to shake.

He did so. Only this time he didn't let himself feel the softness of her skin—just the grip of her fingers. This was a business transaction. Cut and dried.

"Welcome aboard, Mr. Cordova," she said eagerly. "The Keystones are happy to have you."

"Yeah. Sure."

"My father's lawyer will draw up the contract. He can meet with you in Mr. Stykem's office—shall we say eleven o'clock?"

Alex nodded.

"Eleven o'clock, then." She walked backward while she said it, as if she felt she had to make a quick getaway or else he would back out in spite of what he said.

He let her go with a warning not to set him up in the future. "I can be bought, honey, but I can't be had. Cy Young's given up only one home run this year. To Roscoe Miller of the Detroit Tigers."

Her cheeks paled; then she turned in a swirl of skirts and left the wood shop.

Camille attempted to walk away as gracefully as she could, but it was an effort to keep one foot in front of the other. She could feel his gaze on her back, hot and steady. Observant. As if he could see right through her skirt to the frilly petticoat beneath.

She never should have fibbed about Cy Young. But just how had Alex known about Cy when he claimed not to follow baseball? The embellishment had been meant to entice Alex into taking her offer.

But it had been she who'd been enticed by him.

From the moment he'd taken her hand in his, an unfamiliar thrill had swept through her. She'd felt breathless and warm. Almost unable to move. Although she'd been taken by him, she'd done her best to hide her emotions. And was fairly certain she had succeeded.

But it hadn't been easy.

His eyes were dark and fathomless—keepers of the enigma that was Alex Cordova. And for a reckless moment, when he smoothed the wood with a caressing hand, she'd imagined what it would be like for those large hands to skim over her body.

As he worked, black hair fell in a part down the middle of his head; the ends were just shy of being long enough to tuck behind his ears. He probably thought the wild, untamed image suited him. Kept people at bay.

Well, it hadn't kept Camille Kennison at bay.

She'd gotten him.

Oh my goodness!

Rounding the corner of Elm and heading down Hackberry Way, she was able to relax. But her mind continued to whirl. As she walked, she went from laughing to keeping a hand over her heart to still its thumping beats. She couldn't wait to share her news. She felt like dancing on air.

But then she hurtled back to earth as reality struck.

Her father had decreed that whoever got Alex Cordova could be the manger of the Keystones. Of course he would never hold her to that.

She wanted no part of the job. She liked baseball quite a lot, but for the most part, the players were crude. All that spitting and adjusting their athletic supporters. Most of them cursed and few of them apologized for it. They carried on with women in saloons. Drank beer. They thrived on fistfights and arguments with the umpires.

Manage baseball players? No thank you.

She'd be happy to sit and enjoy the games now that the Keystones had a chance. Seeing Alex Cordova play would be wonderfully exciting.

Who was she kidding? When she told her father whom she'd payed a call on before Alex, whom she'd asked for thirty-five hundred dollars, she wouldn't be around to watch Alex pitch in his first game.

Because her father was going to kill her.

*   *   *

The slam of the front door announced James Kennison's arrival home. Camille and her mother sat in the parlor when he came in and went to the liquor cabinet straightaway. Without a word, he poured a himself a short tumbler of sipping whiskey.

As he sank into his favorite lounging chair, he moaned and stared into space with a blank and beaten expression on his face. "We lost again."

Camille waited several seconds before speaking.

"Then my news will be just the thing to cheer you up," she said in a bright tone though her insides were quaking.

"Nothing could cheer me up."

Looking up from the needlework in her lap, her mother said, "Maybe you should hear her news, James. I know I'm interested."

"Very well, what is it, Camille sugar?"

"I went to see Alex Cordova today," she divulged without preamble.

Surprise registered on both her parents' faces at the same time.

"Camille, you didn't," her mother admonished.

Blustering, her father said, "I told you not to go out on Elm Street."

"Yes, I know. But I went out there on Keystones business for you, so I didn't think you'd mind."

"I do mind. I said that it wasn't respectable for a young lady to—What kind of Keystones business?" A questioning expression crossed his face. "You didn't approach Cordova to play baseball, did you? I told you nobody—"

She cut in with a rush. "As a matter of fact, I did. I offered him the standard American League salary. Twenty-five hundred dollars."

"Camille"—her mother leaned forward—"did you really make him an offer?"

She nodded.

"And?" Her father eyed her with the dubious scrutiny he'd give a new hardware catalog with prices lower than his.

"And," she echoed, "he accepted."

Her words hovered in the air and his eyes grew large. "You're not serious."

"I am serious."

"Twenty-five hundred? You asked him? He said yes?"

"Yes."

"My God." The mustache on his lip curved—actually, more like twitched. "I can't believe it." Then his eyes narrowed. "What did you do to make the difference?"

The front bell cranked, chiming through the parlor like a shriek. Her father jumped. So did Camille, but for different reasons. She still had that other matter to mention and she wanted to get it over with.

The caller cranked the bell once more, a long and deliberate spin of the chime key that ground out the monotone note for a full five seconds.

"Leda!" His brows shot into an angry frown. "Answer the door before whoever's out there breaks the bell!"

"Hold your shirttail. I'm on my way," Leda snipped, walking across the parlor rug. She entered the foyer and swung the door open. "Yes?"

A man's voice drifted to the parlor. "Good evening. Bertram Nops to see the rusty hinge who calls himself a merchant."

Camille sucked in a sharp breath and was certain the color drained from her face.

"Nops!" her father spat. "I don't want to talk to that lug nut. Leda, tell him to get his carcass off my veranda."

In spite of his directive, the housemaid appeared

beneath the grillwork that led into the parlor. She wasn't alone. "Mr. Nops is here."

Jerking out of his chair, Camille's father blared, "Nops, I want you out of my house."

Mr. Nops didn't heed him. Instead, he held out his hat for Leda, who took it, then proceeded into the room as if he were an honored guest.

"Kennison," he greeted his rival in a well-pleased tone. "Mrs. Kennison. And Miss Kennison, a pleasure to see you again."

She forced a smile. Mr. Nops had no upper lip, a fact that was brought to attention when he smiled and his mouth grew wide. A brown hairpiece swooped far down on his forehead, making what would have been obvious more so. His eyebrows were a bit too pointy in the middle—as if they'd been drawn by Old Scratch.

What had she been thinking?

"So," he said, rubbing his hands together and clearly relishing the moment. She knew full well why. "I gave Alastair Stykem a bank note for the thirty-five hundred. Everything is neat as a pin. All set for tomorrow."

Her father's stare traveled between her and Mr. Nops. "What's all set for tomorrow? And what in the blue blazes does thirty-five hundred dollars have to do with it?"

Mr. Nops chuckled, then chortled when he apparently realized her father was in the dark. "She hasn't told you?"

"Told me what?"

It was impossible to steady her pulse, so she might as well say what she had to. "You see, Daddy, I needed a bonus to convince Mr. Cordova to play for you. Without an added incentive, I knew I couldn't have gotten him to sign. After all, he has turned you down for the same amount. So I asked Mr. Nops to go into partnership with us on this one small thing."

"Good God, Camille. Why did you do *that?*"

"Because I needed three thousand five hundred dollars."

"So you went to the biggest double-talker in Harmony?" Because her father stood nearly on top of his competitor, his irate voice practically blew Mr. Nops's toupee up his forehead. "Nops, you could argue a gopher into buying a tree."

Mr. Nops snorted with laughter. "That's a good one, Kennison. And quite true."

Bertram Nops wasn't Harmony's most trusted businessman. But he'd been a sure thing when it came to supplying the money Camille needed. For nearly a decade, Mr. Nops had been envious that her father owned his own baseball team. And recently, with the Keystones going professional, Mr. Nops had turned a full shade of green.

The look on his face when Camille had presented him her idea . . . well, he'd gotten so excited he'd had to flip the OPEN sign on the door to CLOSED so no customers would intrude when he made her repeat herself just to be sure he'd heard her correctly.

Her father acted as if she'd schemed up something foolhardy. She'd put a lot of thought into her plan. "Daddy, my intentions were to bring an end to the ridiculous hardware store war you two have been engaged in for the past ten years. This way you both have a vested interest in Alex Cordova and can work together."

Her father yelled, "Nops owns more of him than I do by *one thousand dollars!*"

"But you still own the whole team, Kennison!" Mr. Nops yelled back.

Her mother interrupted. "Gentlemen, I think there's validity to what Camille did, and if you'd both stop shouting at one another, you'd see that this could be a very beneficial arrangement."

Her father braced his hands on his waist. "A beneficial arrangement? I fail to see the benefit in it." Turning to Camille, he lashed out. "How could you promise this flathead screw a part of the Keystones without asking me? It was stupid of you, Camille." He drew in a deep breath and exhaled, "It was beyond *stupid!*"

Her jaw dropped in horror, that he could say such a thing to her. In front of her mother. In front of Mr. Nops. And in front of Leda. Hot tears filled her eyes.

"If anybody is stupid, Kennison, it's *you,*" Mr. Nops said. "For spouting off at the mouth, and as usual, without thinking. But then, one man's stupidity is another man's gain." Laughter shook his chest. "I ran into Duke and Jimmy before your daughter came to see me. They said that you told them whoever got Alex Cordova to play for the Keystones could be the manager." Grinning wide, Mr. Nops showed his cards. "It was my thirty-five hundred that turned Cordova around. So I'm the new manager of the Keystones."

After a long moment, her father barreled back, "I wasn't serious about that!"

Camille was too stunned to say anything.

"It's time to put your words into action, Kennison. *I* am the new manager."

In an attempt to save himself, her father sputtered, "Duke and Jimmy misunderstood me."

"But I heard you myself," Leda said.

Turning to her, he snapped, "You were in the kitchen. How could you hear a thing?"

"With an ear to the door, Mr. Kennison. Like I always do in case you're after me to refill that pot of coffee on the breakfast table. You did tell those two boys, plain as day."

Mr. Nops's guffaw rumbled through the parlor. "I've got you up a tree, Kennison. Allow me to tell the gopher to move over on that limb."

"Leda, you're fired!"

"Humph. That's the second time this month, and I haven't packed a stitch of clothing yet."

"Listen, Nops, if anyone in this room is entitled to be the manager, it's my Camille."

Her stomach lurched; her heart pumped double time.

"She did the talking!" her father exclaimed. *"She* convinced Cordova, not you. This was her effort, and it's going to stay in the family. She gets the credit."

Squaring off, the two men drew verbal weapons. They blasted each other in a shoot-out of accusations, although neither could hear the other above his own voice.

"Gentlemen, if you please." Her mother's tone was coolly disapproving, yet did not lose its silken quality. She needed to voice the plea only once.

In the cease-fire, the spent powder of their anger almost made a visible cloud of gray smoke.

Then Mr. Nops folded his arms over his chest and flared his nostrils. "All right, Kennison, I agree."

"That's more like it."

"You've got yourself a manager." He aimed a finger at Camille. "A *female* manager."

Under his glare, Camille's stomach felt as if it had fallen to her knees and her legs tingled to the point she had to sit down on the divan or lose her footing.

"That's absurd!" her father shouted. "My daughter could never give orders to thirteen men and be taken seriously. She wouldn't know the first thing to do."

Camille had absolutely no designs on the job, but her father touched a sore spot with his lack of faith in her abilities. Especially in light of what she'd accomplished.

"What do you mean I couldn't be taken seriously?" she asked. "There's no doubt one Alex Cordova is a lot harder to talk into something than twelve of your Keystones. Managing the others would be like handling a prickly pear without the prickly."

With his mustache twitching, he said, "Baseball players aren't like your little flower garden. You can't prune and water them and expect to see results. A firm hand, a hard voice, an iron will. That's what gets results. Camille sugar, you wouldn't last a day." He clenched his fists by his sides. "But none of that matters because I'm not taking a penny of your money, Nops. The deal is *off.*"

The simmering argument, about to erupt into full boil again, had to be stopped by Camille's mother once more. "James, really. You're not thinking clearly."

"Grayce, you don't know anything about this."

Not put off, she observed, "You may own the Keystones, but they're the town's team. They've stood by you through all the losing seasons. And now you can give them a winning pitcher. You'd let Mr. Cordova go just to keep your pride?"

Her father could be a grouchy old bear, but he did listen to her mother, more than from time to time. His face grew somber. It took him a while to weigh things out. At length, he said, "All right. Nops has a share of the Keystones. But Camille's not going to be the manager. Watching the game and being in the thick of things are entirely different. She's too much of a lady to be subjected to the rowdiness of athletes."

"Be that as it may," Nops responded with a lift of his forefinger. "I'm going to have to hold you to your word. If she's not the manager, then you don't get a plugged nickel."

"Thunderation!" Her father pinched the bridge of his nose as if he had a blinding headache. "She's not manager material. Look at her. She's soft. She's feminine. She's pretty."

Camille's nerves were at a breaking point. Years of her father telling her that frayed what was left of her composure. Why did he constantly misjudge her? The unfairness of it all filled her with a crushing disappointment. "I *am* manager material, Daddy." She couldn't explain exactly why. She knew only that it was true. "And if you don't give me the job, then you really *aren't* a man of your word."

Chapter
4

Alastair Stykem's second floor office was located on Birch Avenue in an upper-rent building. The lobby had a granite floor and two private mailboxes on the wall. As Alex climbed the stairs, Captain followed.

The hunt-and-peck tap of typewriter keys sounded in the hallway.

"That would be Hildegarde." Cap made the observation. "She told me she can't type worth a whistle."

"Then how come she's Stykem's secretary?"

"She said it's only temporary. She'll be coming back to the mercantile as soon as Mr. Stykem finds somebody who knows how to file the A files in the A drawer, and the B files in the B drawer—all the way to Z. What's so hard about that? I know the alphabet. Do you think I ought to tell Mr. Stykem?"

"Not unless you want to learn how to type."

"Hell no."

Alex came to a glass door that had ALASTAIR STYKEM, ATTORNEY AT LAW spelled out in gold lettering. The typewriter sounds grew clearer as he and Cap went inside.

Hildegarde Plunkett sat at the reception desk, her brown hair piled high on her head. When she looked up, she smiled. Her face was round and she had a full figure, but she was no less attractive for it.

"Hello," she said. The pencil she'd tucked behind her ear fell onto the desk as she tilted her head.

Captain removed his hat and crushed the brim in his large hands. "I wanted to come with Alex so I could ask you when you'll be coming back into your father's mercantile. When will you?"

She shuffled the papers in front of her. "I don't know. Mr. Stykem has had five secretaries since his daughter Crescencia got married." She moved one folder, then another, and then she reached for a pile of mail. "I'm the only one who's lasted—I mean stayed—this long." More paper went from one spot on the desk to the other. Then her hands stilled. She frowned at what she'd done. The stack of papers had looked more organized before she'd rearranged them. She sighed. "My mother says secretarial work isn't my calling."

"I think your calling is being at the mercantile when I sweep." Captain reached down beside the desk and grabbed a trash can. "Your father doesn't talk much. Your mother talks too much. But you talk to me just enough." With a sweeping motion, he cleaned the desk of papers. The documents landed in the waste can. "There. Now you can get fired."

"Cap, you shouldn't have done that." Alex took the receptacle from him and began to take the papers out.

"It's all right, Mr. Cordova." Hildegarde propped her chin in her hand. "I've thought about doing it myself. But the Remington won't fit."

"Who's Remington?" Cap asked.

The young woman had dimples. "The typewriter."

"I could bust it for you. I'm a big guy." He gave her a demonstration, lifting his arms and pumping up his biceps. The defined muscles bulged the sleeves of his cotton shirt.

Hildegarde blushed, her full cheeks turning pink. "That's all right."

Alex shifted his weight, eager to sign what he had to and get on with it. All he'd had time for was thinking about his decision, and for every minute that passed, he'd searched for a plausible excuse to back out. "I've got an appointment to meet Kennison."

"Yes. She's waiting for you with Mr. Stykem."

She?

Hildegarde led them to an inner office. "They told me to have you go right in as soon as you got here." She opened the door and let him pass through, closing it behind him.

In a chair directly to his right sat Camille Kennison. She wore an ivory dress that was softly molded to the curves of her figure. A large hat covered her golden hair; her profile was barely discernable to him beneath the wide brim. A hint of natural rose color brushed her cheek; her lips looked soft and pink. Jesus, she was a beautiful woman. She could make a man forget himself just by looking at her.

Stykem rose from behind a massive oak desk and extended his hand. "Alastair Stykem," he said by way of an introduction.

"Alex Cordova," Alex replied while shaking the man's hand.

"Have a seat, Mr. Cordova, and we'll get right to business."

Alex took the chair next to Camille's. "Where's your father?"

A trace of worry caught in her eyes, but her voice was steady as she replied, "He's put me in charge of this transaction."

Transaction. The word shouldn't have sounded so demeaning, but it prickled the back of his neck. In baseball, players were bought and sold. This wasn't like he'd been thrown on a waiver list and the Keystones were claiming him for the eighteen hundred-dollar waiver price. The offer was more than satisfactory. He just wished that he didn't need to take it. And that a woman hadn't presented it.

Why would Kennison leave this kind of business up to his daughter?

Sitting this close to her, he could almost feel the softness of her skin; the fine fabric of her dress. Everything about her was sophisticated. The way she sat, the way she smelled, the way she looked. Next to her, he felt too big. Too coarse. Too raw.

Alex set his jaw and focused on the man before him.

"Now then," Stykem said while opening a portfolio. "Miss Plunkett has typed everything up, and all that's required is your signature. I'm sure you're familiar with a league contract, Mr. Cordova."

Leaning back into his chair, Alex rested his hands on the worn denim encasing his thighs. "Enlighten me on the details just the same."

Stykem picked up the document and began to read. "The American League contract states that players are forbidden to drink, on the field or off. No staging games to suit gamblers. Suppression of obscene, indecent, and vulgar language will be in effect while the player is on the ball field. No use of fists, bats, or spikes in confrontations. Your uniform, bats, and balls are to be supplied by the Keystones franchise."

The lawyer cleared his throat, then lifted another

paper and scanned it. Light from the window caused the gold signet ring on his finger to flash. "This page lists the terms of monies. Two thousand five hundred dollars for the season with no deductions for the three weeks you haven't played, to be paid in monthly installments. Three thousand five hundred dollars for the exclusive use of your photograph and signature, which the Keystones will use at their discretion."

After defining the rest of the clauses, Stykem handed him a pen and showed him the various places that required his signature.

The gold fountain pen felt heavy in his grasp. Alex needed to believe he was doing the right thing. That he had considered every option available to him. But this was the only way to get a large amount of money. And on that conviction, he signed himself over to the Harmony Keystones.

When everything was neat and tidy, the lawyer stood and shook Alex's hand once more. Camille rose as well and extended her hand to him. Her attempt at being straightforward had a slight hesitancy to it. As if she'd been the one to sign herself away instead of him. "Congratulations, Mr. Cordova, and welcome to the Keystones organization."

The fine white of her glove warmed his fingers. Made his blood pump fast and surge to his groin.

Alex released her hand and left the private office. He had to get out of there.

"Cap, I'm leaving." He spoke as he walked.

Once on the street, Alex shoved his hands in his pockets and felt for a matchstick and cigarette. He came up empty. Seven months ago, he'd quit smoking. But the urge to light up hadn't fully gone away.

Captain caught up to him. "How come you're in such a hurry?"

"Do you understand what happened in the lawyer's office?"

"Yes. You explained it to me yesterday. You're going to play baseball. Just like you used to." Captain stuck his fingers inside his shirt pocket and took out a small photograph, its edges worn, yet not a single tear or tatter marred the paper. The image was of the Baltimore Orioles team. The players in the front row held up a banner that read 1897 PENNANT WINNERS. Pointing to a spot on the picture, Cap said, "That's you."

Alex gave his likeness a cursory glance, a flood of memories coming at him.

"I'm going to ask Mr. Plunkett if I can leave work early tomorrow so I can watch you play."

There had been a time when Alex had given Cap the photograph, that he'd wanted him to see more in it than a group of ballplayers. Now he lived with the paralyzing fear Cap would find the hidden meaning. And that fact made him ashamed.

When Alex turned, he saw Camille Kennison walking toward him and Cap, moving with that fluid stride of hers. Head held high. Tiny pearl-and-gold earrings dangling from her earlobes. Earlobes that looked sweet. Too damn sweet. Very kissable.

Hell.

"Hello." Her greeting was directed more to Captain than to Alex.

"Hello," Cap replied, recognition lighting his eyes. "I know who you are. Kennison's Hardware."

"Yes." She held the handle of her pocketbook. "How are you feeling today?"

Confused, he looked over his beard to the tips of his shoes. He gave his chest a pat, felt his cheeks and the wiry hair on his chin, then said, "I feel the same as I always do. Do you want to feel me to make sure?"

A delicate crease formed on her forehead. "Oh. Well, you do look nice."

Alex knew Captain didn't remember what had happened. At least not all of it. He didn't forget his headaches, but after most episodes, he couldn't recall what had set him off. On days like today when he appeared to be well, it made it harder for Alex to accept he wasn't improving.

A man walking toward where the three of them stood tipped his hat to Camille. "Good afternoon, Miss Kennison."

"Good afternoon," she replied as he strode by.

Alex watched the man retreat. She'd barely glanced at him.

"Mr. Cordova." Her voice pulled his attention back to her. "There are a few things I neglected to mention." She seemed less anxious now that she was free of the book-lined walls in the lawyer's office. "The Keystones are playing the Boston Somersets tomorrow at four o'clock. Cy Young is starting for them."

Another "Good afternoon, Miss Kennison" came when a businessman in a dapper coat headed for the doors of the building.

"Good afternoon."

Alex's mind momentarily focused on the brief exchange, then returned to the conversation at hand. He hadn't figured on facing Cy so soon. He wasn't in the best physical shape he could be in after having sat out several seasons. The prospect of going against the Cyclone when he hadn't used his pitching arm in so long increased his misgivings. Then there were other things. He'd known that by signing on, he'd meet up with players he knew. He wondered how many of his former teammates were in the American League.

What had happened to make him quit was something Alex lived with every day. He wasn't ready to talk about it. Most people could move forward, but the other players didn't get that. They'd been uncomfortable around him, frequently not saying anything at all for fear of saying the wrong thing. At least in Harmony, nobody knew the details. His old manager had paid off the newspapers to bury the speculation surrounding his departure.

"Practice begins at three," Camille continued. "There'll be a uniform for you in the clubhouse at Municipal Field. What size shoe do you wear?"

"Eleven."

"Good afternoon, Miss Kennison." The doffer of the hat this time was a young man whose broad smile took up half his face.

"Good afternoon," she replied. Without a breath, she added, "I'll make sure you have a pair. I don't believe there's anything else. Uniform, shoes, equipment." She inhaled, standing taller. "All right, then. Everything will be fine," she said, as if more to convince herself than him.

The braided brim of her ivory hat kept her face in partial shade. The rest of her reminded Alex of a statue of a Greek goddess. Pure marble; smooth, soft, and desirable.

The barber stepped out of his shop with a broom. Seeing her, he called across the street, "Good afternoon, Miss Kennison."

"Good afternoon."

The overabundance of male greetings got on Alex's nerves for reasons he didn't care to examine. A woman like her had to be used to the attention and probably enjoyed it. Even so, he couldn't curb the exaggerated grin that curved his mouth. "Do you ever get tired of hearing that?"

To his surprise, she didn't blush. "Why don't you say it to me, and I'll let you know." She began to walk away.

He took the bait. "Good afternoon, Miss Kennison."

Without interrupting her stride, she glanced at him over her shoulder. She hit him with a smile that was so beautifully candid, so captivating, he had to fight himself from going after her. From sliding his hand around the back of her neck and kissing her fully on the mouth.

The muscles in his body tightened. He wanted to take her straight to paradise. Run his hands over every inch of her body. Hold her breasts in his palms. Trace the nipples with his—

Her wave cut short his fantasies; then she went on her way. She didn't say "Good afternoon" in return.

She'd made a mackerel out of him.

"I think she likes you, Alex," Cap mused aloud.

"No, Cap," he said, watching her until she was out of his view. "It just seems that way."

When Camille was a little girl, strawberry taffies had always made her feel better when she was anxious. But she felt no different now than after she'd eaten her first one.

She sat in the clubhouse, at the manager's desk, a bag of the candies in front of her and empty wrappers littering on the desktop. As she chewed the sugary confection, she settled into the brand spanking new chair and looked around the brand-spanking-new clubhouse that her father had spent a lot of money to build.

Even while it was under construction, the building had been off limits to her. It was a man's domain. A player's place. That she was in here now, actually had the key to the door in her purse, would be the manager—

She had to unwrap another taffy before finishing the one in her mouth.

The room smelled of yellow pine and varnish. Behind her, a long row of open cubbies spread across a wall. Inside them, knob hooks held freshly laundered uniforms. In the trunks below, were the players' personal possessions. Athletic shoes rested on the lids. A placard with the name of one of the thirteen Keystones hung above each cubby. Bats forty-two inches in length stood on their ends in a wall rack. A large basket of regulation balls lined the floor, some virgin white, but most tar black or at least a dark gray.

Camille swallowed her taffy. She'd come here after encountering Alex Cordova on the street corner. That he could put her out of sorts was an understatement. One small glance from him in Mr. Stykem's office had set her heartbeat to an uneven rhythm. She'd conversed with good-looking men before, but she'd never asked them their shoe size . . .

Eleven. Such a personal detail; its only relevance should have been purely professional. And yet, with the information had come a flustering confusion that had tickled her ribs and woven a cocoon of intimacy around her.

She never should have flirted with him like that. She just should have said "Good afternoon" back. Her silence had implied more. She'd had a lapse in common sense. Blame it on his voice, with its hint of an exotic accent from someplace far away. There was a quality to it that made her want to hear how *he* would say those two words to her. He had a wonderful mouth. She wondered how his lips would feel against hers. How—

She quickly put the new piece of taffy into her mouth.

She couldn't squander valuable time thinking about Alex Cordova or dissecting the feelings he evoked in her. There were far more important issues at hand.

Namely, plotting how to kill Bertram Nops.

Last night, Camille had tossed and turned over the events that had led her into this mess. She blamed Mr. Nops. But every way she thought about his hand in making her the manager, she had to concede the same thing.

It was her fault.

She never should have asked him for the money.

Little did she realize what affect it would have on her life—on her Garden Club plans. When she'd left her father no choice but to take her challenge, the ramifications had sunk in. She'd felt faint. Sick at heart. She'd had to go to her room to lie down or she would have keeled over.

How could she be president of the Garden Club if she had to manage a group of spitting, scratching, and jockstrap-adjusting baseball players? The mere thought had made her woozy.

But today, the problem didn't seem as awful as she'd initially thought. This was a way to show her father she had know-how on a level that he could relate to. Managing might even be fun. Well, as much fun as spitting, scratching, and adjusting could be.

On her off hours, she could plant her garden. She could still run for president. This Friday's meeting was at seven o'clock. Friday's baseball game should be completed by then. Balancing playing schedules and tending flowers and vegetables could be done.

Just thinking about that gave her enough optimism to commit herself to both. That wasn't to say it would be easy. It would be quite difficult. But she could do it. After all, organization was her forte. She'd never met a more organized person than herself. A list for everything. A place for everything. A chart. A box. A notebook.

She moved aside the growing pile of taffy wrappers

to lay her hand on the baseball regulations book. She'd have to study it tonight and learn it by heart. She'd been to many games, but she'd never memorized the rules. She didn't want to come across as unprepared. She knew what to look for to call a ball and a strike. Fielding strategies and batting positions. The basic things. There was a lot in between she would have to grapple with.

But she could do it. She *had* to do it.

She slid the crumpled candy wrappers into the trash, then grabbed the rule book and her purse. Locking the door behind her, she headed for home. The afternoon was sunny and bright; the grass on the field had just been mowed. The baselines had been freshly chalked in white, and the bags in the corners and both the pitcher's mound and home plate had been dusted.

On a satisfied nod, she told herself tomorrow would go just fine.

Camille never fell into a deep sleep that night. At 1:28 in the morning, she woke with a start.

She'd forgotten something.

She tossed the covers aside and quickly went to her wardrobe. Fitting her arms into the sleeves of her kimono and absently stepping into felt slippers, she pushed one of the dangling curl papers from her forehead as she entered her mother's sewing room, a tiny alcove beneath the stairs fitted with a hanging electric light that gave off a bright beam.

She turned the switch and blinked against the flood of light. Cold air skimmed across her skin. She shivered and struck a fire in the small parlor stove so that she could warm her feet. Her mother kept folds of material beside her Singer and Camille riffled through them. For the most part, they were remnants or weren't as long as she needed. Only one would work—the fifteen yards of Paris organdy with lace-on-lace effects and blushing pink rosebuds twined with hunter green leaves. She had been going to sew a summer dress out of it, and now she'd have to use it for ... but Paris organdy?

It would have to do. With a snap of her wrists, the silky fabric billowed open, and she set to work.

Hours later, the floor was littered with snippings of threads and dribbles of ashes from the small heating stove. But she deemed her task complete just as the melodic chime of the parlor clock struck four. Yawning, she returned to her bedroom, crawled back into bed, and closed her eyes.

Now, tomorrow would go just fine.

Chapter

❦ 5 ❧

Rain came down in buckets.

Just after noon, the sidewalks were slippery with mire. Rivers of water spilled over the canvas awnings of businesses, giving the tightly knit storefronts in the town square the look of Niagara Falls.

The torrential downpour was a bad omen, surely one triggered by the shenanigans between Camille's father and Bertram Nops. The fight had begun before business hours, with Daddy squeezing off the first shot, but the return volley was swift and deadly.

Just before nine o'clock, Mr. Nops had begun to pile gallons of willow green paint in front of his store. Spying out his window, her father hadn't missed a move. Minutes later, he'd brought out every last gallon of willow green paint he had in stock and slashed the price to half of what Mr. Nops was selling his for. Nops; seventy cents; Kennison; thirty-five cents. It was an underhanded move on her father's part that infuriated Mr. Nops. No sooner had her father stacked his paint cans in a pyramid with a big sign on the top can advertising the price than Mr. Nops put up an even bolder sign on his top willow green can:

> For cheap vermillion paint,
> look no farther than Kennison's Hardware.

It was a sore spot for Daddy. Last fall, he'd sold Tom Wolcott some of the offensive red paint for the exterior of Wolcott's sporting goods store, just so Mr. Wolcott could aggravate the tenant next door, Edwina Huntington . . . who later forgave him and became his wife. Mr. Wolcott had eventually repainted his side of the building on Old Oak Road to match the canary yellow paint on her side, but not before the townspeople had gotten a good eyeful of that awful red. And not before the townspeople had heard who sold Mr. Wolcott the paint that allowed him to pull a prank on a woman.

Camille didn't have time to keep it all straight in her mind as she shook the rain from her oilskin umbrella and closed it. Even though she wore a jacket and lace-up storm shoes, she was damp. In rain like this, there was no way to keep dry. It was hard enough walking with dignity on dry heels, but wet ones hampered even the best of efforts.

The openly admiring gazes of men had followed her as she'd walked past the opposing team's dugout where the Boston players were gathering to begin practice. The scrutiny had intensified as she bypassed the grandstand. If she hadn't been holding her umbrella, she might have checked to see if her fruited hat had been pinned on straight. She still felt eyes on her now as she reached the Keystones' clubhouse. Taking a quick inhale, she prayed everyone would be decent. She'd purposefully waited a quarter of an hour to return after having been inside this morning to hang—

"Whoa, honey," came a voice behind her. "You can't go in there."

She turned and encountered a man no taller than herself. From the dour expression on his face, he looked like he'd been weaned on an icicle. His eyes were too close together, his nose was on the bulbous side, and his left cheek was packed so full of tobacco, he could hardly talk.

"Who are you?" She rested her palm on her umbrella handle, the point on the step. Without an awning above her, rain fell on her shoulders.

"Boomer Hurley, manager of the Boston Somersets."

Because the Keystones had never played a major-league team before, Camille had never seen this man at prior games. After his introduction, she hastily made her own. "Camille Kennison, manager of the Harmony Keystones. Now if you'll excuse me, I'm getting wet."

He gave off a big roar of laughter that shook his entire body, and for a moment she thought he'd up and choke on his prune-size lump of chewing tobacco. "Manager? No, honey, you're mistaken. You're not the manager of the Keystones. Now you might be a relation to James Kennison—which I don't know for sure or not because he's not, here—but you're no manager."

Camille had wondered where her father was, too. She'd searched the stands for him—which hadn't been hard. The only person sitting in them had been Captain, who'd waved at her. Nobody else had braved the rainy day to watch the batters warm up.

"I am his daughter, Mr. Hurley." Camille dropped her chin to keep the droplets of water from her face. "And I *am* the manager of the Keystones." She held out the notebook she'd tucked beneath her arm. "I have today's batting order to prove it. But I don't need to show you that, do I? I'll see you on the field."

"Wait a minute. Wait just a damn minute. You're no manager." He projected a stream of brown juice, just missing the hem of her skirt. Whether his aim was intentional or not, she gave him the benefit of the doubt, only because she didn't want to get upset on her first day. "Honey, baseball is a red-blooded sport for red-blooded men. It's not teatime, so ladies such as yourself had better stay the hell out of it."

She got upset.

The blunt point of her umbrella stabbed him in the big toe of his thin leather shoes—an accident, of course—as she turned to go inside. "Pardon me," she said, by way of both apology and departure.

Pleased with herself, she went inside the clubhouse and closed the door on Boomer Hurley, leaving him out on the stoop. But if she thought she'd left a problem outside, she ran headlong into another one. Much bigger. Much *barer*.

Half-naked baseball players.

Activity in the room froze, as did Camille. She couldn't even swallow, much less blink, while facing men in various stages of undress. Shirts on. Shirts off with bare chests showing. Pants dropped at ankles. Athletic supporters in hand; athletic supporters in place over drawers.

Within seconds, everyone made a mad grab for their white-and-gold uniforms. Pants legs and shirt-sleeves flailed while the men shoved arms and legs into them. Everyone moved except Alex Cordova. He remained standing in his underwear as if he didn't care what she saw. As if he *wanted* her to see him.

His stance emphasized the strength in his thighs and the slimness of his hips. Worn, ribbed cotton clung to every muscle of his body, hugging his chest, expanding over broad shoulders, and molding to his flat belly. The top two buttons of his drawers were unfastened. Camille's gaze lowered to where the cotton cupped a particular area. For a second, she allowed herself a look. Her quickening heartbeat caught in her throat as she looked at the definition of pure man. She swiftly lifted her eyes to his.

She sensed he was angry with her.

And then she saw the animosity written over Cub LaRoque's face as he gave Alex a long stare. Cub was the Keystones' starting pitcher; apparently he didn't like his position being usurped by a new player. The others noticed it, too. Tension gripped the room. Sharp glances made it clear that Alex was out of place.

That *she* was out of place.

A warning erupted in her head. Moisture formed on her palms. She'd fully expected her father to have been here first, to pave the way. She'd been certain he'd be the one to tell them about her new position, break it to them in a man's terms, straightforward and to the point. There'd have been no arguing about it, because he owned the team.

"Miss Kennison, you gotta get out of here," squeaked Mox Snyder, the third baseman. Never fast on his feet, he'd stepped into his pants backward, the behind part now drooping front and center—an error that pretty much summed up how he played baseball.

Deacon Pfeffer, the right fielder, sat on the trunk in his cubby with his shoes untied. "What's going on?"

"Yeah," Yank Milligan and Charlie Delahanty said at the same time. "What's going on?"

"No women allowed," grumbled Bones Davis, the second baseman.

A chorus of the same sentiment echoed off the walls.

Her misgivings increased by the minute.

"Hey, wait a minute," Specs Ryan said while facing them. "Maybe her father sent her over with a message." With eyes magnified by thick glass lenses, he stared at Camille—rather, he squinted through his lashes, his upper lip extended, as if that could help him see better. His real name was Timothy. She'd gone to school with him, and ever since she could remember, he'd worn spectacles, thus earning him the nickname. "So, did he?"

Everyone waited for her reply. She hadn't been prepared for this. She'd been raised a Southern lady. Genteel. Taught to speak in a buttery tone gentlemen found charming. She was unequipped to confront men in their drawers, a fact it was too late to do anything about now.

So she'd save face if it killed her.

Finding her voice, Camille spoke. "As a matter of fact, my father did send me."

"Did he find a new manager?" asked Noodles Duggleby, the catcher. His hands were nearly as big as the oversize mitt he used to catch with.

"Yes," Camille said, "he has."

Baritone shouts went up through the room, accompanied by a few pats on the back, a nod of a head here and there. Mostly, there were relieved expressions and audible sighs of relief. She wondered just how long that relief would last when she told them the truth.

Cub asked, "So who'd he get?"

"Yeah, who?" Charlie pressed.

"We want to know," Duke Boyle said while trading glances with Jimmy Shugart. "Kennison said whoever got Cordova could be the manager." Duke pointed at Alex. "And there he is."

Jimmy jumped in. "We asked Cordova who talked

him into it, but he said it wasn't a who—it was a *what."*

Speculative gazes fell on Alex. If he was uncomfortable, he didn't show it. Camille waited for any kind of reaction from him. Nothing. His expression was unreadable.

"Why won't he say?" Jimmy wanted to know.

She knew why. Alex's words came back to her. *I can be bought, honey, but I can't be had.*

Money.

Money had made him change his mind, but at least he wasn't boasting about it to the other team members.

"Because the person who contracted him isn't somebody you'd think of." She moved to the desk, then laid down her velvet purse and notebook. Then she stuck her umbrella into the trash can so that the rainwater wouldn't drip on the floor. Turning, she held her posture erect. "It's me."

A stunned silence fell like lead, hard and heavy, suffocating the room. She didn't dare meet Alex's gaze. But she felt it on her as sure as if she were looking directly into his eyes.

Cupid Burns, the first baseman, broke through the strain. "You've got to be kidding."

"I'm quite serious. Why else would I be here?"

"To satisfy your womanly curiosity."

The low and rich voice came to her from the right. Exactly where Alex stood. She faced him. He wore his underwear the same way he wore the smile he gave her: sinfully.

"Certainly not," she snapped. "I can assure you, I have the best of intentions and I take my responsibilities quite seriously. I knew there would be some problems, but I've already found a way around one obstacle." She gestured to the corner where her Paris organdy rosebud fabric hung. The drape looked like a woman's parlor curtain, only it was gathered in a single direction, not the way she'd left it—spread out and able to conceal players as they disrobed. "I put up a dressing curtain."

Cupid howled with humor. "That frilly thing?"

Bones smirked. "We thought Kennison was off his nut. No offense, Miss Kennison, since he is your father. But we were laughing so hard over that curtain, that's how come we're late getting dressed for practice."

"Yank even sniffed one of them bee-you-tee-ful roses to see if it smelled like toilet water," Doc Nash commented with a chuckle.

Yank cried, "Did not!"

Specs seconded Yank. "Saw you myself, Doc."

"You couldn't see a pile of shit in a cow pasture, Specs." Yank pushed on his cap, the brim falling low on his brow. "For a change of pace, why don't you get the right prescription for your goddamn glasses when you play ball? Maybe we might just win a game."

"Not only *my* fault we stink," he shot back.

"If we had a manager who was worth his salt, we wouldn't," Noodles complained.

"But we don't," Cub shot back. "We've got *her.*"

"I quit." Mox threw his glove on his trunk.

"Me, too."

"I second that."

"Make that three."

Calls came from all over the room. "Five."

"Make that seven."

"Eleven."

"Count me in as twelve."

Then came silence. The disapproval that had echoed through the clubhouse made Camille's bones feel brittle. If she had had any kind of sense, then she

would have turned tail and left right then. But she refused, to do it. She couldn't quit—because of one fact.

The thirteenth player hadn't voiced his opinion.

Alex.

Even if he voted with the rest of them, it would
change nothing. She'd still be the manager. They'd
have to give her a chance. Because they didn't have a
choice. And neither did she. It was either her or
Bertram Nops. And Mr. Nops didn't count. So she
was it.

Alex took the jersey from his cubby and slid one
arm through a sleeve. Watching him dress with deliberate slowness brought a tingle across her skin, a rush
of color to her cheeks. Slipping his other arm into the
shirt, he began to do up the length of buttons. "What
the hell do I care who tells me when to pitch? The
game's still played the same."

"But she's a woman, Cordova," Bones complained.

Alex's gaze roamed over her with molten heat,
from the brim of her hat to the hem of her skirt. Just
that one look ignited a flame in the bottom of her
stomach. She fought the urge to press her palm into
her middle to still the warmth within her.

His tone deep and quiet, Alex said, "I can see that."

"But we can't take orders from a woman."

Taking his white pants off the hook, he stepped into
them, completely heedless of Camille's presence as
his fingers slipped buttons in place on the fly. "Get
over it."

The players stared at each other, sending silent
messages through the clubhouse. She didn't move an
inch; she barely breathed. She took the time to size
them up in return.

They were a ragtag bunch, it was true. The Harmony Keystones were local men. Some lived in Harmony, others in Waverly and Alder. They worked at

the feed and seed, the lumbermill. Another farmed with his dad. Several were bricklayers. No matter how much her father wanted to believe they were professional-league material, the fact of the matter was, they were just hometown players. That's all they'd ever been. And right now, clinging to hope and league salaries was all they had going for them.

But the right person could make the difference. She had her work cut out for her, but she could do it. She had to.

With every ounce of conviction she had, she found herself announcing, "I want you to know that my vision for this club is quite ambitious. I may be a woman, but I know the game. I can reverse the direction this team's been going."

Since they were listening, she hastily added, "The margin between a winning club and a losing club isn't always that big. It depends on how the players look at themselves. I've read the rule book and I know how to improve batting statistics. We'll practice fielding better and shagging balls. Everyone will work together as a team."

Alex's eyes met hers as she articulated her message. "And we can go to the pennant if we all try. It could happen, you know. You all have potential. And with Alex Cordova onboard, the Keystones can learn a great deal." She took a deep gulp of air and smiled.

Then she waited for their reactions.

A few mumbles, quiet conversations, and shrugs. After another long moment, the players finished dressing without protest. Specs slid the curtain shut and those men who needed to change into trousers concealed themselves behind it.

Camille didn't think she could resume normal breathing, much less sit down at the desk. So she reached for the leather notebook and opened it.

Feigning great interest in that book was how she kept from thinking about what was going on around her.

With their spike shoes on and bats in hand, and with the basket of balls carried in between Cupid and Charlie, twelve men filed out of the clubhouse.

Only Alex remained. He came toward her; she stilled in anticipation. She didn't know what she expected him to do, and she didn't understand why she'd wanted his approval.

Her discomfort was unfounded. He made no attempt to touch her. He merely propped the ball of his foot on the edge of her desk to tie his shoe. Looking up at her through the hair that fell in his eyes, he said, "You didn't tell me not everyone would be happy to see me."

"I didn't know they wouldn't be." She wanted to assure him he was welcome. "I'm sure Cub will find you to be an asset to the team. They've all known my father wanted you to play with them. So it's no surprise."

"Yeah." He fit his gold felt cap backward over his head, then turned to leave.

"Mr. Cordova, I'm glad my being here doesn't bother you."

"It doesn't bother me because you won't last a week." Then he walked out into the rain, leaving the door open behind him.

The patter of droplets smacked the ground, the sound filling the vacant clubhouse. Her smile deflated, and she gripped the desk's edge before sinking into the chair.

If she hadn't been so knocked off-kilter by his assumption, she would have been outraged. Wait a minute—she *was* outraged. He had no more faith in her than her father did. Alex had let her go on and on about what a difference she'd make, all the while mentally seeing her quit when she'd barely started. That talk about "getting over it" had nothing to do with her. It had everything to do with getting over *her* because *she* wasn't going to be around long.

Camille lowered her chin to her chest and sighed. Her energies had been wasted on a man built of granite. A terrible sense of injustice beat within her heart.

Then she remembered a crucial piece of information, something her father had said to her the night he'd made her the manager. Anyone else would have been disheartened by Alex Cordova's prophecy, but not Camille, not in light of what her father had said. The odds on her survival had just gotten better: her father had declared she wouldn't last one day, but Alex had just lengthened the estimate to one week.

Pushing to her feet and grabbing her notebook, she nodded to the empty room with renewed spirits.

There was something to be optimistic about after all.

Alex remembered his first uniform playing semi-professional for the Buckeye Brawlers when he was seventeen. Hell, he'd been so proud to wear it, he'd slept in it that night. Getting that uniform had been a long time coming.

He'd immigrated to America when he'd been twelve, leaving behind a grandfather in Cuba who'd since died. His childhood was a painful place he rarely revisited. It had been filled with war and bloodshed. Anger against the revolutionist Spaniards, deaths that came too early, and disillusionment with the Roman Catholic church. Once in Philadelphia, he grew determined to be a regular Americano. And he'd slowly succeeded, in a way his cousin Hector would never understand.

Hector Herrera and his family had taken Alex in

STEF ANN HOLM

and given him food and shelter in return for the
money Alex earned. They got him work in a textile
mill rolling bolts and feeding machines with thread,
a job that lasted some eight years. He'd hated almost
every day of it. Baseball was the only thing that
had kept him from leaving his cousin's house and
heading out on his own. Hector's was a place to stay
while he gained some respect among the sandlot
bunch.

Sean O'Brien. Arthur Daley. Fellows he had admired, grown up with in a time that had been both
heartbreaking and heavenly. Along with other boys
from the neighborhood, they'd formed their own
team, the Philly Billy Clubs. Together, they'd go out to
Shelton Field and watch the Hogee Knox team by
crawling under the fence so they wouldn't have to pay
their five cents.

One day Arthur arrived and showed off a silver
dollar his father had won in a poker game the night
before. So Arthur's mother wouldn't find out about it
and give Arthur's father hell, the old man had given
the silver to Arthur. The gang of boys had asked
Arthur what he was going to do with it, and he'd declared he was taking them all out to the ballpark on
Saturday to watch the game between the Philadelphia
Athletics and the Brooklyn Bridegrooms. Well, hell,
you could have heard their cheers all the way to Independence Hall.

It was the first professional game Alex had ever
seen, and it reaffirmed his desire to wear a uniform,
throw a regulation ball, and use a glove. A year later
he played for the Buckeye Brawlers, then the Cincinnati Stars. Two years after that, he'd been bumped up
to the majors. To his amazement, his contract had
been bought by the Brooklyn Bridegrooms before
the Orioles had him.

76

Anybody else would have said it was a dream come true. But for Alex Cordova, it had been the beginning of a nightmare.

Leaning his back against the dugout wall, Alex watched Camille. She kept an umbrella over her head while gingerly stepping over the soggy ground, skirt held high, but modestly so, searching for spare balls that might have been planted in the tall outfield grass. The practice of hiding balls to take away home runs was a common one. But the hunt for them came before the game; not before batting practice. Apparently, she thought her own players would try to stiff her.

She was a curious woman. He hadn't been able to fully get her out of his thoughts since the day she'd come to his carpenter's shop. He'd figured that after he'd signed his contracts, he wouldn't have to see her again. How wrong he'd been. Her showing up at the clubhouse had been a big surprise.

Why in the hell would she want to manage a baseball team?

Maybe he could understand it if she were mannish. On the ugly side. Large-boned. Ungainly. But she was the opposite of that. So opposite, he couldn't figure her out. Not that he wanted to. Not that he should.

He was here in body only. He was disconnected from the emotions that went with ball playing. He didn't feel. He didn't care. All he wanted was his money.

"Well, if it isn't the old shoe man." The greeting came in a contentious tone. "Hey, Regal."

Alex shifted his gaze to the man who'd walked up beside him. With the exception of being in a Boston Somersets uniform rather than in a Cleveland Spiders uniform, Cy "Cyclone" Young looked exactly how Alex remembered. Every angle of his frame was exaggerated by the tight fit of his jersey. His arms were long and almost appeared to dangle from the sleeves of his shirt. But it was that right arm that could shoot a ball into the catcher's mitt with a crack. Below the bill of his cap, his pomaded hair parted down the middle with two inward curls on either side, looking much like commas . . . or horns of the devil— whichever way a person wanted to look at it. Alex knew which one he preferred. That remark about the Regals did it.

"Cy," Alex said noncommittally so as not to kick up a conversation. He didn't feel like rebuilding old acquaintances. Not that he and Cy had ever been friendly.

"How'd that go?" His arrogant smile said he knew exactly how the advertisement went and he was going to recite it. Sure as it was raining, he did. " 'The whole world loves a winner. How would you like to be in Alex "the Grizz" Cordova's shoes? "The Grizz" wears Regals.' "

Alex cursed the day he ever agreed to wear Regals as part of the shoemaker's campaign. For a solid year, that advertisement board had been on every outfield wall, in every stadium he'd played in. He'd had to wear the shoes, too. They'd given him over a dozen pairs.

"Don't wear Regals anymore, Cy. Don't have to."

"Guess you don't." Cy reached into his back pocket for a tin of chew, opened the lid, and stuffed a large wad of the flaky tobacco into one cheek. As he worked it into a wet mass, he spoke through the lump. "You dropped out of sight, Cordova. Where the hell have you been for the past three years? Not in this standing-water town, have you?"

Alex never discussed where he'd been. Where he'd come from. That was his business. "Been around."

"And landed on this dung heap. Like a bottle fly."
He chortled.

Alex's jaw ached from the tight clamp of his teeth.
Son of a bitch.

Batting practice was called by both managers and
Young departed for his side of the field. Alex wanted
to take a piece out of his ass. So much for hiding emotions from himself.

The next thirty minutes were spent fielding balls,
pitching fast ones, practicing double and triple plays,
and keeping the mud from seeping inside shoes. Alex
went through the motions without thought, as if doing
something he learned as a child. He hadn't forgotten.
But he did it without heart or conscience.

When it was time to return to the dugout, Alex
glanced up at the grandstands, which had only a handful of fans. They wore coats and capes, had open umbrellas, and sported rubber shoes. Mostly men; a few
women. Alex took off his hat and acknowledged Captain's clapping.

Sitting on the bench, his uniform soaked through
and rain dripping from the ends of his hair, Alex
waited as Camille came beneath the dugout. Her
appearance hardly showed the effects of the
weather. Hat still perfect; dress hem just a little
muddy on the bottom; hair in place. All neat and
tidy.

"All right ... let's put that practice out of our heads
and concentrate on winning the game."

"How can we win if Specs can't see out of his
glasses?" complained Yank, the relief pitcher. "They're
all fogged up."

Agreement came in grumbles.

Specs defended himself. "I keep wiping them off.
And it's not only me who stinks. Maybe some of you
other fellows need glasses, too."

"Ballplayers don't wear glasses. It makes them look less than men," Doc sniped.

"Well, thanks a damn lot, Doc," Specs countered.

Deacon broke in. "We all look like blind idiots when we're out there."

"Speak for yourself, Deacon," Jimmy admonished. "You couldn't find your nose if your fingers was up it."

Alex brought one leg over the other, resting his ankle on his knee. If he were manager, he'd kick Specs in the butt and make him get the right strength spectacles. But he wasn't. And he didn't give a damn about it anyway.

The Keystones were at bat first. Just as Camille prepared to read the batting order, James Kennison came rushing into the dugout as soggy as a wet rug. Rain fell in a tiny river off the brim of his derby.

Out of breath, he rushed his words. "Fellows, I have some news—"

Yank cut in. "If it's about your daughter . . ."

Cub finished the thought. ". . . we already know."

Kennison's brows leveled as he ran his gaze over the men on the bench. "I figured you would know by now." His voice rose an octave as he explained, "I would have been here to tell you myself, but it's all Nops's fault. In more ways than one, believe you me! That gas pipe emptied half his infernal store onto the boardwalk and marked it on sale. The next thing I knew, I was hauling things outside myself."

Camille glanced at him.

"Deputy Faragher made us put everything back inside." From his coat pocket, he brought out a handkerchief and wiped off his face. His waxed mustache drooped. "On top of it all, I got slapped with a two-dollar ticket for sidewalk violations."

"I'm sorry about that, Daddy, but you can't be in the dugout. You'll have to tell me about it later."

"What do you mean?"

The rose in her complexion paled, as if telling him what she had to was difficult for her. "The dugout is for managers and players only."

"What about owners? I own the team."

"Nothing in the rule book says an owner is entitled to a seat on the bench."

"Folderol!"

"It's not folderol. It's the rules."

All the Keystones but Alex looked at Kennison, and Alex got the clear impression this was one thing they sided with their new manager about. From past run-ins with Kennison, Alex knew the man was as hotheaded as a furnace.

He stared at the players, then blustered, "Well, how do you like that? Chased away by my own daughter."

Then he turned and left. Alex swore he could hear audible sighs of relief.

"All right. Now for the batting lineup . . ." Camille continued, seemingly unfazed, as if her father's interruption hadn't affected her. But Alex saw the slight quiver of her fingers, the barely evident droop in her shoulders. After she'd read them the batting order, she sat down.

Primly. Expectantly. Head held high. Gloved hands folded in her lap.

Waiting for the game to begin.

The first inning, the first three batters were retired in order. Cy Young struck every last one of them out. Alex had been positioned ninth to bat, so he hadn't yet gone up against his former nemesis. He'd sat back, observing, letting himself become a little amused at how easily Cupid Burns, Mox Snyder, and Doc Nash let Cy intimidate them. They didn't know the first thing about hitting against the Cyclone.

Alex had been assigned to pitch the bottom of the first. Cub gave him a look that would have peeled the bark off a tree. Putting Cub out of his mind, Alex took the mound.

He stood on the rubber, a place that felt forbidden to him. Glove in hand, fingers through the webs of leather, he stared down at his first batter for the Somersets. Hobe Ferris.

With rain spilling over the bill of his cap, Alex raised the ball in both hands, looked at Specs, who stood at the shortstop position, and then relaxed. He had to take deep breaths to try to focus his concentration. He looked at the ball. He fingered it, working it to get the best grip he could. The ball was as black as the ace of spades. As black as the place in his heart.

He tried to pitch the ball once more. And again, he froze.

His muscles bunched and pained him. Digging his toes into the wet ground, he reasoned better footing would help.

It didn't.

When Alex had told Camille he'd play baseball for the Keystones, he'd been so desperate for money that he hadn't thought about actually following through and standing in the pitcher's box. He now found himself thrust back in time to a place that had altered him beyond any emotion. For all the money in the world, Alex didn't think he could go through with it. But then he glanced up at Captain.

He had to do it.

He tried once more, staring down at Hobe, reading the deaf and dumb signal from Noodles. Three middle fingers down. A tap and an angle left of the thumb: knuckleball.

Winding up for the pitch, Alex coiled his leg back, put his right foot on the ground, and . . . stalled.

He swore. Disgusted with himself.

The next thing he knew, Camille had come out to the mound. He could hardly face her. His stomach churned. He was sick and angry with himself. He couldn't even have give her an explanation. How could she understand? Only Captain did, and Alex couldn't talk to him about it.

"I'm out of the inning, honey." He started to turn away from her and head for the dugout.

"No, you're not out of the inning, Mr. Cordova."

The light touch of her hand on his upper arm stopped him short. He looked into her upturned face. Her eyes danced with lively fire; her lips parted—no doubt over the sheer gall of his statement. "You're not out of the inning, Mr. Cordova, until I tell you you're out." Droplets of rain glistened on the fruit decorating her hat. She'd forgotten her fancy parasol. "Now, throw that ball as if you want to kill somebody."

She didn't mean literally. He knew that. But the implication sunk beneath his skin and rattled him. Rattled him more than he could handle. Squeezed inside his chest and just about suffocated him. How could he tell her he'd already taken a man's life while playing ball and it haunted him every moment of his life?

Call him a goddamn quitter, but he was finished for the day. He threw the ball. At her feet, not even giving her the courtesy of slapping it in her pretty little gloved hand. "I'm out of the inning."

If she said anything, it was to his back and soft enough for him not to hear. Then again, he'd already tuned out the jeers that followed him as he sidestepped the trash that littered the field in his wake.

"The Grizz" was gone. And nothing could make him come back.

Chapter
❧ 6 ❧

Using a hoe to take out her frustrations, Camille made uneven rows for her hollyhock seeds. She stood in the rear garden, her rubber gaiters caked with muddy soil. Having long grown cold and wet, her work gloves did nothing to warm her hands. Or her frame of mind. She made a mess, but she didn't slow down. She had no time to spare. She'd called for an earlier practice this afternoon. The Keystones needed every minute to improve themselves.

The manager's job was more than she thought it would be.

She should have known nothing she could do or say would impress the fans. Not that she had anything to say to them when she'd been introduced by one of the umpires. She'd smiled at her mother and her father sitting in the front row. Mr. Nops had glared at her, clearly wishing he'd stood in her place.

On the few occasions Camille had glanced at her father, his teeth had been clenched. She'd hoped his anger wouldn't be aimed toward her after the Keystones' poor performance. Under the circumstances, she knew she hadn't prepared them to face off with the Somersets. Knew she had not a prayer even before the first ball was pitched.

The umpires had taken the field.

The two assigned to the game were Roy Phillips, whose jowls hung to his shoulders, his body tall and thick; and Monte Green, a small man, bent half forward with an eager face. Only that eager face had fallen as soon as the managers' names had been submitted to him.

The two officials had dropped their jaws. She hadn't batted an eyelash when she left the bench to wave to the crowd—a crowd that had gone deadly silent. Only Captain and her mother had applauded. Her father was busy looking around him, as if to gauge the fans. She hadn't expected him to give her a rousing welcome, but it would have been a pleasant surprise if he had.

That nasty Boomer Hurley, the Somersets' manager, had gotten the fans laughing. He'd caricatured a woman's walk across the field, one hand on his hip, his other arm swishing by his side. It had taken every lesson of decorum ever drummed into her to keep from going out there and jabbing him in the stomach with her umbrella tip.

If that weren't enough, the person she'd counted on to make her look good had done nothing. Alex had walked away off the mound in his first game as a Keystone, leaving her to question his abilities for future games. She was still stunned that he'd sat in the dugout and watched, refusing to play. "The Grizz" was no more. Alex was a shadow of that man, of the legend that had been larger than life.

She wished she knew why.

After the game, she'd asked him what had gone

wrong, why he hadn't pitched like he was supposed to. His explanation had been brief. His arm hadn't felt right. Then he'd walked to the clubhouse, looking strangely worn for a man so massive and powerful.

"Camille sugar, where are you?" Her father's voice rang as he rounded the corner of the backyard. Engrossed in what she was doing, she hadn't even heard the picket gate slam closed.

Without stopping her work, she replied, "What's wrong?"

"Did you leave the door to the clubhouse open?"

For a moment, she had to think. But then she frowned. She had been extra careful with the key. "No, I didn't. Why?"

"The door wasn't closed when I was there a minute ago."

"But I locked it myself last night. I double-checked." A tide of panic brought her hoe to a stop. "Is anything missing?"

He shook his head. "No. That's the strange part about it." With eyes narrowed in suspicion, he said, "I bet it was that Boomer Hurley. I wouldn't trust that bean eater as far as I could hurl him." Then in a voice so soft she had to strain to hear, he mumbled, "The bum mocked my daughter."

She leaned toward him. "What was that, Daddy?"

He looked as if he wanted to say something more—something she'd be glad to hear. But then he only lectured her. She tried to put aside her disappointment.

"The professional league is a whole different box of nails." He adjusted his tie. "It's nothing like hometown ball. You've got to watch for underhanded tactics."

"I will."

"At least the weather's better for today's game," he said, gazing up at the sky.

Endless blue rose heavenward, with only a lacy tuft of cloud here and there. Sunshine brightened the yard. The grass was growing in thick and green from spring rain.

"Yes, much better."

"The score will be better, too."

She propped both hands on the knob of the hoe handle. It couldn't be much worse. They'd been defeated yesterday 12–0.

Her father slipped both hands into his pinstriped trouser pockets. The gold of his fob chain glistened in the sun. Camille found it curious that after having said what he had to, he didn't head right back for his store. He wasn't one to make idle conversation. "Getting anything planted?"

"Not yet." As she resumed her task, she gave him a quick glance.

Looking at the plot of dirt, he commented, "You sure can make things grow." He didn't meet her gaze. Instead, he stared at the bushes along the fenced yard. "It takes a lot of patience to take a seed and nurture it into a plant. Not many people can do that."

Again, she was sure he was trying to say something else, to tell her, in his own way, that maybe she wasn't a bad choice for the manager's position after all. The actual words would mean so much. She needed his assurance that she was going to be fine. "Daddy, I—"

"I'd better get back over to the store." The gruffness in his tone didn't fit with the softness shimmering in his eyes. "I have to stay on my toes with Nops. The man is lower than an Acme brass threshold."

After her father had gone, Camille sat down on the rose arbor bench, the hoe laid before her on the grass. She stared at the plot of dirt that was to be her crowning glory this year. But its rows were complicated by players and baseballs and rules and a pitcher who hadn't been able to pitch.

If only making the Keystones flourish could be as easy as coaxing a bloom from a begonia.

Somebody had gummed up the Keystones' bats.

A liberal amount of pine tar had been rubbed into all the bats. The sticky dark substance used to create a better grip worked well when applied correctly. Too much, and the batter's hands stuck to the wood; he lost control and couldn't release after a swing.

The probable culprit snored at the Brooks House hotel, sleeping off a night of whooping it up in the Blue Flame saloon. Camille had no way to prove Boomer Hurley had done it. However, as far as following the codes of honor, the Somersets hadn't last night. Drinking went against the ethics of the American League, and of all the possible people to be the ringleader of last night's fiasco, it had been the Boston manager.

The smell of thinner lingered in the air of the clubhouse as she left with her notebook in the crook of her arm. The Keystones had lost practice time unsticking the bats. She hoped Mr. Hurley would be suffering today. Maybe he'd have such a sick headache, he wouldn't be able to create a lineup. Maybe his players, with their minds hazy from the aftereffects of liquor, wouldn't be able to hit a tin can with a two-by-four.

"All right, gentlemen." She addressed the players on the bench but purposefully eyed Alex. The speech she'd rehearsed in her head was to the point and indisputable. "We're going to spend the next half hour on calisthenics."

"Cali-what?" Bone mumbled.

"Calisthenics," Alex supplied, flexing a lean leg. "Exercise. Sit-ups, trunk twists, toe touching."

"Crapola. If you don't mind my saying so, Miss Kennison." Cub LaRoque propped his feet on the foot railing. "Red Vanderguest, the manager three managers ago, had us lifting weights at Bruiser's Gymnasium over on Birch Avenue and we still lost nearly every game that season. Frankly, we stink. We don't ever seem to have a chance. I'm tired of hoping we do. We don't. Plain and simple."

"From now on, any man with that kind of attitude will be fired from the Keystones." The words were out before she'd thought them through. Could she really fire somebody?

Regardless, her threat worked, because Cub cooled on the issue. "I'm not saying I'd quit, Miss Kennison. I'm just saying we smell like an outhouse and nothing's changed that fact so far."

"Things *will* change. Starting today. From now on, you have to believe that winning is the most important thing."

"The most important thing on my mind right now is getting that brick fence up over at the Elks Club on schedule," Jimmy stated. "That's how I get in my calisthenics. I break my back hauling bricks, then break it some more trying to hit baseballs."

She regarded him, then the others who were in the same predicament, working outside jobs and then being expected to play baseball as well. "Some of you have been playing for my father for nearly ten years. In that time, you've had some fun. I know that when the team was called Kennison's Keystones, you would take the field and laugh and joke around. I watched from the stands and I enjoyed myself. Nobody thought about pennants and big money and the prestige of winning a trophy."

"Your father really wants the pennant, Miss Kennison," Doc said. An older member of the team, he was one of the original Keystones.

"Do any of you want the pennant?" she asked, hoping that a majority would reply yes. "If being in the American League is taking the fun out of the game, then there's no point in playing it anymore."

Specs spoke up. "Everyone knows there's only a few of us who're any good. The rest of us are here because the money can't be beat."

Charlie said, "You got that right."

Camille kept her hands clasped together at her waist. "If you could get something from playing baseball, what is it that you'd want? Aside from the salary."

"To impress women."

"The only women *you* impress are ones with buck teeth."

"But do we have to do calisthenics?"

"You couldn't touch your toes if there was a beer sitting on them."

"The pennant would be quite a thing."

"Pennants are for professionals."

"We're professional now. American League."

"American League is where the great fellows play."

The answers were as diverse as the players and Camille let them voice all opinions before adding, "The Keystones can be a great team. Everyone out on the field. And I want to see you in rows and touch your toes thirty times. Bend at the waist and don't buckle your knees. Keep them stiff."

The bench emptied, but the procession out to the grass was a slow one.

The idea of calisthenics hadn't been hers. It had been Meg Gage's.

Camille had been late for the Garden Club meeting

last night because of her duties with the team. She knew there would be talk from the ladies. She'd prepared herself for some backlash. But when it came, she'd still felt bruised. At least Edwina Wolcott and Meg Gage had taken her side, saying what she was doing was wonderful.

Meg had mentioned *Whitley's* fitness magazine. The men on the pages were in fine physical form after exercise and hearty diets. All thirteen of the Keystones were bachelors, and most ate at Nannie's Home-Style Restaurant. Camille was going to ask that they order steak and eggs, bacon and fried potatoes—real man food.

Standing at the sidelines, she observed the players as they bent down. Specs and Deacon ribbed each other. Charlie couldn't make a forward fold over his stomach. It was too wide. Cupid bent his knees to reach his toes. Yank went through his exercise far too quickly, missing his toes by a good four inches. What a sorry sight.

Sorry except for one man who moved with the strength of bendable hot iron. His body looked sculpted, lean and well worked in spite of years away from the game. He must never sit idle. Never slouch. His uniform fit him like a glove. He was tight, taut, hard, and sinewy. Taller than the rest, he stood nearly a head above them while moving his limbs in a way that said he didn't put thought into it. He just told his muscles what to do and they did, bulging and straining.

Dreadful thoughts had filled her mind while she was walking to the ballpark—what if Alex didn't show up? But he'd been there with the others, waiting for her.

For a blushing moment, her thoughts went back to earlier in the clubhouse, and she felt a tiny flicker of curiosity to see Alex boldly standing half dressed again. The scene that had greeted her this morning had been different than yesterday. None of the players had been undressed. They'd been suited up and ready to go. She should have been relieved. But her gaze had lingered over Alex longer than it should have.

After the players went through a series of exercises, she had Cub and Yank throw balls. Each player took a turn at bat, making a rotation on the field so that the outfielders and basemen could practice fielding. When Alex stepped up to the plate, Cub just about knocked him out of the box with a screwball. It was a clear case of animosity—Alex was on the team in Cub's position. After the third pitch, Alex struck out. Her heart sank. For all his powerful muscles and lean body, he didn't put any of that strength into his swing. They couldn't win on bad swings or throws.

By game time, she'd assembled the team on the bench. Fans had come out in droves. The weather certainly helped, not to mention it was Saturday. But they came partially, she supposed, because they were curiosity seekers.

The men scooted and maneuvered to fit between the items that already occupied the narrow length of wood.

She asked them as a whole, "Is all of that necessary?"

"Certainly is." Charlie held up a fist of black licorice. "Gotta have something in my mouth."

"Durham is better than that godawful candy," Duke remarked, raising a Bull Durham pouch. He took a pinch of tobacco and added to the lump already stuffed in his left cheek.

"Adhesive tape," Deacon said. "I busted two fingers once on a ground ball and was sorry the rest of the day I didn't have something to wrap my fingers with."

Specs worried a horseshoe in his grasp. "Horseshoes. I've got five more in the box beside me. From horses I've known and loved."

"Four of which are dead," Charlie responded, "so how much luck is that, Specs?"

"Luck enough." He twisted the rusty piece of metal in his fingers as if to get as much good luck out of it as he could.

"Four-leaf clovers." Doc showed her a jar of them. "I found most of 'em out at Fish Lake by the bank where the fly-fishing contest takes place. I got one just last week, so I should be able to hit the ball better."

Cupid laughed, his half-bald head shining like an apple. "You can't even hit a tree when you piss."

Specs blushed a deep crimson and stared at Camille.

Cupid mumbled, "Sorry."

Mox frantically rubbed an oil lamp, much akin to the kind Aladdin must have found. "Oil lamp. Only thing around here that will bring good luck."

"Mox, you've been rubbing that thing for years and the only fog to come out of it was your fart when you had it between your legs." Cub didn't apologize for his language. He looked at her and she looked right back.

She wouldn't make a fuss. They were crude. They were men who scratched themselves in places that ought not to be scratched in public, much less in private. She had expected as much.

Although she did appreciate Spec's blush.

"Rabbit's feet." Bones had a dozen of them on a chain. Gray, white, black, and tan. He pulled out his shirt collar and dropped the feet inside his uniform.

His stomach now appeared lumpy. "I keep them close to me at all times."

"I don't go in for all that good-luck business. A man's got to feel like he's fit," Jimmy said, opening the cap on a bottle of Ayer's Cherry Pectoral. "And that breakfast I ate didn't do much for my innards, so I've got to take pectoral to aid in my digestion. I hit and run better after I have a teaspoon or so."

Duke noted, "Booze is in that. Read the label, Miss Kennison, and take that snake oil away from him."

"Is not!"

Cupid held up a dark amber bottle. Carter's Liver Pills. "I have a constant ache in my gut when I come to the ballpark. This helps."

Noodles came up with Bull's Cough Syrup. "For medicinal purposes only, ma'am." He took a pull on the mouth of the bottle, swallowing with a shiver of— as far as she could tell—revulsion.

Yank showed his Bromo Seltzer, took a swig, and followed up with a long burp. "Clears the lungs."

Cub nursed his elbow with a hot water bottle. "Bad joint."

Alex was the only one empty-handed. All eyes landed on him. With a quirked lift to the right corner of his mouth, he said, "I drank a fifth of Danish schnapps before I came to the park."

"On ice or off?" asked Mox.

"Off."

That got a rise out of Cub, who jabbed Cordova in the ribs, the friction between them momentarily set aside. "Yeah, right."

Camille didn't get the joke. Unless schnapps was something that put hair on a man's chest when he drank it at room temperature. But the meaning of the riddle was moot. If Alex had drunk a fifth of liquor, he'd be flat on his face.

Or half dead.

"While these items might be of some value to you, gentlemen, they clutter the bench. Perhaps we could put it all in one big crate. You know, mix it up so everyone would receive the benefits." She thought her suggestion quite practical. But it was received with twelve angry scowls. "All right. Hold onto it if you must. Just don't sit on anything and hurt your behinds."

Their laughter caught her by surprise. She gave them a hesitant smile—unfortunately, one they didn't hesitantly return. They reverted back to scowling at her.

Of course she dared not hope the begonia had just formed a tiny bud.

She'd said to meet him at the livery.

Alex could think of a better place to meet a woman. Camille had made an appointment to have his photograph taken in Waverly. Fan cards. There had been a time when posing for them would have been a real yahoo. The only good side he could see to having them now was that Camille was coming along for the ride.

But if she started to talk baseball, he'd have to balk at the subject. He had done what she'd wanted yesterday. He'd gone to the mound and thrown. Put himself in a frame of mind that overrode the fears of that first game. By going back out there, he'd allowed the fans to say Alex Cordova had done his job. Even if he reeked.

Every ball he threw had been over the plate. Any lackey could hit one. And the Somersets had. Cy had homered off him five times. Christ. Alex hadn't struck out a single player. Boston had crucified them 14–1.

The one run had come off of Bones Davis. A fluke. He'd been hopping up and down, his rabbit's feet having slipped into the groin area of his pants. When the pitch came at him, just that slight hop lifted him up enough so the bat—not the man—whacked the ball out of the park. He'd been so stunned, he'd stood at the plate a few seconds before taking off in a run. In his excitement, he missed second base and had to be called back by Cub, who ran out of the dugout to yell, "Touch the bag! The bag, rabbit ass!"

The nonzero score in the home team's column had been a victory in itself. A small victory that Alex had watched bring smiles to the players. If that's all it took, damn—if the Keystones ever busted out of their slump, they'd split a gut.

Analyzing the errors and plays wasn't for Alex, but he couldn't help sizing up fielding, base running, and coordination, or rather, the lack of it. Defensively, there had been tough hops for Deacon, and Duke dropped every last ball he managed to catch. Cupid mishandled a bouncer off to his right. Offensively, hard swings and pop-ups were weakly sent to foul ground by third. A peg-down was off-line, allowing a base runner for Boston to move into scoring position.

Beyond that, nobody was in good enough shape. Himself included. His body was stiff, his right elbow joint ached. He wasn't used to throwing.

He wasn't used to caring about baseball.

But he stood firm on his vow of indifference. The reasons behind that vow raged inside him. Each time he began to feel the vitality of the game pulse through him, guilt pulled him back. If that weren't enough, he'd been that close to bumming an Old Judge off of Charlie. But one cigarette and he might as well buy a pack. The other day, he'd bought a couple bottles of beer and drank them on the walk home. Some habits died hard, and he found himself sliding into them like fingers into a comfortable leather mitt.

As Alex leaned into the hitching post, he saw Camille coming toward him. She looked like a snowflake. Cool and lacy and white. The bottom of her dress lightly skimmed over the tops of her pearl kid shoes; her hips were outlined by some kind of fancy lace material. She held an open parasol, its sheerness nothing but a thin veil against the sun.

"Thank you for being here on time," she said, reaching his side. "Is the buggy ready?"

The light blue of her eyes were limned by a darker hue of blue. They tilted slightly upward at the corners, making her gaze sensual. Her eyes distracted him. As did her lips.

"Max said it was ready to go whenever we were."

A moment later, Alex tossed the bag containing his uniform and gear into the bed of the rig, then sat beside Camille. He guided the rented horse out of town. The buggy springs weren't in the best repair and each rut and pit in the road had them bumping shoulders. While she held herself stiffly, he propped one foot onto the driver's box.

She'd poised herself on the lumpy seat, arm raised with the parasol in her hand. The buggy had no hood, so she'd had to resort to shading herself with the umbrella. Sun didn't bother Alex. When the weather was warm, he worked outside with his shirt off. He wondered what Camille would do if he took his shirt off right now.

He glanced at her profile, finding the hat netting that came over her forehead provocative. Lots of ladies wore hats similar in style, yet to him, this one was irresistible. What he didn't like were the reasons why. They had little to do with the hat and everything to do with the woman wearing it.

The country rolled by. Sunlight stippled through the branches of leafy maple trees overhead. They hadn't said anything to each other since leaving Harmony. Alex wasn't one for small talk. But now a few words would cut the monotony of the harness tack as it jingled and creaked.

She addressed him properly. "Mr. Cordova, we have a problem."

He didn't much like the sound of her tone. Maybe the monotony would have been preferable. "We would if we were going over to the next town to do something private." Because she didn't give a gasp of surprise, he couldn't resist teasing her further. "There really isn't a photographer in Waverly, is there, honey?"

She flushed. "There most certainly is."

"Then I'm disappointed." He held onto a laugh over her shock. "I was sitting here thinking about what we were going to be doing in that hotel room."

"There's no hotel room," she quickly replied. Clearly nonplussed, she knit her fingers. "That is to say, there is a hotel in Waverly, but we aren't going there." She licked her lips in slight confusion. The gesture drew his attention—more so when her teeth caught on her plump lower lip. She had the nicest mouth he'd ever seen on a woman. "To the hotel, that is."

"I know exactly where I'm going," he said, his eyes staring into hers.

"Well, then, if you know so much," she replied, once again brisk and businesslike, "you'll know I'm going to talk about your attitude, Mr. Cordova. You aren't showing the Keystones a fraction of what you can do. You aren't even trying. Why not?"

He looked at the outline of her face. Noticed the way the brim of her hat tilted forward, its feathers and bows moving on the breeze. A golden curl touched her brow; sunlight played over the shades of blond.

As he imagined how her silky hair would feel in his hands, his jaw went rigid.

He couldn't explain to her that the Alex Cordova she was asking to see was no more. He'd once been glorified in stadium programs and articles, the paper having long ago yellowed. She wanted the legend.

The legend was gone.

"It's been a while. I'm out of shape," he suggested.

Her gaze slowly lowered to the expanse of his chest, then briefly to his hips before rising. He felt himself reacting. Tightening, growing heavy and thick. When she looked at him like that, all he could think about was pressing her body against his own. About cupping the curve of her buttocks.

She drew a deep breath. "You don't look out of shape to me."

He studied her expression. Wild and sweet. She made him think crazy things when he was around her. After he'd quit the Orioles, he'd tried to lose himself in a string of meaningless sexual encounters. But over the years, no woman had been able to make him forget.

Camille came damn close. When he was with her, he could forget his obligations to Cap. Forget the reasons he should resent her. She gave him the means to solve his money problems, but it was a solution he didn't want.

"That's right," he replied in a lazy drawl he'd heard many a ballplayer use. "You took a long, hard look at my *shape* when I was in the clubhouse."

As she stared at him in that innocent way—wide-eyed and lips parted—a rush of desire went through his veins. He was halfway to running his fingertips along her jaw and bringing his mouth over hers when the buggy wheels bounced off a groove and jerked his thoughts away.

The reins nearly slid from his fingers, and he tightened his hands on the leather. He had to force his attention on the road.

"You act as if I know you." When she nursed her chagrin, her accent was more pronounced.

"You know more about me than I do you." He let the horse walk at its own pace. "I don't wear red underwear. Do you?"

Her hand rose to her throat. "I'm not going to answer that."

"Then answer this," he replied, loosely resting his elbows on his knees. "Where'd you get that accent? You don't talk like you're from around here."

"Neither do you."

"That's because I was born in Pinar del Río, Cuba."

Turning her head, she looked at him. "I wondered."

"Did you?" He hadn't expected that to interest her.

"Yes." She crossed her ankles and kept the parasol steady. "Have you lived in America long?"

"Sixteen years. Took my oath of citizenship on July the Fourth when I was nineteen."

"What made you leave Cuba?"

Alex tried to shake off childhood memories, but he heard his grandfather's voice, telling him that he'd be better off in America, where he could live his life without hatred. To look back now, he knew his grandfather had been right. If he'd stayed in Cuba, he'd have tried to bring down the government that had killed his father and brother—and had killed his mother, by the sheer grief of losing them. Avenging their deaths would've only brought on his own.

"Too many reasons," he eventually said. "So how come you have that *sugar* in your voice?" He tried to say it the way she did. But he didn't even come close.

"I'm from Shreveport, Louisiana."

He'd never been there. Heard of it, though. "River-boats."

"Among other things."

"You live there most of your life?"

"Until I was nine. Most all of my relatives are still there. I've got a lot of aunts and uncles. Cousins. Almost all boys. Actually, they're grown men now." Her reflective mood emphasized the drawn-out way she spoke her vowels. She seemed to be comfortable, so he let her talk.

But he barely heard the words; he was mesmerized by her mouth, by its fine shape and color. Like soft pink rose petals. He listened to the story about her father's not being handed down the family hardware store by Granddaddy Kennison, who gave it to her Uncle Calvert instead—who hadn't wanted it anyway. That's why they'd moved from Louisiana to Montana so her father could start his own store. But she missed Shreveport at times.

She reflected about smelling the orange blossoms from her Uncle Bridge and Aunt Royaleen's groves before the riverboat even rounded the bend. He could see the rocking horse mounts she described in front of every house on her street.

Her life had been so different from the one he'd known when he'd been nine.

The canopy of trees gave way, revealing a clear azure sky. Alex turned his face to the sun, enjoying the pleasant warmth. If Camille thought that little nothing of a parasol could keep a tan away, she was mistaken.

"Is Captain your only relative?"

Her question bumped up his pulse. Without thought, he nodded. Then he motioned to her parasol with a slight lift of his chin. "Close that."

"Don't you find women with milky white skin appealing?" She looked entirely too surprised by her comment, as if she'd spoken before she thought. But there was no taking back the picture she'd presented him.

He felt his voice go low. "It depends on the woman and the parts of her body that are milky white." He smiled as color lit her cheeks. "I'm sure your milky white parts are lovely."

Staring straight ahead, she let him envision what he wanted.

He gazed at the tiny hollow of her throat. Then lower to the contour of her breasts. Naked in his hands, they'd be as pale as alabaster. With dusky pink nipples that would turn into tight buds beneath his fingers. She'd taste just like warm lavender next to his tongue. Her slender waist gave way to a nubile suggestion of hips. Her legs would be nicely shaped, nudged apart by his knee for him to stroke the tender skin on her inner thighs. And the golden curls between them.

The blood converged to a single place in his body. Its roar echoed in his head, making his thoughts reckless.

"How come you're not married?" he asked, his voice thick and uneven. He shouldn't have cared one way or the other about her lack of a husband.

"I prefer not to be."

"You sure as hell have enough men interested." He switched the reins to one hand and touched a finger to the underbrim of his Stetson. " 'Good afternoon, Miss Kennison,' " he mimicked.

She smiled. But said nothing.

He had to smile in return. She'd gotten him to say it again.

Keeping the leather ribbons together, he settled his arm over the seat—a thumb's width away from caressing the slope of her back.

The depth of his curiosity about her unnerved him. "Who was the first man who asked you to marry him?"

She gauged the heat, glancing lightly at the sky. Then with efficiency, closed her parasol and laid the frothy thing on her lap. "Henry Griffon, but he was ten years old, so he doesn't fall into the 'man' category."

"Who was the last?"

The buggy wheels hit a chuckhole and they jostled a little on the seat. The sunshine-warm fabric of her dress met his palm, and his thumb traced a small pattern over her spine. Slow and feather light. A controlled circle.

She didn't flinch. She sat beautifully tall.

"Archie Douglass, a National Corset salesman."

"I'll bet his samples went beyond plain white." This time he repressed his smile. "Did he kiss you?"

She nibbled on her bottom lip; there was a brief display of pearly teeth. If she didn't quit doing that—

"Why do you want to know?"

"Did he?"

"Yes."

Her brazen answer had him swallowing hard. "When was that?"

"A year ago." She frowned, a pout to her lush bottom lip. It was too damned much for him to resist. "I don't see why any of this—"

Without warning, he stopped the buggy. "Then you're long overdue to be kissed again, honey."

He slid his hand around the back of her neck and crushed her mouth to his. Her lips were soft and pliant. She tasted faintly of candy. Strawberry taffy.

She braced her palms on his chest as he moved to pull her tightly against him. She made a soft moaning sound that sent a shot of heat below his belly. The fullness of her breasts branded him. She felt tantalizingly slim. Smelled good. Tasted good. Every sense he had was heightened. She burned through him.

Kissing her was like drowning in honeydew.

He murmured against her mouth, "You never answered me. Do you wear a red corset?"

She returned his kiss, her lips light over his. Still touching, tingling. "I'm tired of you asking all the questions. Why are you called 'the Grizz'?"

The Grizz. The ghost of the big brown bear suddenly loomed over him, large, and with fierce, teeth and claws. He felt the instant pain in old scars, scars that made him remember and sucked him back to the reality. Back to baseball and his manager—not just any woman.

He drew back and looked at her. "Maybe I'll tell you some day."

"And maybe some day I'll tell you what color my corset is." Her blue eyes were half lidded, passion kindled in them. "Until then, we'll just both have to wonder."

Chapter

❧ 7 ❧

Camille walked to Plunkett's mercantile under a sky with dumpling clouds, happy in the fact that she'd proved her father wrong. Not only had she stayed on as manager of the Keystones beyond his projected one day, she'd lasted seven—refuting even Alex's prophecy.

Alex . . . the thought of his name disturbed her more than it should.

Too many things about Alex disturbed her. Most notably, her reaction to his kiss. He hadn't even had to invest any effort in it before she'd surrendered. His mouth over hers had wiped out every kiss she'd ever had. In the past, the brushing of lips over hers had been nothing to make her toes curl, make her heartbeat feel as if it were going to catch in her ribs.

So much for her doubting fiction. She'd assumed that kisses with heat and fire and passion enough to make a woman's breath hitch were ones invented by creative imaginations. All her kisses from men up until now had to have been of the nonfiction variety—because the real thing was infinitely better.

Obviously, she'd been kissing the wrong men. . . .

In regard to the matter at hand, she might have had staying power, but so did the Keystones' losing streak. There had been no letup in sight, in spite of her enthusiasm for changing the outcome of games.

To be fair, she could understand the players' being down in the dumps. But the injustice was that they didn't look to themselves for the answers. They blamed *her*. As if she should have had a magic tonic to sprinkle on them and all would be well.

If she'd had some kind of miracle cure, she would have used it by now. At home, her father constantly complained. Although his daily outbursts weren't directly aimed at her, she knew he was miserable. And in turn, he was making her miserable. He was still angry about Mr. Nops and the bonus.

As soon as Alex's fan cards were ready, she'd have him autograph the photographs. Once they were in circulation, that should smooth over some of her father's upset.

Until then, Daddy's ranting was something she had to deal with. But she could do something about having to hear his voice over the breakfast and dinner table. Earlier in the day, she'd paid a call on Otto Healy of Home and Farm Realty and inquired about houses for rent or purchase. She had a manager's salary coming to her. Money was no longer an issue. And she wanted a place of her own.

A tiny bell sounded above her head as she let herself inside the mercantile. Mr. Plunkett helped a customer in the grocery department while Hildegarde stood behind the counter arranging lace collars on a velvet display board. Her mother tidied items in the case.

"Hello, Camille," Hildegarde greeted her.

"It's nice to see you, Hildegarde."

They had known each other for years, having gone to both primary and finishing school together. Like Camille, Hildegarde wasn't engaged. Unlike Camille, Hildegarde wanted to be. She involved herself in various activities in the hopes of catching that special someone's eye. There had been a man from the Woolly Buggers, a fly-fishing club in town, who'd called on her for a time. But a romance never developed, and Hildegarde hadn't gone back to any meetings.

Her love life wasn't helped by the fact that her mother meddled in it and dictated Hildegarde's thoughts most of the time. In turn, Hildegarde pretty much did and said what Mrs. Plunkett told her.

Taking a glance at Mrs. Plunkett—who eyed Camille with an assessing gaze—Camille felt obligated to greet the woman. "Good afternoon, Mrs. Plunkett." Camille rested her handbag on the counter in front of Hildegarde. "I need to buy thirteen school slates and two boxes of chalk."

Mrs. Plunkett was a large woman with brown hair who suffered from a mysterious and sudden pain in her side whenever she overindulged in sweet treats. It was an unexplainable phenomenon that Camille had witnessed on more than several occasions, but so far, the ailment hadn't stopped Mrs. Plunkett from accepting cakes or cookies whenever they were presented.

"Why do you need slates?" Mrs. Plunkett asked as she counted out the correct number from a spot on the floor-to-ceiling shelves behind the counter.

Camille shouldn't have thought she could buy them without question.

"I'm going to nail them above each ballplayer's cubby."

"What for?"

What for? To write down special orders, that's what's for.

They were playing the Chicago White Stockings this afternoon—the last game of a four-game series. The previous three games had seen the Keystones in the cellar. Having a rotation of only three utility men didn't give her much room. One injury would foul up the entire order, so she needed to stay organized—and that's where the chalkboards came in.

To tell Specs Ryan his spectacles weren't the right strength—that he needed to get a new pair. To write a note to Duke Boyle about his fielding. To remind Bones Davis not to oil his glove so much—that's why he dropped the ball. Things like that. Things Mrs. Plunkett wouldn't appreciate. Things that were none of Mrs. Plunkett's business to begin with.

"Hildegarde, is that a new dress you're wearing?" Camille changed the subject, disregarding the even stare from the young woman's mother.

Hildegarde looked down. "No. Does it look new?"

"It looks lovely on you."

"Really?"

"I think so," Captain said as he appeared from the storeroom carrying three large crates that could hold thirty dozen eggs. Though the crates were extremely heavy, even empty, he gripped the wooden boxes without a struggle. He took them out the front door, to be placed on the boardwalk for the farmers to pick up and refill.

Hildegarde watched him retreat.

Without preamble, Mrs. Plunkett said, "Mrs. Calhoon is going around spreading rumors about you, Miss Kennison. I think you ought to know."

Camille already knew what the local women were saying about her. Nothing good. She was used to hearing how perfect and pretty she was; a little buzz and hum about her being a baseball manager didn't scandalize her. The gossip gave her a reason to be defiant—something she'd never been in her life.

"Now, Mrs. Calhoon," Mrs. Plunkett continued in a warning tone, "is a born gossip if there ever was one. I don't know how she can look people in the face, the things she says behind their backs. But butter wouldn't melt in her mouth. And she told me not to tell, so don't tell I told you. *But* . . . she said that the only reason you're managing the Keystones is to find yourself a husband. The lengths some women go to."

Camille wondered if she was referring to the lengths Mrs. Calhoon went to to slander a good name. Or the lengths desperate women went to to find husbands. Not likely the first option, as Mrs. Calhoon and Mrs. Plunkett were thick as thieves.

"I'm afraid I'll have to disappoint Mrs. Calhoon." Camille put a note of sarcasm in her voice that Mrs. Plunkett failed to notice. "Those baseball players aren't what I'd call gentlemen. They don't wear proper union suits." With an exaggerated arch of her brow, she lowered her voice. Mrs. Plunkett piloted in like a moth flying at a street lamp. "Two-piece underwear, most of them. There's one who does wear a union suit, but I couldn't say who. It's a color you'd never guess. That's all I can divulge. It's a good thing I have no desire to find a husband." She managed to keep a straight face and sound serious while adding, "I wouldn't marry a man who wore a union suit, much less drawers with a hole in them. But don't tell Mrs. Calhoon I told you that."

Mrs. Plunkett had been glued to every word. The vigorous shaking of her head and her wide-eyed wonder spoke louder than words: as soon as she had half a second to escape, she was going to broadcast every syllable to the postmaster's wife.

Mrs. Plunkett suddenly blurted, "My, my, but I forgot I had to . . . to meet with Mrs. Kirby about the selection of the hymns for this Sunday's service." She untied her apron and rounded the counter so quickly, she knocked into the velvet tray of collars and sent them sailing. "Hildegarde, write up Miss Kennison's order. I'll be back later."

She dashed out the door just as Captain came in. He took a few steps, stopped, then rubbed his temples. His eyes squeezed closed. A twist of pain caught his mouth.

"Captain," Hildegarde said with concern, "do you feel bad?"

"My head hurts just a little."

Worry reflected in her eyes. "Maybe you should go home."

He quickly lowered his hands, smoothing his beard and mustache. "No. I'm not going home. I'm working." Then he proceeded into the storeroom. "I'm all right," he called out from the depths of the stock area. "I'm working. W-o-r-k-i-n-g."

Helping Hildegarde pick up the lace notions, Camille asked, "Have you stopped typing for Mr. Stykem?"

"Yes. He found a permanent secretary. I almost wish he hadn't."

The collars back on the counter, Hildegarde sighed. "Ruth is busy with a new beau. I don't see her at all these days. I've been a little beside myself. I know I should be happy for her . . . but I can't help . . . Never mind."

Compassion worked through Camille. She understood the longing to find a husband. Ruth Elward was also one of Mrs. Wolcott's finishing school ladies. A woman who didn't have a man to take care of by the time she was twenty—it was almost a shameful thing.

Captain came back, shouldering two eighteen-quart Cooley milk cans. On his way outside, he said, "Hildegarde can't type worth a whistle."

The dimples in Hildegarde's cheeks deepened. She laughed, a merry sound that she rarely indulged in. She'd told Camille she thought her own laugh sounded like a schoolgirl giggle. Men didn't find giggling appealing. But as Camille watched Captain, it was apparent that he was one man who did. He was smiling broadly.

Hildegarde's gaze followed him through the door with more than passing interest. "He always speaks his mind. I find that . . ."—she shook her head as if pleasantly surprised—*"wonderful."*

Alex sat in the dugout, alone, watching jets of water from the sprinklers chug over the grass. He leaned his back into the bench, legs propped up on the short wall of dirt in front of him.

He'd come to the park early.

Before practice, before the fans came, a ballpark was a place of peace. A place to sit and think. Mentally get ready for the game. Work through the pitches he was going to throw.

He'd told himself that's not why he'd come today. That it had been the heat driving him out of the wood shop. But the warmth inside the shop had never bothered him before. He should have been working on the oak rocker he'd been commissioned to make, instead of letting his legs take him over to Municipal Field. It was a broadax he should have been holding in his hand instead of a bat.

He blamed his lapse in judgment on the measly three hours' sleep he'd had last night. Cap had had a bad episode that left him shaken and paranoid, unable to go back to sleep until his headache medicine relaxed him enough to let his mind rest.

Alex took a drink of cool water from a beer stein. The Orioles had presented him with the colorful enamel-and-silver mug for pitching a perfect game in 1897. July the seventh. Nobody in the league had ever accomplished that—before or since. They'd celebrated until sunrise at Patty O'Rourke's Fine Irish Tavern on Spring Street. Patty had pledged he could have the stein filled with anything—anytime—on the house. For life. Beer, whiskey, schnapps.

At the latter thought, Alex vaguely smiled.

When he'd joked about the schnapps with the team, he'd wanted that old baseball camaraderie again. And for a moment, on the bench that second day with the Keystones, he'd fallen into it. But he knew it wasn't the same as before. These men weren't the Orioles, the players he'd brought to the pennant two years running. The Keystones had no ambition.

But Camille Kennison did.

She'd surprised him. Seven days. She hadn't quit, no matter the circumstances. And the Keystones had given her reason to walk away without looking back. They were lousy. Hell, he was just as lousy as the rest of them.

Alex "the Grizz" Cordova had struck out more times at bat in one week than he had in a month with the Orioles. He hadn't gotten a single hit. But he hadn't chased a single ball, either, a fact that Camille, in her always well-schooled voice, got after him about.

Just once, he wanted to see her crack. Fall apart. Crumble. Buckle under the pressure. Misplace her gloves. Lose the hat. Let her hair down. Maybe even utter a ladylike "damn" once in a while.

"Mr. Cordova."

Alex looked up. *Christ.* Miss Honey herself. Standing on the lip of the dugout. After smoothing back strands of straight black hair from his eyes, he felt the stubble that roughened his cheeks and chin. He'd neglected to shave. For a second, he regretted it. But only for a second.

"Miss Kennison."

"You're here early." She came down the few steps to meet him on his level.

"So're you."

"I have to do something in the clubhouse." She didn't enlighten him as to what. And he didn't ask. She held on to a heavy, paper-wrapped parcel.

Alex rested the base of the beer stein on his thigh.

She wore her usual pale colors and appeared as angelic as ever. Did she ever raise her voice? Ever get her skirt dirty? Ever lie in meadow grass with her hair in a cloud around her and dream up at the sky? Her mouth was too damn full. Her eyes too damn blue. Her nose too damn perfect.

He wanted to dislike her.

He wanted to run his hands over every inch of her body.

Her eyes fell on the beer stein. Reproachfulness gleamed in them. "Mr. Cordova, you know that I don't allow drinking on the day of a game. And you have to play in four hours. What do you have to say for yourself?"

He gave her a slow grin. Let her think what she wanted. Then he purposefully took a long and leisurely drink. Going so far as to wipe his mouth with the back of his hand. Her eyes never left his lips. Was she thinking the same thing as him?

"Give me that stein," she demanded.

Apparently not.

With a bland smile, he handed it over. "You caught me, honey."

Shifting her package in her arms, she lifted the mug to her nose. Then delicate sniffed. Three times. A frown marred her smooth forehead. She knew something wasn't what it seemed, so she went as far as tentatively bringing the rim of the stein to her mouth. She took a short sip. Then with a gasp, said, "This isn't beer."

"Never said it was."

"But you led me to believe . . ." As she shoved the stein back at him, he noted her pulse thrumming at the base of her throat. Right at the lacy dip of her collar. Right at the top of her shirtwaist where the buttons were tiny and white. So tiny, he thought about trying to see if he could help one escape through its tiny buttonhole. "Why did you do that?"

"Because I like to watch you when you think you know something." He slowly gazed at her. "Your breasts rise and fall. Really soft, but you're mad and you won't show it. See—there."

She'd been doing exactly what he'd been talking about when he'd been talking about it. He grinned as she abruptly pulled a quick intake of air into her lungs.

"You're going to have to breathe sometime." Alex took another drink of water, his mouth exactly where hers had been. "And I'm still going to be sitting here watching."

He'd expected her to do all the shocked-woman things. Huffing a bit. Stamping her foot. Acting outraged. She merely stood before him, tall and poised. And when he was finished taking an unhurried drink, she asked, "Are you satisfied?"

"I'd be a lot more satisfied if my lips touched yours directly instead of where they'd been on my mug."

She hefted the package higher in her arms. "I'm not in the mood for this. I don't make jockstrap innuendoes to my players, Mr. Cordova."

He brought his head back, then tilted it to her.

She'd taken his cue, but her remark had not been anything like what he'd thought it'd be. "The weather too hot for you?"

"I think the pressure of pitching is too hot for you." He felt the bite on that one.

"We're going to try something different today," she said. "I want you to warm up away from Cub. Clear your head of everything else but baseball. Focus on one thing only: getting the ball in the strike zone."

She looked across the field. He looked with her.

Bordering the park was a weathered and unused stockyard. It butted against the railroad tracks, the corral broken in spots. A few timbers, crooked and knocked down, fell about ten feet from the third-base foul line.

"See that bullpen? That's your warm-up place from now on. I'll send Yank over with you to catch."

She took the few steps up to the top, then paused. Centerfield had begun to flood. With a shake of her head, she walked to the network of hoses and twisted the valves off; then headed for the clubhouse.

He stared at the stockyard once more. What froze his abilities couldn't be fixed by isolation.

A bullpen would have as much influence on him as a steer had at a barbeque.

Chapter

❧8❧

"What's that smell?" Noodles asked, sniffing loudly. "Good Gawd, it smells like a dead rat."

Mox snorted. "Jesus! Now that you mention it."

Deacon blurted, "Who the hell didn't take a bath?"

Camille had just explained the slates to the players and they'd broken up to read their respective notes. But there had been that unpleasant odor in the clubhouse.

A search for the offensive smell commenced. They sniffed the air, took long pulls into their lungs. The only person not interested was Alex, who leaned against his cubby, his slate above his head with one simple word written on it: *Try*.

The hunt narrowed in on Cupid Burns. He shrugged but gave no apology. Doc yanked Cupid's cap off. "Damn, Cupid. What do you have on your head?"

No hair. Cupid was going as bald as a Spalding baseball. He had the baby face of one of those naked cupids that artists drew on Valentine cards, so the name Cupid had stuck. For a man who was twenty-two, it was a terrible thing to be losing hair. Camille hadn't given it any thought, but Cupid, obviously, was quite sensitive about it.

"You shaved your head!" Bones laughed.

"Give me my hat back, Doc!" Cupid yelled, making a reach for his team cap. "I don't go around snatching yours."

"Go ahead. I've got nothing to hide." Doc had a bushy head of blond hair and a whopper of a mustache to match.

Charlie shook his head, his nose wrinkling. "Why did you shave your hair off?"

Cupid blushed a sweetheart red that crept across his face and colored his ears. "A fellow told me that if I shaved it completely off and rubbed this liniment on it's supposed to help grow hair."

"Who told you that?" Cub asked.

"Eureka Dan." Alex's deep voice quieted the room and caused heads to turn in Alex's direction. Arms folded over his chest and one shoulder resting against the wall, Alex half-smiled.

Cupid grew wide-eyed. "How'd you know?"

"He comes by and tries to sell me horse liniment." The other corner of Alex's mouth lifted. "But I don't own a horse. So figure it out."

The others guffawed.

"Cupid's got horse liniment on his head!" Jimmy slapped his knee while laughing it up.

Disorder followed, the men roaring with laughter. Camille rose and called over their shouts. "Gentlemen. We can't waste time with this issue. We've got a game to play against the White Stockings, in case you've forgotten."

This slowly sobered them. Expressions went from merry to somber. "I can't forget," Cub said, "Zaza Harvey's pitching for them. He's good—"

"You're good, Cub," Yank broke in. "When you concentrate, you're good."

Noodles added caustically, "Trouble is, he hasn't concentrated all year. Why don't you try throwing the ball at my glove instead of wild-pitching it?"

"I try that, but you move around behind the plate like you've got a constant itch you're after."

"I'd like to win once in a while," Jimmy said, then took a swig of his cherry pectoral.

"I think you fellows keep forgetting"—Mox examined a cloudy spot on his oil lamp, then shined it with the elbow of his sleeve—"Kennison bought our ticket into the American League. This is a once-in-a-lifetime deal to play with the best. We'd better get our heads together."

"Better get *something* together," Duke said, then spit.

Cub pressed a hot water bottle to his arm. "Fellows in Philly and the like are good players because that's all they do—practice around the clock."

"Then we have to make the most of our shorter practice times," Camille said, her gaze passing over Alex. Though she answered Cub, she spoke as much to Alex—if not more so—as to Cub and the others. "You don't have to live in Philadelphia to be good at what you do. Deep down, if we believe we can, we will be good. Contenders. Not pretenders." She smoothed the rosettes on her cuffs and gave them a quick perusal. "May I suggest we go out there and tell ourselves that we'll win?"

"You can suggest it," Specs said, ever the pessimist, "but I don't think it's going to happen."

"Specs, I hope you're wrong," Cub replied. "I say let's get those White Stockings."

A rally of seconds sounded through the clubhouse.

*   *   *

The horse liniment caused the riot.

In the bottom of the third inning, Cupid got a single and went to third on a hit by Deacon. Once Cupid occupied the bag, Frank Isbell, the Chicago third baseman, gave the air a loud sniff. Then he kicked Cupid in the shin. Just like that. Out of the blue.

Cupid looked at him in surprise. From where Camille stood, she could hear Cupid holler, "What'd you do that for?"

Frank didn't say a word. He backed away. Cupid began to follow him, and Camille hurried from the dugout and waved with both arms for Cupid to stay put. Zaza Harvey threw the ball to third. Luckily Cupid got back to the bag before he was tagged out.

Bones got a walk and took first.

The crowd stomped their feet on the bleachers, the grandstands thrumming with their enthusiasm.

Alex was next to hit, and as he practiced some warm-up swings, she went to him and offered some sage advice. "Deacon is on second and Cupid is on third. The score is zero to two. We could do something in this inning. You've got to focus." She shouldn't have let her anxiousness come through, but this was the first flicker of hope they'd had since she'd taken over. A cold knot formed in her stomach. This was it. She could prove herself worthy of the job. But she needed Alex's help.

His cap rode low on his forehead, a portion of his dark hair having fallen over his forehead. The Keystones lettering on his shirt stretched over his chest, the crisscross laces down the front a contrast of white next to gold. A black belt circled his lean waist. White pants, molded against his hips, ballooned slightly at the knees where stockings came up his well-defined calves.

She stared into the dark black depths of his eyes.

The gaze was more of a caress she didn't care to explain—not to herself, not to him. Perhaps she'd been thinking too much about the words that they'd had before the game, talk of lips together, because when she spoke, her voice came out low and throaty, thick with unspoken meaning. "Tear the leather off the ball, Cordova."

He gave her a smile, his teeth white and straight. "Yeah. Sure."

Then he took his position.

The crowd jeered. Booed. Hissed. Empty paper cups from lemonade rained from the grandstand to litter the grass. Mighty Alex Cordova hadn't shown them a thing since he'd put on a Keystones uniform.

Zaza pitched him a knuckleball.

Swing and a miss.

Camille cringed. She brought her hand to her temple and sighed. If her attention hadn't been focused on Alex, she would have seen the ruckus going on at third base sooner. By the time she looked in that direction, Frank Isbell had Cupid's cap in his hand and was waving it while belly-laughing. Mortification reddened Cupid's face as he flailed his arms, trying to get his cap back.

"Wait a minute. Time!" Camille called to the umpire as she walked to where the official stood behind home plate. "He can't do that."

As she was speaking, Frank cuffed Cupid on the top of his bald head. The action evoked a curse from Alex, who threw his bat down and lunged after Frank with his fists tight. The next thing Camille knew, both benches had emptied and she landed in the middle of wild fisticuffs.

Turning this way and that to get out of the line of fire, she managed to escape to the dugout, where she clutched the awning post in horror. She saw Cupid give Frank a healthy kick in the shins, only to have Frank aim a ham fist in a roundhouse punch to Cupid's eye.

The melee lasted some ten minutes before order was restored. Shaken, she called her players back to the bench, where they sat, with the exception of the men who had to return to their bases. She looked at the ragtag group, her jaw dropping. Charlie's swollen brow was darkening. Doc had a lump on his forehead. A bloody cut marred Bones's forearm. Down the line, caps were askew, uniforms were ripped, and several shoes were untied.

"Well . . . this is something," was all she could say.

She'd never witnessed a full-fledged major-league brawl before. When the Keystones had been a small organization, they'd never went at the opposing team with their fists.

Camille tried to quell the skip in her heartbeat. She hadn't dared look at her father, who sat in the front row. What would he have done? There was nothing anyone could have done. Things had just . . . taken off.

Unsettled, she watched as Alex took his position. And much to her complete surprise, he drew the bat back and hammered the ball over the infield and beyond, well over the wall and out of the park.

Home run.

The fans let out cheers so loud, they just about shook the roof of the dugout. If Alex thought there was any glory in what he'd just done, he didn't reveal it. He merely made a slow run around the bases, his toe touching each bag. When he crossed home plate, the team was waiting for him. They slapped him on his back, whooping it up and hollering, carrying on as if they'd just won the pennant.

The congratulations continued as the men came into the dugout, Alex the last to take his seat. She turned to him, but the right words failed her. She smiled. Grateful. Although she was almost certain that his hitting the ball had nothing to do with her.

As the game proceeded, the Keystones' fielding just about ruined what had been a good game so far. A fly ball sailed to center field and both Specs and Deacon galloped after it without regard for life or limb, hollering all the time, running like maniacs after the ball. Playing side by side like that, they plowed into each other with the impact of runaway freight trains. It wasn't until after Deacon lifted his head off the ground that his glove arm followed. Inside the pocket, there lay the ball—for the second out of the inning.

The score was 5-2, Keystones. Camille's pulse hadn't quit its racing since that third inning. They were in the eighth now, with such a chance, she could barely think straight.

The time Alex had spent in the bullpen had done him little or no good. He wasn't pitching any better than he normally did. So Camille walked to the mound to have a talk with him.

"Quit doing that." The command just rushed out. She hated to be short with him, but for the past five minutes, all he'd done was pitch slow sinkers and blow on his bare hand.

"What?"

"You're stalling when you keep doing that. We don't have all day. We'll lose the momentum."

He raised his wide, tanned hand to her as if she were supposed to inspect it. "You mean this?" Then he brought his open fist to his mouth and blew.

Camille didn't like to speculate why the sight of him blowing on his bare hand caused her to break out in gooseflesh. "Yes, that. It's not necessary."

"I'm keeping the ball dry."

"It's not raining."

"My palm's sweating."

"Well, unsweat it or I'm putting Yank in to close for you."

Then she turned and headed back to the bench. She disliked threats. She disliked having to follow through with them. But she'd meant what she said. And in the bottom of the ninth, she made good on her words and put Yank Milligan in to finish the game.

While she sat, ankles crossed, shoulders leaning forward, she watched Yank throw an effective dipsy-doodle that the batter missed.

And afterward, Yank adjusted himself. Again.

The habit was distracting, and he did it before and after each pitch.

Alex sat beside her, and she heard his low laugh next to her ear. "Does that bother you as bad as my blowing on my hand?"

"It certainly does."

"Then why don't you go out there and tell Yank to knock it off?"

"I most certainly . . ." But the denial trailed off. He was daring her. Baiting her. Of course she didn't want to mention anything of that kind to a man.

"You won't do it." His smile made her insides tingle. Sweat dampened his brow; the band of his backward cap caught the moisture at his hairline. "You couldn't even say the words. *Adjusting* and *quit revising the hang of your privates* are two different things."

Camille about expired. On that, she abruptly left the bench and went out to Yank.

He looked at her, surprised. "Yeah?"

"I want you to quit . . ."—unbidden, her gaze dropped, then she quickly snapped it upward—". . . quit adjusting yourself. Nothing's going anywhere."

Then she retreated and primly sat back down beside Alex. "I told him."

His laugh made her want to pour the ice water bucket over his head.

The last five minutes of the game were a blur. There was an error involving Doc and a play at second was called into question. If it had stood, the Chicago White Stockings would have earned an out, tying the game and making it necessary for a tenth inning. But Camille had gone to discuss the controversy with the umpire, while Eddie Gray, the Chicago manager, just about shredded her senseless with his vile language. He went berserk, spit spraying out of his mouth, cursing, yelling, getting right into her face as he argued his case. And in the middle of all that, calling her a woman.

Then he'd told her she was a nitwit, and that Boomer Hurley had told him all about her. That she was nothing but a piece of honeycake who couldn't possibly know a bat from a ball. Still, he hadn't gotten her to raise her voice back at him, although inside, she was shaking. And she felt the hot sting of tears filling her eyes. When he was finished with using his violent mouth and the umpire deemed it not against the rules for Doc to go back to second from third, the game went on.

Utterly frazzled, she'd returned to the bench. But she tried not to show just how affected she'd been. If she started crying, she'd be a laughingstock.

In those last seconds of the inning, they'd held onto their lead and won.

Good Lord in heaven, they'd won.

A rush of excitement buzzed the air and jovial cheers of goodwill rose. Amid the throng of people on the field, Camille's eyes met Alex's. He'd saved the day—not because of anything she'd told him, but because he'd defended Cupid Burns and had gotten the team to work together. Yet, the expression on his face said that he hadn't done it for the heroics.

Vying for his attention, a group of women rushed toward him wanting his autograph, their signature albums in their hands. Camille turned away.

Her mother met her and they hugged.

"Where's Daddy?" Camille asked. She'd seen him sitting in the front row.

"Right here."

Camille spun around, a smile on her lips. "We won."

"That was one heck of a ball game! The fans finally got their money's worth. And so did I. A delight to watch." Then ever the opinion giver, he added, "But you could have gotten more runs in if you'd played Jimmy instead of Cupid. He hits better."

Her smile fell. If she'd played Jimmy, Cupid wouldn't have smelled up third base and caused a commotion. Rather than explaining that, for clearly her father had made up his mind, she merely nodded. "I'll remember that."

Moments later, her father had been the recipient of hearty pats on the back from his fellow Elks Club members and from other men in town. Not a one of them patted her on her back, heartily *or* mildly. Or shook her hand, or acknowledged her in the slightest.

The next edition of the *Harmony Advocate* would say that the win had been a fluke, but every player on the Keystones knew it had been the horse liniment that had fired them up. In light of that, it had been a unanimous vote from the teammates for Cupid to continue his baldness treatment.

Baseball players took their superstitions very seriously.

*   *   *

"You're not going on a train with thirteen men, un-escorted!" her father announced later that evening as Camille packed a suitcase.

She moved around her room, brushing past the man who stood in its center with a deep furrow in his forehead. "Of course I am."

Her mother sat on the bed beside the stockings Camille had rolled into neat buns. She placed them next to her chemise and petticoat that already were nestled in the case. "Camille, your father might be right."

"Of course I'm right. I'm always right."

A pair of shoes in hand, she addressed her mother, disregarding her father's comment. "How can you say that?"

"Because Mrs. Plunkett and Mrs. Calhoon called on me earlier today and they voiced concern about something you told them." Her mother rarely, if ever, grew discomfited. "Something about . . . men's drawers."

"That was nothing."

"It doesn't sound like nothing," her father barreled back. "What about men's drawers?"

"I fibbed about something and I realized after the fact that I shouldn't have done it." Camille fit the shoes into her suitcase, then reached for her hair-brush and mirror. "But Mrs. Plunkett told me that I was chasing after a husband when I became the man-ager of the Keystones, and that set me off. So I played along with her, and now it's getting me into trouble." Putting her hands on her hips, she faced her parents. "I refuse to cower. And the fact of the matter is, there wouldn't be any of this talk or any problem if I could grow a beard."

"Mrs. Kirby has a mustache," her father pointed out, "and *she* doesn't talk about men's drawers."

"Mrs. Kirby is well into her seventies," her mother countered, "and I don't think she's seen a man in his drawers in over a decade."

Her father grunted. "I don't care about that old crone anyway. She can't sing a hymn worth a blessed beat. The issue at hand is your daughter's going off on a train full of men."

"*Our* daughter has reminded us that she's capable. And sensible." But to Camille she said, "Even given that . . . don't you think it would be a good idea for your father to go with you?"

"And who would watch the store?" Camille pulled a nightgown out of her wardrobe drawer. "The reason he needed a manager was so he could stay here and tend it."

"I could close it while I'm gone."

Dumping the nightie into the open case, Camille declared, "You would not."

"No, James, you wouldn't."

"I would if that roof gutter, Nops, wasn't across the street plotting how to steal my business right out from under my eaves!"

"I'm going alone." To Camille, the discussion was a waste of breath. She was going to be on that train. First thing in the morning, she'd be on her way to Philadelphia, and after that, Washington, D.C. And she was going to be on it without somebody to hold her hand as if she were a child. "It would be humiliating to have my father come with me. I won't be escorted by him or anybody else. You're forgetting, I'll have the players to protect me from unwanted attention."

Her father's loud voice filled the floral-papered bedroom. "You're missing the entire point! Who's going to protect you from *them?*"

Chapter
9

"We have to get rid of her."

The clatter of the train's wheels could not upstage Cub LaRoque's words. The matter-of-fact statement sounded through the vestibule where Alex stood with the majority of the other players. The enclosed hallway between the rail cars pressed in on him. He never should have agreed to come out here when Bones asked him to.

Accordion-like appendages at each end of the vestibule united the individual cars into a single unit where passengers could walk from one train to the next without losing a hat.

Alex would have preferred the beating wind on his face and a cigarette between his fingers. Charlie had been lighting one right after the other, and Alex was on the verge of hitting him up for one.

"I agree," Charlie seconded, drawing in a deep pull on his Old Judge. "Did you see how Eddie Gray read her the riot act yesterday and she didn't do a durn thing about it?"

"Called her a cupcake," Bones said.

Cub corrected him. "Piece of honeycake."

Bones shrugged. "Fergawdsake. Same thing. Both are too sugary to be used on a baseball field."

"Any other manager wouldn't have taken that crap from Eddie," Mox proclaimed. "They would've punched Eddie in the gut."

"And got ejected from the game," Cub concluded. "A good manager gets himself ejected from the game."

Cupid added his two cents. "With a fat fine."

"She was crying," Bones said.

"Nothing to use a hankie on," Mox put in, "but she watered up like a leaky faucet, just the same."

Noddles nodded. "Them other teams are laughing at us because our manager doesn't have balls. *Literally.* If we run her off, then we'll have to get a new manager."

"And not a woman," Mox added. "Let's give her hell."

"Old man Kennison would be better than her," Jimmy ventured to say, "and we know how bad he is."

"So." Noddles pursed his lips. "What can we do?"

"Hold on." Specs raised his hand, light reflecting off the wire frame of his spectacles. "I don't know if I want to be a party to this. She did teach us those calisthenics. I'm feeling a lot more limber."

"Would you rather be a party to being called a sissy ass?" Cupid all but spit the insult.

"Nobody calls me a sissy ass. At least not to my face."

"Well, I suppose it's okay to be called one behind your back, then," Yank snapped. "According to the *Chicago Tribune,* 'The Harmony Keystones have flopped into disgrace in more ways than one this season. Not only do they lead the league in losses, but

129

they are managed by the first ever—and we hope the last—female baseball manager. Buy your tickets now, folks, for the games July first through third at South Side Park. Admission, fifty cents and one pink posy.' " His expression soured. "I saw the newspaper in the station. Bold as brass, right there on the racks. We're making the news across the country and it's goddamn embarrassing."

Nods showed that several others concurred with Yank's sentiments. Alex neither agreed or disagreed, but that wasn't to say he wasn't interested.

He butted his shoulder next to the aft passenger car, the precise one in which Camille sat. They'd made a line switch from the Northern Pacific to the Pennsylvania in Chicago. For some forty hours, they'd been on a train, sleeping and eating with hardly a moment to get off and stretch their legs. And they had twenty-one hours more to go.

The National League had played away games, but they were mostly along the East Coast lines. This going from one end of the states to the other was hard on a body. It was only natural that tempers flared.

"I missed that newspaper," Specs said, folding his arms over his chest. "You're right. It's embarrassing."

Deacon shrugged. "So what do you propose we do, Cub?"

"First off, we have to all be in agreement," Cub said. "Show of hands, gentlemen."

Hands lifted. Alex merely tipped his Stetson at a lower angle over his brow. He glanced through a window in the car door. He saw Captain, doing just what he'd been doing when Alex left him—looking out the window with a worried expression. Cap had been excited to come on the trip and had done nothing but talk about it for days, but as soon as the train rolled out, he'd done nothing but ask Alex when they were going back to Harmony. Alex hadn't anticipated Captain's reaction. He wished he had; he could have made other arrangements.

The car was filled with few passengers at this time of the evening; the hour was just shy of nine. A pair of lovebirds, newlyweds from the way they cuddled and cooed at each other, had gotten on at the last stop. Now they slept, the wife's head resting on her husband's shoulder.

Camille sat in one of the middle seats. Couldn't miss her. That hat. Bluebirds and sprays of floral stuff. She looked out the Venetian blinds into the darkness, then back at something in her lap.

Alex absently faced forward.

Cub narrowed his eyes at him. "Cordova, are you in with us or not?"

"I've never hit a lady."

Cub spouted off. "We aren't going to hit her! Just get her fired."

"Same thing in my book." Alex watched Charlie light another smoke from the burning end of the one he'd just finished. Grinding the butt with the instep of his shoe, Charlie inhaled and let a stream of gray smoke pass between his lips.

Cub pursued Alex. "Why did you tell us to 'get over it' back in the clubhouse a week ago? Do you know something about Miss Kennison that we don't? Do you have a plan of your own to get rid of her?"

"Actually, I thought she'd get rid of herself. I didn't think she'd last."

"Well, she *has* lasted. So are you with us?"

Alex sucked up some of the thick smoke into his lungs, taking from the air what he could of Charlie's Old Judge cigarette. "I don't really care what you do about her."

"Then will you keep this information to yourself?" Specs asked.

"Yeah, why not."

"Here's the deal, then," Cub began with a conspiratorial smile. "We make her look bad every chance we get. On the train, off the train, in restaurants and hotels, in the ballpark. Kennison is going to have to fire her when he sees how shabby things are looking."

Yank felt the stubble on his jaw. "So what do we do first?"

"Well, Doc's in the john." Cub gave a slight chuckle. "Duke's waiting outside and'll take his place as soon as Doc flushes the crapper and the train stops."

Alex listened without enthusiasm. Pranks. He didn't go in for them. Many players pulled this stuff, even when they *did* like the manager. Alex knew all about the pneumatic brake system on the car and how it tapped into the air-water apparatus when flushing the john. If a person flushed at the right moment, the brakes locked. A big sign hung above the sink that said not to pull the chain on a curve.

Cub, who sidled up to the door, gazed through the window and nodded to Duke, who in turn rapped three times on the water closet door.

Holy hell. Alex moved past Cub and let himself out of the vestibule to take his seat beside Cap, who'd finally nodded off. His face was contorted in some dream, but it didn't look as if it were a nightmare—merely the stress of keeping himself awake for so many hours at a time.

Alex glanced at Camille. She sat four rows ahead of him. She'd barely slept all night. Alex had stayed up most of it with her, not one to sleep deeply on a train. He guessed Camille was worried about the team. She should be. They were going to make her life unpleasant. Alex almost felt sorry for her. But he pushed that thought back. There was no place in baseball for foolish sentiments. If men—or women—couldn't handle the pressure, then they'd better get the hell out.

A screech of metal brake against iron rail scratched through the car. Alex clenched his jaw while Cap sat up, hair in his eyes.

"Are we going back to Harmony now, Alex?"

"Naw, Cap. Go back to sleep."

Cap frowned, his eyelids drooping. "I just got comfortable. These seats are bad."

The hard seats, with barely any leather to them, did leave little to be desired. Being as tall as they were, both he and Captain were pressed for comfortable space; the knees on their long legs touched the back of the seat in front of them. Alex stood, shrugged out of his traveling duster, and wadded it in a ball. "Use this to rest your head on, Cap, and go back to sleep."

Almost instantly, Cap did.

Camille had risen to her feet, bending forward to look out the window. Alex appreciated the way her breasts molded against her white shirtwaist. How her waist seemed slender and curvaceous at the same time. She looked over her shoulder at him. A tiny curl fell in front of her right ear, exactly where her cheek had pressed on the wood panel of the wall when she'd napped. That heavy-lidded gaze, and a low voice made throatier from exhaustion, was purely sensual. "Do you think we've hit an animal on the tracks?"

Alex couldn't contain a smile. "We're barely out of Chicago. The only animals out here are criminals."

She gave him a frown, her lips looking soft and lush. He would have liked to knock her hat off, pull the pins from her hair, and sink his fingers into the blond curls—then kiss her for a long, long while.

The brakeman, a big ox of a man, stomped through

the car from the front vestibule, his eyes zeroing in on the water closet. The shiny patent-leather bill of his navy hat acted as a mirror, reflecting the displeasure in his face and giving it a bluish tinge of anger.

Alex casually turned in his seat as Ox Man rapped on the lavatory door with a big fist. "You in there— can't you read the sign?"

"Oh, I can read," came Doc's muffled voice. "My mistake."

Snickers sounded from the players. They'd gathered in the back of the car, trying to smother their guffaws.

"Who's in charge here?" the brakeman called, looking at the players.

"I am."

Camille walked toward them, her steps a little unsteady from having been sitting for so long. Alex was almost tempted to take her by the elbow, but he refrained. He didn't want any part of this.

"I'm certain the use of the closet on a curve was a genuine mistake."

"Who are you?"

"Camille Kennison, manager of the Harmony Keystones." She made a quick adjustment of her frilly collar.

"Manager of baseball?"

At that, her tone grew slightly defensive. "Yes."

The brakeman began to lumber back through the aisle, muttering, "It'd better have been mistake, lady. Now we have to reset the air pressure."

"It won't happen again," she called after him, then looked at the men who hung around the closet door. "Will it?"

Nobody answered.

But it did happen again. Four more times. Each time the brakeman had come in, her demeanor had changed. She'd gone from being demurely polite to being incensed over the joke. The fifth time the train was stopped by a flush, she came apart. She was already standing as Ox Man marched into the car.

"I understand you're upset," she said before the brakeman could get out a single word. Her eyes flashed with outrage. "I feel the same way. And believe you me, there's going to be aces to pay."

She tread heavily—gone was that efficient walk—over to the water closet door, glaring at the players who milled around, then rapping with glove-covered fingers on the door. "Mox! You get your keister out of there right this instant!"

Turned in his seat, Alex watched the sparks that seemed to crackle off her like a charged wire. Jesus. He'd never seen a lady mean business the way Camille Kennison meant business. She looked dangerous. Desirable. If this is how she got when she didn't hold her temper back—holy Christ—what would she be like if she didn't hold her passion back?

Sheepishly, Mox stuck his head through a crack in the door. She all but grabbed the handle and swung it open on him.

She berated him. "This is intolerable."

"You've got that right," the brakeman agreed in a growl. "The next time this crapper is flushed and the brakes lock because of it, each and every one of you will be off this train. I don't give a damn where we happen to be. Even if it's twenty miles from the next station!"

His voice bellowed through the car as he stomped out.

Camille rested her hands on her slender hips, looked at the hoodlums, and made a threat of her own. "If we are thrown off this train, it will cost each and every one of you the price of your ticket, *plus* an additional fifty dollars by way of a fine from the Key-stones management."

Then she went back to her seat, where she took slow, deep breaths to calm herself. She remained gazing out the window as the train began to roll again.

Cub had passed the word that the high jinks had been a success. It was probably a good thing it was over: all that opening and closing the john door had loosened the screws on the door's handle, so the next man in who had to use it for real had better be careful not to lock himself inside.

Three hours after the first flush, Captain awoke and was now chewing on a sandwich a waiter doled out for a few cents.

"When are we going back to Harmony?" he asked again. "I've got to be at work."

"I thought you wanted to come with me," Alex replied.

"I thought so, too. But I don't want to lose my job at Plunkett's. I like it. I like having Hildegarde back."

Alex rotated his ankles in an attempt to stimulate the circulation blood, the lack of which had numbed his feet. "Mr. Plunkett said you could take some days off. We'll be going back home soon."

"When?"

"In about two weeks."

"How many days is that?"

"Fourteen."

"Spell that."

He did, and Cap recited the letters a few times.

Alex continued to monitor Camille's every move, every gesture. A lift of her hand to her lips, her fingers brushing them in thought. Slow sweeps of her lashes. An adjustment of her collar, then an absent graze of the button at her throat. With each little motion she made, he felt his body stir, until he had to stand and look at some different scenery.

Alex walked down the aisle and tapped Charlie on the shoulder. "Have an extra smoke?"

"Yeah, sure."

Hiding the cigarette and match in his hand, Alex glanced at Cap. Cap would give him hell for smoking again; he hated cigarettes. So Alex headed for the vestibule to light up in private. Once at the door, he glimpsed the lovebirds sharing a newlywed kiss. Damn.

He wasn't about to go another minute without smoking this cigarette, so he went inside the comfort station and gently closed the door so as not to pop the screw on the lock. It was a cramped closet barely three feet square with a slash of a window that had been left open. A washbasin with nickel fixtures and zinc floor were about the only things that spruced it up. Above the sink words had been emblazoned in a big sign:

Warning!
A water closet flushed at the wrong
moment could upset the pneumatic
balance of the Westinghouse system.
Do not operate it while train is on curve.

Alex had no intentions of flushing the john, curve or not.

Striking the match against the frame of the door, he brought the flame to the end of his cigarette. Then drew in a cloud of heaven into his lungs. He casually lounged against the edge of the sink. He meant to enjoy every last puff.

Christ, it had been much too long.

Camille paid the waiter several coins for a raspberry jelly sandwich wrapped in wax paper. She'd save the meal for later; she wasn't hungry now. All that horseplay with the water closet. Whatever had gotten into the players sorely disappointed her. She'd thought better of them. She'd actually thought they had begun to accept her position. Their apparent about-face nicked her feelings.

Well, if she were being truly honest, she had to admit they'd never really warmed up to her, not in the way she'd hoped. Although there had been those moments when she thought they'd shared a smile or two. Maybe they'd been laughing at her. If that were the case . . .

She shook off the thought. No sense in making herself crazy about it. They had just under a day left of travel. They'd check into a hotel and get ready for their game against the Philadelphia Athletics. There was no time to doubt her abilities.

She scanned the seats in front of her, where several of the players were occupied with a game of cards. Then she looked a little to her left, and lastly over her shoulder. Captain sat alone. Camille frowned. She looked at the players once more and began to count them off. One, two, three . . . six, seven . . . twelve. One was missing.

Since she hadn't seen Alex leave through the front car, he had to have gone out through the back—if he'd left at all. That meant only one other place he could be. She chilled at the thought.

Quickly, she rose and went to Specs, who sat in the last row of the car with Cupid Burns. She'd thought Specs had been an advocate of hers, but clearly she'd been mistaken. She had to make sure the prank didn't happen again. If it did, they were going to get thrown off the train. And how would she explain *that* to her father? Being cast adrift meant inconvenience, and even more than that, not getting to

Philadelphia on time. They'd miss the game. She'd be in big trouble.

"Mr. Ryan," she said to Specs, "where is Mr. Cordova?"

Specs lifted his brows as if he really wasn't sure. "I don't know."

She moved her gaze to Cupid. "Have you seen him?"

Cupid's eyes darted to the water closet, then his Adam's apple wobbled up and down the front of his neck when he spoke. "I saw him going into the—"

She didn't wait to hear the rest. She turned on a fast heel. She never should have bought that sandwich and grown distracted. While she'd been paying for her meal, Alex had snuck into the water closet. She couldn't let him do anything to get them bounced from the train.

At the door in an instant, she frantically knocked on the wood panel. Her gloves muffled her rapping. "Mr. Cordova, I want you to exit the facility immediately."

No answer.

She knocked again. Urgently.

The train swayed and rocked, careening toward a curve on the rails. She could feel it beneath her feet. She jarred a little to the right and had to put her arm out against the wall. Her pulse danced. Her mind spun with the consequences. Panic swept through her.

"Mr. Cordova, what are you doing in there?"

She knocked harder.

When he finally answered, his voice was dry and deliberate. "Come in and see for yourself."

She was left with no choice but to grip the knob and swing the door open. The moment she did, the train rounded a bend and the door swung closed on her behind, shoving her headlong into the tiny, smoke-filled cubicle. The next thing she knew, she was pressed up against Alex, breasts to chest. No room to move an inch.

The oil-burning globe lamp didn't give off a lot of light from its position over the washbasin. She looked into Alex's face, her hands on his chest—the only thing to brace her fall. She was a tall woman, but he was much taller. Without his Stetson, his ink black hair fell in a tumble over his forehead as he gazed down at her.

"You miss me?" His voice sounded deeper, richer in the small space.

"That's not it at all. I'm checking on you."

"Nobody's checked on me in the john since I was two and learned to pee standing up. So what did you really want?"

Camille felt her cheeks heat hotter than a cast-iron skillet. "I thought you might be fl—" She stopped midsentence. "I just thought you might be up to no good."

He smiled suggestively. "I am up to no good."

That he'd admit it struck a chord in her. "Thank you, Mr. Cordova, for nothing. I thought you were above this kind of foolery."

"Don't get a twist in your petticoats, honey. I was only smoking."

"Smoking?"

"Captain doesn't like it and I didn't want to get him excited."

"Really?" Curls of tobacco smoke did fill the space. She had noticed it before but had put the thought out of her mind. Just the same, she questioned, "You're quite certain that's all you planned to do in here?"

A slow, disarming smile curved his lips. "Not unless the urge hit me to do something else."

Unbidden, a blush stained her cheeks.

Now that the matter of what he was doing in here had been cleared up, she was conscious of every place on her body where Alex touched her, especially the hard cords of muscle in his thighs that were separated from her own thighs by only the pleats of her skirt. Filling out a worn-soft cotton shirt, his wide shoulders seemed even wider in the small space. She noted his shirt didn't have a collar—just a simple band in pale blue to match the pale blue of the shirt itself. She had the strangest urge to touch the base of his throat, where the pearl buttons fastened the top of his shirts. Alex seemed so warm. So . . .

"Uh, Miss Kennison . . ." Specs said through the door.

She almost forgot that there were over a dozen people outside the door. All of whom knew that she and Alex were in the comfort station. Alone.

"We have to ask for help," she whispered, unable to trust her voice. A tingling worked its way into the pit of her stomach and was creeping over her skin and making her feel lightheaded. "Don't you see how compromising this looks?"

"All I can see is the faint light in your eyes, part of your lips"—his face had come very close to hers as he spoke—"and the handle on that door missing."

With that, she all but stammered, "What?" She turned as best as she could to see that the handle was indeed missing. There was a small hole where the locking mechanism was supposed to go, but there was no handle.

"The screws got knocked out when you slammed the door."

"I didn't slam the door. It slammed me."

"However you want to look at it." He slipped his arm around her waist and drew her tightly next to him. His breath was warm against the side of her neck. "I don't care how you got in here. And now that you are ..."

She pushed at his shoulders, knowing exactly what he was going to do. But the push had about as much strength to it as a shadow when his mouth covered hers. Her heart pounded, and as much as she wanted to tell him no, she couldn't. The light brush of his mouth brought a current of pleasure through her. Just as intense, if not more so, than the time he'd kissed her in the buggy.

Her reaction to him shocked her. She should have had better sense. A chaotic dizziness grabbed her, and in turn, she grabbed onto Alex. He slid his hard fingers around the nape of her neck and pulled her closer. His tongue slid over the seam of her mouth, tracing her lower lip, then deepening the kiss in a way she had never experienced.

His tongue slipped inside her mouth. Something turned over inside her that was a mixture of surprise and anticipation that this was only part of how he could make her feel. Only part of what he could do to her to make her melt beside him. Already, she felt the heat of him through her clothes. Almost searing. For a startling moment, she wondered what it would be like to kiss him this way with no clothes between them. Just skin next to skin, warm and hard, every contour of his body exposed to her where she could see its definition, feel every curve and supple muscle.

She thought she might swoon.

Never in her life had she fainted, and she wasn't about to start now.

But his kiss snatched her breath. It was a delicious fusing of his lips over hers. His tongue swept through her mouth, teasing her tongue to meet his. She dared to, slowly, hesitantly. As she relaxed, his hand cupped her buttocks, bringing her sinfully close to him. But she didn't stop him.

This was madness.

"Miss Kennison . . . we can't find the screws to the handle."

The words barely registered. The train reeled and careened over the tracks, much like her heart was beating. Insanity. If the door opened right now, she could forget about everything. Her job. Her reputation.

Alex's hands drifted to the sides of her neck, then higher. "I want to take off your hat."

Breathlessly, she answered next to his mouth. "You can't."

"I will one day."

The way he said it, so certain and with a sense of inevitability, made the knot in her stomach tighten even more. She fought to come to her senses and break away—not that there was anyplace to go—but enough to say something she should have said moments ago.

"Hurry up!" she cried.

"Doc just found one screw, Miss Kennison," Specs called.

"And I got the other one," came a reply a few seconds later—Charlie must have come up to the door.

Camille forced her breathing to resume its normal state, averting her gaze from Alex's. She felt him looking at her, drinking her in with his eyes. He had no right to make her weak just by a mere glance, a mere caress with those warm brown eyes of his.

In what seemed to take an eternity, the door handle was reassembled and the door opened. Camille practically tumbled out of the room. Freedom. Why, then, did she feel so imprisoned by her own emotions? She didn't dare look back at Alex. She couldn't risk his knowing that she was feeling something for him.

"Thank you for getting us out," she said in a rush. "The door swung closed on me and I was trapped. The only reason I was knocking on it in the first place was to make sure that nobody else stops this train." She gazed at the players in turn; then, because she was so overwrought with the aftereffects of Alex's kiss, she grew angry. "The next man who *dares* to use that water closet and stop this train by inappropriate actions will be fined—not the fifty dollars I previously stated, but *one hundred* dollars." She lifted her hand to her hat, feeling it slipping sideways from her ordeal. Righting the stiff crown, she added, "And don't think I don't mean it. I do."

Then she resumed her seat and tried to still the frantic beating of her heart. She never once looked back.

By midnight, the passengers in the train car slept. All of them except for Alex. He looked at the woman who had changed seats so that she could occupy the last one in the train. To keep a close eye on them, he assumed—although with her eyes closed, that would be hard. But nobody crossed her. Not even in a small way. Maybe she had gained some ground.

Rising to his feet, he walked to the end of the car and gazed at the sleeping woman before making his way to the vestibule for another smoke. Her ankles weren't crossed in that delicate way. Actually, one tan Oxford shoe had come untied. And where her hands rested on her lap, a jelly stain marred the pristine white of her right glove. A half-eaten sandwich lay on an embroidered handkerchief that had been spread over her skirt.

He smiled. Miss Honey had come a little undone. The sight took his heart someplace he didn't want to go.

He slipped out of the car to smoke his cigarette and contemplate why this woman did the things she did to him.

And that also was someplace he didn't want to go just yet.

But he would. Because he'd really meant it about taking her hat off. It was only a matter of time.

Chapter
❦ 10 ❦

The Keystones were trampled in their first two games against the Philadelphia Athletics. Camille had written off Monday's loss to fatigue. Their train arrived at the station an hour before the start of the game. There'd been no time to go to their hotel first. They'd ridden directly to the ballpark in a four horse-drawn tallyho. Once at Columbia Park, the players barely had a chance to change in a small office, then take the field without the benefit of batting practice.

On the coach ride, Camille had taken in the scenery, wishing she'd had a moment to really enjoy it. She liked to travel. She'd taken trains before to Shreveport with her parents to see family. But the big-city sights were so different from the town she'd grown up in and from the streets of Harmony. Here, buildings soared skyward to the clouds. She'd wondered where the Museum of Art was located, if it was close to their hotel. She'd never been to Philadelphia before. If she'd had the chance, she would have liked to tour it. See Independence Hall. The Liberty Bell.

The grandstands in Columbia Park seemed mammoth compared to Municipal Field. Just opened this year, the entire park smelled new, of fresh paint on the fences and fresh varnish on the oak seats. The fan area was almost ten times larger than at home. And the people filled the stadium in a way they didn't in Harmony. The dirt connecting the infield was red clay; the field was covered with tightly clipped grass. A pole with two flags flew above the seats behind home plate. A riser high over the grandstand must have been reserved for the press. Looking at it all, she'd felt intimidated. Then to lose two in a row.

For today's game, their last third, the park had been sold out.

At practice, Camille had had Alex throw soft, underhanded pitches so that the players could get the feel of hitting the ball. And they did. They connected with each pitch, one right after the other. Her reasoning for doing such a thing was more emotional than physical. She wanted them to *want* to hit the ball, to want to hit home runs. If pitching easy to them would make them excited to chase after hard ones, then her plan would prove successful. At times, though, she wondered why she'd bothered trying to get them motivated.

The men had been testing her patience to its limits. When they finally had checked into the Euclid Avenue Hotel late Monday, they'd stopped the lift between floors, rung for maid service then said they hadn't, and had a false telegram sent to her from a "Mr. Cupcake." Their behavior had been so unruly, they'd been banned from eating in the dining room—not that they'd been welcomed in the first place. Ballplayers were usually frowned on in eating establishments. Meals—as far as she knew, breakfast, lunch, *and* dinner—were bought at the frankfurter stand outside the hotel's front doors. At least that's where the players ate. Camille had food brought up to her from the hotel kitchen and ate alone in her room.

She hated to admit it, but they were getting to her. She hadn't slept decently since leaving Harmony. She felt on the verge of crying at the slightest thing, but she vowed never to let one of them see her in such an emotional state. What hurt the most was that she really tried to do right by them, by building them into a successful baseball club. She'd rearranged her goals for the Garden Club to help the team. The fact that they were now going out of their way to make her miserable added insult to injury. She resented it and had half a mind to tell them they could just manage themselves from now on. But if she did, she'd have to tell her father she quit. And she just couldn't bear to see that look of "I told you so" in his eyes. Worse yet, Mr. Nops would demand his money back, money that had been partially spent on fan cards.

"Dummy Leitner is pitching today," Camille told the players as they huddled in the dugout. The day was gray and foggy, exceptionally cool for this time of year. Camille had bundled herself into a wool jacket and thick kid gloves. "He's good. But we can be better."

Duke chewed an uncommonly large wad of tobacco and spit from the side of his mouth. The brown juice dribbled down his chin and he wiped it with the back of his shirtsleeve. It was all Camille could do to stand quietly and not reprimand him. She had to chose her battles, and right now, tobacco wasn't one of them. But she did make a mental note to write down the infraction in her notebook and come up with an alternative to spitting.

The players took the field, and the game started

amid cheers. A home run by Philadelphia late in the first inning brought three runs in. Alex held back every time he pitched, and she was at her wit's end about it. When the Keystones came up to bat, she concentrated on the efforts being put forth by Dummy Leitner, trying to figure out a way for Alex to emulate him.

Leitner never gave off a hint of nervousness, even though he could neither hear or speak. Watching the catcher, Morgan Murphy, give Dummy the deaf-and-dumb signs for pitches, Camille followed along through the booklet she had on hand gestures. She'd been studying the many finger and thumb positions, trying to make sense out of the signals.

In the sixth inning, two walks killed Alex and she took him out of the game. By the seventh, however, her spirits were renewed. Bones hit a triple and brought in two runs to even the score. As he rounded the bases, she saw that he ran like he had flat feet. Camille made a notation in her notebook.

"Hey, Alex," came Captain's voice from above the dugout where the first row of seats began. "Why aren't you playing anymore?"

She arched her brow at Alex. She'd grown tired of having to pull him from his starting position. But with a pitching staff of two, it left her little choice. "Why don't you tell him it's because you can't throw the ball?"

His dark brown eyes appeared sarcastic. "I can throw it."

"Not in the strike zone," she shot back. "I used to think that it was because you weren't trying. Now I think you're trying too hard and that's why you're ineffective."

His jaw stiffened.

"I've been watching you, and you go through the

windup just fine. But when you have to release the ball, you stop halfway. Like you hit a glass wall. And then your body goes tense. I can almost see the muscles in your neck popping."

He swore. And it wasn't a "damn."

She'd struck a nerve. She wasn't all that happy she'd figured him out—or at least figured out as much as she could. She went back and forth in her mind over whether she should tell her father to just fire him, to some way get Mr. Nops's money back and call the whole thing off. But whenever she thought about letting Alex go, she visualized the power he did have. That point in his pitch where he stopped. What preceded that moment was greatness. She wished he'd see that, get past it.

She tried to focus on the players. She knew she was being snappish with Alex, but she didn't care. His kissing her on the train still upset her. Not upset in a way that she felt taken advantage of, but upset in a way that turned her upside down. She still thought about his lips on hers. Still thought about his hard body next to hers. Still thought about what it would be like to touch his bare skin. She had no business thinking like this, and that upset her, too—in a different way.

Alex stood and looked over the dugout's rooftop. "I'm just taking a rest, Cap."

"When are we going back to Harmony, Alex? I have to go to work."

"In a couple of days." Alex's calm tone sounded forced.

"I want to go back now."

"In a couple of days." This time the words were tightly spoken.

The exchange had been going on between the two of them the entire game. Every few minutes, Captain would ask the same question and Alex would give the same answer. In the beginning, he'd been pleasant with his reply. Now Camille detected a rigidness to it, as if his patience had gone beyond being tested but he was doing everything he could not to give way to anger.

Leitner threw a medium fastball, letter-high, where K-E-Y-S-T-O-N-E-S was emblazoned on Deacon's chest. The crowd booed and hissed when Deacon hit it clear over the right field fence.

The rest of the inning played out with fervor, the Keystones gaining five runs. The bottom of the ninth could bring the second win of the season to them. But first, they had to get three outs against the Athletics. Camille worried the inside of her lip, hardly aware she was doing it. She stood, paced, and even recited a quiet prayer. The outfielder, Bob Lindemann, had come up to bat; bases were loaded.

Inhaling and resting her hand on the post of the dugout, she closed her eyes a moment. She almost couldn't watch the pitch. Behind her, the players on the bench, Cub LaRoque, Cupid Burns, and Mox Synder, jousted with one another, counting their chickens before they were hatched. But she knew that things could change in the blink of an eye. That's why she didn't want to open hers.

"When are we going back to Harmony, Alex?"

"Cap, I told you. Now quit asking me."

"But I have to go to work!"

"Goddammit, Cap—you don't have to be at work today."

The noise of the fans rose to excited heights, Camille tried to blot it all out. Then a voice spoke close to her ear.

"Lindemann grits his teeth when he's going to bunt."

Her eyes shot open, and she turned her head to Alex. "How do you know that?"

"I've played against him before. Tell Yank to move in."

Dismayed, Camille said in a rush, "But I can't go out there while the ball's in play."

"Then get his attention. Whistle."

"I don't know how." Frustration made her voice lift in volume.

Alex brought his forefinger and thumb to his lips and loudly whistled. Once. Watching the gesture seared her skin like a hot whisper—just like when his mouth had consumed hers.

He whistled a second time. The third one caught Yank's attention, and Yank faced their direction.

"Give him the signal." Alex left the rest to her.

She pinpointed her concentration on getting the signals right. With slow hand movements, she spelled out the letters: "Move in. Bunt."

Yank reluctantly took the message. Nodding, he resumed his stance. As soon as the Philly pitcher released the ball, Yank sprang up to catch it as it dribbled up the grassy field. Gulping the ball with his glove, he took one step and threw it to first and got Lindemann out.

Shooting his gaze at Camille, Yank was almost as surprised as she was. The tactic had worked. They'd gotten the out.

The fog had lifted. Literally. The Keystones won the game.

"Take me home, Mama," Cub cried, "and put me to bed!"

Camille eased the stress from her shoulders and was astonished at the sense of fulfillment she felt. But it had less to do with her and more to do with Alex. He'd given her sound advice, aided her. He'd made her look like she knew what she was doing. She found him in the crowd. He stood alone. As usual. Cub, Cupid, and Mox ran out to congratulate the other players with hoots and slaps on the behind.

"Hey, Cap, come on down. Let's get some dinner." Alex rounded the dugout's edge and looked into the seats. Camille watched him do a quick scan of the area. Tension stretched over his features. He put his hands on the railing, and in one hop, jumped into the seats.

"Where's that man who was sitting here?" he shouted to a spectator.

The spectator's eyes widened beneath his bowler. "That crazy fellow with the beard?"

His arm lifted so fast, Camille hadn't been prepared for the aggression. Alex grabbed a fistful of expensive suit fabric and knotted the man's lapel in his fist. "He's not crazy."

"H-he left."

"When?" The word was sharp and urgent.

"I don't know exactly when. He said he was going back to some place happy."

"Happy?"

"Uh—called Harmony."

"Oh, God." Alex stumbled back as if he'd been struck. He jumped to the ground and, without another word, began to sprint toward the exit gate.

Camille faced the players who'd returned to the dugout. "Gentlemen, you'll have to see yourselves back to the hotel. Make sure you gather the bats and balls. No visiting saloons this evening."

"We didn't visit a saloon last night," Yank complained.

"That's right. And you won't tonight, either," she went on. "We have to be on a train for Washington, D.C. at ten o'clock in the morning. *Tomorrow,*" she emphasized.

Then she looped her pocketbook in the crook of her arm and snatched her notebook. Picking up the front of her crepe voile skirt, she began to run, in a way in which she'd never done before. She searched the crowd for Alex. She quickened her pace when she caught a glimpse of white-and-gold ball cap.

Alex had helped her win the game.

She'd help him find Captain.

Blinding fear gripped Alex's heart. The logical place to look for Cap was the train station. Having lived in this city, he knew how to get there from here. But how would Captain know? Alex had nothing else to go on aside from a hunch and maybe a witness who'd seen which direction Cap had gone in.

Alex was stopping a constable at a vendor's stand outside of the park to ask when Camille came toward him in a rush.

"Two people can look faster than one," she said, her breath coming in quick pants. Her cheeks were pink, her eyes soft with sympathy.

He should have told her to get lost. But his first priority was Captain. And she was right. With both of them looking, one might catch something the other missed.

"Have you seen a tall man with a full beard come this way in the last half hour?" Alex asked the man, who was uniformed in dark blue from his gold-emblemed hat to his crisply creased trousers.

White-gloved hand resting on the butt of his billy club, the officer gave Alex a quick study. "As a matter of fact, I did."

"Which way did he go?"

The officer pointed to the street bordering Columbia Park. "Up toward Broad Street. Say, are you one of the ballplayers?"

Alex didn't answer. Automatically, he took Camille by the hand, and he propelled them down the block.

"Look for him while we run," he said. "He could be anywhere."

"All right."

He was glad she kept up with his pace. If she hadn't, he would have dropped her off at the nearest shop and told her he'd come back for her later.

"Do you think he could have found the train station on his own?" she asked from his side, her steps light over the sidewalk.

"I don't know. It's on Broad and Glenwood. We'll look there first."

Alex didn't want to think about the possibility of not finding Cap at the Broad Street station. Enough time had gone by that Captain could be anywhere—disoriented, wandering, scared.

Dammit.

He never should have been short with him. Alex didn't think Captain would leave Columbia Park to find the train station in an unfamiliar city. The possibility had never entered his mind. It should have. He'd failed Cap.

Alex barely glanced at the street signs, the building numbers. The sights were familiar to him, yet they'd changed in the years he'd been gone. He saw 26th Street and veered through the intersection, cutting between carriages and coaches. The cobblestones beneath his feet felt slippery because of the spikes on his shoe soles.

"You okay?" he called across his shoulder.

"Yes." But she'd lost her hat and her hair was falling free of its pins.

The musty smells of the Delaware and Schuylkill Rivers pressed in on the evening air.

"I don't see him," Alex said, and in seconds, he was

flagging a hackney. "We'll get there faster this way."
Within fifteen minutes, they were inside the train station, combing separate ends of the terminal, the ticket booths, the baggage collection areas, the arrival and departure platforms.

There was no sign of Captain.

When they met back at the central clock tower, Alex looked at Camille. "I don't know. I just don't damned know. He's not here. He could be anywhere."

"Maybe the police—"

"You think the police might have picked him up?"

"It's worth finding out."

The closest police station was the 12th Precinct on Monument and 33rd Streets.

The clatter of horses hooves rang across the damp street as the carriage sped along. The sky had blackened, glowing lanterns on street corners lending a hazy yellow light to the returning fog.

Alex set his jaw, unable to speak as the wheels rolled over the cobblestones. Guilt consumed him.

Silence blanketed them like the heavy mist that had begun to creep through the streets. If he'd thought about it long enough, he would have realized he was so cold, he had to keep his knees pressed together.

"Monument and Thirty-third," the driver called as he reined the horses to a stop.

"Wait here." Alex bounded out of the hackney and was inside the police station before he could breathe. He went straightaway to the tall desk, where a uniformed sergeant sat on a hip-high stool.

"I'm looking for a man my height, black hair, black beard—"

"Alex? Alex!"

Captain's screams came from a hallway. Cap appeared, two men on either side of him, escorting him toward the front of the police station.

In a condescending tone, one of the officers explained, "We're taking you to the hospital, laddy, where they'll take real good care of you. Woo-woo." He chuckled.

"H-o-s-p-i-t-a-l! No shave!"

The other officer laughed while jerking at Cap, who fought to get free. "Somebody stole his rudder. He's not on an even keel."

The officers' chins shot up as Alex went straight for Captain.

"Shut up," he warned them, advancing. "It's okay, Cap. I found you."

Captain's gaze was glassy. His hair fell wildly about his face, and his screams were ones of sheer terror. "No shave! No hospital!"

Bracing Cap by the shoulders, Alex glared at the men restraining him. "Get your hands off him. "Cap, we're going back to the hotel now. Not the hospital."

"Alex," he sobbed. "I was mad at you. Just like you were mad at me. I tried to find the train home. I got lost." Gazing through his rumpled hair with forlorn eyes, he asked, "Are you still mad?"

"I'm not mad, Cap. You're all right now."

"I want to go home."

"We are. Soon."

But the weight of that promise settled heavily on Alex's shoulders. He wondered how he was going to tell Cap they were going to Buffalo, and never going back to Harmony again.

Camille couldn't sleep. She couldn't think about anything but Alex. And Captain. And what had happened.

Alex had come out of the police station and taken Captain into the hackney, his arm wrapped tightly around him. The ride back to the hotel was broken only by Cap's quiet mumbling and shaky sighs.

Once at the Euclid Avenue Hotel, they'd entered the lobby together, taken the lift, and parted company on the fourth floor, she to her room at the front of the hall, Alex to his and Captain's in the other direction. Alex hadn't said a word. It had been as if she'd ceased to exist. His energies had been spent on calming Captain, making sure he was comfortable.

In the quiet of her room, Camille had washed up but she hadn't undressed for bed. She couldn't. Not until she made sure Alex was all right. Reassuring Captain had been his sole purpose, but she'd seen the look of utter grief on Alex's face.

Taking up her key, she left her room and walked down the near-dark hallway to knock on Alex's door. She slowed her steps midway, noting a tall man's silhouette outlined by the window at the end of the hall. A glowing red ember burned; the smell of cigarette smoke lightly drifted in the air.

Alex.

She began walking once more. She reached him, but he didn't turn to look at her. He continued to stare out the curtainless window, the globe of light above him hissing. The wick had been turned down, the illumination a faint spot of flame. His profile to her, she noted his lips clamped around the cigarette, firm and hard, as if he was trying to maintain a composure that was slipping.

In the darkness, she followed his gaze to the lights outside that looked more like milkweeds in the low fog, fuzzy and white, unclear. Much like her thoughts at this moment.

Should she have come to him? She had no business . . . and yet. . . . It was like Cap had brought them together tonight. But it was more than that. She'd been drawn to him. Physically. And now emotionally. Unable to help herself.

The window had been opened, and now the chill of night seeped into the hall. Dew glittered off the fire escape. The coo of pigeons could be heard from a perch on the side of a nearby building.

"Thank you for helping me."

She hadn't been expecting him to speak, much less say that. His voice sluiced over her almost as if he'd skimmed gentle fingers up her arms and across her lips.

He brought the cigarette to his mouth, inhaled, and let out a slow and steady stream of smoke. She watched him. The way he stood, the way he was dressed. He wore no shoes, just socks. The hem of a ribbed cotton undershirt was tucked into his trousers. Three buttons met at the throat. He'd kept them open. Barely discernable was a sprinkling of dark hair. She'd wondered if his chest would be smooth.

"You would have helped me, too," she replied at last staring through the window once more.

"Maybe."

A tug of irritation made her frown. Why did he feel like he had to do that all the time? Make himself look beyond caring. He did care. She'd seen him with Captain.

"I know it's none of my business, but what's wrong with Captain?"

Although she couldn't see it, she could sense the muscles in his body grow tense and inflexible.

A long moment passed where Alex thoughtfully smoked his cigarette. She didn't think he'd answer her. She was about to return to her room when his words came to her.

"He had an accident some years back. It damaged his brain."

"What happened?"

He held the cigarette between his forefinger and thumb and flicked it out the window. "His mind went, that's what happened. He hasn't been right in the head since." He still hadn't looked at her. "Cap's got to take a certain amount of medicine every day."

"Do you think it helps?"

"Yeah." But then he slowly shook his head. "I don't know. I thought he'd get better. I thought—" His voice broke. "He has his good days. And his bad."

"I'm sorry." The words seemed so simple. She wished she had more to offer him. "I heard him say 'no shave' again. What does that mean?"

"It has nothing to do with his beard. He was in a hospital that shaved his head," Alex said while blinking at the lights across the city. "They rubbed mercury over his bare scalp. You can imagine how that must have stung like hell." His deep voice dropped to a mere whisper. "With all the things he can't remember, he has to remember that."

Camille felt helpless.

Alex lowered his chin, running a hand though the hair that fell in his eyes. "I can't do anything. I can't make him better. I can only watch him get worse."

She cupped his cheek with her palm. It seemed the right thing to do. He leaned into her hand, a troubled sigh breaking on his lips. He finally looked at her. His eyes glittered. Her heart broke.

They stood there that way. Silent, a spell of kinship having cloaked them. It was a moment like none she'd ever experienced.

In the past, she'd flirted with men; she'd been coy. They, in turn, had come to her with flowers and candy. It had been a ritual of sorts. Neither she nor her suitor had taken things all that seriously.

But now, the men that had been in her life seemed

so insignificant. So trifling. She felt a stirring deep within her heart, a place that had never been touched. She feared and yearned for the feeling at the same time.

Alex moved away first, bringing himself back to the aloofness she was used to. But she could see the shudder of his chest as he drank the night air to his lungs.

She dared to broach a topic that she thought she now understood. "You can't pitch because you worry about Captain's illness."

She didn't know what she expected from him, but laughter hadn't been it.

Humor lacing his words, he replied, "That's not why."

"Then tell me what's wrong."

He faced her, an easy grin on his mouth—a grin she wanted to erase. "There's nothing wrong."

"There is." She went as far as speaking what she'd been thinking for the past hour—even though it would probably come back to haunt her. And she'd never hear the end of it from her father. "If you need me to let you out of your contract, I can do that."

Before she knew it, he'd laid a hand on her shoulder. He didn't hurt her, but his displeasure was clear. "Don't even *think* of letting me out of my contract. We have an agreement."

"I just thought that if you're so distracted—"

"You distract me." Then he brought his mouth over hers, in a quick but effective kiss that left her reaching for the window casement when he moved away from her. "G'night, honey."

Then he left her there, reeling from the warm touch of his lips.

Chapter

❧ 11 ❧

"Is there any way you can get back issues of a Baltimore newspaper for me, Mr. Gage?" Camille asked.

The clunk and whoosh of the press echoed through the tiny shop as the latest edition of the *Harmony Advocate* was printed. Strong odors of ink and wet pulp filled the air.

Matthew Gage, the editor, reclined behind a desk, fingers meshed against his neck and his feet kicked up. He was quite attractive. He wore his black hair clipped short and fashionable; he'd grown a mustache in the past month. A dark blue silk vest covered a white shirt with the sleeves rolled up. Curls of a smoke from his cigar swirled toward the ceiling.

Meg Brooks had done very well when she married this man. He was ambitious and yet fit into the slowness of small-town life. Camille did, however, have one small bone to pick with him. But she wouldn't bring that up until after he answered her question about the newspapers.

"It's possible, Miss Kennison." Standing, he said,

"But it may take some time." He went to the press to check the long sheets of paper running through the machinery. He raised his voice above the loud clackety-clack. "How soon do you need them?"

"As soon as you can get them." She reached into her pocketbook and withdrew a piece of paper. "This is the year I'd like you to find."

Mr. Gage took the sheet and gazed at it. "1898." His brows furrowed. "Any specific month? A search like this is going to take just about as long as 1898 did."

She snapped the clasp closed on her purse. "April to June—I think. Go to July, just in case."

"I can tell them to look, but what exactly," he said, lowering the paper, "are they looking for? Do you want copies of the dailies from those months? Going to be expensive to get them and have them mailed."

"How expensive?"

"Really expensive." He leaned a knee into the low spindled railing that separated the pressroom from the office. "If you told me what, specifically, you want to find, I could save you a lot of money. And time."

She didn't want to have to come out and say it, but she was left with no choice. "Could you have them look for any articles written about Alex Cordova?"

Mr. Gage didn't ask her why. In fact, he didn't seem all that interested. "All right. Give me a couple of weeks. I can have the telegraph request sent today. I know one of the editors on the *Sun*. He may be able to pull some strings. It's still going to take somebody a lot of hours reading over those back issues, Miss Kennison."

"I understand." She fussed with a row of buttons on her gloves. "Do I pay you a deposit for your services now?"

"You can pay me when the newspapers come in."

"Thank you."

As he began to turn to the press once more, she blurted, "Mr. Gage, I enjoy reading the *Advocate*. Harmony needed a newspaper. I do, however, have to take issue with the fact that you keep printing unflattering headlines about the Keystones."

When she had his full attention, she continued. "Take for example, last Friday's edition when you reported on our game with the Detroit Tigers. I wasn't here, but my father saved a copy for me." And with great huff and bluster, he'd handed it over to her. "Headlines like THE KEYSTONES GO DOWN IN A BOATLOAD OF MISTAKES is bad for morale."

His eyes, a mixture of gold and green, leveled on her. "Pardon my saying so, Miss Kennison, but I didn't think the Keystones had any morale."

She drew herself taller, quietly bristling. "We might have lost eight on the road in the past sixteen days, but we did win three."

He brought his cigar to his mouth. On a puff, he said, "Next time you win, I'll make a special banner."

"You do that." She smoothed down the front of her skirt. "Good day."

She exited the newspaper office and headed toward the restaurant. Now that that piece of business was taken care of, she could move onto the next. Which would be about as pleasant as having Dr. Teeter drill out a cavity.

"I'm buying the cottage on Elm and Hackberry Way," Camille announced, taking a fortifying sip of water. "Mr. Healy is handling the transaction. I've put a down payment on it."

"What?" Her father's reaction was precisely what she had thought it would be. He threw his napkin on the table. At least he couldn't break anything.

She'd invited her parents to lunch at a public place:

Nannie's Home-Style Restaurant—safe ground on which to announce her plans.

She'd stalled for a while. They'd placed their meal orders, talked briefly about how the team was coming along. Vehemently, she'd had to deny there was any trouble on the road. But her father had heard about the train incident and hotel pranks. Most likely, the players had told him in an effort to get her canned. She'd assured her father that she could handle the situations as they arose.

Choking, her father stared at her. Her mother leaned forward a little over the table, eyes wide with surprise.

Camille proceeded in a rush. "I have that small amount of money in the bank from Granddaddy Kennison that I used for the deposit, but the majority of my living expenses are coming from my salary of twelve hundred dollars." She didn't pause for a breath. "Of which I'm owed one hundred and fifty dollars as of today, Daddy. I haven't pursued the financial aspect of my position because I wasn't sure how things would work out. But now that I'm certain I'll be in the manager's position for the season, I have an income that can support me."

"How much is this house?" her father asked.

"Nine hundred dollars."

"Nine hundred dollars," her mother repeated. "Camille, that's so much money."

"I know, but I'll have the mortgage paid off by October." She fingered the handles of her clean utensils. "After that, I'll rethink my options. If Daddy doesn't find anyone else for the manager's job, maybe I could keep it for another year."

"I can't believe you'd make such a decision and not talk it over with us first," her mother said, worry lines marring her forehead.

"A woman doesn't buy her own home," her father bellowed, then, on her mother's warning—sent with just a look—lowered his voice. "She waits for her husband to buy one for her."

"I don't have a husband," Camille reminded him.

"And whose fault is that?"

"I'm not interested in marriage at the moment," she replied, refusing to let him interfere with her resolve. "I bought the house because I felt like it was time I became independent. The cottage is in some disrepair, but the location is very respectable."

"I know how much *disrepair* it's in—I've seen it." Replacing his thrown napkin on his lap, her father said, "Healy hasn't been able to unload it for over a year."

"But it is in a nice part of town." Her mother grew thoughtful. "Oh, Camille, you'll be alone. I'll worry."

"I'll be fine."

"A woman doesn't buy her own home," her father reiterated.

"And a woman doesn't manage a baseball team either. But I am."

"Don't get me fired up about that again."

The debate went on for nearly half an hour, the conversation quite rocky at times. Their lunches came but were barely touched. After her father paid the bill, he'd stood and frowned. He hadn't revised his opinion an inch, calling her actions irrational. He did, however, relent on paying her a salary. She'd have the money in her bank account this afternoon.

"The thinking of modern women baffles me," he exclaimed, pushing in his chair. "The next thing you'll be telling me is you want to take over my hardware store."

Her mother placed a hand on Camille's arm. "Are you quite certain this is what you want to do?"

She was quite certain. The decision wasn't a rash one. And it had to do with the players. The fact that they'd played tricks and practical jokes on her while in Philadelphia and Washington, D.C., was a determining factor. Men couldn't respect a manager—female or male—who still lived with parents. It wasn't independent. In the players' eyes, her being their manager probably looked to be a whim. An indulgence by a father. She'd come across differently if she had to depend on the baseball team for her livelihood. And now she would.

If she was going to be a spinster, she'd better be one in the truest sense of the word.

"I'm very certain, Mama," Camille said at length. "I'll be happy living alone. I'll come visit you often, and you and Daddy can come visit me."

And that's how things had been left between them.

An hour later, Camille stood in the empty parlor of the cottage, glad she was daring enough to buy it. The cottage was charming. Empty, but charming. In need of tender care, but perfect for her.

The first floor had a piazza that ran around two sides of the building. Callers entered directly inside the living room. There was no foyer. A corner fireplace drew the eye with its floor-to-ceiling brickwork; the cobwebs and ashes needed to be swept out. Two pocket doors led to the dining room, which had four windows; from there was the kitchen with a pantry and porch. A shed had been attached by the last owner. It housed a water closet and small shower bath with tub.

The upstairs had ultimately drawn Camille to the cottage. At the top of the stairs was a loggia with latticework. From the position of the house, she would receive just the right amount of sunlight for her ferns and other delicate plants. The area was protected against the wind but would heat up nicely on a warm summer day. Perhaps she'd try her hand at orchids.

Aside from the loggia, the second floor had two large bedrooms, and one smaller one, which she wasn't sure yet what she'd use for. A long hall ran between them, and the bedroom she'd picked for herself had a balcony that connected to the other bedroom of the same side. Inside, a large closet shared space between them.

The exterior needed paint. The drab colors had faded and were peeling in places. She wanted to go with Indian red for the accents, medium olive for the trim, and fawn for the body. The leafy green foliage of her plants would look wonderful against that kind of scheme. When the Garden Club came by for teas, she would have a beautiful setting in which its members could view her garden.

She had sent out invitations for this Friday's meeting to be held at her new residence. They'd be taking the vote for the next president. Her name was on the ballot, along with Mrs. Calhoon's and Mrs. Treber's. She had no illusions that by inviting them over, she'd gain votes. She'd already missed two meetings because she'd been out of town. When she allowed herself to, she doubted her ability to manage both team and club. But she didn't want to think about that. She wanted to be able to juggle the two positions.

It was important for her to maintain a good impression. These women's lives were steeped in tradition. To be president meant you had the fortitude to lead such a group. To display a garden worthy of renown, which she would have because while she'd been away, Leda had watered her plants. They were coming along nicely.

But it would take time to get things in order. First, she had to move her bedroom furniture and buy a few things—divan, chairs, tables, fireplace tools. There was a nice plot of dirt in the back of the house that wasn't overrun with weeds. Which was a good thing. Because secondly, she had to dig up her garden and move it to her new home. Just how, exactly, she wasn't sure.

If Alex didn't know any better, he'd say Captain was perfectly normal. That he didn't need the daily bromide the State Orthopaedic Hospital and Infirmary insisted he take. Didn't need the Dover's Powder for his headaches. And didn't need Silas Denton in Buffalo.

Since returning to Harmony, Cap had been fine.

But what happened in Philadelphia reaffirmed to Alex that going to New York in the fall was the right thing to do. So he continued to make plans. In the meantime, he put himself into his woodworking.

He had lots of orders to fill and fewer hours in which to work on the projects these days.

He'd come into town to pick up his mail; he was waiting for a letter of confirmation from Silas Denton's hospital. But no correspondence had come yet. So he was headed back to his wood shop.

Nearing Elm, he spotted Camille. She pushed a wheelbarrow and had to struggle to keep it steady. The unbalanced load wobbled from left to right, then at one point nearly tipped over. She set the legs of the barrow down, adjusted her grip on the handles, and proceeded. She'd overloaded the bed. With what looked to be dirt.

Moving dirt down Elm Street didn't seem like a normal activity for a lady.

She wore gardening gloves and a simple straw hat. It reminded him of the one she'd lost on the streets of Philadelphia. This one was simpler in comparison. Not a single fruit or bird decorated it. Plain straw with a wide ivory ribbon that caught beneath her chin in a bow. She wore an apron over a plain gray dress.

Even without her flowing pale skirts and light-weight shirtwaists, she looked ethereal to him. Camille always exemplified the femininity that some women tried hard at capturing but never quite had. Looking soft and stunning was simply a part of her, like the refined way she walked. He liked the entire package—far too much.

He stopped directly in her path. She clunked the wheelbarrow on its feet and glared at him. A smudge of dirt marked the bridge of her nose.

"Mr. Cordova."

"Miss Kennison."

Looking at him through the thickness of her lashes, she asked, "Did you have a baseball question?"

"No."

"Well, then, can you move out of the way? I'm in somewhat of a hurry." She raised the wheelbarrow handles once more and grappled for a solid hold on the wood.

"You've got too much dirt in the bed," he replied, bumping her out of the way as he took hold of each handle and began walking in the direction she'd been going. Behind him, he heard her give a little gasp as she caught up.

"What do you think you're doing?"

"Where're we going with this load of dirt?" he inquired, ignoring her question.

A slight skip caught her steps as she kept up with his pace. "It's not dirt. Can't you see there are seedlings in there?"

He gave the dirt a quick glance. Tiny green shoots erupted from the earth in various places, as if they'd been dug up.

"Those are cucumbers, muskmelon, sweet peppers, and tomatoes."

Shrugging, he took her word for it. "Okay."

"I'll be going back for my gladioli, ranunculuses, and anemones, as well as some hedges." She practically cut directly in front of him as she turned up Elm. "This way," she said, directed him toward a run-down cottage that needed its lawn clipped and porch cleared of leftover fall leaves. "Around the back."

The wheels of the barrow jumped and bumped over the uneven grass. Alex didn't know much about flowers, but there were a lot of them coming into bloom along the serrated bricks that edged the path to the porch. Bricks also circled the tree trunks and beds of some kind of lily-looking flower.

He walked around the side of the house where a large plot of dirt had been recently raked and little plants had been dug into the freshly tilled ground.

Stopping the wheelbarrow, he reangled the brim of his Stetson. "Why are you putting plants in this yard?"

She snatched up a trowel and began to make long furrows in the dirt. "This is my yard."

A contemplative silence held him as he stared at the surroundings.

"I bought this house, Mr. Cordova. I'm moving in. Lock, stock, and plants."

Before Alex could comment, Betram Nops entered the yard with a frown on his mouth as wide as the hairpiece that covered his forehead.

"If it isn't the Regal man without a regalness to his name—or shall I say feet?" Dressed in a neatly tailored suit, Nops wore a plaid necktie that Alex would have liked to choke him with because of the crack he made. "I should have let Regal Shoes have you, Cordova. I'm sure not getting my thirty-five hundred dollars' worth."

Alex's thoughts jammed on the monetary amount—the exact sum he'd been offered by Kennison as a bonus. "What are you talking about?"

Nops looked at him, then at Camille, who looked at Alex.

"Cordova doesn't know?" Nops suddenly laughed. "It surely isn't a secret. What's the matter with Kennison? Didn't want to look like he didn't have the ol' greenbacks?" Then to Alex. "I'm paying your bonus. Therefore, I should have been the manager of the Keystones instead of her."

Camille paled. "I didn't want the job in the first place, Mr. Nops. You insisted."

"Only after your father reneged on his word about the manager's job. Enticing Cordova out of retirement had everything to do with my money and nothing to do with the way you handle yourself—aside from the fact that you are nice to look at, and who could say no to a pretty face? But the scores tell everyone what they need to know about your baseball smarts or lack thereof."

Alex was on Nops before he could take another breath. Tightening the man's plaid necktie, he slid the knot up a fraction.

Nops's eyes widened in stunned horror. "Take it easy, Cordova. I was only stating facts."

"Then here's another one for you. You may think you own a piece of me, but you're not entitled to insult the lady."

With a shove, Alex let him go.

Nops put on a display of exaggerated sputtering as he smoothed out the wrinkles in his tie. "Cordova, you aren't worth a plugged nickel, much less thousands. The Keystones are in the same place they were weeks ago. Last in the league. The only bright side is I get to see Kennison's public humiliation."

On that, he turned and walked from the yard in a disgruntled huff.

Alex held his gaze on Camille. She didn't readily look at him. "Is it true? Did Nops put up the bonus money?"

"Yes."

He didn't know why it should make a difference, but it did. Not only did Kennison own him, but so did Nops. He felt manipulated. He smiled. Grimly. "I must be the golden apple to you. You get me, you get the manager's job."

"I'm managing the team because Bertram Nops was going to pull out his thirty-five hundred if I didn't. He had designs on the manager's position and that's why he agreed to invest in you. When I came to see you that day, I honestly didn't know things would work out this way."

"Lucky for you they did."

"Lucky?" she said, astonished. "I wouldn't say I'm lucky at all. My life's been turned upside down because of this. And when you play bad baseball, you make me look bad in front of my father, the players, and the town." She tugged off her gardening gloves and slapped them into her palm.

It struck him that this was the first time he'd ever seen her hands without gloves. Her fingers were slender. She wore a ring on her right hand. A tiny sapphire with diamonds around it. The ring looked delicately romantic. He momentarily wondered who'd given it to her.

He had no defense for her statement. At least none that he'd care to explain. He did make her look bad. But not for reasons that could be fixed by a pep talk and a steak over at the restaurant.

Camille sighed. "I have your photographs in the house. I'm sure you have more pressing things to do at the moment than think about baseball, but maybe you could take a quick second to sign some of them now."

"I could do that."

"Good." She untied her apron as she started for the house.

Alex followed.

The rear entrance led directly into an attached shed where partially unpacked boxes lined the walls. Camille went into the kitchen, the sideboards covered with wrapped dishes and other cooking items. He noted the red gingham curtain that covered the sink plumbing was open. A slow, steady drip from one of the pipes fell into a galvanized bucket.

"I have them in here. The photographer sent them over this morning," she said, entering a dining room where a very small, and very well-used, table was made smaller by the large room. "I can have the autographed ones given out at tonight's game."

He drew up behind her, standing close enough to smell the lavender of her perfume and the sweet earthiness of garden dirt. The backside brim of her hat nearly hit him on the cheek as she turned her head toward him.

In a low voice he whispered, "So what kind of pressing engagement do you think I have?"

Her breath practically tickled the side of his mouth before she backed away a few inches. "I could pick anything and it probably would apply."

He wanted to take her in his arms. Take her into another room in the house. He looked into her extraordinary blue eyes and imagined how it would be lying beside her on her bed. Naked. Caressing. Touching her body—everywhere.

"I can't pick one," he said, rubbing the pad of his thumb over her nose to wipe the dirt smudge off. Her breathed sucked in at his touch. "There aren't any reasons why I have to leave."

That was a lie. There were many. He had to finish sanding a chair. He had to size lumber for a cradle he'd been commissioned to build for the Wolcotts. He had to fix the handle on his adze eye hammer. He had to look over his orders. He had to mix up glue for his broken wood clamps. But none of that seemed important to him right now.

"Get me a pen." Alex pulled out a mismatched chair from the table.

"Here." She slid the pile of photographs in front of him. "Can I get you a glass of water? I was going to make some lemonade, but I haven't had time."

"Yeah. Water's good."

She went through the doorway to the kitchen. He could see her at the sink. She turned sideways to look beneath it, then put her hands on her hips as if wondering what to do. He was no plumber, but he figured a few twists and a little putty would fix the problem. It was on the tip of his tongue to offer to fix it for her, but he refrained. He couldn't afford to get personal with her. And yet, because of Nops, here he sat at her dining room table as if he belonged in her house.

He couldn't take his eyes off her. The way she moved. The way she searched for just the right glass for him. She discarded a rose one; then an amber. She settled on a cut crystal.

He liked the line of her back, the way her spine was straight and tall. The way she paused, as if she suddenly remembering she'd left her hat on. She lifted her arm, and gave the ribbon a tug. He wanted to see her profile. The slant of her nose, her forehead, the fullness of her lips, the shape of her breasts. She set the straw hat on the counter.

The rusty sound of the faucet handle turning shrieked through the kitchen as she poured water into the glass. He hadn't watched a woman so intensely since he'd been a boy and he'd peeped across the alleyway into the sixth-story neighbor's window with Sean O'Brien and several others from the sandlot gang. The woman had been in her chemise and in the arms of her lover.

This was different. Camille was fully dressed, yet he felt the same sensations pulling at his body.

She turned. He didn't look away.

From the expression on her face, she knew he'd been watching her.

"You haven't signed anything."

He returned to the photographs. He cursed himself for letting his thoughts and emotions get the better of him.

"Well," she said, putting her hands on her hips once more. "While you do that, I'm going to unpack some other boxes."

Alex took up the pen. "All right."

As she moved about in the room, he signed his name. Alex Cordova. It seemed so meaningless to do this.

From the corner of his eye, he followed her movements. A lift of a vase here; a setting down of a knickknack there. He didn't have to try hard to come up with the illusion that this could be something more.

Before Captain had gotten hurt, Alex hadn't thought about female companionship beyond a leisurely dalliance. An overnight stay, then a kiss good-bye. A new city. A new woman. He had never regretted his lack of serious involvement. He'd done what he'd felt like doing in the heat of the moment.

He'd never been without a woman if he'd wanted one. Never had to stay and worry about breaking her heart. The women who followed the game hadn't wanted his heart anyway. They'd wanted a part of him, much like the photograph. A memento. A token of Alex "the Grizz" Cordova.

Now that he saw that clearly, he didn't like himself much for how he used to behave. After being away from the game for three years, he was free to explore the fact that he wasn't getting any younger. That he would grow old and die without knowing what it would be like to spend his days with a woman who loved him and whom he loved equally in return. To pass their days walking, holding hands, watching sunsets, making love outdoors, indoors, wherever they desired. Waking up together. Going to bed together.

These were all things he couldn't wish for because they weren't to be.

Because no matter what, he owed Captain.

Chapter

❧ 12 ❧

To the uninformed observer, the men in baseball uniforms throwing a ball around the bases at Municipal Field while an Edison phonograph played Scott Joplin's "Maple Leaf Rag" looked like buffoons. But there was a good reason for the two-step even rhythm that had them flinging balls to one another. Or at least that's what their manager had told them. There were those hold out skeptics who'd scratched beneath their chins, but they'd eventually given into her demand.

"Syncopation, gentlemen," Camille called from home plate, where she stood next to a table that held the phonograph. Out of the colorfully painted black horn came the piano notes to the double-time rag tune.

With a tap of her toe to the beat, she named the positions the ball was to pass from. "Six. Four. Three."

Shortstop to second baseman to first baseman equals the double play.

They sloshed around in Spalding Featherweight

shoes on a field that had been flooded with sprinkler water once again. She was going to find out who kept turning it on and forgetting to turn it off.

As the music's tempo jaunted along, she directed, "Seven. Five. Two."

Left fielder to third baseman to catcher equals an out at the plate.

They'd been practicing like this for over a half an hour. In the three games they'd played since returning to Harmony, they'd lost two and won one. Today was their first game against the Baltimore Orioles. Yesterday's win against the Milwaukee Brewers had been joyful.

She called out the numbers *eight* and *nine,* then *three* and *one.* Her gaze fell on Alex, who stood on the mound. He was the number-one position man. Since he'd arrived at practice, he'd been preoccupied. Only a moment ago, she realized why.

The Baltimore Orioles were his former team.

They'd yet to show up at the field, but they'd arrived in Harmony late last night. She wondered if any of Alex's old teammates were still playing for the Orioles. She'd never met the manager, George Dunlap, but she'd heard he was a fair man—if there could be fairness where she was concerned. She hadn't met a manager yet who treated her as his equal.

She discreetly stifled a yawn beneath her fingers. She'd stayed up into the wee hours of the morning fixing her home for this evening's Garden Club meeting. Everything had to be just right, down to the last flower in the centerpiece on the table. If she could help the men win this afternoon's game, she'd take it as an omen that tonight would go splendidly.

"All right, gentlemen," she said, lifting the needle from the recording. "That will do." She walked to the dugout and called them in. "There are a few things we need to go over."

She went to the canvas bag she'd brought from home. From inside, she produced a shoe box and gave it to Bones.

"What's this?" he asked while lifting the lid.

"Shoe inserts. You run with flat feet. That ought to help your speed."

His brow rose, as if he couldn't believe she'd noticed that about him. How could she not? He ran with the uneven balance of a duck.

Deacon spat tobacco. As did Yank and Charlie. Then the others. It seemed to be a go-around. One player began, and the others followed on down the line. It was nasty and disgusting and she had a solution for that, too. She brought out a paper-wrapped package from her bag. But first, an empty soup can—gumbo soup, to be exact.

"Gentlemen, as of now, there will be no more spitting."

Grumbles rose from the ranks.

"I know you may find it hard to give up, but it's a vile habit and I think you'd be better players if you didn't worry about spitting." She held the can out to Cub to pass down. "Dispose of that tobacco you have in your mouths."

Cub peered into the tin can, then looked at his fellow players. "I don't want to."

"A fifty-dollar fine says you don't have to," she returned evenly.

Cub spit his tobacco out.

As the can was handed from player to player, she continued, "I know it will be hard to give up your tobacco, so I've bought you all a replacement." She opened the paper package, pulling the string and revealing the inside to the players. "Chiclets."

"Gum?" Specs squinted at the colorful packets. "You want us to chew gum instead of tobacco?"

"It's gum or nothing."

"Yeah, but—" Cub began.

"Gum or nothing," she repeated with resolve.

The players took the Chiclets.

She brought out another box, this one imprinted with the words MONTGOMERY WARD OPTICAL GOODS DEPARTMENT. "Specs, I've ordered and received nine pairs of spectacles for you to choose from. Try each one until you can clearly see the outfield lines. That will be the correct pair."

Specs looked inside the box, then squinted at her. "Gee—you didn't have to go to so much trouble."

"Believe me, it was no trouble."

Minutes later, Specs stared at them through quarter-inch-thick lenses. He had beautiful hazel eyes that were now magnified three times over. "It would seem these are the right ones. But can I keep the spares just in case these turn out to be the wrong ones?"

"Please do."

Three hurdles overcome. Camille held out hope that everything else would fall into place just as smoothly.

The Orioles had arrived and she caught a glimpse of George Dunlap. A tall man with wide, proud shoulders, he looked like he could guzzle Tabasco pepper sauce without getting indigestion. Just about the time she noticed Mr. Dunlap, he noticed Alex. He paused, as if uncertain, then walked to the Keystones' dugout and extended his hand.

Alex barely moved. Then finally, he gripped the elder man's hand firmly. "George. Been a while."

"Three years."

"Yeah."

George took off his cap, wiped his brow with the back of his hand, and gestured to the Orioles' dugout. "Jerry's here, but Harry Howell's pitching for me today. Steve Brodie, John McGraw, and Wilbert Robinson—they're the only four left who played on the '98 team with you. They'd probably like to buy you a beer after the game. Hell, I know I would."

Indecision briefly fell over his face. Then Alex nodded. "That'd be good, George."

Camille remained on the bench, wondering once again about Alex Cordova's past. What had happened to make him quit? Why he was called "the Grizz"? There were a variety of other things that she didn't know about him. She hoped the old newspapers would give her some answers when they came.

But right now, she wondered if he'd even try to beat his former team.

His first pitch was a curve that broke too high up the batter's knees. The ball came at the hitter like an apple rolling off a crooked table. Then it sank right outside the strike zone. By the bottom of the second, the Orioles had scored two runs.

In the top of the fifth, the Keystones came back with three runs of their own. Camille sat on the bench, notebook in her lap, feeling as if there might be a chance if she could keep the players focused.

Alex stood on the mound, the ball in his grasp behind his back. As he coiled his arm and made ready to follow through, he glanced at Captain, who sat in the stands. Captain looked at him with such despair, Camille could feel it in her heart. And because of that look, Alex fell short of delivering the ball where he should have.

Innings later, she still observed him as he sat on the bench, restless, slouching, one foot on his knee. She watched how he would turn to see if Captain was still there. Then he'd face forward and stare off into the field. At his former teammates.

She wanted to know his thoughts. Wanted to understand the chaos that seemed to run through his mind.

Doc struck out, and Cupid, who couldn't hit water with a paddle, took his place in the batter's box. The horse liniment on his head hadn't done a darn thing for him in this game. He struck out as well.

In the top of the eighth inning, Mox Snyder went to field a ground ball on the grass, slipped, and fell on his thumb. His wail carried through the air as he rolled onto his back and grimaced in agony. "Sweet jumping Christopher!"

Running out to him, Camille knelt down beside him. "What happened?"

He woefully gazed up at her from beneath the brim of his cap. "I just broke my thumb."

Right then, for the first time in her life, she said "dammit."

Inside the Blue Flame Saloon, Alex was welcomed by the team he'd once called the greatest bunch of players in the entire National League.

"Cordova!" they shouted, and the old camaraderie was back in place like the fit of a worn uniform. They ribbed one another, joked, and stood up at the bar.

George drew up to him and ordered two beers. "Alex, I want to put in an offer for you. Get you in with the Orioles on a trade. Take you out of Montana and bring you back to Baltimore where you belong."

Alex's heart stilled. He didn't belong anywhere in the world of baseball.

But in that fragment of time, he thought about all George had done for him in the years he'd played for the Orioles outfit. He'd taught him how to play hitters. Judge line drives. How to shift on different hitters and even the same hitter. How to run out after a fly instead of backing up. George Dunlap had been able to offer Alex the most he'd ever been contracted for. He'd signed on at a staggering $1,750.00 a season. At the time, that kind of money for playing ball had been unheard of.

"George, that's a hell of a thing you're offering."

"I want you to take it, Alex. You should be wearing an Oriole uniform."

George had a heart as big as a watermelon and made out of pure gold. He was a great manager because he knew how to handle men. Some players he rode, and others he didn't. He brought out the best in each man that way. It wasn't so much about his knowing the game. It went beyond the fundamentals. What made the difference was George knew each player and how to get the most out of him.

"It's generous of you, George," Alex said, tipping back his beer. "But I can't take you up on it, even if the Orioles organization went for the trade. I've got some commitments here that I can't turn my back on."

"I wish you felt differently about it. You know that if you put on the Orioles uniform, it'll be your choice if you take it off."

"I know that."

George hadn't traded him, even when he'd pitched his worst season in 1895. It had been George's idea for Alex to take the winter off in Montana. He'd known of a lodge in the mountains and told Alex to do some hunting and fishing. Get his head straight.

Alex had been twenty-two and, up until then, had had the world at his feet. Yet he hadn't been able to decide what he'd wanted from baseball. He knew one thing, though—that he wanted to kick Joe McGill's ass. He'd hated the New York Giant more than he could put into words. That hatred might have been what had kept him alive after what had happened on that cold fall morning in the woods when Alex had nearly died from a grizzly bear attack.

He'd returned to Baltimore, following some of the other great players in their quest for notoriety by coming up with a nickname of his own. There was Rube, Lefty, Spitter—to name a few. And then came "the Grizz."

He'd played the best season of his career that year. Pitched forty-seven complete games, won twenty-eight of them, and had the most strikeouts. Batters got the least hits off him and he'd pitched the most innings of any pitcher. He'd also hit ten home runs.

In '96 and '97, they'd won the pennant. In 1898, George assembled the best players ever for the Orioles. If not for that day in June, who knows what would have been. But all that had been covered over. Just like dust choking up home plate. George had seen to it Alex's early retirement was nothing all that notable, playing it down to the press. Accidents happened in the game. Players were injured.

Ah, hell.

"I can't, George," Alex said again. "I just can't."

Over beers, Alex rehashed old times with George and the others. They talked about games they'd played, won and lost. Talked about other teams. About women, the American League, the National, Pop Foster, Zaza Harvey, Roscoe Miller, Pink Hawley, Snake Wiltse.

"Hell, Alex," Harry Howell said with a grin, "it's damn great to see you."

The others from the team of '98 smiled in agreement. Steve Brodie gave Alex a fond shove on the shoulder. "Just like old times. We haven't seen you since we played—"

Steve cut himself short, his brows furrowing and his eyes growing dark.

Alex felt his own mood darkening because he knew without having to be told what Steve remembered. The shock of it all. The devastation. At first, the disbelief, then suddenly no denying. It had to have been a dream—but the trouble was, Alex never woke up.

Because Joe McGill never got up.

Alex softly finished Steve's sentence. "Since the day we played the Giants."

A stillness fell over the bar. Alex thought back to that June afternoon. Joe's powerful presence at the plate was something that stayed with a person. He'd been tall and strong, a slugger if there'd ever been one. It went without saying that Joe was missed in the league, and many wondered what would have happened if he'd stayed in the game. But nobody had ever spoken about it in front of Alex.

After all these years, he was finally able to add, "Since Joe McGill. You can't talk great ballplayers and not mention Joe."

Then Alex headed out of the saloon soon after, his hands slipping inside his pockets as he walked.

Night had fallen, the buzz of incests droning in the darkness. Crickets sang while winged bugs danced on window screens. Breathing the warm air into his lungs, Alex tried to clear his head of smoke and beer and talk about things that had once been. And would never be again.

His mind wandered to Camille and he found himself headed toward her house instead of his own.

She was even. Balanced. She knew what she wanted and went after it. She had confidence in herself. Her abilities. God help him, he needed that tonight. Needed to be with her. Hear her voice. See her face.

He raised his arm to knock on her door just as it opened. A group of ladies stood in the living room staring at him on the other side of the porch screen.

The half dozen or so ladies inspected him. He saw a few glares, some curiosity, some brows raised and some lowered.

Camille stood to the side of the other women, holding open the wooden frame door.

"Mr. Cordova," she said through the screen, hand on the wooden frame. "Has something happened?"

"No. Ah, yeah. It's work related." Holy Christ. He'd never been in a situation like this.

Shifting his weight from one foot to the other, Alex looked down, then up. He had a legitimate excuse to be here, but it wasn't one he was going to broadcast to a host of gussied up ladies. So he made something up. "The boys were discussing a play that could improve fielding and I thought you should know about it."

That was a lie. Bald as a baby.

"Oh, well." She straightened importantly. "Yes, that is of interest to me."

"We were just leaving," came a voice from the vestibule.

A tall woman made her way out the door, the others following behind. He counted eight big trimmed hats, each accompanied by gloves, smart dresses, and tidy appearances. He recognized a couple of the faces.

"Good evening, Miss Kennison," Mrs. Plunkett called.

"It's been pleasant," Mrs. Calhoon said, a cat-in-the-creamery smile on her face.

Although their tones were cordial, Camille's smile was forced. As if she were merely going through the motions of being polite.

Alex watched the ladies march down the walkway and onto the sidewalk, where they turned to Elm Street and dispersed at the corner. Camille remained in the doorway, the screen propped open by her hip. Light spilled across her back, outlining her in golden hues, yet keeping her face in partial shadow. Her hair looked blonder, softer, piled high in curls and twists with beaded combs on either side of her head to keep the style in place. Tiny gold earrings dangled from her earlobes; the jewelry looked delicate—much like the contours of her face.

"What kind of play?" she asked.

It took him a moment to recall what she was talking about.

"Can I come in?"

"All right." She stepped aside. When he entered the living room, she closed the door behind them.

The house had shaped up since he'd last been here. Pictures hung on the walls; furniture made the room homey. The divan and chairs were just enough to make a person feel comfortable without being closed in with the junk that some women liked to keep in their parlors. In the bay window, dozens of plants filled the tiny area, some blooming, some in different shades of green, some in colored pots, and some in glass pots. Some kind of fragrant flower scented the room.

He noted the teacups and cake plates placed on tiny trays and the side table, the folded napkins, the teacart. Books on gardening were placed on a center table where they couldn't be missed.

Walking to one of the tray tables, Camille began to gather up the teacups and saucers. "What is it, Mr. Cordova, that you felt couldn't wait until tomorrow's game?"

There was a quiver in her usually no-nonsense voice. It wasn't like her to be unsteady.

He didn't immediately answer her. Instead, he watched as she flitted from one station to the next in the room, gathering, collecting, never once looking at him.

"Did you get a hat delivered to you today?"

"Yes. How did you know?"

She wore yellow, pale and creamy like summer butter. Her breasts were molded by the long panel in the front that went to the floor, buttons on either side. They were tiny white pearl buttons. A collar came to her throat, white lace with two embroidered points on either side.

"Because it was me who sent the hat."

"Oh. I haven't opened it yet," she said, carrying the tray as she went into the dining room and directly through to the kitchen.

He remained still, trying to decide what to do. He could hear the clatter of china in the kitchen from the living room. Alex followed her.

Once in the doorway, he paused. Camille stood at the sink with her back to him. He could have sworn her shoulders trembled. She was definitely upset.

A mason jar full of fresh cut flowers rested on a doily to her right. The counter was clean and neat with a soap shelf that had a tiny flower-shaped piece of soap on it. Glasses were stored on the shelves with tiny paper cutout borders. The stove gleamed in its metal enamel glory. A *drip-drip* sounded through the space, the gingham curtain hiding the leaky pipe.

He knew that she needed comforting. But for the life of him, he didn't know how to approach her. He'd never once held a woman in such a way.

"Ah, Camille—"

She visibly pulled herself together. "If you want to tell me about that play, I'll get my notebook and write it down."

She started to move, but he stopped her. "No. I didn't come for that." His eyes landed on the bright red and gold-striped hatbox with its wide red ribbon. It rested on one of the kitchen chairs, partially covered by the tablecloth as if it were hiding. "I just wondered if you liked the hat."

"I'm sorry I haven't opened it yet." She reached for the hatbox and set the gift on the counter. "It came when I was busy, and then I had guests over tonight and . . ." Her composure seemed to be hanging on by a thread.

Slowly, she lifted the lid. He stood taller to peer inside with her, as if seeing it for the first time himself.

"I felt like I owed you this," he explained. "You know. Captain and Philly and all that."

Her eyes drank in the hat. He'd had the milliner, Miss Taylor, make it up special. He'd told her to put a little of everything on it. Feathers, beads, sprig of green stuff, stiff lace, and even a rhinestone buckle with a velvet tie.

The hat itself was some kind of deep-braided straw with a really wide brim that curved sideways. He remembered that tilt of Camille's hat when she'd sat in Stykem's office. He'd liked that and wanted to buy a hat for her that would always look like she was tilting her head. He'd been pretty specific about his wants to Miss Taylor, and he'd been damn self-conscious about it. But the end result was a hat he thought looked pretty good. At least in the box it did.

"To make up for the one that got lost," Alex felt compelled to say when Camille hadn't spoken a single word. "In Philadelphia," he added, even though he'd already said that.

The drip of the faucet seemed to get louder the longer she didn't speak.

"Those big hats you wear look good on you," he

added, feeling like an imbecile, "so I had her make a big one for you."

Camille reached out and traced a length of feather. The blue of her eyes was wistful. Then she began to cry—cry so hard, her shoulders shook.

Well, hell . . . maybe the hat didn't look good in the box after all.

Alex went to her as she turned away from him and looked down into the sink with its soiled china cups and saucers and cake plates with their little rosebud patterns on them.

Hesitantly, he put his hand on her arm. She cried harder. Jesus.

Alex took her in his arms, cradling her head with his hand so that her cheek rested on his shirtfront. "What's the matter, honey?"

She didn't answer. The sound of her crying cut into his heart. He held her closer, running his hand softly up and down her back. Soothing. Trying to coax her to talk to him. Her shoulders gently quaked as she cried. Tears wet the front of his shirt; her hands were two fists pressed against his chest, as if she were afraid to get closer to him.

"What happened?" he asked once more.

On a shuddering breath, "My life's not going so well," she replied in a muffle next to the oxford of his shirt.

Instead of dwelling on what might have been wrong, he opted to point out the plus side of things. Maybe that would get her to stop crying. "It might seem that way, but you're the manager of the Keystones. And doing a damn good job." The latter was a slight stretch, but women needed to be told they did good in times of crises. He'd learned that much from his mother.

"It has nothing to do with baseball," she cried, then

loosened her fists so her breasts crushed against him, burning an imprint of femininity.

Trying to keep his mind focused, he listened. "Actually, it does have something to do with baseball. And yet it doesn't. It's just . . . *everything*."

Then she broke into another round of sobbing.

Alex felt a tick spring to life along his jaw; his teeth clenched to quell it. He did the only thing he could do. He let her cry it all out. Between the gasps for air and the shuddering of breaths, she began to talk—babble was more like it. He just kept quiet and let her go on.

"I've wanted this for a l-long time. It j-just isn't fair." She moved her arms higher; her palms lay on his shoulders, her cheek still against his chest.

He could feel her uneven breathing—and feel himself catch fire.

"She's had her turn as p-president. So has Mrs. P-Plunkett. I thought the ladies would see it's time for a n-new voice." The tips of her slim fingers absently touched the sides of his collar, toying, teasing. She was completely unaware of it as she rambled on—or he knew she wouldn't be doing it. "New ideas. I don't know the exact v-vote outcome. It could have been close. We take a c-closed ballot vote. I'm certain that two of them voted for me. They confided when I was s-serving the lady Prussia. It's the older ladies. They just can't accept change. People who're different. And I'm apparently too d-different."

Alex drew in his breath as her hands brushed at his hair, very gently. Lightly. And without thought. "I've always prided myself on my impeccable deportment. I *like* being neat and orderly. It's never been a problem for me. And yet, as soon as I do something different—like manage my father's ball team, suddenly my deportment is questioned. Do I carry myself differently because I tell men to throw a baseball? That's the b-bottom line. That's . . ." —she gulped in a mouthful of air—"that's what's b-behind all of this. I know it. Nobody dared speak the words to my face, but that's the p-problem. I never should have made that jest about the players' drawers." She buried her face against his collarbone. "That's the *real* reason I wasn't elected as the Garden Club president. It has nothing to do with my g-garden."

Players' drawers? "What's that about underwear?"

"Never mind. I said it. It's over and done with."

Alex tried to string the words together to make some sense out of them. *Baseball . . . Garden Club . . . president . . . deportment.* It all seemed disjointed to him.

"What galls me most is that Mrs. Calhoon doesn't need a second term. She has lots to occupy her time with." Camille's warm breath kissed his neck as she spoke into his collar. "She probably implied to the club that those who didn't vote for her would have their mail misplaced. Even though there's a law against mail tampering." She grew thoughtful. "All right . . . maybe she wouldn't go that far."

She quieted sniffling a bit. Then nothing.

At length, she continued. "But if that's true . . . then she won because people liked her over me."

He thought she'd just about cried herself out, but on that last thought, she began anew with the tears. He held her snugly, his hand around the back of her neck. The heel of his thumb stroked the side of her throat, then higher to where her hair began. The strands felt like a smooth network of silk, swept neatly into the combs. Slowly, lightly, he massaged the pulse point of her skin where the curve of her neck met her shoulder. She gave an unconscious sigh of pleasure, then wound her arms around his waist, locking her hands behind his back.

"None of this would have happened if it wasn't for Ned Butler." A cry eclipsed her words. "Actually, that's not true. None of this would have happened if it weren't for my father's temper. I can honestly tell you that I really didn't have any d-desire to be the manager of the Keystones." She pulled away to look up at him. "B-but you know what?"

The fact that she asked him a question threw him off guard. "What?" His voice sounded thick and heavy to him—much like the lower part of his body.

"Now that I'm the manager, I'm going to do better than my best just to prove a point. And to give me something . . ."—her voice broke—"something to do because baseball is all I have now."

Alex braced himself as her eyes flooded once more. His hands slipped up her arms, bringing her close again. Every inch of him was aware of her. She drugged his senses with her voice, her touch, her smell.

He brought his mouth to her forehead and kissed her. The feel of her skin next to his lips was like the purest silk. Superfine and flawless. He had known beautiful women in his life, but Camille Kennison was stunning. In his glory days, he would have wanted her just so he could say he'd had her. In the past three years, he'd matured. Now, he found himself wanting more—and to his overwhelming surprise, it wasn't just the physical. He wanted to be inside her, inside her body, her mind, her heart.

He kissed her brows, his large hands explored the hollows of her back. He caught her chin with his finger and brought her face toward his. Her eyes shimmered blue like a frosted pond, yet there was no coolness in her gaze. Just bare emotion, layers of vulnerability.

She breathed lightly between parted lips dusted with rose, as if painted by dewy petals. Her voice was so soft, he could barely hear her words. "I don't like living alone. I think I've made a big mistake."

He knew about mistakes. He clung to the thought of them just about every day. But memories weren't life preservers. You couldn't keep holding onto them and not expect to drown. That's what he'd been doing.

"People can fix mistakes." With his finger, he traced the side of her cheek. He moved his mouth over hers. "Or die tryin'."

His lips explored the velvet warmth of her, touching her like a whisper, slow, drugging. He could feel her inhale and drink him into her lungs. It was a sensuous thought that got his pulse to thump madly through his body. Her hands rose, curling around his neck and drawing him tightly to her.

The kiss changed, no longer light like a summer breeze but electric and devouring. He opened his mouth wide over hers, coaxing and drawing her tongue to meet his in sensual swirls that pounded through his blood. She made him feel things he'd never felt before.

It was that thought that had him lifting her into his arms, her shapely behind beneath his hands, as he sat her on the countertop. Her legs slipped apart and he nestled himself between them, bringing her closer. Tilting his head to one side, he brought her fully against him. He traced her lips with his tongue, then slipped inside her. She tasted like sweet frosting and cake as she kissed him back, matching his hunger.

The airy fabric of her dress lay beneath his palm as he skimmed her sides and brought his hands higher. He relaxed his hold on her enough to graze his fingertips over her breasts while kissing her. A sigh escaped her mouth, and she arched toward him. The whaling of her corset and the layer of underclothes that covered her kept him from fully appreciating the satin of her skin.

He lifted his hands. His fingers were too large, the buttons too small. The combination slowed the process. The first one worked free. Then the second. Down one side of the panel. Slowly. All the while kissing her. Her hands were on his shoulders, keeping the two of them together.

It was heaven and hell at the same time.

He unfastened enough of the buttons to part her dress to her waist. He broke his mouth from hers to push aside the buttery folds of cloth. With his breath ragged in his chest, he viewed her in her white chemise, its square collar caught together with a tiny ribbon. The light above them cast her in ivory, pure and perfect, cleavage in just the right places to create hollows of light and shadow.

He reached out and took the combs from her hair, mesmerized as thick curls clouded around her waist just like spun honey. His heartbeat throbbed in his ears. He felt his legs tremble.

"Camille." He breathed her name in awe. With respect.

The fact that she let him undress her filled his mind with a myriad of thoughts, mostly dishonorable. But amid all his fantasies and carnal desires came one decent thought. Even if she said he could have her, he couldn't do it. He had a conscience, whether anyone else might believe it or not. She had virgin written all over her and he was a son of a bitch if he ignored that.

"You're beautiful, Camille. So beautiful, you make me ache," he said in a low tone, kissing her softly. Against the curve of her lips, his murmur filled her ears. "But if I don't do this"—he began to slip a button back into place—"you'll have to fire me. And then I'd miss your telling me I stink as a ballplayer." Then he slowly put the front of her dress back together while she sat in stunned silence.

When she was in order, he kissed her once more. Just a peck that said he was sorry, or so he hoped she'd take it. Damn but if her eyes didn't begin to moisten.

He didn't carry a handkerchief, so he grabbed an embroidered white napkin from the counter. She took it. "I think you're all cried out for tonight, honey. But for what it's worth, if I were that Lady Prussia woman, I would have voted for you."

She dabbed the corners of her eyes with a tea towel, its edge colorfully embroidered with songbirds. "Lady Prussia is a white cake."

"Yeah, well." He meant to brush the comment off, but then he paused and said, "It is?"

"Yes." Then out of left field, she asked, "Would you like a piece?"

Alex stood motionless, Camille still sitting on the counter in front of him, her hair a river of gold about her shoulders. His chest hurt, as if he'd been slugged in the ribs. *Would he like a piece?*

He reached up and caught her beneath her arms and lowered her gently onto her feet. "Sure," he caught himself saying, mentally kicking himself in the ass. He should leave. Go home. And once there, dunk his head in cold water and forget about what had happened between them. He should have done a lot of things instead of pulling out a chair at the small table.

But that's what he found himself doing. Then he watched her as she moved about her kitchen, getting a cake plate and cutting a slice of lady Prussia for him while the dripping water plunked into a metal bucket.

"You want me to take a look at the leak in your

pipe?" *Double wrong move. First he stays for cake, then he says he'll fix her plumbing.*

"I can fix it myself." She set the cake in front of him, along with a fork and a napkin.

"Okay." He took up the utensil, self-conscious with her gaze on him. He cut into a bite and brought it to his mouth. Nodding, he swallowed. "It's good."

"I know."

She sighed, back in control. She took out a chair and sat across from him looking like a fancy woman on a tease postcard with her hair parted down the middle and spilling over her shoulders. Then she glanced at the hatbox. "That was thoughtful of you to buy me a hat. It's not that I don't appreciate it. It's just that . . . it's on the large side."

The fork in his hand suddenly felt clumsy. "You don't have to wear it. In fact, do me a favor and don't wear it." Then unbidden, he asked, "You get a lot of hats sent to you?"

"Actually, this is the first."

For some fool reason, he was glad.

But the feeling was short-lived when the light caught on her sapphire ring as she moved her hand.

"I guess you're used to rings," he said, damning himself for bringing up the jewelry.

She looked at the blue stone with its circle of tiny diamonds. "My father gave this to me on my sixteenth birthday."

She didn't say anything further. Neither did he.

He ate his lady Prussia in silence. How in the hell had he gone from making love on the kitchen counter to eating cake at the kitchen table?

Jesus. He really had reformed.

Chapter

❦ 13 ❦

Camille had no reason to go see Alex Cordova at his wood shop at the end of Elm Street. Especially on an afternoon that was perfect for sitting in the shade sipping lemonade; perfect for tilling and weeding gardens, repotting houseplants, fixing leaky pipes, or a variety of other things. She should have been doing any number of them rather than paying a visit to Alex.

But she'd concocted an excuse to see him.

Why, she didn't care to analyze. She should have been mortified by her behavior last night and done anything she could to avoid him. Obviously, they'd have to see one another again, but in a crowd she wouldn't be tempted to do anything aside from talk to him. Last night, she'd lost her head. And herself in his arms.

Just thinking about him standing between her legs, kissing her, touching her . . . brought a rush of gooseflesh over her skin and a hotness to her cheeks. She felt her knees grow weak as she walked; her heartbeat seemed to echo her ears.

Even with all that, she felt that facing him alone would be better than facing him with the other players watching her every move. At least this way, she could get it over with.

Get it over with ...

As far as she was concerned, last night had ended too quickly. She had only one regret—that fit of crying, which in the light of day seemed so utterly spineless and embarrassing. Aside from that, and beyond the kissing, she'd enjoyed having Alex sit at her table, eating lady Prussia cake and listening as she rambled about her life. The companionship had been like a quenching drink after a dry thirst. She hadn't even been aware of how much she'd needed to talk to him. Alex had patiently let her go on about the Garden Club and her new living arrangements.

Much to her disappointment, he'd declined a second piece of cake and gone home. Then she'd been left with four walls and a sinking feeling in the bottom of her stomach. She was alone.

Suddenly, a house of her own had lost a bit of its appeal.

She hadn't foreseen how much that would affect her. At her parents' house, Leda was always nearby, as was her mother. Her father was around in the mornings and evenings. Even his tirades at breakfast seemed something to look forward to now that she ate at an empty table with only a coffeepot to keep her company.

Several months ago, if somebody had told her she'd own her own house and be managing the Keystones, she would have laughed and said they were badly mistaken—or even delusional, because never in a million years would she consider such a thing as surrounding herself with sportsmen.

Spitting, cursing, scratching. She cringed.

So much for rational thought.

It was irrational kissing on her sink counter that brought her out on a mild summer day, heading over to see a man who could put her out of sorts with a mere glance. A man who made her fantasies pale in comparison to the real thing.

The paved road and neat boardwalk came to an end. In its place was a dirt lane with elms that grew in no particular pattern. Through the network of oblong leaves, sunlight dappled the earth. No breeze stirred the air. Flies lazily hovered over dandelions and meadow grass. Butterflies flitted from bluebells to wild phlox.

Camille, fringed parasol raised, gloves neatly buttoned, and hat angled smartly on her hair, approached the old building where she hoped to find Alex.

The shop's shingled roof and siding shimmered gold from a linseed oil wash. Quiet blanketed the yard. A totem pole under construction rose high and strong, as if it were a sentinel guarding the building and its occupants. Flawless detail set off the completed blocks of animals, plants, symbols, and objects. One figure in particular caught her attention—a grizzly bear with its mouth open, snarling furiously.

She moved to the entryway that led to the wide double doors. No sounds from a sanding plane or saw reached her ears. She peered inside the shop, squinting to adjust to the change in light. Her gaze scanned the work area, and the back where lumber was stocked on shelves. No Alex.

Wondering what to do next, she stood still. It was then that she heard the dull *thump* coming from behind the wood shop.

Thump.
Thump.

Thump.

Methodical in its repetition. *Thump,* pause, *thump,* pause, *thump,* pause, and so forth. As if something were being hit.

Camille exited the building and walked to the rear. At the corner, she stopped.

Alex stood with his back to her, a metal bucket of baseballs at his right foot. In the ground some fifty feet in front of him, he'd created a high slope of dirt and blocked it with lengths of shop wood to create a strike zone. Wearing a pair of loose-fitting trousers and a shirt without its tails tucked in, he bent down and grabbed a baseball, coiled his arm back, and threw it. The ball flew in a brief blur of gray.

Thump. Dead center into the strike zone.

Another ball. *Thump.* Strike.

Strike.

Strike.

Strike.

One right after the other until the pail grew empty.

"That's the Alex Cordova I signed to play baseball for the Keystones," Camille said, walking toward him. "Where have you been?"

Alex turned with a start. He looked up at her through the sweat-damp black hair that fell into his eyes. Square jaw clamped tight and chest rising and falling from his exertions, he glared at her.

"How long have you been standing there?"

"Long enough to know my father got his money's worth." With an efficient snap of her wrist, she collapsed her parasol.

The sleeves on his pale blue shirt had been rolled up to the elbows and the tan skin on his arms glistened. He reached for a towel beside the bucket and wiped his face—first his brows, then his forehead, and then behind his neck. A shadow of stubble darkened his chin and throat. A tingling pushed at her ribs as she watched him wipe the sweat from his skin.

Tossing the cloth, he combed his hair from his forehead with his hands. "Why'd you come out here?"

Caught up in the sight of him, she fought to find her voice. She ended up foolishly blurting, "I had to see you alone."

Growing still, his dark eyes ran the length of her. Long and slow. "Really?"

Her heart slammed against her chest. "I mean, I need to discuss something with you and I didn't want to do it in front of the other players."

His gaze seemed to smolder, his full sensual lips quirking up at the corners. "I'm not particularly interested in *doing it* in front of the others either."

On a short staccato breath, Camille's mouth fell open. "I—I, well . . ."

But before she could make a bigger fool of herself, Alex crooked his finger under her chin and tilted her head up until she was forced to meet his eyes. The touch as sweet and soft as a caress.

There was a faint smile on his mouth. "What did you want to talk to me about, Camille?"

She wasn't sure what made her knees go weaker— his finger against her skin or his low, deep voice wrapped around her name.

She shook her head as if she could clear all her errant thoughts. Her words came out in one big rush. "Your signed photographs are increasing attendance at home games."

Abruptly, he dropped his hand away.

"Well, the fans aren't coming in droves," she clarified, thankful to be back on more familiar ground, "but I do believe more are coming to watch us."

"Watch us make jackasses out of ourselves."

"It doesn't have to be that way." She looked at the

mock strike zone he'd made. "Alex, I just saw what you're capable of. You're wonderful." *In more ways than one.* Kisses and touches and her name drifting on his tongue. Heaven help her, she should have stayed home and pulled weeds.

"I'm not wonderful."

"But you are."

He began to walk away. "Forget about it, Miss Kennison."

She was no longer Camille to him. She hated the flare of disappointment she felt.

She forced her thoughts back to baseball and followed him to the front of the building. "I don't know why you're doing this. Why do you hold back?"

"I don't hold back. I just happen to foul up when you put me on the mound." He gave her a disarming smile. "I choke under pressure."

She frowned. "That's ridiculous."

"That's"—he chucked the underside of her chin, this time in an entirely unromantic manner—"the truth."

"It is not." She ignored the shivers that his touch sent through her. She followed him inside the building. "You never choked before. What happened in June of 1898 to make you quit?"

His steps abruptly ceased. Turning, he regarded her through wary eyes. She could almost see the memories reflected in his gaze. She didn't think he'd answer her; when he did, his voice was hard and cold. "It's easy enough to find out."

"Save me the trouble and tell me."

"Maybe one day."

"You said that before."

He made no comment as he went to the workbench and picked up a length of wood that had been cut into the shape of a crescent moon. There were a pair of them, and he suddenly engrossed himself in the pieces as if she wasn't there.

She wouldn't get answers from him.

On a sigh riddled with discouragement and frustration, she offered a parting bit of advice, "Don't be late for this afternoon's game."

"Have I ever been?"

"As a matter of fact, yes. Four weeks late."

"I don't want to go to Boston with you, Alex," Captain repeated as he and Alex walked across from the white-spired church on Hackberry Way to Dr. Porter's office.

"That's why we're going to the doctor's office, Cap, so I can give him your medicine and he'll help you take it while I'm gone."

Captain wore a Stetson identical to Alex's. "I can remember things sometimes. I think I could remember my medicine." His fingers splayed through his full beard. "But I can forget things, too. Huh, Alex?"

"You can."

"That's why we'd better give the doctor my medicines."

Crossing the street, Alex said, "You have to promise me you'll go to Dr. Porter's office every day."

"I promise. Because if I had to give myself my medicine, I might take too much like I did that one time. Or I might lose the bottles. I got lost in Philadelphia. It's a good thing you didn't stay mad at me, or you'd have to kick my ass. Right, Alex?"

Alex smiled. "I'd never kick your ass, Cap."

Captain grinned. "Maybe one day I'll kick yours."

The words landed hard on Alex, but he pushed them off his shoulders. "Yeah, you could do that, Cap. You're a big guy."

"So're you."

"Yeah."

Alex held on to a small bag containing the two bottles he'd been given from the Baltimore Hospital. One was administered daily. The other, a powder, was given only when Cap had a particularly bad headache. Alex had the medicines mailed to him in Harmony when he ran out.

Between the two, Captain seemed calm most of the time. But that calmness came with a price. His coordination had been affected, he grew drowsy and sometimes confused, more easily agitated—on rare occasions, hostile. But Alex had to give him the medicine. The doctors told him it would help Cap, and Alex knew of no other solution until he could get him to Silas Denton's hospital in Buffalo.

Alex pulled open the door to the doctor's office and was greeted by the doctor himself. He sat at a desk in the front office. A curtained partition led to the examining room. Glass cabinets with glass shelves held instruments and various items dealing with medicine.

"Mr. Cordova," Dr. Porter said, standing and extended his hand. "I've been expecting you."

He was an elderly gentleman with thick white hair and scraggly eyebrows that looked like tree bark. His face was kind and compassionate. Alex would never have agreed to do this if it weren't for the fact that he trusted the doc. He'd never taken Captain to him in an official capacity before. There had been no need, as Alex got his medicines from Baltimore and Captain didn't need physical exams.

"Doc," Alex replied, taking the man's hand.

"And you are the patient?" Dr. Porter said to Captain in a tone that didn't belittle Cap's capabilities.

Captain stood his full height, seeming to dwarf the room. His gaze had traveled across the four walls, looking and staring, then finally focusing on the doctor. "I'm Captain." His eyes darkened, uncertain; a little afraid. "I don't like shaving."

"You don't have to."

"That's good."

Alex set the bag of medicine on the desktop. "The bottles are labeled with instructions." He took a piece of paper from his pocket. "I wrote down the names of the hotels I'll be at in case you have to find me."

Dr. Porter nodded. "You come see me every afternoon, Captain, and we'll take care of everything."

"All right."

"If he's not here," Alex said, "you'll have to track him down. Check the mercantile first."

"I will."

"Alex," Captain said with a scowl, "you're embarrassing me. I never get lost here. He won't have to come looking for me."

"I doubt he will." Alex did a quick calculation in his head. Today was June 17. He wouldn't be back until July 5. "I'll be gone eighteen days, Cap. That's a long time."

"No it's not."

"He'll be fine," Dr. Porter insisted. "Do you play checkers, Captain?"

Smiling, Cap replied, "Yes."

"We can play some games if you'd like." The doctor motioned to the board set up on a small table next to the front window.

Morning light spilled in through the pane of glass, reminding Alex he had an hour to get to the depot to make the train. "I've got to head out, Cap."

"All right. I'm going to go to work now." He added in an excited tone, "Then I'm going to the restaurant for dinner."

Alex had arranged for Cap to eat his meals at Nannie's Home-Style Restaurant every day. "See you when I get back."

"See you."

Alex nodded, hoping all would go well. He was reluctant to leave, but for more than the obvious reasons. A date was looming, a date with which he didn't cope well. Every year on June 25, Alex thought about Joe McGill.

And about what should have been for the Giants catcher.

Alex's pitching remained the same. Camille coached him, encouraged him, talked to him—all to no avail. What she'd seen that day at the wood shop had stayed there. The only hope she had of uncovering the reasons why were the newspapers.

She'd seen Matthew Gage before she'd left for Cleveland. He'd told her the archive room at the *Baltimore Sun* had sustained water damage and the back issues she was interested in weren't readable. Mr. Gage had taken the liberty of contacting the *Sporting News*. But it would take more time to get the information she requested.

They'd since played the Cleveland Blues and won one game because of fielding errors by the opposing team and hits from Duke and Noodles. But they'd lost four. Tomorrow marked the first of a four-game series with the Boston Somersets.

Their train arrived in Boston shy of eleven o'clock at night. Camille and the players went straight to the St. James Hotel, only to learn their rooms weren't ready.

At the check-in desk, she sighed. All she wanted was to go to bed. But they did have to eat, so they might as well do that while they were waiting.

They were shoved into the back corner of the hotel

restaurant. Fifteen minutes later, and still every waiter in sight avoided them like the plague. The twelve ballplayers grew more disgruntled. There would have been thirteen, but Mox had stayed behind in Harmony, unable to play because of his broken thumb. Kennison's Hardware couldn't afford to bring the second baseman along just to sit on the bench.

"What's the holdup?" Cub grumbled. "Just because we're ballplayers doesn't mean we're a bunch of pigs. "Red Vanderguest used to take care of stuff like this. He'd holler over at the guy so loud his head would spin."

"Yeah," the others agreed.

Camille gazed at Cub, then the rest of them.

For the first time, she had to confront a situation where ladylike manners weren't adequate to handle the problem. When she'd had to deal with facing scantily clad men in a clubhouse, she'd come up with the idea of a screen to shield her modesty. But suddenly, she realized her father had always been in charge when they'd sat in a restaurant. And his way would have been Red Vanderguest's way. She searched her mind for a solution because she absolutely wouldn't holler for service.

With a gentle smile, she turned and summoned a waiter by raising her hand. To no avail. When she swiveled back, her gaze connected with Alex's. He relaxed in his chair, his maddening eyebrows arched as he toyed with his knife. Parted in the middle, his hair fell into his brows and his eyes. The chandelier light above him gave the inky black strands a slight russet hue. When he looked at her, he gave her a slight shrug as if to say: *Do you need my help?*

No. Absolutely not.

Camille determinedly conducted a visual search for a waiter. Finally, one in dress black walked toward them, and she sighed her relief. But it was short-lived as he continued on to a party that had been seated after them.

Smoothing her napkin with pronounced strokes, she averted her gaze from the players who stared at her, waiting for her to yell. The best solution would be to leave the restaurant. But where else could they go? Nothing was open at eleven o'clock at night. In the end, she said, "I'm sure he'll be right back."

Cub lifted his coffee cup and held it over the floor. "I'm sure he won't. But this'll get him back."

Horror made her heartbeat skip. "You'll do no such thing. I'll handle this."

The waiter walked past them once more.

Ire began to tick like a clock in her chest, and it took considerable effort not to do as Cub threatened herself. Her fingers itched to drop a coffee cup on the floor. But that would only prove the hotel management right—they were baseball players and as such, had a reputation for being destructive and obnoxious. That's why in Philadelphia the Keystones had had to live on frankfurters bought from a vendor's stand.

She looked at the maître d', who was conversing with a couple. She waited for him to come their way. When he did, she kept her composure in place while saying, "Excuse me, sir, but we've been waiting twenty minutes for service. Is there a problem?"

The man had the nerve to smile, as if he didn't know what was going on. "No, ma'am." His eyes leveled on her as if he thought she were a minor inconvenience. "I was going to send a waiter to your table."

"When?"

"When I had one available." He gave a long, slow perusal to each man at the table. His nose wrinkled in disapproval.

Her thoughts raced dangerously to images of hurling her coffee cup at him, but she maintained her curt composure when censuring him, "Many people violate some of the observances of etiquette, whether from ignorance, thoughtlessness, or carelessness. The Keystones have never been thrown out of a hotel or charged with any kind of public disruption. For you to assume our manners are lacking because we are from a baseball organization is prejudice and beyond appalling."

Although she made an excellent point, one that her finishing-school teacher would have applauded, Camille had to admit she sounded like a deportment textbook. And worse—ineffective.

The maître d' grew flustered. "Let me assure you, ma'am, we don't base our level of service on the occupations of our customers."

"Oh?"

"Certainly not."

"Then you don't dislike baseball players."

"As a matter of fact, I like the Somersets. Nobody plays better than Cy Young."

"Then it's just the matter of our being the rival team."

His face turned red. "I wouldn't say—"

"But you already have by not giving us service."

"Ma'am, you are putting words in my mouth."

"I would rather put an order in your hand, sir."

Mottled from annoyance over the quick exchange, his cheeks grew redder. "I will have a waiter here in a moment."

"That won't do." The thumping of her pulse pounded the inside of her wrists. "*You* may write down our selections."

"I couldn't possibly. It's not my station to write orders."

This was getting her nowhere. She had to think fast

and outwit him. Drawing in a breath, she snapped, "Then I'm quite certain it isn't your station to accept a gratuity."

His brows peaked. "Ma'am, I don't take tips."

"Of course not. And if you don't, you couldn't possibly take tickets to tomorrow's game. It's a shame, because Cy Young is pitching."

He stood there, wide-eyed. "The game is sold out."

"Yes, I know. But I have several complimentary seats. I suppose I'll have to give them to that nice gentleman at the front desk who checked us in."

All but stammering, the maître d' said, "I could make an exception in this case and—"

"I wouldn't want you to compromise yourself. We'll wait for a waiter."

"No need." The red on his cheeks faded to a shade of pink. Delighted pink.

Within seconds, the maître d' had taken their orders and scurried off to the kitchen to submit them. She lifted her eyes to Alex, who saluted her with his water glass.

He spoke across the table. "That's one way to handle it."

"And I didn't have to yell to get my point across," she reasoned.

"No," Cub said, then chuckled. "You just had to resort to bribery."

"Yes . . . well."

But then the most unexpected thing happened. Cub winked at her and said, "It worked, didn't it?"

Shortly thereafter, five waiters appeared at their table bearing trays of hot food, and they were served with quick efficiency. Succulent roast beef, whipped potatoes, glazed carrots, bread and butter. For dessert, there were thick wedges of triple-layer chocolate cake.

As they ate, jovial laughter went around the table. Camille heard her name mentioned over and over, in a way that she'd never thought she'd hear.

"I have to admit, listening to her was better than watching Red throw his dinner plate."

Laughter and smiles.

"She put words in his mouth he didn't know he had."

More smiles.

"That fellow didn't know what hit him."

Nods of agreement.

"When she mentioned the tickets, he sure changed his tune."

Then from Specs, "You got him to do something without yelling, Miss Kennison. You stuck up for us."

Fork in hand, Camille paused. "Of course I did. Because we've got a right to the same service as anybody else. Just like," she added softly, "I've got the right to have the same chance as any other manager in charge of the Keystones. I know I don't do things the way Red Vanderguest or my father did. Just because I don't swear or spit or yell doesn't mean that I don't care about what happens to this team."

The players looked at her, solemnly and thoughtfully, and for a long moment, nothing else was said. The seconds passed. Silent understanding measured out the time. Camille felt rekindled hope that she could be taken seriously.

Then the smiling came back and the men resumed eating. Talk began anew. They traded jokes, laughing and expressing their enjoyment.

The men included her in their conversation.

It was a rapport she'd never experienced before in her life—most certainly not with the Garden Club women.

She lowered her head, a full smile on her lips that

she couldn't contain. She was a part of something and it felt wonderful.

When she looked up, she found Alex staring at her and her excitement slowed to something else—deeper, more intense. She had the fleeting feeling that he thought her . . . worthy.

And that meant a lot to her.

Chapter
❧ 14 ❦

They looked like bumblebees.

The uniforms the Keystones had brought with them to the St. James hotel weren't the same ones that had gone to the laundry in Harmony. Alex looked at the putrid color of the fabric encasing his arms and legs, then glared at Camille.

"I can't imagine what could have happened," she gasped, giving them all a glance. "I took the dirty uniforms to the laundry, the same way as I always do—in the canvas bags. Then I picked these up the next day. How could something like this have happened? It's not as if the colors have faded. These are *new* uniforms."

"These are puke-i-forms," Noodles whined.

They'd left the hotel for the Huntington Avenue Grounds without checking the uniforms. There'd been no reason to. But now the Keystones had no choice but to suit up in the bumblebee gear.

Camille was perplexed. "The colors may be a little . . . bright, but it will be easier for you to spot one another on the field. Old gold with dark slate for the lettering."

"This isn't any Old Gold and Dark Slate," Yank commented, scowling at the clash of colors on his chest.

Noodles broke in. "This is squash yellow and black plum."

Cupid frowned. "Put the two together—"

"—and you've got a bumblebee," Bones finished.

Grumbles circulated in the small room.

"I honestly don't know how such a mistake could have been made," Camille said, standing before them, her peach dress falling in a light swirl of fabric over her long legs. "But mark my words, I'll get to the bottom of it when I get back to Harmony. In the meantime," she said encouragingly, "are they *that* bad? The Tigers and the Senators wear bright colors."

No comment.

Dressed as she was, she reminded Alex of an Italian ice—enticing on a hot day. He wanted to put his mouth over hers to see if she tasted as cool and sweet as she looked.

She wore a simple braided hat that on closer inspection looked vaguely familiar. Damned if it wasn't the hat he'd given her—minus most of the gewgaws the milliner had put on it. Just a sprig of lace here and there remained, and one ivory flower.

"Well," she went on, her eyes resting on Alex a moment. "We'll just have to make the best of things. There isn't anything else you can wear."

"Our birthday suits," Jimmy suggested with a grin.

"Yes," Camille replied, "that would go over very well. Why don't you?"

It took the players a few seconds to realize she was teasing them. Afterward, they laughed along with her and shook their heads at Jimmy.

Alex sat down on the bench and began to lace up his shoes. Uniforms were the least of his worries. It was all he could do to keep his mind clear and his thoughts from being pulled down a dark path. But hard as he tried to keep away visions of Joe, Joe McGill filled his head. Alex saw Joe at the plate, catcher's mitt in his grasp. As the years had melted away, so had some of the words he'd once traded with the Giants' catcher. He couldn't remember exactly everything they'd said to each other that day. He knew they weren't pretty. It was part of the game, of the way they were toward one another.

Laces knotted, Alex sat back and inhaled deep lungfuls of air. He'd get through the day, just like he had on the two previous Junes. Only today, he had to get through it with a bat in his hand. He had to fight the personal battle raging in him. He had to stay uncaring, remain unfeeling.

If Joe were here, he'd probably say to spare him no mercy. To knock him right out of the batter's box because he was going to hit the ball out of the park. The admission was dredged from a place Alex didn't like to go—memories of the old days, the glory days.

His glory days.

To get out on the mound, to pitch like he meant business, to see the batters take a powder, one right after the other, strike, strike, strike—He was capable of doing it. Just like he'd done that afternoon Camille had caught him hurling balls at the dirt.

He thought back to the question she'd asked him: Why had he quit baseball? He'd wanted to tell her, to take her into his confidence.

But there was nothing anybody could do to change things. No matter how hard Alex tried, he couldn't revive Joe. And he would have given anything—*anything*—to bring him back. In body. In mind. In spirit.

"Hey, busher."

Alex froze. His heartbeat tripped, then surged; his blood grew hot in his veins. Slowly, he glanced over his shoulder. Nobody was there. Who in the hell was he expecting? Joe McGill?

It was just like Joe to play a trick on him. To make him think one thing and do another, to make him want to shove his fist in his chops and kick his ass— and maybe have his ass kicked in return. That was the way of things between them because they'd both been bruised by the other at the plate and on the field, starting with the first day Joe batted in a Giant's uniform. He'd ripped a pitch right at the mound and shot the ball into Alex's shoulder. The injury benched him for a couple of weeks. Intentional or not, that incident had set up seasons of antagonism.

"Cordova, if you can't play the game stay the hell off the field."

Alex shot his chin around, his gaze darting across the wall. There were open lockers, closed lockers, clothes on the floor, bats and balls in buckets and tall boxes, towels, water pitchers.

No Joe.

Facing forward, he was assailed with a sense of relief. He shouldn't feel that way. Grief should have torn at his heart. But it didn't. His heart pulsed and his blood flowed, strongly and without the usual tightening in his throat. A weight had lifted from his shoulders. Somehow, it just felt easier to breathe. His awareness of the sensations was so acute, it was almost a physical pain. And with the tenseness eased in his body, he allowed himself to mentally prepare to pitch.

He was going to win today.

Because Joe McGill understood why he had to. Even though he wasn't in the room, he was here.

He'd been with Alex since the day of the accident. In his thoughts. Words. What he did. Why he did things.

And oddly, Alex's decision to do his best came from Camille. She was good at standing up for what she believed in. He could do no less. By failing himself and the team, he failed her.

It was time to either get into the game, or get out.

"Gentlemen, I'm going to bring the lineup to the umpires." Camille's voice broke into Alex's thoughts. "Let's make the best of things, shall we?"

Then she left.

Alex looked at the group of men shuffling on their feet and taking their own good time getting ready.

"We're going to win today's game," he said, tucking the tails of his shirt into his pants.

Charlie, cigarette dangling from the side of his mouth, asked, "How do you know that, Cordova?"

"Because we owe her. After what she did in the restaurant."

"Well, that's a nice thought." Doc buttoned his jersey. "But when we win, it's not like we really set out to do it. I think we get lucky, that's all."

"Yeah, that's right." Specs squinted. His new glasses didn't seem to be working.

Alex went to the small desk, grabbed the box on it and lifted the lid. It was Camille's and he knew what was in it. "Today we'll do things her way. And I mean everything."

He fingered the packages of Chiclets and began to toss them out to the players. "No sneaking tobacco. We'll do the music thing where we pass the ball to one another with that two-step crap. Bones, wear your shoe inserts. Specs, plaster a different pair of glasses on your nose."

Specs grunted. "I like this pair."

Yank chuckled. "That pair wouldn't help you find the foul line if you were standing on it."

"Shut up, Yank."

"Both of you put a lid on it," Alex directed. "Cupid, make sure you put a lot of liniment on your head. Maybe we can piss off Cy and he'll throw a punch—get himself ejected from the game."

"I don't want the Cyclone hitting me in the head," Cupid objected.

"Then duck if you see his fist coming at you." Alex reached for the basket containing their luck charms, remedy bottles, and the other essentials that fueled their phobias. Alex, though, had never once relied on any of that stuff. He always counted on himself to pull him through a game.

"Take all this sludge and make it work for you." He held the basket out. "Other than that, I don't know what else we can do."

"We could pray," Deacon said, his cap low over his eyes.

"Yeah, we haven't tried that." Yank had shoved the entire package of gum into his mouth and talked around the wad in his cheek.

Cub snorted. "Why would the Lord listen to anything we have to say?"

" 'Cause we're asking," Doc said. "He'll listen to anyone who asks."

Alex took up his cap, grabbed his bat, and went toward the door. "Do what you have to do."

Then he went outside. He'd done all his praying when Captain was in the hospital. And it hadn't done any good.

He put more faith in Bones's string of rabbits' feet.

"Mr. Regal man," Cy Young called to Alex with a mocking tip of his cap.

Alex shot back, "How's the farm, *Denton?*"

Cy's face grew red from being called his given name and having his Ohio country roots mentioned. "Same as it always was, Regal. Doing well. Just like my pitching. Not like yours, which is in the crapper."

Camille listened to the exchange between the Somerset player and Alex Cordova. Alex wasn't amused. In fact, he glowered and would have probably fired off an obscenity if she hadn't been standing beside him.

"You're going to wonder why you can't hit the ball today, rube," Alex said. "Because the Keystones are winning this game."

Cy smirked. "What are you going to do? Knock my head off like you knocked off—"

Alex tackled Cy to the ground before he could finish his sentence. Their fists flailed and some punches landing. Dust clouded the air. Camille shot to her feet, but her call to stop went unheeded. It was the umpire who broke them apart and sent them to their respective benches to cool off.

Sitting beside Alex, Camille looked at him as he pressed a wet towel on the corner of his mouth.

"What was that all about?" she asked.

"Winning." His eyes narrowed across the field to where Cy sat in the Somersets' dugout. "I'm going to beat him pitching today."

Camille was taken aback by Alex's sudden confidence. "Are you really going to beat him?" she asked, gazing into his face, her breath catching as it had a way of doing when his brown eyes peered directly into hers.

"Watch me." Alex snagged his glove and jogged out to the pitcher's mound.

Camille observed her players, taking notations.

The Huntington Avenue Grounds, newly constructed this year, had opened in May, with railroad tracks along the full advertisement wall behind first base. In back of third base, tall offices and warehouses sprung up, some as tall as ten stories. The ballpark, built on a former circus lot, had patches of sand in the outfield where grass wouldn't grow.

There was a toolshed in the far middle of center field, and as the Somersets took the outfield, the players grabbed rakes and groomed the ground around their positions to give their spiked shoes more grip on pebbleless dirt.

Outraged by the unfairness, Camille went to her feet to have a word with the umpire behind home plate.

Walking toward him, she called out. "Mr. . . . er—" But she stopped, having to think a moment to make sure she didn't call him Catfish. It didn't help that his name had an aquatic sound to it. If she addressed him incorrectly, he'd take her out of the game. Just that one word, *Catfish,* and you were ejected. He was quite sensitive about it. Probably because he had rather prominent lips, and because when he'd call a ball or a strike he'd let a fine spray of spit fly from his mouth. It gave the general impression of a catfish.

"Uh, Mr. . . . ." She'd reached him now, and he gazed at her with quiet reprobation in his eyes. Then his name came to her. "Mr. Carpio, I find this display of raking the dirt unacceptable."

"On what grounds?" Boomer Hurley, the Somersets' manager, asked with a guffaw as he drew up to them. "Get it? Grounds. As in dirt."

"I get it, Mr. Hurley," she remarked tightly. Her second meeting of the man was fast proving to be just as antagonizing as the first.

"The Somersets always rake their dirt between innings," Mr. Carpio declared.

"Then I propose the Keystones have the same advantage." She looked at her team members, who sat on the bench, waiting for her to tell them what to do. Noodles was next to bat, but she'd held him back until a decision could be made about the rakes.

"Did you bring your own rakes?" The tobacco lump in Boomer's cheek put a lisp in his words. He spit. "The Keystones can't use the property of the Somersets."

Mr. Carpio nodded his head in agreement. "You had the opportunity to even things out."

"Of course we didn't bring our own rakes, and to imply that it should have been a consideration is ludicrous." She lifted her chin and spoke crisply. "Mr. Carpio, this is very offensive to me and to the Keystones organization. To all of baseball, for that matter. A manager can't make up rules. And nowhere in the books does it say the home team has control of rakes."

Mr. Carpio pursed those fleshy lips of his, then looked at Camille and then at Boomer—who inched one deviant brow up his forehead like a crook on the prowl for something to steal.

"Miss Kennison," Mr. Carpio stated judiciously, black fedora over his bald head, "I can't force Mr. Hurley into sharing his rakes. They are official property of the Somersets."

In a silent standoff, Boomer sardonically grinned at her, to the point of gloating. She fought the urge to sneer.

Without another word, she resumed her seat. It was horrid. It was vulgar. It was baseball wearing its worst face. The home team was getting away with something that was unfair. Her father would have lambasted Mr. Carpio with language that would have gotten him severely fined, if not thrown from the ballpark. Were she to do such a thing, he'd probably be proud. Camille wondered if spouting a mild oath would make her feel better.

On the bench, she gave it a polite try mumbling beneath her breath, "The big dumb stiff."

Reclining next to her, one leg out in a long and lean stretch, Alex commented, "I would have said worse."

"I know."

He laughed, the sound rich and deep-timbred.

She grew aware of how close he sat—not indecently so, but just near enough to have his muscular thigh meet the material of her skirt. Just enough to have her sleeve lightly skim over the outline of his hard biceps as she raised her hand to shade her eyes. She saw the field, but she didn't see it. She could smell the soap Alex had used this morning, a woodsy masculine scent that jumbled her senses and made her almost forget what she was doing.

"Noodles, go out there and hit a home run," she mumbled, not putting much emphasis into her words. They seemed wasted on a team that was always the underdog—not even granted the courtesy of rakes. Much to her surprise, though, Alex had pitched a fine first inning. Only one man had gottened a hit off him, but the man hadn't scored because of great fielding from Cupid. Alex had struck out the rest up to bat. He looked like the Alex she'd seen at his wood shop. Virile and dominant. In prime form.

Her advice to Noodles had been given in near jest. In the twenty-eight games they had played since she'd taken over, he'd gotten a few hits, but not a single home run or even a double. He never beat the ball to second, and it seemed he was chronically out at first even if he hit a bobble that rolled into third base territory.

So when he stood and took his first strike, it didn't surprise her. Nor did the second. As he positioned himself for the third pitch, he dug his spikes into the dirt, but then he held his hands up to call time. She sat forward, wondering if there was a problem. But he gave her a quick gaze and a nod, then reached into his back pocket. His hand withdrew a package of Chiclets. He tipped his head back and poured the tiny candy-gum pieces into his mouth; then he stuffed the wrapper back into his pocket.

Carpio fined for littering. He wouldn't fine for illegal rake use, but he'd get you on a trash violation.

The fans booed and hissed at Noodles, waving him off and jeering at him. Their laughter and mockery made Camille angry. Noodles took his stance again and Cy fired a knuckleball. Noodles took a swing. It sounded like he was hitting a squash when the tip made contact and sent the ball sailing high. Higher. Over the backfield wall.

He'd hit a home run.

The voices of the red-hot Somersets fans were abruptly silenced. On the Keystones bench, a wild cheer rose, along with the players who ran out to home plate to wait for their unlikely hero.

When Noodles came in, cheeks ruddy and jaw working on all that chewing gum, he doffed his cap to Camille and said, "You were right, Miss Kennison. Those Chiclets are the ticket."

She laughed, unable to keep the smile from her lips as Cupid went up to bat in the hopes of adding to the 1–0 score.

Alex resumed his position beside her, leaning against the dugout wall, one ankle lifted over his knee. The sound of gum popping as he snapped it between his teeth made her turn toward him. His smile was as intimate as any kiss.

"You're responsible for the gum, I'd bet."

He shrugged. "I might have brought it to their attention." He twirled a finger through the ivory flower petals on her hat, then trailed it lower down to the piece of lace that it brushed her jaw. "But it was your idea."

Her heart skittering, she brought her attention back to the game, heat and pleasure dusting her cheeks.

The game progressed with startling effort on the Keystones' part. Camille could only hope it would keep up. In the top of the third, Charlie swooped low after a brilliant going-away grab. Into the fifth, Duke shot the ball out to the mound after an inning-ending strikeout. The Somersets' first baseman made a hand-pop over to second after his line drive into the right field corner. And after each play, the Keystones did a round-the-horn toss of the ball. In two-step ragtime.

Jimmy Shugart, who along with Cub and Yank, were the only players not in today's game, grinned at the unexpected plays. His prominent teeth gleamed and glistened. "We're showing them, Miss Kennison."

Yes, they were.

Midday heat made Camille's chemise stick to her skin; perspiration rolled between her breasts. She felt sticky and in need of a cool bath. She took out her handkerchief to dab her forehead. Then she did the unthinkable: She removed her gloves, pulling on each damp finger and setting the gloves on top of her pocketbook. It was just too hot to stand on ceremony.

She chanced looking at the players as she lightly patted her face. They stared at her, but quickly looked away when she caught them.

The bottom of the seventh began, and not five minutes into it, Alex pitched a breaking ball that the Somersets' batter got a piece of. He ran to first as the ball shot to Bones. He gulped it, throwing so hard to Cupid, he'd scooped up pebbles that sailed with the leather to first base. The runner slid and a substantial amount of dust and confusion arose at the first base bag as the Somerset runner's left foot crashed into Cupid's ankles and threw him off kilter. He fell, but the ball was in his glove.

Mr. Carpio didn't immediately make the call. Camille didn't take anything for granted. It was obvious to her the Somersets' player was out. But from the look in Boomer Hurley's heavily lidded eyes as he stormed the field, he thought otherwise.

Camille dashed out to meet him at first base.

"He's out," she stated, not giving Boomer the opportunity to speak first.

"He's not out," Boomer countered.

Thus ensued an argument that had Camille gathering every single detail she knew about the game—and then some. In the end, Mr. Carpio ruled that the Somerset player was indeed out. That the umpire had found in her favor gave her bottomless satisfaction.

But her excitement evaporated when Boomer blared, "You've been a pain in the ass since the day you set foot in a ballpark. You aren't manager material and you never will be. Skirts or no skirts."

She'd always been taught to treat her elders kindly. To respect their views, even when disagreeing—but her mother had also taught her never to let a fool make a fool of her. "Going by the criteria you set for yourself," she said in an even tone that masked the tremor in her voice, "then you're right. I'm not manager material."

The nostrils of his overly large nose flared. He stammered and flapped his gums, but no words came out. Then he blathered, "Just look at those players of yours. They look like a hive of honeybees in those uniforms, and you're the queen bee herself, *honey*. You aren't the Harmony Keystones. You're the Harmony Honeybees!"

The barb shouldn't have stung, but it did. The uniforms were a sore subject. "A uniform doesn't make the player. The player makes himself. And if he's good, the fans will know it. We're going to beat the pants off you today, Mr. Hurley."

Boomer's face seethed in anger. "Carpio doesn't allow cursing on his field. But if he did, I'd like to *really* give you a piece of my mind."

"Oh," she said, frowning in feigned sympathy, "I couldn't *possibly* take the last piece."

Then she turned and sat back down—to the supportive laughter of the Keystones, who'd heard every word. It was a long time before her heart quit its racing, but she was proud she'd stood up to Hurley.

The ball went back into play and a late-inning rally by the Somersets threatened the ninth. The bases were loaded with two outs. The game was Alex's to hold or lose. Cy Young came up to bat.

Camille held her breath. Alex raised both hands until they were level with his left eye. Striking a pose with attitude, he gazed at the ball for a long moment. He stood like a tower of iron. Like a man who could make the baseball in his hand do whatever he wanted it to.

He turned the baseball around once or twice to get the best grip, his biceps hard and tight. After a scowl at Specs and a glance at home plate, he nodded. Then he delivered the ball with the precision and rapid fire of a cannon. It was a pitch Cy clearly hadn't been expecting. All he could offer was a feeble, off-balance slash at the ball and bloop it. It rolled to Cupid for the last out.

The game was over: 7–6, Keystones. They'd won.

The players whooped and hollered, racing to the mound and jumping on Alex, knocking him over. The display was juvenile and silly, but Camille couldn't help wanting to jump right in, too. She stayed in the dugout, an immense feeling of satisfaction putting a smile on her lips.

Alex had had terrific fire and unbelievable drive today. He'd brought them out of the dungeon and into the light. And each player had been a part of it. This win wasn't a fluke. It had come to them because they'd played hard and worked together.

The players came into the dugout, animated and full of laughter. She tried to keep her professional composure, but it was difficult not to get caught up in all the merrymaking. Cradling her notebook in her arms, she told them in turn what a great job they'd done.

"And to show your appreciation," Charlie said with a wide grin on his face, "you can let us indulge in a round of beers tonight!"

She gave him a small smile. "If we win the next three games against the Somersets, then you can buy yourselves beer on our last night in Boston. How's that for incentive?"

Good-natured grumbles came her way.

Duke threw a towel around his neck. "Since we can't celebrate with suds, how about we buy you a steak for dinner, Miss Kennison?"

"Yeah. Show those St. James dining room folks we've got class," Doc added.

Camille glanced at Alex, who'd removed his cap, wiped the sweat off his forehead, and replaced the yellow hat to sit backward over his hair. "That would be nice. I'll wait for you while you change and then—"

"Egads, girls! Here they are!" The sudden excited screams of women filled the field as the other Boston fans were released from the ropes that kept them in the grandstands.

The group of glamorous ladies came straight to the

Keystones dugout, much to the delight of the players, who suddenly stood straighter, groomed their hair back with their hands, and shoved their chewing gum in their cheeks.

Female fans.

The Keystones hadn't been accosted thus far during their away games, as they hadn't done a whole lot to impress the crowd. Camille knew that there were women who followed baseball—more specifically, who followed the baseball players . . . and wanted more from them than just their autographs.

"Could you sign my hankie?" one woman asked Alex while shoving a lace-edged handkerchief and a fountain pen at him. "I thought you were so *wahn-da-ful* out there, Mr. Cordova."

Camille disregarded the niggling little tingle of jealousy she felt.

Alex obliged the lady. Impeccably dressed in a gray day suit, the titian-haired woman wore cosmetics, but it was apparent she wasn't a floozy—just a very modern dresser. Camille looked at her lips that were soft and colored quite artfully. Rose Delish. She'd seen the lip rouge this morning when she'd walked into Jordan, Marsh & Co. to gaze at the department store's lavish displays.

No doubt Alex liked the attention. He smiled, his teeth flashing white. He talked with the women, as did the other players. The ladies went on complimenting and flirting, some giggling and tittering behind their hands and some staring boldly at the players.

Camille stood back, her notebook in her arms. Miss Rose Delish was quite interested in Alex. She wouldn't let him get away—not that he was showing any signs of wanting to get away. He let her go on about how *wahn-da-ful* he was. How he was so strong and such a great pitcher and it was a crying shame that he didn't wear a Somersets uniform. Camille heard her go so far as to offer to show him Boston. With the other ladies trying to talk over each other to vie for his attention, Camille couldn't make out his reply. Not that it was any business of hers.

How could women not naturally flock to Alex? How could he not like it? He was a man who appreciated a pretty woman. Just because he'd taken a few seasons off didn't mean he'd changed his opinion of the women who congregated on the field after the game.

She found it hard to stand and watch as the women showered Alex with accolades in their coquettish voices. She didn't care to explain why the scene bothered her. It just did.

So instead, she thought about what she would wear to dinner.

Not that she'd be trying to impress Alex . . .

Chapter
❧ 15 ❧

Alex didn't show up for dinner.

Dressed in her finest mauve batiste, Camille ate, pretending the three tiers of flounces on her embroidered skirt were nothing special. That the blouse with its puff sleeves and tight wrists was just everyday attire. As was the crushed-velvet belt and the tease of underblouse that showed through the deep yoke of her waist.

She dabbed her mouth, and the thought of the lady with rose-colored lips popped into her head. She could just imagine what Alex was doing to those lips.

She made small talk with the players and tried her best to cover her disappointment. Every so often, she'd discreetly glance at the dining room doorway to see if Alex had arrived.

But he never appeared.

True to their word, the players had generously followed through and bought her a thick T-bone steak. The trouble was, she hadn't felt like eating it. She tried to enjoy her meal but was grateful when the waiter cleared her plate. This time, they hadn't had the trouble they'd had the night before in the dining room. The waiters gave them excellent service.

She declined dessert, thanked the players for her meal, then excused herself, but she didn't want to return to her room. Just as the sun began to slip behind the tall buildings, she left the hotel to run an errand. It didn't take long, and she soon returned with a tissue-wrapped parcel, small enough to fit inside her pocketbook.

Once in her room, she stood in front of the low dresser and its silver-backed mirror and withdrew the pins from her hair. Her blond tresses fell in loose spirals to her hips. Absently, she unbuttoned her cuffs.

She hadn't turned the wall sconce light up all the way, so the corners of her room were gray. With nimble fingers, she unfastened the belt from behind and draped it over her chair, then slid her arms out of her sleeves and hung the blouse in the wardrobe.

Wearing her skirt and the thin-strapped taffeta chemisette, she opened her pocketbook and took out her package. She unwrapped the pretty colored paper. Inside lay the small oval of cosmetic lip rouge she'd bought at Jordan, Marsh & Co. The color: Rose Delish.

Using a fine brush, she carefully applied the lip rouge. Leaning back, she viewed herself with a critical gaze. She didn't look overdone, did she? She did look different. Her lips seemed fuller, the bottom one broader. She moved this way and that to get a better look. She had never before realized she had a cupid's bow at the top of her lip. Now she did. Not overly exaggerated, but defined.

Sighing, she shook her head. She didn't know why she'd done such a silly thing as to buy lip rouge. She should wipe the cosmetic right off. And yet . . . she looked at her reflection once more.

She looked somewhat provocative.

The room was hot, its air unmoving. She dragged the vanity chair to the open window, sat, and turned on the electric fan that rested on the sill. She unbuttoned her shoes and removed her hose.

Outside, the night was dark and colored a deep blue-black. Lamplight from various buildings, the street corners below, and the skylight rooftops in the distance twinkled like candle flames.

It had been a long day. She was tired. But she couldn't help thinking about Alex, where he was, who he was with. The name Miss Rose Delish floated in her head. Maybe she was a floozy after all . . . floozies spent their evenings showing baseball players the town—showing them other things if the ballplayers were interested.

The fact that Alex had taken the woman up on her offer should have come as no surprise to Camille. She shouldn't have been bothered.

She wouldn't think about it.

Instead, she looked out the window for a long while. She wondered if Alex was in one of the buildings she could see, with the lights . . . off. It was none of her business. And yet, she thought about the times he'd kissed *her*. Her determination to remain solely professional was slowly being shattered. All it took was one look, one touch by Alex and she was ready to give way too much of herself to him.

She was wound up, but her eyelids grew heavy. Perhaps she'd wait up and listen for him to return to his room. It was only several doors down from hers. The players had come up a half hour ago. Since then, it had been quiet in the hall.

Quiet as a rundown clock.

Her lids closed. She fought sleep. But it had been a long day . . .

The next thing she knew, she was startled awake by a door closing in the hallway.

Unfolding her arms from the windowsill, she sat upright and smoothed the hair from her eyes. She momentarily forgot where she was, the interior of the room semidark. Furnishings came into focus, and the fan stirred the air in its whirling blades. Camille remained still a moment, then stood. She fumbled for her watch to view the hour. Bringing the timepiece next to the light, she read its face. Almost midnight.

Indecision had her thoughts drifting in a variety of directions—mostly conflicting. At length, she took her wrapper from the wardrobe and put her arms through the sleeves. She made sure the silk lapel edges came across each other securely to fully cover her underblouse, then she cinched the tie with a firm bow.

Leaving her room, she closed the door behind her and walked down the hallway. The cool, waxed wood grain of the floor under her bare feet caused her to pause and look down. She'd neglected to put on her slippers.

Once at Alex's door, she knocked.

The door opened. The physical dominance of Alex Cordova standing in the frame displaced her motives for seeing him. She fought against the invisible pull of his powerful magnetism. Her foothold on the floor actually faltered, and she took an unthinking step that was more of a backward trip. It hadn't been his gaze that rocked her senses into a plunging spiral. It was his state of dress. Rather, undress.

He wore pair of denim pants. The fabric was worn thin at the slashes of pockets, at the knees, and at the button fly as if he'd leaned up against one too many counters. The rich navy color had grown pale, almost the shade of snow with winter sun reflecting off it.

The way he filled out the cloth was indecent. She shouldn't have let her gaze linger over the sinful way the material molded his thighs. Or the way the waistband fit around his trim waist, the belt loops empty. His rock-hard physique held the fabric snugly against him.

And yet, it wasn't just the fit of his pants that caused her breath to catch.

He was shirtless, the flame from glass globes in the hall lighting every contour, every taut ripple and dimension of his chest. She'd never seen his bare chest before, although she had wondered what he'd look like.

But not even in her most uninhibited thoughts had she imagined the true extent of his beautifully proportioned body. His biceps strained with a pronounced strength. Flat and corrugated with muscles, his belly looked as if it could stop a fist without even flinching. Nipples the color of warm earth nestled in a covering of dark hair that tapered in a soft line to his navel. A small gold medal hung from a chain around his neck. The dim light caught on the shining metal when he folded his arms over his chest and crossed one foot over the other to lean into the jamb. She couldn't quite make out the image on the tiny round piece; it almost looked like a robe-wearing man with a staff. She'd never seen anything like it.

Alex stood somewhat sideways to her, giving her a shadowed view of his right side, his back to the opened panel of the door. She lifted her eyes to his and found his gaze fixed on her. Most aptly, her lips. She'd forgotten about the lip color. His study of her descended, slowly, to her breasts and waist, then to her hips, and finally, to her bare feet. What must he think of her? His eyes lifted and he waited for her to say something. His black hair had been swept from his forehead, the ends damp and appearing as if he'd just run a wet comb through them.

Camille fought to put a coherent sentence together in her head, and when she spoke, she sounded ridiculously breathless. "I was awake going over tomorrow's lineup and I heard you come in. What I mean is . . . I assumed it was you coming in because you missed dinner." Never before had she been so flustered in a man's company. She was rambling like a silly young girl, yet she couldn't seem to pull her thoughts together. "I wanted to let you know that the front desk can send a fan up to your room if you're hot."

One dark brow arched upward; his mouth curved. "I wasn't a minute ago, but now I am."

"Oh, well . . . yes. It's hot in the hallway, too." She was utterly confused. Her gaze lowered once more to his chest, to the medal, to the muscles that worked over his arms as he straightened. Uncontrollably, the muscles in her lower belly tightened. "I just wanted to let you know about the fan . . ."

"I appreciate the thought, Miss Kennison."

Miss Kennison.

They were back to that again. Miss Rose Delish was probably Rose, or whatever her real name was. Camille couldn't explain to herself why she felt disappointed with the formal address.

She absently twisted the sash of her robe in her fingers. "I'd better let you get some sleep . . . we want to win tomorrow's game."

Is that perfume I smell?

Then a thought jolted her. What if he wasn't alone? What if there was a woman in his room? Right now. How stupid could she be to stand out here and go on about fans when he could have company?

"I'm sorry I disturbed you. . . . I have to go now. . . . I mean, you're busy and I just wanted to mention the fan because it's hot and I—"

Unexpectedly, he gripped her wrist, gently pulled her inside the room, then quietly shut the door behind her. She was so startled, she could hardly breathe, much less move.

She sputtered in confusion, "Mr. Cordova, what's this all about?"

"I couldn't leave you out there reciting all that crap about the fan. Somebody might hear you, open their door, see you out there in your unmentionables, see me in here without mine and come to conclusions."

In a rush, she denied, "But I'm not in my unmentionables."

His warm fingers touched the edge of her wrapper and slipped beneath the fabric at her throat, causing her to gasp with surprise. "Close enough."

Roughened from playing ball, his knuckles skimmed over her bare skin where the taffeta underwaist did little to cover the tops of her breasts. Then the back of his hand slid lower, toward her waist, slowly loosening the silk.

With a will of their own, her eyelids lowered and her lips parted. She felt herself swaying toward him. What was she thinking? That was the problem. She *wasn't* thinking. "I didn't mean it to look like I was inviting myself into your room. I honestly wanted to tell you about the fan and . . ."

. . . *And maybe I was curious about you and Miss Delish.*

She gazed about the interior, which was bathed by two keyed gaslights, one in the ceiling, one on the wall beside the bed. The only people in the room were her and Alex. No other woman. No sign of a woman. Men's clothing was scattered over the chair's arms and back, as was Alex's uniform and his shirt. A suitcase with the lid open rested on the floor.

And a fan had been set on top of the bureau. The blades purred.

"Oh . . ." she whispered, "you already have a fan."

"Yeah." His mouth mesmerized her when he spoke. "But it isn't cooling me off."

She rose a hand to her throat and swallowed.

The air in the room felt thick and sultry. Her wrapper seemed to cling to her. Although she was fully covered she felt naked in front of him.

As if he could read her mind, huskiness lowered the volume of his next words. "You look like you're going to melt from wearing too much."

She didn't speak, unable to think of a decent reply. She couldn't very well deny she was without her blouse. It was true. And it was also true that she had no business being in his room. At this hour, or any other. If she wanted to maintain propriety, she should turn around and leave right now.

"You need a long, cool soak in a bathtub," he suggested, the sight of his bare chest making it hard for her to follow what he said next. "One August in New York when we were playing the Giants, I had the hotel bring up an old-fashioned bathtub to my room and fill it with cold water. I put the fan on the windowsill and soaked while the air breezed over me. Stayed in there for the afternoon reading *Good Housekeeping,* smoking cigarettes, and drinking beer."

In a tub naked. Reading a magazine. Good Housekeeping? *Drinking beer. Smoking cigarettes.* The vision of Alex that filled her mind was virile and unabashedly at ease, with heat-quenching droplets running over bronzed, bare skin. She really should leave . . .

Alex went to the bureau, toward the fan. When he turned away from her, she saw the scars and instantly grew unsettled by the fierce tattoo on his shoulder. She could feel the blood drain from her face. All of her past bewilderment and confusion welded together. He was a complex man, not easy to know because he let so little of himself show. But with the turn of his back, she now knew where one piece of the puzzle fit.

She knew why he was called "the Grizz."

Alex turned up the speed on the Emerson fan. Thick air churned behind him and sluggishly crept through the room. Facing her, he asked, "Can you feel it?"

When she didn't answer, his eyes followed hers to his shoulder. He didn't initially say anything. The image itself said everything, as did the scars. They were claw marks. The tattoo was that of a grizzly bear's head and upper body. What made the drawing so vivid was the fact that the grizzly's arm had been penned midswipe, making it appear ferociously real with the fluid move of Alex's body.

"It was no big deal," Alex said, his jaw suddenly tight.

"It is a big deal. It's who you are. Alex 'the Grizz' Cordova." She moved toward him, her gaze never wavering. "What happened?"

He inhaled, ran his hands through his hair. "It was a long time ago and it was a stupid thing to do. I wish I could say I was drunk when I got it. But I was stone-cold sober."

"I wasn't talking about the tattoo." She'd drawn up to his side. "What happened to *you?*" Tentatively, she reached out and touched the curve of his shoulder. The hot skin jumped beneath her fingertips, but she didn't stop her exploration. She skimmed the smooth, marble-hard flesh of his shoulder and back; then traced the five subtle ridges.

Their noses nearly brushed as he looked down and she looked up, their breath fused together. "I had a run-in with a bear who seemed to want me dead," he said, the tone of his voice belying his light words. "When I didn't die, I thought the spirit of the grizz was in me—was with me and made me a better player when I went back to Baltimore after the attack."

"Where did it happen?"

"Up near Alder."

Her chin lifted a fraction, their noses met. "Really? In Montana." That he'd been there before and she hadn't known it made her feel queer. Like they'd been meant to know each other, but it hadn't been the right time until now.

"Yes." His arms encircled her waist and he brought her flush against him. As if he needed her.

Her arms remained at her sides, but she made no protest. The flat of his belly pressed the knot of her robe's tie. Through the thin fabric, she felt the hard contours and definitions of his body as he settled next to her. She felt herself dissolving, but she did her best to tamp the feeling down. "Why were you in Montana?"

"My manager, George Dunlap, sent me out there after the ninety-five season. I had a bad year and he told me to get out of town and rethink why I played ball." His mouth all but touched hers. She could practically feel the vibration of his lips while he spoke. "I went. What the hell did I have to lose? So I stayed at a lodge and I had nothing to do. I'd get up and walk out to this meadow I found and I hit baseballs. No one was around to hunt them down for me, so I had to find them myself." He brought his lips over hers. So briefly, so lightly, she almost thought she had imagined the kiss. "What do you have on your mouth?"

His sudden change in topic had her lifting her lashes to stare into his eyes. At the time, it had seemed a silly whim to have bought the cosmetic. Now that she'd been found out, she felt ridiculous. "Lip rouge."

Alex scowled. "What the hell for?"

"Because . . . it's called Rose Delish."

Raising his arm, he rubbed the pad of his thumb slowly over her lower lip, removing the traces of rose pink rouge. Her breath came out in a shaky exhale as he touched her as intimately as if they were lovers. "Am I supposed to know what that is?"

"Maybe . . ." Her voice was but a choked whisper. She wouldn't dare say why she thought he should. It seemed insignificant now. Nothing else mattered but the two of them. In this room. Together. At this moment.

He kissed her once more, with a lazy exploration that made her bones feel like they were melting. "You do taste delicious. But then you always have to me, honey."

Oh God. That made Camille bring her arms around Alex's neck and hold him. For some strange reason, she wanted to cry. The broad expanse of his chest became her pillow; her cheek lay against him, her head was tucked beneath his chin. A heady, musky scent clung to his skin, making her so aware of him, it was almost anguishing to be this close. "Is that how the bear found you? In the meadow?"

"Yeah." His voice rumbled beside her ear. "I heard a crack above my head and a low growl. I barely had time to see what was coming down on me from the tree. The next thing I knew, she'd straddled my chest and I couldn't go anywhere. Once you hear that snarl, you never forget it." The blunt ends of his fingernails moved over the silk of her wrapper as he lightly stroked her back. The slow, deliberate motion raised the gooseflesh on her arms.

In a voice just barely audible, she asked, "Then what happened?"

"I didn't move. Maybe I should have tried to run, but the honest truth is, I was too scared. I felt my legs grow numb and I didn't know how badly I'd been cut until I felt the stickiness of blood at my shoulder." He pressed a kiss at her temple, making standing difficult. "My first thought was, *Don't let it be my pitching arm.*"

Camille lifted her face to his. "How did you get away?"

"The grizzly just went off on her own after a few minutes. I figured I could walk back to the lodge, take a few stitches, and be all right in a day or two. Damned if I didn't get fifty-six of them and end up stuck in bed for a month. I don't remember how I made it back. Determination, I guess. She cut me good. On the shoulder." He stood back and pointed to the side of his abdomen, where rows of tiny scars were barely visible. "On the stomach. On the back." He turned so that she could see the opposite shoulder. "On my legs." His hand went for the button fly of his denims.

She blurted, "I don't need to see."

"Don't you?" The beginnings of a smile tipped the corners of his mouth.

The distraction he presented was difficult to resist. Trying to keep her thoughts clear, she said, "So you stayed in Montana for a while, then went back to Baltimore?"

Bringing her close once more, he murmured, "Something like that."

"What do you mean?"

"I mean I watched the sun rise and set for the first time in my life and I appreciated it. I felt a soul connection with that grizz. It had more to do with being a survivor than anything else." He ran his palms down her arms, then slid his hands upward inside the sleeves of her wrapper, until he caressed her shoulders. "I stayed in Montana for the rest of the winter." His lips claimed hers again in a kiss that lingered. "I had the tattoo put on by an Indian man. At times," he said, his mouth continuing to graze hers as he spoke, "I can still feel the grizz's paw on me. That quick and sinewy power. That's why I wanted the tattoo before I left Alder. To make sense out of the attack. If I could see the grizz with me, it would be real and I'd be better for its having happened to me. And that's how Alex 'the Grizz' Cordova came back to the city."

His hands pulled her closer. The swells of her breasts crushed against him in sweet agony. "And you never told anybody the reason why."

"Nope." His fingers massaged, easing away her tension. "I pitched the best season of my career afterward. We won the pennant. Year after that, we won it again . . . and then we might have the next . . . but . . ."

His words trailed off and he kissed her, slipping his tongue between her lips. The kiss turned heated and wanton, their mouths clinging together. Alex pushed her wrapper off her shoulders. It floated to her ankles. His tongue probed the recesses of her mouth sensually. It was quite drugging—quite the most extraordinary feeling she'd ever had.

She reached up to slip her fingers into his hair, holding his head close to hers, kissing him without thought or regard for consequences. His hair was long and glossy, silky to her touch. She loved the feel of it. She loved his mouth on hers, his tongue dueling with hers.

"I recognized your hat today," he said between kisses. "I told you not to wear it."

"I wanted to."

"You fixed it up."

Her mouth caught his. "I unfixed it. I like my hat."

"You do?"

"I do. When I wear it, I think of you."

He backed her toward the bed. She made no protest as he leaned over her and lowered her into the comforter to lay beside her. His fingers slid up her waist, then tilted her face so he could kiss her with a lazy and swirling penetration of his tongue. She should have taken this moment for what it was—stolen, fleeting. It was harmless. Or was it?

In spite of telling herself it shouldn't matter, she asked against the wet fullness of his mouth, "Why didn't you come to dinner?"

"It just wasn't the right day to celebrate."

"Why not?"

He combed her hair with his fingers, catching a fistful and bringing it to his lips. "I had something to do."

Looking up into his face, she searched his eyes. "What?"

"You ask a lot of questions." He took her jaw between his hard fingers.

He was about to kiss her when she raised her fingertips and pressed them on his mouth. "Because today you've been answering them."

For a long moment, he said nothing. His voice was low and deep, thick with desire when he answered. "I was at church."

She didn't move. His reply took her utterly by surprise. "Church?"

"Yeah. I've been known to go in one every now and then." The ends of his hair tickled her nose as he dropped down to kiss the side of her neck.

"Really? Church?"

Putting his weight on his arms, he straightened his elbows. "Church of the Immaculate Conception on Harrison Avenue."

Embarrassed, she blurted, "You weren't with Miss Delish?"

"Who?"

His finger traced the edge of her underwaist. Her breasts strained at the tight fit of fabric, leaving little more than her nipples hidden in the piece of underwear. "Never mind." She shivered with unbridled pleasure as he slowly grazed her damp skin, exploring the curves and valleys, looking at her.

Light caught the medal around his neck. It swung on the chain away from his chest. She lifted her hand to capture it. It was indeed a man wearing a robe, staff in hand and crossing what looked to be water, carrying a child on his back. "What's this called?"

"Saint Christopher."

"Who is he?"

"The patron saint of travelers. My grandfather gave him to me. He's supposed to keep me safe."

"Does he?"

His mouth curved. "Not when I'm with you, Miss Kennison."

She heated like an ignited match when his fingertip teased her nipple. It rose, hard and swift, beneath the circles his fingertip made. "Why don't you call me Camille anymore?"

"If I don't call you Miss Kennison, I'm liable to get real comfortable with you. Do you want that?"

She swallowed. Right now, she didn't know what she wanted. Yes, she did, but it came with a price. Change. Change in the way Alex would view her. The way she would view herself. Flirtations, coquettish laughter, and her arm through a man's while strolling . . . that had been the extent of her experiences with men.

Until Alex.

No man had ever kissed her the way he did, touched her breast, her nipple. No one had ever made her want to feel every inch of his naked skin, be with him in a way she never should have thought about.

He'd shown her she could be passionate. Could crave intimacy and the pleasure it brought her body. But if she let him know her in the way that a husband knew his wife . . . She didn't want to confuse what she was feeling now with love. Love couldn't be reasoned out of. It was a woman's greatest bliss—but her deepest sorrow when lost. She'd read poetry. She knew that more times than not, it came with bittersweet pangs.

Beyond that, marriage wasn't something she thought about. Perhaps in the future . . . With one touch, Alex made her feel like she was the only woman he'd ever desired to be with.

Her heart fluttered wildly as she gazed up at him. "What I want is for you to call me Camille."

He lowered his head within inches of hers. The air stirred by the fan passed over them and did little or nothing to cool her skin. She lay there, drowning in a flood tide of heat. Her whole body felt thirsty.

Several seconds lapsed, then Alex softly kissed her.

Her arms came over his shoulders as if they belonged there, now and for always, holding him close as he kissed her.

Time was suspended.

Alex pushed up her underblouse until it came to her collarbone. From the way they lay beside one another, the whalebone of her corset barely kept her breasts firmly in place. He pulled the top hooks, freeing her breasts from their tight confinement. He bent his head over her, stroking one nipple with his tongue. Camille sucked in her breath, her back arching as he traced a slow circle around her with his tongue.

His touch felt so good it almost made her chest ache. Her mind reeled. Feeling this way made her crazy, and at the same time, she didn't want the feelings to end. She wanted to have him in her arms forever.

Between the damp caresses he gave her breast, he asked, "You want me to stop?"

"No!" Her reply was too quick, too telling.

He pulled her into his mouth again, hot darts of pleasure warming the center of her. The flat of his belly pressed snug against her side. When he spoke, his head was still bent forward. "Are you sure?"

That he had to ask . . . "Yes." His hair tickled her skin and caused her to shiver.

She clutched his shoulders. The fine stubble on his chin abraded her as he nuzzled the valley between her breasts.

"No man has given you a hat but me," he murmured. "And I'd bet that no man ever has"—he caught the fabric of her skirt and inched the hem up to her waist—"done this."

Her heartbeat pounded in her ears. "No."

A smile bracketed his mouth. "Then I'd better make sure you like this better than the hat."

Oh God.

Without her being completely aware of what he'd been doing, he'd taken her skirt and petticoat and brought both folds of fabric to her waist. His hands slowly caressed, teased . . . explored. His fingers trailed up her inner thigh and made her shudder. The building pressure in her was so intense, she couldn't speak.

"You lost your stockings and shoes," he said, gazing down at her.

"I left them in my room."

"A good place for them." His fingertip traced the hooks and eyes down her corset front. She couldn't help arching her back. His brown eyes darkened, as he watched her face, gauging her reaction as she gasped for breath in response.

Exposed to his hot gaze were her French-patterned pantalets that were so delicate, they did little to cover her. His warm palm cupped the apex between her legs.

His touch shocked her. She should have told him to stop. Without conscious thought, her thighs separated when they should have clamped together.

"Want me to stop?"

She closed her eyes, tightly. *Say yes. Say yes. Say yes.* "No. I don't want you to stop." The words were throaty; they didn't feel like they belonged to her.

"Then open your eyes, honey, so I can watch you."

She lifted her lashes, grateful the room wasn't all that bright. If it was, she would have—No, she wouldn't. A sigh escaped her lips and she lifted her hands into his hair. It was silky and cool and warm at the same time. She wanted him to kiss her, to—

With only the near-sheer lawn of her pantalets covering her, he massaged the most intimate place on her body. Thoughts of kisses fled. She'd never let her imagination go this far. She hadn't been prepared for how she'd actually feel when it happened. For how the touch would consume her, make her pulse.

"Alex . . ." She held him in her hands pulled his mouth to hers. She put her lips to his. Soft. Barely touching. She gave him a light kiss, then pulled his head back.

The way Alex moved his fingers over the barely nothing fabric was maddening. This was taking a kiss and turning into something she had no experience in.

The need she felt for him to touch her made her senses spin. She'd been brought up a proper Victorian woman, and these feelings, these things he did to her, they upset her balance, her reasoning. And yet she had to confront where this was leading.

"I can't . . . that is . . . I—" His palm rubbed her sensitive flesh and the hot ache in her intensified. "This is wonderful, but I . . . can't—"

"I'm not asking you to do anything." He slowly twirled his thumb over her, jolting her so that her jaws clenched. "I'm giving this to you. Like I gave you the hat. Just enjoy it."

He tortured her slowly at first, then with an artful stimulation that had her making small, helpless sounds in her throat. She didn't want him to look at her face and know how glorious she felt, how wanton . . . or to hear the gasp that she caught with her teeth . . . or to see how her eyelids slid closed in utter ecstacy.

His voice came to her, low and whiskey smooth. "Do you like when I touch you?"

Oh help, that wasn't a question she wanted to answer. The truth was painfully embarrassing. Why would he want to know? Why did it matter to him anyway? There was no reason to give him a verbal confirmation of what clearly must be written over every inch of her body, of her skin.

"Do you?" he asked once more when she didn't reply.

Eyes slipping open, legs stretching taut, her pelvis straining against his hand, she dared look at him. Hoarsely, she whispered, "Yes."

With that one word, he slipped his hand inside her pantalets and increased the tempo of his thumb and forefinger. She didn't even think about the sheer intimacy of it. What he did to her was like nothing she'd ever felt before. That he could do this, evoke such desire in her without her being undressed, left her feeling fragmented—not whole until she reached that place he was destined to take her by the way he stroked and touched.

"Then don't fight me."

"I'm not."

"You are." He kissed the sensitive spot behind her ear, his breath hot in her ear. "Your teeth are clenched, honey."

Everything in her was clenched, and if she didn't let it go, she wasn't going to be able to breathe. An ache in her breasts tugged, drawing her into an exquisite harmony with the motion of his hand. His expert fingers moved in a tempo that made her toes curl.

Alex's voice was tender, almost a murmur, as she melted beneath his touch. "It's okay, Camille."

She shattered, releasing the tension wound so tightly within her. And as she rocked against his splayed fingers, her pulse spun. She was helpless to halt her breath from coming out in long, surrendering moans. A climax of indescribable heat surged through her. Fulfillment she couldn't have begun to describe made her tremble, made her pant, made her reach out to Alex and bring him to her.

He captured her moist lips with a kiss. "You're beautiful to watch." His words shook her, just as tangibly as the shudders that centered between her thighs.

She could barely trust herself to speak. "Don't say that."

"You *are* beautiful, Camille."

Unbidden, her eyes filled with tears. How many times had she been told that? But right now, what did she want him to tell her? *Camille, you are the smartest woman I've ever brought to fulfillment.* So she took his words, embraced them, and believed—truly—that he meant every part of her was beautiful to him.

He traced her upper lip. "You don't need Rose Delish to pinken your mouth. You need only me."

Too many emotions collided inside her at the very thought that she needed him. She didn't want to. How could she? She had to prove herself to her father first—*and* prove to herself she could make the team better because of her know-how—before she could fall in love. Why, then, didn't her heart listen to her? Why, then, did it trip and skitter whenever she was near this man? She couldn't love Alex. It would ruin everything—her purpose, and his. It would be horrible.

It would be heaven.

She struggled to sit up. As if he understood, he pressed his forehead to hers. She let the warmth of his skin soak into hers. Then he pulled back. "I know. You have to go."

Not wanting to leave and yet wanting to—both clashed within her. He helped her put her underwaist on as she sat beside him. Tugging her skirts down, she felt her cheeks grow warm once more. The fan did little to cool her skin. Its breeze passed over them, intertwining her skirt between his legs, billowing her hair across his shoulder. Touching, yet without touching.

Alex got up from the bed, went to the center of the room, and picked up her robe. As he came back to the bed, she rose. When she stood, her knees nearly gave out. He steadied her, brushing her lips with a gentle kiss. Then he put her robe on for her, tying the sash in a neat bow.

Tucking a curl behind her ear, he offered, "I'll walk you to your room."

He kept the door to his room ajar while taking her down the hall. Once at her door, she turned and pressed her back to the panel. He raised his arm above her, resting his wrist on the jamb over her head.

A smile lazed on his lips. "I'm glad you liked your hat, honey. See you in the morning."

Then he left her standing there feeling thoroughly debauched . . . and, heaven help her, wanting him to debauch her again.

Chapter

❧ 16 ❧

The train broke down in Dorothy, Wisconsin, on the Fourth of July. A piston froze and quit on the Chicago & Northwestern a day away from Harmony. Since the disk had been antiquated to begin with, and Dorothy was ancient itself, the small town's railway yard didn't stock that particular part at this time.

Nor at any other time.

But given the fact the No. 1653 had stalled on rail lines smack in the city limits, the C & N was obligated to put passengers up for the night in a hotel of the company's choice. Their choice was the Buffalo Bill House, which happened to be the only hotel in town—in which Buffalo Bill had never stayed. But the residents of Dorothy were still hoping he'd show up one day, seeing as they'd named their only hotel after him.

The Keystones had been sitting on the crippled train for two hours with no news when the porter had come onboard and told them it wasn't a problem that could be fixed that day. The part had been ordered by telegraph and would arrive on the next train, which wasn't due in for twelve hours. Then it would take time for the engine to be repaired.

Alex disembarked from the train, stretching his tight muscles. This particular line of the rail didn't have upper berths like the New York Central, and he'd had to bend himself into a wicker seat to sleep. Hot as it had been while they were traveling, they'd kept the windows open. He'd been eating soot and cinders all night long and half the day.

Once on the platform, he lit a cigarette from the pack he'd bought for himself. There was no point in bumming them off of Charlie all the time. He'd all but resumed the habit. But when he got back to Harmony, he told himself he'd quit again.

As he waved out the match, he watched as Camille dusted her blue skirt while stepping down with help from the porter. Her ever-present parasol was missing, as were her white gloves. She hadn't gotten rid of the hat, though. Although not huge like the one he'd given her, this one was big enough. It looked like birds were taking a bath on the low crown. Not exactly his style, but he had to concede it was a step up from the basket of fruit she'd had on the other day when they'd played the White Stockings.

She discreetly yawned, then tried to extend her cramped limbs without being obvious. They were all dead beat from the road travel, but to Alex, she wore the fatigue well—kind of sleepy, kind of sensual.

He remembered how she'd looked on his bed. How her lips had tasted. How her pale blue eyes had slid closed when he'd brought her to satisfaction. He'd wanted to be with her. He'd wanted her, wanted to give her the kind of pleasure he was sure she had never experienced. But he'd known then, just as he'd known the first day he saw her in his wood shop, she was a lady—a lady who didn't trifle with men and didn't give herself away.

If he wanted Camille Kennison, then he had to give himself to her as a husband. Because anything less wasn't good enough for a woman like her. He could accept that. Didn't mean he was going to propose. But he was smart enough to know when he couldn't get his heart involved.

He could have gone out and found a woman to ease the hardness in his groin after he'd walked her to her room. But he hadn't. Because no other woman would have been the one he wanted. The only face he would have seen beneath him would have been Camille's.

"Sir, could you direct me to the stationmaster's office?" she asked the porter. "I've got to send a telegram right away."

The porter showed her to the office behind Alex. She averted her gaze as she walked by, just as she had been averting her eyes every time she had seen him since the night in Boston. They hadn't been alone in eight days, so whatever had been between them that night no longer existed. He didn't care to rationalize why that thought disturbed him.

As he drew on his cigarette, he assumed she was sending her father a message that they'd be late. He didn't think they'd make it to Harmony in time to play the Philadelphia Athletics.

The Keystones had swept the Somersets four straight games, and true to her word, Camille sent them out for a night of beer drinking. Alex had gone; it felt right to fall in with the Keystones, to have some rounds of beer, play a few hands of poker, and talk about the games in which they'd whipped the Somersets because they'd been good enough those four days.

Early the next morning, they'd caught the New York Central rail to Chicago. Their wins against Boston had been miraculous—too miraculous to maintain. They'd lost all three games to the White Stockings.

When Camille walked past him from the office, her perfume lightly on the air, Alex fought the tightening in his belly. He pitched his smoke, then ground the butt beneath his heel while gazing across the street.

There wasn't much to the town, just a wide-open plaza without any trees or shrubs and just dirt road and the wagons that rumbled down the span of dusty earth. From where he stood, he could see the building labeled CITY HALL with its brass bald eagle perched on the roof peak. There was no way to miss the patriotism emblazoned on the exterior. It looked as if the structure had been wallpapered with American flags.

"Hello, folks," came a man's deep voice that sounded as if it belonged in the bottom of a barrel. "I'm Mayor VanHorne."

Alex turned his attention to the man who wore a coat that was just as colorful as the building across the square. On its padded shoulders were red and white stripes and on the lapels were stars; the sleeves were blue. A tophat sat on his crop of yellow hair.

"All right, the first question I have to ask is . . ." —his glance slid across them with a wishful gleam— ". . . is anybody by chance Buffalo Bill?"

No one replied, so the mayor's mouth slipped into a crestfallen frown. "Well dang. All right then, we're going over to the Buffalo Bill House hotel." He began to walk, legs bowed, his polished shoe heels stirring up the dust. "Let me be the first to extend our fair town's hospitality. Lucky for you, the train broke down on the Fourth of July—you're invited to this afternoon's activities and evening's fireworks. You missed the parade, but I might be able to convince the fraternal orders to give it another run-through."

"Well, I'd rather skip that," Camille said behind Alex, her voice low so as not to carry. He wondered if she'd spoken the words to him, or to herself.

"You don't like parades?"

"Not today, I don't. I just want to cool off, slip between the clean sheets of a real bed, and call it a day."

"And miss the Fourth of July?"

"I don't need to watch a parade to celebrate," she muttered. "I'll wave a hand flag in my room before I retire."

Grinning at her lack of enthusiasm, he looked at her over his shoulder. "But what about the festivities? The footraces? The tug-of-war? All that stuff that's required to celebrate a holiday like the glorious Fourth?"

"I'm not the athletic type."

Alex measured her with a quick, appraising gaze. *No, you don't look the athletic type.* She looked the "kiss me" type to him. Lush lips, soft eyes, alabaster skin, high rounded breasts, slender waist, and hips that flared just right to fit in a man's palms. She was more suited to fine dresses and big hats, to parlors and socials—indoor things that brought out all that fancy deportment she wore on her sleeves.

She might not be an outdoors woman, but he was thinking Miss Honey ought to have a little outdoor fun.

Even if she didn't think so.

An hour later, Camille found herself on a field of grass, right leg tied to Alex's left, hopping toward a chalk finish line.

"I don't know why I'm doing this," she said in a rush, holding her skirt up with one hand while trying to stay in sync with Alex's long leaps. Their shoulders bumped, elbows tangled, and thighs rubbed. Each contact of his hard body with hers shot through her like a charged wire.

Without sounding winded in the slightest, he replied, "Because I dared you."

"Yes, that's right." The crimped hairpins securing her curls in place slipped lose. "I should have let the dare go unchallenged."

"But you didn't."

No, she hadn't. So here she was, her legs kicking up her blue muslin skirt as she ran. The lace edge of her snowy petticoat was exposed in plain view, but she was having a hard time feeling improper.

Alex slipped his arm around her waist to keep her from putting space in between them. Being this close to Alex in front of people . . . she wondered what they would think of her—of them.

She supposed her discomfort had more to do with her guilty conscience than anything else. She'd had to put on a bold front to face him the morning after she'd been in his room. In the stark light of day and with a mind that was perfectly clear, she was embarrassed by her behavior. It was hard to think about herself as the woman lying on Alex Cordova's bed, Rose Delish on her lips. She couldn't bring herself to think about her blouse and skirt, rumpled and disheveled, or his hands on her body.

Because then she'd have to face up to the fact that she'd encouraged him . . . just as she felt like encouraging him now while tied to his leg in a foolish footrace.

She should have said no when he'd asked her. Giving in to him made her face the undeniable and dreadful facts: She was far too attracted to Alex. And not only in a physical sense. She liked being with him, talking with him, touching him, watching him laugh, listening to his voice—having his hands on her.

She didn't know how to deal with her teetering emotions. Before, she would have liked the attention. Now she felt vulnerable, naked, a target for his speculation about what had possessed her to knock on his door wearing a robe.

At that last thought, Camille stumbled into Alex and leaned heavily on his shoulder. She would have fallen if he hadn't tightly gripped her waist. Her face heated and she mumbled an apology. He merely gave her a smile that rocked her to her soul.

Another pair crossed the finish line by a long margin. Nobody was even close to the winner's speed. Camille concluded the couple must have been practicing since last Fourth of July. She and Alex were horrible at it because she went out of her way to avoid body contact—an impossibility with their knees bound and pressed together.

Cupid came running over, along with Jimmy and Duke. "You didn't even come close," the first baseman complained.

Her breasts rising and falling from the effort, Camille shrugged and made a futile attempt at shoving her hairpins back in place without her hat sliding down her forehead. "We tried."

She stood still as Alex lowered himself to one knee and lifted her petticoat up. The starched linen had a dry rustle to it. He untied the rope that she'd felt snag her stockings at the calf. His knuckles skimmed over her in a way that could be seen as accidental. But she knew better—she knew his touch.

Searing heat clung to her damp skin, and she did her best to hide her disquiet. His fingers traveled down her calf to where the kid lace stay of her shoe began. He checked the lace, as if to see if it was secure. Of course it was. She'd double tied it before the race, fearing she'd fall flat on her face if one of the laces came undone. His thumb made a quick circle around the top of her ankle where the shoe leather started, then he released his hold. The scratchy rope removed, she stepped away from him and smoothed down her skirt with a little too much vigor. Cupid gave her a puzzled look.

She merely arched her brow at him; he said nothing.

"Tug-of-war is next," Noodles said, drawing up to them. "Who's in?"

Camille spoke up quickly. "Not me."

Cub grunted. "It's not for ladies. Only men."

"Oh. Well, good." She adjusted her sleeve cuffs. "I'll watch from the shade of that tree."

And so she did, glad to be on the sidelines. Alex took part in the rope pull, his muscles straining as he held on. He smiled, his white teeth contrasting with his tan face. He actually joked around with Cub when their team won against the opposing side. This was something that would not have happened at the start of the season. She noted that Alex had been welcomed into the club somewhere along the miles of train travel and was no longer considered an outsider, an intruder.

With that thought, she wondered about her role with the Keystones. A disciplined manager was never supposed to form an emotional attachment to the players. At least that's what her father always went on about. Camille feared it was too late for that advice. Fondness made her smile as she watched Specs wiping his spectacle lenses on the tail of his shirt before putting them back on—only to squint. Cupid and his bald head with the sun shining up the top after he removed his hat. Doc casually perusing the field grass for clovers. Duke and Bones limbering up for the tug-of-war by touching their toes. Yank, Jimmy, and Noodles laughing at a joke. Charlie and Deacon drinking lemonade. Yes, it was too late to heed her father's advice. She was unable to prevent herself from keeping her distance. She'd already invested her heart into this team.

At first, she'd wanted to take them to the pennant to show her father she could do the job. But she now wanted the players to see just how good they could be, how deserving they were to play for the coveted prize. They could do it. Boston proved that. What happened in Chicago . . . that was disappointing.

As she pondered how to get the spirit of Boston back into the team, her gaze fell on Alex. It would seem he held the key to their success. When he wanted to be, he was a brilliant player. And so much more.

"Folks, next is the bicycle races," Mayor VanHorne announced through a megaphone. "Five people to a race, on account of we only have five bicycles in the whole town—compliments of Mr. E. Whippy . . . who has said that after the race he'll be renting them out for fifty cents an hour." The mayor's stars-and-stripes suit flashed beneath the sun as he waved his arm. "So come on over and sign up."

Camille waved to Specs, who secured one of the bicycles and was giving it a test run—right into a picnic table.

Several of the town ladies stood by a soda fountain stand and Camille wandered over to get a cool drink. She watched the bicycle races play out in groups. Jimmy was rather good at it—good enough to win. Alex rode one as well, the wind billowing his shirt as he pressed for the finish. He lost by a small margin, got off, and waved Yank in, who wobbled and finally tumbled before coming close.

The bicycle races wound down, and were followed by performances by a band on a decorated stand. For the past few minutes, they'd been playing their renditions of "Stars And Stripes Forever" and "Battle Hymn of the Republic." Then the mayor introduced a young woman by the name of Miss Idella Appleby who wore a flowing white toga, a grape wreath in her high-piled hair. She sang "My Country 'Tis of Thee" with such flourish, she'd stunned the crowd into silence. As soon as she quit, an encore was quickly called for—and received. She sang the song once more. When she came to "let freedom ring," she raised her arm high and her voice shot up an octave.

Most of the Keystones practically tripped over one another to get a better look at the woman whose bare arm resembled pure alabaster. Camille opted to bow out on the fourth encore. She wouldn't be missed.

She began to walk toward the hotel, the music fading behind her. She had barely reached the boardwalk when an elongated shadow crossed from behind her. She turned to find Alex grinning at her from a bicycle. The spoke wheels gleamed in the late-afternoon sunlight, as did the buckles on a leather basket that had been attached to the back fender. Alex's thumb rang the bell on the handlebars.

"Get on, honey, and we'll go for a spin."

She gazed at him askance. Actually, she gazed at the bicycle. She'd never ridden one in her life, but she knew that there was only one seat. And it was occupied.

"Yes, certainly," she quipped. "I'll sit on your shoulders."

She had no intentions of sitting anywhere on that thing.

"Interesting idea. But not what I had in mind." He circled her tightly, keeping her trapped in place. Each pass he made, he jingled the ringer like a child. The picture he made on that bicycle—long legs pumping the pedals, Stetson hat sitting high on his forehead, sleeves rolled up to his elbows—had her smiling. "Get on the handlebars."

Her eyes flew to the narrow bar of metal. "What?"

He stopped pedaling and put his right foot on the ground to hold the contraption steady. Extending his hand, he waited for her to take it. "You can do it. Just climb on."

"I'll fall off."

Her protest fell on deaf ears. "No you won't. I won't let you get hurt."

Her heartbeat slowed and her gaze drifted to his lips.

"You'll enjoy it," he said, his voice like gravel.

Her eyes shot up, her heart racing. She couldn't possibly enjoy the ride. She'd be scared to death. There was no place to hold on. "I can't."

"Can't or won't?"

"You're not going to dare me into anything again."

"I think so." She grew keenly aware of his eyes seeking hers. A slow and thorough assessment of her was clear in his expression. Her heart took another perilous leap; she couldn't let him affect her this way. "That night in my room you trusted me. Why can't you now?"

Biting her lip, she looked past him to the hotel. "I don't want to talk about what happened in your room." Then she said, "It shouldn't have happened. I . . ." She could say no more.

Alex reached out and took her hand. His fingers closed over hers. "I'm glad it happened. And I'm glad you felt the way you did. Not every woman does."

It took her an awkward moment to comprehend

what he meant. When she did, she was shocked by his words. Not only were they blatant but they were alarming. What was wrong with her? Why did she feel such passion in her and not all women did? She'd assumed her feelings were normal . . . but such a topic was just never discussed. She'd never asked another woman in her life about the details of lovemaking. Not even her mother, with whom she shared a close relationship.

Heavens, he was saying she was overly passionate! Suddenly she didn't know which was worse—the fact that she'd encouraged him to touch her or the fact that she had found release in his touch.

"Honey." His voice lowered and he brought his face close to hers. "Don't tell yourself you shouldn't have."

Camille drew in her breath. Why was it he could read her thoughts so perfectly at times?

"Now get on." His arm bent, pulling her to the bicycle, and she scooted closer. "I've got good balance on this thing. You won't fall off."

She looked at the handlebars, then at Alex. "I wouldn't even know how to get up there."

"Hike your skirt a little and hop up. I'll keep the bike steady."

"I'm suspicious. This is the second activity today where I've had to hike up my skirt."

"And it may not be the last," he said with an easy grin.

She'd walked right into that one.

Looking over her shoulder, Camille bit her lip. The group was still at the field beyond the plaza listening to Miss Appleby. None of the players would see her if she and Alex kept to the back streets and she took only a short ride.

She turned her attention back to Alex and the bicycle. Then she gave a soft sigh and grabbed her skirt and petticoats in her hand. That done, she stared at the handlebars and the large wheel just under them. What was she supposed to do now?

"Straddle it." Alex motioned to the tire. "Back up over it and then hop up."

If she was supposed to straddle a tire, she have to do more than hike her petticoat up. She'd practically have to bunch it to her waist. Lifting the fine blue fabric higher, and then even a smidgen higher, she gazed at the bottom edge of her pantalets. Gingerly, she backed up over the wheel, standing on tiptoe so she'd clear the rubber. Her skirt dragged over the sides of the wheel and caught on a spoke. She managed to free the hem.

"A little higher."

She shot Alex a dark frown, then inched her skirt higher.

"More."

She moved it up a tad more.

"More."

Exasperated, she blurted, "I might as well take my dress off."

"You could do that. But wait until we're alone."

She didn't comment on that as she stood taller and clutched the hand grips so that she could hoist herself up. "We'll go only down that street and back. All right?"

"Yeah, sure."

"You promise." She gazed at him. "Just right over there, then back here and you'll let me get off."

His inky hair fell over his collar, his ears, and his forehead. She never tired of looking at his face, the way he smiled. Even when she doubted his sincerity. "Absolutely."

"You promise?"

"I do." His eyes held hers. He was quite convincing.

She nodded, then faced forward and gave a bouncing leap so that she sat between the grips, where her hands held on with a death-clutch. The bicycle momentarily wobbled under her weight, but true to his word, Alex kept them from tipping over. Her backside wasn't very comfortable at all on the thin tube, but when she leaned back a little and got her balance, she felt all right.

"Okay. Just down there and back," she repeated in a shaky voice. Her skirt and petticoat were stuffed into the shallow dip of her lap, and her legs were open too immodestly. But if she brought them in any farther, her clothing would wind up in the spokes and then they'd certainly crash.

"I'm going to bring my foot up now, just hold on."

As if she'd let go.

His voice was deep and reassuring as he said, "Don't lean left and don't lean right."

"I won't."

He pushed off, bringing his feet to the pedals. In a matter of seconds, they were rolling smoothly down the street. Alex aimed them toward the end of the block, pushing hard on the pedals and gaining them speed. A breeze tickling her cheeks, her hat ribbons making fluttering noises on top of her head, and a smile on her mouth she was unable to contain, Camille laughed. Her voice held a giddy quality that was uncharacteristic of her. She was acting ridiculously unrefined.

But she didn't care.

Once at the juncture of the road where it forked east and west, Alex didn't turn around. He veered right.

Camille had let herself have fun because she knew the ride would be short. Now it didn't look that way and a quiver of panic made her elbows ache. "Where are you going?"

"Down here. Over there. A little of everywhere."

"But you said we'd go back."

A rich rumble of laughter came from his chest and rose to her ears. "I lied."

Chapter

❧ 17 ❧

Camille opened her mouth in dismay as the bicycle sped on. "Well, unlie. Take me back."

Alex only chuckled as the scenery rolled by.

"But—"

"I don't think so" was all he said as he pedaled them past the closed-for-the-holiday buildings on Main Street. The boardwalks were empty, no horses at hitching posts. They passed a white-spired church and weathered buildings. The dwellings went by in a soft blur of grays and browns—red brick for the firehouse. At the end of the street, the road turned into a lane marked by wildflowers on either side.

Alex turned the bicycle into a meadow of black-eyed Susans. The trail was narrow, only about a foot wide, as if it was used for horses. As the bicycle cut through the meadow, the hip-high flowers waved, their petals orange-yellow and their centers dark purple, lending a light fragrance to the air.

The wheels hit a rock and the bicycle bumped and

rattled. A squeal left Camille's throat. Surely she was going to fall off.

"I think we ought to turn around," she suggested. "It's too rocky."

"Sorry. No place to turn around."

There would be if they both got off the bicycle and faced it the right way—back to town. "We could—"

"Nope. Don't think so."

Camille adjusted her death grip on the handlebars, too scared to worry that her skirt might slip down her knees. "Are we going much farther?"

"Just a ways."

"How much of a ways?"

"See that barn over there?"

Tilting her head so that the brim of her hat kept the last remnants of blinding sun from her eyes, she viewed a red-and-white barn surrounded by outbuildings and a fenced pasture that held cows.

"That looks like private property."

"It is."

"But we—" Another bump jarred the two-wheeler, this time strong enough to loosen the pin from Camille's hat. "Oh, my hat's falling off! We have to go back."

"Yeah, looks like it's going to take flight."

Holding tightly for fear of falling into a rut, she felt her hairpins in her hair begin to slip. "I don't think you meant that very nicely."

"I didn't."

The fact that he wouldn't deny it proved he was the wrong type of man for her. A gentleman would have begged her pardon. A gentleman would be respectful of her wishes to turn around. A gentleman . . . would have been a lump of boring stuffiness.

Black-eyed Susans thinned out, taken over by

rolling hills alight with warm orange color and rich greens. There was a hay pasture and sporadic sunflowers. Alex turned onto a wagon wheel–grooved road and steered them to the barn's drive. At the top of the incline, he stopped the bicycle. She quickly hopped off.

On firm ground, she looked around. The knoll on which the farm stood was just high enough so she could see over the rooftops of Dorothy. They'd gone away from the crowd, but occasionally, Camille could hear a shout or laughter as it drifted up from the flatlands. Horses grazed on alfalfa in one pasture while tan cows did in another. A house was tucked behind a copse of cottonwoods. The barn had been freshly painted and a sign hung above its high double doors.

E. WHIPPY FARM

RENTALS: BUGGY, SURREY, BICYCLES

STUD SERVICE

Alex laid the bicycle on its side and came to stand beside her. His gaze followed hers to the sign. "You think he's talking about himself?"

She fought the urge to roll her eyes. "No, I don't think so. I saw him in town and he didn't look like a ladies' man."

He tucked a wisp of fallen hair behind her ear, sending an avalanche of tingles across her skin. "What does a ladies' man look like?"

With him this close, she could hardly think. She could fib, but there was no point. He knew it. She knew it. The cows probably knew it. Conceding, she said, "You."

"Is that so?"

The way he looked at her, he might as well have kissed her. She didn't know why he was doing this to her. "Do you want me to write it down?"

"Maybe you already have in that notebook you keep." He left her side and went to the bicycle's basket and undid the straps. "You say it's just for lineups and stuff. But there might be some good reading in there."

"I can assure you, there's not." Her mind quickly raced. Had she not once doodled a heart on one of the pages and put Alex's name in it? Or did she dream that she did that? Either way, it was mortifying that he'd come close to the truth. "What's that?" she asked as he revealed a small canvas bag. She hoped to distract him from the topic.

"Dinner."

"Dinner?" she blurted.

"Yeah. Come on."

"But I . . . that is, we can't just barge in here and make ourselves at home."

"Sure we can." Alex started up to the barn—more precisely, to the ladder anchored on its side. "I paid for the use."

"Paid for it?"

"I rented the bicycle for the night. And the barn."

"The barn?"

"Vantage point."

"For what?"

He paused, foot on the bottom rung of the ladder. "Fireworks." With a hand on one section of the rail, he extended his other. "Come on. You go up first. I'll be right behind you."

She took his hand, noting the calluses that had formed from months of holding the shaft of a pine-tarred bat in his grasp. "Afraid I'll run away?"

"Thought about it."

She ascended the ladder, wondering if he was looking at her ankles as she rose . . . or worse, at her underclothes. But he'd once seen them both in plain view. And more.

Once at the top, she stood on firmly planted feet. The roof was quartered, each section with its own pitch. Alex came up behind her and motioned to a flat section just below a weathervane. She went to it and sat.

She tucked her knees level with her breasts and looked out at the view. She had to admit, it was inspiring. The sun was setting, its orb of yellow like a burst of summer dahlias. She didn't mind that some of her hairpins had given way, leaving curls to dangle loose in places. This was nice. Quite thoughtful. Very sweet.

It was her first kidnapping. A shivaree without the fuss and noise. Or wedding license . . .

Alex opened the bag. She realized now that she was hungry for dinner after such a long day on the train. "What did you bring?" she asked.

"Cornflakes and beer." He came up with a box of Kellogg's cornflakes and two amber bottles of crown-capped beer.

"Cornflakes and beer?"

"It travels well on a bicycle." Running his finger beneath the fold of the box, he opened it. "Cereal's good. Do you eat it?"

"Yes. With milk and strawberries. In a bowl. For breakfast." She lowered her legs when he tapped her knee to indicate that he wanted to pour cornflakes into her lap. "I don't drink beer, though."

"Have you ever?"

"Well, no. But I've had sipping whiskey before." She remembered the time she'd snuck a splash of her father's when he hadn't been home—just to see the appeal in the liquor. She'd found none, although she'd definitely felt the whiskey go right to her head, along with a shiver of revulsion up her spine. "I got a little glow from it."

"Glow?"

"A lady of character doesn't refer to overindulgence as being drunk. The better word is *glow,* which indicates a combination being tipsy and not being oneself."

A side of his mouth lifted in amusement. "I never knew that."

"Now you do. Whiskey made me feel like a lightning bug, glowing from the inside. All dewy-eyed and warm."

He smiled. "Well, beer's entirely different from any kind of whiskey. But you can warm up to me anytime you like."

"I'm not altogether certain I want to chance beer. I don't believe I'm cut out for alcoholic refreshments. Not to mention," she added, giving him a stern frown filled with reprobation, "I have instituted restrictions against liquor, you know."

"And I have the day off, honey." Using an opener, he removed the cap and a soft burst of air came from the top. Handing her the beer, he opened the other one; his knuckle cracked as he did so.

She didn't immediately take a taste of the beer. She stared at his hand. His fingers. His knuckles, which seemed swollen.

"Every finger in my right hand has been broken at least twice. You just put adhesive tape on them and keep on playing. Two fingers together make the good one work the bad."

"Have you hurt yourself a lot while playing?"

"As much as any player."

"Do you get aches and pains?"

"A guy like Cy would say no." Alex took a long, slow drink of beer. The slight swell of his Adam's apple intrigued her as he swallowed, then lowered the bottle. "I'll admit to having them. Right now, I've got a tightness in the knob of my pitching shoulder. I could use a good rubdown at Bruiser's Gymnasium back home."

"I don't think they have a gym in Dorothy."

"Probably not."

They sat for a while, then Camille brought the bottle of beer to her lips and took a try. It wasn't wholly as bad as she'd expected. It certainly didn't carry the same bite as her father's liquor. This had a rather pleasant mellow, if not quenching, taste as the heat began to wane in the twilight.

"Well?" Alex gazed at her while removing his Stetson and setting it on the cap of his denim-clad knee. "What do you think?"

Truthfully, this was a slice shy of heaven. Sitting here with him, the now deep blue-violet silhouettes of clouds scudding by, the distant glow of fire sparkles on wands waved by children. She could hardly lift her voice above a whisper. "I think this is the most wonderful time I've had since we left Harmony."

After a short moment of silence, he said with a tinge of regret lacing his words, "I wasn't talking about that. I meant the beer."

Blushing, she chided herself for having revealed something more than was needed.

He brought the back of his hand to her cheek; she fought the instinct to lean into him. He rubbed his knuckles down to the column of her neck. The caress was gentling, reassuring. "But I'm glad you told me, Camille."

They sat in silence a while, eating cornflakes and drinking beer.

Alex's voice broke the spell. "I wonder how Cap's getting along."

"Hmm, yes. I'm sure Dr. Porter is making sure he takes his medicine." Camille chewed on a few flakes. "I wonder if my gladiolas have come into bloom. Leda's watering my garden while I'm gone."

"You got over that ladies' Garden Club thing?"

"I suppose as best as I will."

They grew quiet once more.

Camille dared to broach a subject that had never been settled between them. "Were you disappointed that you quit baseball?"

If she expected a ready answer, she'd been deluding herself, because one wasn't forthcoming. In fact, he didn't give her an answer at all. In the sky below, sky-rockets and torpedoes and salutes of various calibers began to fire off in showers of color. The bombs and whistles bombarded the night, and after a moment of calm, a fresh assault began, seemingly aimed at what looked to be the bell tower of the schoolhouse rather than straight up.

As the noise level rose, cheers reaching them up in their private retreat, Alex said something in such a low voice, she wasn't sure she heard correctly.

An explosion of white and blue rained down as he repeated, "I killed a guy."

She said nothing, her pulse having slowed until it seemed to cease altogether.

He spoke the words again; his voice was without inflection. "I killed a guy. That's why I quit base-ball."

She stared across at him, her heart lurching. "Alex . . . you didn't." Shock caused the words to wedge in her throat and she had to force them into sounds. "You couldn't have."

"I didn't mean to."

Through the din of the roaring fireworks, she breathed two words: "What happened?"

Alex rubbed his jaw with his fingers, then thoughtfully scratched at his throat. He kept his gaze ahead, as if he couldn't look at her. "I've never talked about it out loud. What happened is in my thoughts every day. But I've never spoken the words, heard them with my own ears. It's condemning enough to have them haunt my mind."

She was shocked. Devastated. Oh God, the man she had feelings for was a . . . killer. *My God.*

"Did you know him? What did he do to you?" Her questions came out in shaky rush.

He put his palms on his knees, the Stetson falling beside him. "We were playing the New York Giants in Baltimore Park. I was up at bat with their catcher riding me. We didn't get along well. In fact, I hated him. He hated me. Rusie was pitching and he gave me a spitter too far on the outside corner and I took it. I wanted a piece of it so bad, I overswung and knocked the catcher on the side of his head. He went down." The anguish in his heart was audible in his tone. "A catcher's mask doesn't save a guy's head. The bat whacked right through the wire and knocked him out. Right there, on home plate, I ended a man's life."

Her throat closed; the beat of her heart steadied to a hard pounding. An accident at the plate. *That wasn't something cold-blooded.*

Camille quietly asked, "Who was he?"

Alex stared at the stars and the powder smoke fanning over the clouds. "Joe McGill."

A breeze touched them. How utterly horrible for Alex. Horrible. She felt his despair.

"It happened three years ago. The day we played our first game against Boston last week."

"Oh, Alex . . ." She reached out and took his hand, squeezing, wanting badly to comfort him.

"His spirit was out there when we played the Somersets." As he faced her, the fireworks illuminated his somber expression. "That's why I went to church. I lit a candle for him."

Warm moisture filled her eyes. "I don't know what to say."

"What can you say? I ended a man's life, then wanted penitence for it by lighting candles. It's nothing compared to Joe's being here."

"But it was an accident. You didn't mean to."

"Doesn't matter. I still swung the bat. I took everything from him. He had a good career. He could loop them over the infield better than anybody I ever saw." He grew thoughtful a moment, then continued after a sip of beer. "He could do a lot of things well." Alex looked up at the sky, as if searching for Joe McGill's heaven star. "He was a checkers champion on the road. He could play several opponents simultaneously and beat them all. He was a good billiard player, too. A fair fisherman, and a hell of a poker player.

"You know," he went on reflectively, shrugging slightly, "we had a hell of a lot in common, but we never knew that about each other when he was playing for the Giants."

A skyrocket flared in the blanket of night that swaddled the Fourth. "His father was a drunk, roughed him up. His mother was never around, so he ran away from home when he was twelve. He grew up in a sandlot, just like me. Things like that, it makes people understand each other. Only me and Joe, we never talked about it. We were never friends."

"I never knew any of this . . ."

"People only talk about the legend. The stats, the pennants. George had the papers play up my career rather than that June day. It was dusted over. Accidents in ball happen. You don't dwell on it. It's bad for the team. For the owners." His voice faded. "The attendance."

He grew quiet once more.

"That's why you quit baseball," she said softly.

Alex went for a cigarette, lit it, and talked through the smoke leaving his mouth. "And that's why I should quit today."

"But you won't, will you?"

"I can't."

She understood his words to mean that baseball was in his blood, his body, and his mind.

When she looked at him, she could almost see the grief running in him so deeply, it was a physical hold on his heart.

They sat without talking further. Smoke curled above Alex's head. A firefly flickered past. A missile whizzed by, shuddering in a flash of red. She was grateful he told her about Joe McGill. Now she understood.

Blinking back tears, Camille knew she would never forget this night—being with Alex Cordova, sitting on the roof of a red-and-white barn, their knees brushing, drinking beer and eating Kellogg's cornflakes out of the box. Watching fireworks as they bloomed into a palette of colors on a night sky's canvas. Listening to the shrill shrieks of the rockets, the oohs and ahs of the crowd in the distance, the lowing of cows in the pasture, and the steady rhythm of her heartbeat in her ears.

This was the closest she'd ever felt to another human being. It was humbling. A gift to cherish. And it made her fully aware of how easy it would be to fall in love with Alex.

If she hadn't already.

"Cap?" Alex took in the clean-shaven jaw of the man sweeping in front of Plunkett's mercantile. Facial features that had been hidden for so long were now defined, jolting Alex from his walk and holding him in place. A tightness caught in his chest, and the blood in his veins chilled as he stared. Little by little, warmth returned as a war of emotions raged within him. It was like looking at a photograph of what once was—a person Alex had once known.

"Hey, Alex." Captain stilled the broom and gazed at him with a wide smile. His rich black hair had been clipped short and combed into place with pomade. "You're back."

"Yeah." He proceeded slowly, unable to take his gaze from Captain's altered appearance. Without the facial hair, small lines at the corners of Captain's mouth were noticeable. "We just got in a couple of minutes ago."

"They told me your train broke in Dorothy, Wisconsin. *Wisconsin* is an easy word to remember. I don't have to spell it."

Captain didn't usually remember details like town names.

The brown eyes that had looked at Alex with confusion over the past few years now seemed somewhat sharper. "That's how come you didn't play the Athletics yesterday afternoon."

"That's right." Alex looked hard at Captain, his thoughts going in all directions with uncertainty. It wasn't just his lack of beard and mustache and his trimmed hair that made him seem different. He stood taller; his skin color wasn't as pale as moonlight anymore. "We had to forfeit the game."

"Forfeit. F-o-r-f . . ." His dark brows furrowed. "How do you spell that word, Alex?"

"F-o-r-f-e-i-t."

Captain rested the broom against the mercantile's wall and took out a pencil and small tablet from his back pocket. "I'll remember that word now because I'm going to write it down." He carefully wrote out the letters, then folded the cover over the page and stored the tablet back in his trousers.

"Are you doing okay, Cap?" Alex took in his white shirt, sleeves rolled to his elbows, and the string apron around his waist. His body filled out his clothing better than it had before.

"Now I am. I wasn't feeling very good for a while after you left. I was sick every day." He spoke with resonance and clarity. "I couldn't come to work. I've been staying with the doctor at his house. Today's my first day back. I was worried Mr. Plunkett would fire me. But he didn't."

Alarm pulsed through Alex. "What happened? Did you get a headache that was worse than other times?"

Captain felt his jaw and smiled as his fingertips worked over the skin. "Did you notice I shaved?"

Alex went along with Cap's change of topics even though his mind was spinning. "I did, Cap."

"I shaved myself. The doc watched me to make sure I did it right."

"You look swell." Alex gave him an approving smile, then slowly asked in a quiet tone, "What made you do it?"

Captain's expression turned serious. "I wanted to see what I looked like."

Alex lifted his head with a brief nod. "Well, that's good." There was more to this than Captain was telling, or maybe even understood. Not once since his accident had Captain expressed an interest in seeing his face. He'd been too afraid of a razor to give shaving any consideration. What had made him change? "Do you know why you got sick? Did something upset you and you have to take a lot of your medicine?"

"No." Captain reached for the broom and began to sweep once more. "I haven't had my old medicine very much lately. Dr. Porter said—" The thought was cut short as his face lit with excitement. "Hey, Alex, I kicked his ass at checkers. Every time. The doc never won a single game. When my stomach hurt, to make me not think about how bad I felt, we played checkers." Each sweep of his broom was executed with fluidly moving muscular arms; it reminded Alex that Cap was still a very strong man—something Cap had forgotten at times when he had hidden behind his hair. "I'm teaching Hildegarde how to play. She's not very good yet. I kick her ass, too. But sometimes I let her win because she's a woman and because I think she's pretty. Do you think that's cheating, Alex?"

No medicine lately? Playing checkers with a pretty woman?

"No, Cap, that wouldn't be cheating." Listening with bewilderment, Alex found it hard to stay focused on what Cap said. His thoughts were frozen amid the questions of why Captain looked and sounded different. Why the doctor had quit giving him his medicine. "I've got to go do something."

"Okay. I'll see you later at the baseball game. I'm going to watch from the front row."

"That'll be good. I'll see you."

Alex headed directly for Dr. Porter's office, confused and filled with an anger that put a briskness in his walk. Who did the doc think he was, altering Captain's medicine? The physicians at the Baltimore Hospital had urged Alex to keep Captain on the doses they'd written for him or else he could suffer seizures. He made sure Cap got the proper amounts each day, at the same time of day, and he'd done so for the past seven months since taking him out of the hospital.

Certain things agitated Cap at times, but he stayed in a routine in most cases. Keeping him comfortable on his medicine while Alex got the money to take them to Buffalo was the most important thing.

And that damn doctor had slacked off. What if—

But Jesus. Captain looked and sounded better.

Alex grabbed the knob to Dr. Porter's office and yanked the door open. If it hadn't been for the fact the doctor had a patient sitting at his desk, Alex would have unloaded on him. The woman turned to see who'd come into the office. In his current state, Alex could barely recall who she was even though he was working on an order for her and her husband.

After several seconds, he said, "Mrs. Wolcott."

Her smile was pleasant. "Hello."

"Mr. Cordova," Dr. Porter said, rising from his chair. "I'll be with you in a moment."

"I'll wait outside." Alex shoved through the door, stuck his hand in his trouser pocket and withdrew his pack of smokes. He shook one out and lit up, gazing across the street at the newspaper office. His thoughts went in different directions. Captain, baseball, money, hospitals, medicines, what was, what could be.

He still wondered about the wisdom of telling Camille about Joe. It was a hell of a thing to admit . . . To a woman who made him feel hope.

Hope that he could fix Cap.

Hope that maybe he could come back to Harmony one day.

Hope that there could be a chance.

But hope was a dangerous thing to have. When dashed, it could wear a body down.

The door to the doctor's office opened and Mrs. Wolcott stepped outside with the doc behind her. Her condition showed, a soft swell of her belly from the baby she carried. Motherhood suited her, gave her a radiance that put a rosy color in her cheeks.

He tipped his hat to her. "I'll be finished with the cradle this week and I'll bring it by for you, Mrs. Wolcott."

"We won't be needing it for another five months, but I'll be glad to have it early so I can make up some quilts the right size." She gave her thanks to the doctor and went on her way.

Alex was inside the office before being asked, and as soon as the door closed, he went off like a trip wire. "Captain told me you didn't give him his medicine on a regular basis while I was gone. That he got sick."

"He has been sick," the doctor said, and he would have continued.

But Alex cut off the man's words with an angry yell. "What in the hell happened?" He strode to the desk and turned with a quick jerk. "I gave you the medications with directions. The state hospital told me that if Cap didn't have that elixir every day, he could have an attack and get really bad off. God-dammit, I'm not going to let him slip back into that man he was that first month in the public hospital."

He'd worked himself into a cold sweat, his palms damp. He was barely able to control his hands from trembling.

The doctor's compassionate voice intruded on the room. "Sit down, Mr. Cordova."

"I don't want to sit down," he replied in a hard tone.

"I think you'd better. I have something to tell you." Dr. Porter rounded his desk and sat in the large leather chair. He took a fob from his vest pocket. On the end was a tiny key, small enough to fit into the double-door pine cabinet on his left. Once one side was open, Dr. Porter reached for the bottles on one of the shelves. They were Captain's medicine bottles.

Alex still stood, watching the doc set them on his desk. Foreboding clamped over him. He told himself his fears were premature. Nothing was wrong. There was no good reason to be feeling as if his breath had been cut off. But looking at those bottles, then look-ing at the doc, his confidence ebbed. He grew filled with such self-doubt, it was a physical pain that tensed his muscles.

"How long has he had this medication?" Dr. Porter asked.

"Three years."

With his weathered hands folded before him on several charts, he gazed acutely at Alex when next he spoke. "Then for three years, Captain was slowly being poisoned."

Alex stared at the man in utter disbelief. Several strokes of the clock's pendulum went past before he found his voice. "That's bullshit."

"It's not, son." Dr. Porter turned one of the bottles toward him so that Alex could see the label.

He didn't have to read it. He knew what it said.

"Foetor arsenicum," Dr. Porter recited, then lifted his gaze to Alex and added, "Those are the Latin words for bromide arsenic."

Alex's mind tripped into shock over the startling translation. He'd wondered about the word *arsenicum* but had dismissed any thought about its being arsenic. Arsenic was poison, and doctors wouldn't use poison on their patients.

With his stomach clenched tight, he sunk into the chair opposite the doc's. "That can't be right."

"I'm afraid it is. I sent a sample to a druggist friend of mine in Boise so he could give me the compounds in this." Dr. Porter tipped the bottle; light caught on the deadly liquid inside. "There is bromide in it, which is commonly used to treat brain injuries. There are also chlorides of potash, sodium, phosphate, and lithium. But there's a small trace of arsenic, too. Lithium has been proven affective in severe cases; however, too much over a long period of time can dull a patient's senses. It's the arsenic, Mr. Cordova, that is of great concern. I gave Captain an exam. Beneath the surface, there is a man with a mind that allows him to think quite clearly for himself. But for three years, the arsenic has put him in what I believe to be in a walking catatonic state."

Gooseflesh rose on Alex's skin in hard, tingling points. He could barely swallow, barely handle the rush of heat that went to his bones. He had nothing to say. Words failed him. Holy Christ, if this doctor was right, then by his own hand, Alex had been poisoning Captain for the past seven months.

His mind reeled in denial.

"These past few weeks, I've been lowering the dose daily to wean him off," Dr. Porter said. "He was very ill from withdrawal. I had him stay at my home with me so I could bring him through. He still suffers headaches. The Dover's Powder is opium. In moderation, he can take that on an as-needed basis. I don't know how long it will take to bring him around. But I do see that he's much improved in color and mind as it relates to daily things." The doctor chuckled. "He's a very good checkers player."

Alex couldn't laugh. There was a question he didn't want answered, but he had to know. "Would I have killed him, eventually?"

Dr. Porter sobered, settled a pair of spectacles on his nose, then leaned back in his chair and folded his arms over his chest. "Yes."

A stabbing tore through Alex's heart. He thought he would be ill. The horrible knowledge hit him full force, swelling his throat and making him blink back the rush of moist heat in his eyes. "Dammit, what kind of doctor prescribes poison? Didn't he know I'd be killing him?"

Doc Porter said quietly, "I'll get you a glass of water."

He heard the doc moving in the room, making sounds that, in his state of shock, seemed both muted and sharp at the same time. Then a drinking glass was put into his hand and Alex took long sips to cool his insides. When he felt his lungs expand once again and his breathing come somewhat normally, he spoke. "I didn't know."

"It's not your fault, Mr. Cordova. I know it's hard not to take blame, but you were only following instructions." Dr. Porter sat down once more. "As I said, some treatments in medicine are common even though we physicians don't always know the full extent of their effects. We know what works at the time of injury." Removing his glasses, he wiped his eyes. "I will say that the doctors you talk about did Captain a disservice. I'm not a brain expert, but I think I can help bring him back to a semblance of what you and I consider normalcy." He opened a journal and picked up a pen. "I'd like to know what caused his injury— every detail of what happened and the treatments that he's had."

Alex had never spoken about Captain's days in the hospital to anyone, those first hours when he'd laid there unconscious. Alex would have to be brutally honest. He would reveal secrets, things past and things buried, old wounds. But as he lifted his gaze to the doctor's, he knew that the only way to move forward would be to return to the past. So he told Dr. Porter everything. He left no detail out, no emotion or feeling. And when he was finished, the doc didn't look at him any differently. Alex did not understand the reason for the doc's unspoken forgiveness, for it was nothing that Alex could forgive of himself. But the fact that doc didn't say he was a son of a bitch meant a lot. For that, Alex was grateful.

The doc steepled his fingertips. "Then when Captain woke up from his accident, he was never allowed to heal his brain without medication. I'm not saying the bromide was the wrong course to take. It's the arsenic that I can't justify. And yet, it is often prescribed."

"But the fact remains," Alex said, his voice hoarse, "Cap's been taking it."

"He won't be anymore, and any ill effects may very well go away. I just don't know. I had my colleague mix up a new combination for Captain, and it arrived the other day. Captain's had two doses already and he hasn't shown any distress. In fact, I think he's tolerating it well." Dr. Porter went to the cabinet shelf and took out a clear bottle with a cork top. "This has bromide in it and the other components we discussed. Use the opium sparingly, and we'll see what happens."

"Do you think Captain could remember what he used to be like?"

At length, Dr. Porter sighed. "The memory is a remarkable storehouse. Captain's had the door to his clouded by narcotics. Behind that door, he may very well know who he is."

His hands, hidden from sight in his trouser pockets, twisted nervously at the pocket seams. "You think that's why he wanted to shave and cut his hair?"

Dr. Porter smiled with optimism. "I'd like to think so."

When Alex left the office, his feet felt weighted. He felt like he'd been thrown to the ground by the entire lineup of the Philly Athletics. They sat on him, squeezing the air from his lungs, until he couldn't see. Until the world went black with one realization:

He'd almost killed Captain.

As Alex gulped in the warm summer air, he kept his shoulders straight and his head high. Cap was getting a second chance. Alex should have been embracing the news, happy, encouraged. But smothering those emotions was a fear so strong, it was a blinding white sheet inside him.

If Captain remembered the day of his accident, he would hate Alex for sure. And who could blame him.

Shame clutched Alex, enveloping his soul and dragging him closer to hell ... because a very small part of him didn't want Cap to get better.

A rush of water came out of the faucet pipe, dousing Camille with a cold spray. She lay on the floor, partially beneath the kitchen sink, wrench in hand, her legs stretched out before her, her back cushioned by a pillow. Her body contorted in an awkward position so she could reach the pipe that had sprung a leak while she'd been gone. She thought she'd fixed it before she left, but the oakum caulking hadn't held. After days of a slow drip that had overflowed, her storm room floor was ruined from the spill.

Quickly putting a bucket beneath the drain, she rolled over and stared at the bottom side of the cast-iron sink. The concentrated fragrance of dish soap tickled her nose and she sneezed.

"I told you you needed the long lead trap, not the half." Her father's words came down from above— through the three-inch-wide hole in the sink bottom—to be exact. She looked up and saw his eyes and nose as he peered at her through the opening.

She didn't want him to be right. She'd *fought* against him being right. But he was right.

"Hand it over." She extended her arm from the cupboard and then a heavy pipe came into her grasp. She could have hired a handyman, but she wanted to do this on her own. And actually right now was as good a time as any. She needed the distraction as soon as her father had come over wanting a full report on the road trip. So far, she hadn't told him anything. He was the one doing all the talking.

"It's in every newspaper across the country." His voice came to her amidst the plumbing. "They're calling us the Harmony Honeybees. So you say you checked with the laundry?"

"I checked with the laundry," she repeated for what seemed to be the dozenth time. "They said that the uniforms they put in the duffle bags for me to pick up were our regular worn-out, drab uniforms."

"It makes no sense," he muttered. "How can a laundry lose thirteen uniforms? And even more baffling, replace them with ones that are godawful old gold in color."

"I don't know."

"Well, we're going to have to find out and make whoever is responsible pay for new ones. Until then, the players will have to wear what they have." He muttered. "The newspapers are having a field day. I'll bet we're news in all the train terminals. On every street corner. I tell you, it's an outrage. And Bertram Nops is loving every minute of it. I caught him walking away from Municipal Field the other day. The sprinklers were on, soaking the outfield. He denied doing it, but I'm not stupid. I know he's out to ruin me because he didn't get his way. Camille, you really were thoughtless when you got that bum involved with my baseball team."

She fought to get the wrench grip over the wide pipe and turn it loose. "Maybe he switched the uniforms."

"Interesting speculation. I'll tell the police." He warned, "You've got to watch your back with him. He's as slippery as axle grease."

"I'll be careful. But right now my mind's not on that. I just got back and I came home to a flood in my kitchen."

"It could have been worse. Leda told me she saw water running from under your porch door, so I turned off the main pipe to the house."

"I appreciate that." And she did; but in his cutting the water supply to the property, her flower garden didn't get watered and the flowers that had been flourishing before she'd gone on the road now resembled a wilted salad. She had assured Leda that it was no great loss, but the housemaid had still felt terrible about the plants' dying.

That flowerbed and vegetable garden had been the last link Camille had to the Garden Club—and now it was gone. Interestingly enough, she wasn't overly despondent about it.

"My investigator found that lovestruck pitcher, Will White," her father barreled on with a fair amount of bristle. "South of the border in the hoosegow, held on charges unknown. Hogwood says I can't touch him."

"You don't need to touch him," Camille said, liberally applying oakum to the end of the pipe joint. An itch caught her nose and she made a face. "You've got Alex Cordova. He's ten times the man."

And he was. In every sense.

"He's been a losing pitcher."

Camille lost her hold on the pipe fitter and it fell onto the floor with a hard *clunk*. Defending Alex's playing abilities wasn't easy—it was impossible, since she would never tell her father about the reasons why Alex didn't put his all into the game. It was a conflict that she grappled with—sympathy for what he'd been through, versus frustration that the past stood in the way of his talent, a talent for which she had paid a pretty penny. She felt bad even thinking of the two together.

Picking up the wrench, she moved it back in place, twisted, and cut her knuckle in the process. "Oooooh."

Her father's head filled the sink opening once more. "Camille sugar, quit this nonsense and move back home."

She watched blood seep from a small cut in her skin. "No, Daddy. This isn't a passing fancy. I'm going," she said while grabbing the tool, "to make something of the Keystones"—and jamming it in place—"if it kills"—but the wrench immediately slipped and nearly whacked her on the head—"me." Leaning her head back and sighing, she closed her eyes. "And it may very well do that."

A quiet moment passed, almost as if her father was trying to think of something encouraging to say in light of her bleak admission. But that couldn't possibly be true. He had difficulty cheering her on.

"What happened in Boston . . ." he began, and Camille tensed, preparing for the worst, "was nothing short of brilliant."

Her gaze flew to the drain hole where kitchen light, instead of her father's face, filled the opening.

"The *Sporting News* called the sweep a seamless victory," he said. "Scores were high, batting was quality, runs were earned, and the boys played like the win was only the icing on the cake. It was being out there together that was the whole hurrah." She heard his footsteps as he went to the icebox, opened the door, and apparently took a peek inside. "There was pride in that team. And it didn't come from nowhere." A draft from the ice block cooled its way across the knit of her exposed stockings. "How did you do it, Camille?"

Her first compliment from him, and she was beside herself. "Sometimes there are days when a person just gets it right. They know what they're supposed to do and how they're supposed to do it. That's what Boston was all about. The Keystones grabbed onto those four days and made them belong to Harmony." Her father stood in front of her once again and looked down. Her gaze lifted to view his face, flanked by a round cast-iron frame. She was touched by his praise. She shouldn't get her hopes up. And yet, even with years of disappointment, she couldn't stop herself from asking, "Did you really think they were brilliant, Daddy?"

"I did, sugar. I wish I could have been there to watch it pan out." She couldn't see his mouth, but she knew he was smiling; humor lines fanned at the corners of his blue eyes, eyes the very color of her own. "That Boomer Hurley is one hard egg. Not even an anvil could crack his skull."

"He doesn't scare me."

"I didn't suppose he would. You've got gumption, I'll give you that." It was a long moment before he added, "Those Boston games . . . you did good, Camille." He left the counter, and from the sounds, he was checking out the goods in her poorly stocked pantry. "I wish you could bring that enthusiasm back to Municipal Field. I'm sure you can if you prepare. You always did do that well—prepare for the day."

Her breath seemed to solidify in her throat. He was actually talking to her as if she were the real manager of the team. As if she really was a viable candidate to permanently oversee the Keystones. "I'll see what I can do."

"You see what you can do," he said, mirroring her words.

Her voice betrayed her, wavering and showing far more emotion than she cared to. The moisture in her eyes threatened to blind her. "Thank you, Daddy."

She blinked the emotion from her vision. She fumbled for the heavy iron wrench, its jaw pinching her fingers as she grasped the handles, giving her a new injury. She winced and dropped it.

Her father lowered to one knee and looked inside the cupboard where she lay. "I can fix this for you."

His sincerity meant the world to her. "That's all right. I have to do it myself. It's become a matter of me versus the pipe, and I can't let this hunk of iron win."

"Of course not." Sunlight caught on his watch chain and he glanced at it without checking the time. "I've got to get back to the store before Nops sets it on fire."

Camille tried to hold onto a grin.

Her father rose and brought his hands down to dust the seams in his trousers. "I'll have your mama tell Leda to fry you some hushpuppies and bring them over. Your pantry is nothing but shelves of glassware and gadgets. You don't have anything in your icebox but a wheel of moldy cheese and a crate of lemons. What in the deuce do you need so many lemons for?"

"Lemonade."

"I don't recall you drinking lemonade at home."

One statement about the Keystones being brilliant didn't change a lifetime of inattention. So she dared to add softly, "I don't recall you paying any attention to what I drank at home."

Clearing his throat, he didn't answer right away. "Then I should work on that." The soles of his shoes made a crisp noise over her clean floorboards. "I'll see you later this afternoon for the game."

"All right."

The back door opened and closed, leaving the kitchen quiet.

The persistent itch on Camille's nose grew annoying, but she was loathe to use her greasy finger to scratch it. She brought the back of her hand to her nostrils and rubbed. The sleeve seam on her blouse gave a harsh rip. She cringed. At least the shirtwaist wasn't one of her better ones.

An hour later, she stood in front of the faucet and fully opened the cold valve. Leaning sideways, she looked inside the cupboard for signs of leaks. The pipes were still dry. Jubilation made her give a little hop of delight.

"Success!" she shouted to the empty kitchen just as she spotted the silhouette of a man behind the dotted swiss curtains covering her back door window. A knock sounded. She went to answer it without thought of how she must look.

Opening the door, she found Alex standing on her stoop.

"Alex."

Suddenly, she grew concerned over her appearance. Maybe she didn't look all that bad aside from that rip in her sleeve. But when she took a quick glance at the plumber's mud stains on her ivory shirt-waist and the tiny tear in her skirt she'd gotten when she closed the lid on the toolbox and caught the fabric in the hinge, her outlook dimmed. She did look that bad.

"You surprised me," she said, refraining from smoothing her hair. She didn't want to point out the obvious.

He leaned back, looked up at the eaves, then alongside the mudroom door. "Your clapboards could use some paint. You should take care of that before winter."

His usual easygoing manner was missing. The faded blue of his shirt stretched tight over his chest. Denim pants defined his legs as he stood rigidly on the porch. His mouth was grim. Something had happened.

"I was going to," she replied, knowing from his face that he hadn't come over to discuss the paint peeling on her house.

"After that last time, with your lady friends leaving, I didn't know if I should come to the front door."

She wasn't quite sure what to say about the courtesy he was presenting her. It seemed so unlike him. He was a man who didn't usually concern himself with how others viewed him—with how she might view him. He just was who he was. No pretenses.

She stepped aside, then said, "Please, come in."

He shook his head. "That's all right; I can't stay. I have to get home and take care of some things before the game." He lifted the brim of his hat with his finger and angled his chin toward her. "I just wanted to see you."

Confused, she murmured, "See me?"

"See your face." He shifted his weight from one foot to the other, then hooked his thumbs in his belt loops. "Look at you."

This time she ran her hands over the curls that felt like a lopsided mass of corkscrews on her head. "Yes, well . . . I'm not looking that great."

The power that was usually in his voice was muted; he spoke softly and almost with a degree of reverie. "I think you look fine, Camille."

Under his quiet appraisals, she wasn't sure what to say, what to do. All the pieces didn't fit together. He'd never acted this way before. As the seconds seemed to stretch out, she felt a restless need to move.

Just when she was about to open her mouth, Alex said, "Captain could be getting better. The doc's put him on a new medicine."

She looked at him with surprise. "Alex, that's wonderful." She motioned behind her. "Please, come in and I'll make some lemonade. You can tell me everything."

He did and she closed the door. While he sat at the small kitchen table, she fixed a pitcher of lemonade.

Handing him a glass, she asked, "How did the doctor know to change the medicine?"

His jaw tightened. "The old medicine wasn't doing him any good."

"Oh?"

When he didn't elaborate, she said, "You must be thrilled that he could take a turn for the better."

"Yeah. I'm a lot of things."

She got the impression he wasn't telling her everything. "Alex? What's wrong?"

The deep color of his eyes warmed, but he didn't enlighten her. "You should see him. He shaved."

"Really?" She tried to imagine Captain with a clean-shaven face.

"He looks . . . different."

She watched the lemon slices floating in her glass, then lifted her gaze to Alex. She felt strangely comforted by his desire to tell her the news. "I'm so glad you told me."

He stood. "I've got to go. I just came by—because I came by."

She tilted her head in confusion, then followed him to the door. Once there, he turned to her and raised his hand to her cheek, trailing his fingers down the line of her jaw. Then he gave her a kiss. Very gentling. Barely there. Just a whisper of lips brushing together, making her forget that she didn't understand the full reason why he had come by. The depth of what she felt in the kiss touched her. That sense of closeness created in her a euphoria that nothing else did.

He moved his lips over hers again, then spoke. "I needed to feel you, touch you. You make me want to be more than I am."

Then he walked down the steps toward the side of the house. Camille put her hand on the doorjamb and stared after him until he was gone from her view. She already missed him.

She closed the door and left the kitchen, passing the dining mirror on her way to the table. Absently, she glanced at her reflection. There was a line of black grease beneath her nose where she'd rubbed that itch, making her look like she had painted a mustache on her upper lip.

Once in the dining room, she looked at the mess of mail and papers waiting for her on the tabletop. She'd already read the articles of interest in the newspapers, their pages yellowed but sturdy. But no matter how many times she'd digested the words, they still didn't make sense.

Sitting, she opened one of the back issues of the *Sporting News* that Mr. Gage had given her when she'd gone to the newspaper office earlier in the day. Once more, she read the words in the narrow columns, skimming down to the last paragraphs. Then she viewed the next edition's headline.

The Slugfest Ends

Their relationship fouled up from the beginning, Alex Cordova of the Baltimore Orioles and Joe McGill of the New York Giants ended their slugfest at this afternoon's game on an ominous note when Cordova leaned into a pitch delivered by Amos Rusie. The swing hit the Giants' catcher on the side of the head and knocked him unconscious.

Overly aggressive behavior, fighting, and prolonged violent incidents are nothing new to these two players. In fact . . .

She didn't read further because she already knew what happened. She scanned the next issue from the day after the accident. And the edition the following day. And the day after that. She had a week's worth of newspapers. Not a single one supported Alex's story. Joe McGill never died on home plate.

He simply disappeared.

Chapter
❧ **19** ❧

She didn't reds

August arrived with the drowsy scent of flowers and sun-warmed glove leather. The citizens of Harmony became more caught up with the national pastime as the summer played out. The Keystones had won a three-game home stand against the Detroit Tigers in mid-July, and ever since, the seats at Municipal Field had been packed with fans.

As the first game with the Cleveland Blues progressed, Camille asked from her seat on the bench, "Specs, do you have your horseshoe?"

He held it up. "I never sit here without it."

"Good. You're batting next. We're going to win this. We're two runs up." Looking down at Doc, she inquired, "How about you, Doc? Four-leaf clovers?"

Doc shifted on his backside to get to the hind pocket of his pants. "I'll check, but I'm sure I've got my special one here."

Camille didn't want to leave anything up for grabs. Mox rubbed the oil lamp in his lap; the adhesive tape on his thumb was a white blur as he put some vigor into the motion. His finger had healed enough so he could come back into the game. The chain of rabbit's feet Bones used for inspiration hung around his neck. He'd added two more feet to it—for insurance, he'd told her—after they'd beaten the Milwaukee Brewers a week ago Saturday. The air smelled of bad liniment, compliments of Cupid's shaved head. And Yank swigged back a Bromo from the beat-up tin cup he always used.

To the unenlightened, the scene would have looked bizarre—certainly nothing to get hopeful about. But to Camille, everything was just right.

The momentum had begun when Noodles came running out of the clubhouse, his uniform on inside out. He'd arrived minutes before the coin toss and had been in a rush. But he socked a triple his first at bat.

If he hadn't shot the ball deep into left field, Camille would have taken him to task for missing practice. But the fact that he started them off with a great hit made her decide not to give him a lecture. Especially when Yank ripped off his jersey, flashed his ribbed undershirt, and proceeded to put his yellow jersey back on—inside out.

"Never seen Noodles lead off with a triple, Miss Kennison," he said as his fingers worked over the buttons. "If it works for him, it might work for me."

No longer skeptical when it came to their good-luck tactics, she smiled. "Good idea."

Yank hit a flare into right and took first base with a single.

As soon as that happened, Jimmy, Mox, and Cub put their jerseys on inside out as well.

"I can't find my clover," came Doc's distressed cry from the end of the bench. "I had it in my pocket, but it's gone. Oh good Lord . . ." He stood and looked beneath the bench. "Dammit all. Oh good Lord."

Camille immediately rose to help him look, as did Cupid and Charlie. Alex gazed beneath his seat, then shrugged.

"It's gone. It's as simple as that," Doc moaned as he straightened.

"You can use my rabbit's feet," Bones suggested.

Doc just about took his head off. "The hell I can. I'm not wearing any feet of dead animals around my neck." He moaned. "Oh good Lord. I can't go out there and hit the ball without my clover."

"What happened to the jar of them you had?"

He put up his hands in defeat. "I lost it yesterday when I was out on the lake. And now look—bad luck is coming my way."

Camille thought a moment. There was no point in wasting time trying to convince him he'd be all right without a clover. She didn't want to leave the park, but there was nobody she could send. The lineup was set and she couldn't disrupt it.

"Stay here," she insisted, "and keep things going. Specs, you get out there and stall. Adjust yourself. Do what ever it takes to add some time."

Specs wrinkled his nose. "I never adjust myself in public. Things stay where . . . they're supposed to stay on me once . . ."—his cheeks bloomed the color of an imperial red geranium—". . . once I put things where they should go."

"Then pretend your . . . shoelace is untied."

On that, she ran all the way to the mercantile and bought one of those souvenir clovers in pressed wax paper with a tiny round frame around it. In a matter of minutes, she was back at the dugout and presenting Doc with the new clover. "You're all set now, Doc." She was heaving as she tried to calm her racing heartbeat. She'd never moved so fast in her life.

Doc stared at it. Looked up at her. Then down again. "I can't use this."

Specs had untied and retied his shoe at the plate so many times, the umpire threatened to call him out. But Camille and Doc still debated the luck quality of personally found clovers versus store-bought.

Doc was adamantly against his new one until Alex intervened saying, "Doc, you know who has a clover just like that one?"

"Who?"

Alex had one leg over the other, knee to heel, his arm stretched out on the back of the bench. "Art 'the Dodger' LaFlamme."

"No kidding?"

"Kicked some butt with that framed clover. Batted three-oh-two the first season he had it."

Doc's expression lightened. "Well, if he used an artificial clover, I guess I could, too."

Specs had struck out, the crowd booing and causing Doc to look over his shoulder. "I'd better go out there and clean up the mess junior made."

"You do that, Doc." Alex adjusted the slouch in his stocking. "Go get 'em."

After Doc grabbed his bat, Cub gave Alex an elbow in the arm. "You were yanking his chain, huh, Alex?"

"I never lie," he stated while looking at Camille.

She got mad at herself for blushing, the day on the bicycle coming back to her. In the weeks that had passed, she hadn't forgotten how close they'd been on that July night. Or the shared moment in her kitchen. She missed him in that way, missed his company. She shouldn't have expected it, or wanted it, but Alex was the closest thing to a best friend she had. There were times when she wanted to talk to him, to tell him small things. Silly things. Things that didn't matter to anyone but her, like her pipe not dripping, or the fact that she'd ordered the paint for her house.

When she ate dinner alone, she imagined him sitting beside her. She was being foolish and ridiculous, overly romantic. Neither one of them had made promises to one another . . . and yet . . .

Sometimes at night, she wished Alex were in bed with her. She longed for his hands over her body, his lips on hers. But she couldn't tell him such things. So the feelings he'd evoked in her remained private memories.

It was hard, though, when he did things like this with Doc for her. He was helping to make the team all that it could be.

The other day, he'd brought his sanding paper and a small wood plane. He'd gone up to Charlie and told him, "You've got too much meat on your bat, Charlie." With his woodwork tools, he made minor adjustments, reshaping the bat's barrel. "That ought to help you out."

It had. Charlie's hitting stats had increased. Alex used his skills on the bats of the other players as well, altering, adjusting, customizing the bats to each player's height and weight and to the power they put into their swings.

Her mind was pulled back to the present as Deacon came in from being tagged out, a frown souring his face. "I couldn't hook the bag or he'd ride me right off."

Cub snorted at the brawny first baseman for Cleveland. "Next time, run into him."

"And kill myself?" Deacon took his seat and wrapped a towel around his neck.

From above the dugout, the sound of a laugh filtered through the raspberries and hisses.

Bertram Nops.

Recalling her confrontation with him, Camille's eyes narrowed with displeasure. She'd asked Mr. Nops if he'd noticed anything flashy about their uniforms. He'd said he thought they looked good. As he spoke, the corner of his left eye occasionally twitched. Had he always had that tick?

And the fact that he'd laughed when Deacon slid out only increased her suspicion he wasn't honest. Her father had been right about him. Mr. Nops was untrustworthy. Unfortunately, he'd come up with the cash she'd needed, and that couldn't be changed.

She pushed that thought to the back of her mind as the game went on, and the stakes got higher. Extra innings factored into the afternoon, as the score tied in the twelfth and fifteen innings. With each team at eight runs apiece, the bottom of the sixteenth was met with the threat of darkness. The Keystones *needed* this win for morale.

They were tied against Milwaukee for the most losses this season. But if they could put this game in the win column, they'd be ahead of the Brewers by one. That would put them in seventh place for the pennant. Not wonderful, but hopeful.

The umpire's voice, hoarse from calling balls, strikes, and outs, fought the dust as he hollered a strike on Mox—who was nearly mowed down by a fastball.

The relief pitcher for the Blues was a young hotshot, tall and slim, light-haired and buck-toothed. He practically burned a hole into the catcher's glove with each throw.

Sitting at the end of the bench, Cub observed, "That guy can do everything except steal first base."

"He does that," Alex remarked in a low tone from beside Camille, "in the dead of night when nobody's around."

From the tightness in his voice, it was apparent he didn't like the way the pitcher was throwing. Camille had noticed the killer sliders, too, and was keeping a close watch on them. Some pitchers were notorious for bean balls; some players actually *liked* them. Once hit on the body, the players could take the base without having an at bat and risking a strikeout.

The Cleveland quick-delivery artist wound up for the next pitch to Mox and unloaded a zap of lightning. Mox jumped out of the way and went down in the dirt.

Camille rose, mouth open. Mox clambered to his feet, wiped the dirt off his sleeves, and retrieved his bat.

Alex swore, threw off his cap, and paced in front of the bench. He stalked, his eyes narrowed in a scowl as he paused to look at the field once more.

Mox took his stance in the batter's box and the pitcher let go with a fast one. The ball caught Mox on the shoulder, bounced up at his head, and nearly took off his ear. It was no accident.

Before Camille realized what was happening, Alex had leaped over the edge of the dugout and had knocked the pitcher down. In a tangle of legs and arms, the two engaged in a fiery fistfight.

"Holy cripes!" Jimmy blurted from behind her. "Cordova struck that guy like a roadrunner going after a rattler!"

Camille yelled for her players to stay on the bench and not get in on it. But as soon as the first Blue jumped in, the rest of the players on both sides made a heap of flying fists.

She ran to the edge of the brawl, calling for them to stop, but her cries went unheeded.

Pandemonium ensued as the umpire yelled over the upset. "You want to get thrown out of the game,

Cordova? I'll throw you all the way into the club-house." When Alex made no attempt to get off the pitcher, the umpire shouted, "You are *out* of the game!"

Suddenly, Captain appeared, tall and undaunted by the display of upper cuts and jabs. She'd seen him in the seats with Hildegarde and was thankful he'd come down to try to stop Alex from hitting the pitcher. He went right up to them, cutting his way through the knot of players without being struck—even though he pushed men this way and that to get to Alex.

"Alex! Hey, Alex!" Captain grabbed the back of Alex's shirt in his big fist and pulled with enough force to get his attention. "Alex, you're going to hurt him. You're going to hurt him bad. Cut it out."

Alex, drenched in sweat, looked up—just as the pitcher laid one on his jaw and snapped Alex's head back. Dazed, he stopped and staggered to his feet. "Sweet Jesus."

The others quit their fists, began to nurse wounds, and ambled back to their respective benches.

Alex's lip had been cut by that punch from the op-posing pitcher, and the corner of his left eye had begun to swell. "I'm sorry, Cap. I didn't mean for you to see. I'm sorry."

"It's okay, Alex . . . that pitcher did wrong. But still . . ." Captain put his arm around him and the pair started back to the dugout. "You're a big guy. You could have knocked his head off. I don't want you to get ar-rested. I know what that is. J-a-i-l. It spells *slammer.*"

"I'm sorry," Alex repeated.

"You didn't hit me, Alex," he replied, patting him on the back and trying to get him to smile. "I'm not mad at you."

Alex's next words were barely audible. "Ah . . . God, Cap. You should be."

Camille stood there, watching the two, shades of a sunset glowing off their shirt backs. It was an odd irony—Captain calming Alex.

The game resumed and the Keystones won, but Alex was suspended for the next five days.

As Camille walked home that evening in the twilight, she couldn't help thinking about Joe McGill . . . and wondering.

Camille opened the front door, wearing her robe and with her hair falling about her shoulders, to find Alex. Although the screen separated them, he could see by her disheveled appearance that he must have awakened her. Her eyes blinked back the bright morning sunshine that spilled over the porch veranda. She put a hand to her brow to shade her gaze.

Her words came out in a sleepy Southern drawl. "What's the matter?"

As she stared past him to her lawn, he smiled. The players had set up shop on her grass, holding buckets of paint, brushes, turpentine, and protective sheeting. Then her gaze rested back on him.

A ray of hope lightened her sleepy blue eyes. "Did you get the umpire to lift your suspension?" Her accent reminded him of sugared peaches.

He had to shake his head. "Nope. But you're going to have your house painted today."

"I am?"

He dipped his voice down low. "Get dressed, honey, and tell us how you want the colors."

She paused, looked at the yard once more, then nodded. "Okay." She shut the front door.

He turned and viewed his crew of recruits. Captain had joined in. He sat on a tree stump studying the color chart Kennison had given them when they'd picked up the paint.

Captain's recovery had continued—amazingly so since those days in July. His headaches had subsided, but he suffered from blocks of memory loss. His day-to-day recollections had improved. He could tell Alex what he had for lunch the day before and remember the meal with detail. He hadn't been able to do that before.

He conversed about things he hadn't in a long while—basic topics, like cooking scrambled eggs, riding a sled in the snow, playing cards.

And he asked questions, too.

A lot of questions. Why did the doctors give him the wrong medicine? How did Alex's bow drill work? What do you call the machine with the wide trumpet where music comes out? Who is the president of the United States? Where is the hospital he used to be in? When did he get sick?

Alex wondered when these questions would eventually lead to: What happened to me, Alex? When the time came, Alex would be honest. And it was going to kill both of them. But he owed Cap. He'd tell the truth.

In the meantime, each day remained an uncertainty. Alex still thought taking Captain to Buffalo was the answer. If the doc here could help Cap so much, Silas Denton ought to be able to bring him back to his old self.

So Alex didn't want to get used to sticking around in Harmony. He'd already sent what he had of his bonus money to Buffalo. At the end of the season, he was going to walk out on his contract. Only now, it was going to get him in the gut to do it. Before, he didn't know Camille, didn't care if he ruined her father's team. He'd cared only about helping Cap. Now, he thought differently.

But the bottom line always came back to having to put Cap first.

He kept telling himself he couldn't risk falling in love with Camille. In the long run, he'd hurt her. And he didn't want to do that. He'd do anything *not* to do that. She was too good for him. He didn't deserve her. Not when he went off in a rage yesterday and nearly beat a guy senseless right in front of her.

What kind of a man would do that?

A man who'd seen this kind of arrogant pitching before—because he'd lived it, done it himself. Watching that Cleveland pitcher had been like looking into one of those glass snowballs that kids shake. Inside, Alex had stood on the mound, a mean streak and an arm that let him knock the batter out of the box. He didn't play that way anymore; there just wasn't any justifiable excuse for trying to cut a guy down at the plate.

At least none of the Keystones were cutthroats.

Looking at Cub and Yank arguing over what size brush to use on the porch posts; Noodles, Cupid, Jimmy, Bones, and Mox comparing mustache growth because of the bet they'd made with one another to see who could sprout the fullest one fastest; Doc on his knees, running his hands over the grass blades to look for clovers; Specs wiping off another trial pair of spectacles; Deacon, Duke, and Charlie puffing on ten-cent cigars and making smoke rings—Alex felt a pang grab him in the ribs. He was going to miss these fellows more than he could have predicted—much less have imagined. They were a good group of players. They weren't the best he'd ever played with, but winning, to them, didn't mean killing anybody to get the trophy.

The Keystones played with heart. It was something to be proud of, and Alex was. And Camille had the grit and determination to bring them to the playoffs. For her, Alex would have liked to get the pennant.

He wanted to do everything he could for her before October. It seemed too close, to be coming too quickly. On the day he pitched his last pitch of the inning, he would leave. Until then, he'd fill the gaps in his life with thoughts of her. She occupied his mind all the time—when he sculpted wood or carved a new design on his totem pole, when he walked over to the ballpark, when he lay in bed at night wishing he had her to cradle in his arms, to kiss and make love to.

He looked forward to seeing her each day. He liked being with her and watching how she moved, walked. How her hands gestured when she talked. When she was with the team and telling them how to play, she was funny and smart. She didn't always show her emotions, which made her all the more alluring, more complex.

The screen door's rusty hinges made noise behind him as Camille came out wearing one of those dresses he liked. They looked light and breezy, feminine in all the right places in the way the fabric draped her body. The dress had smooth lines and fancy trimmings. Its color was lavender, like the fragrance she wore so often. The pale violet hue seemed to turn her eyes that same shade.

She hadn't done up her hair in pins, just loosely braided it. The curls looked soft and sensual, although he doubted she realized that. A few tendrils caught at her forehead and ears, where he noted she'd put on a pair of tiny pearl earrings.

Jesus, she was beautiful.

"How did you get the paint?" she asked, stepping out to meet him.

"Your father." He breathed in, savoring her perfume, noting she did smell as good as she looked. "We went over to the hardware store and told him we wanted to paint the place for you and he said your order had come in the other day."

She gazed into his face. "That was thoughtful, Alex."

"Hell, I don't want to be thoughtful. After the way I got suspended, I owed you."

"You owe more to Cub. He's going to have to pitch five days in a row now." Her lips were pink and shiny. He wanted to kiss her, the memory of her lips against his not enough. "Maybe you should be painting his house instead of mine."

"I like Cub fine enough, but he's not as pretty as you."

He always thought she blushed nice; he wasn't disappointed, because she blushed now.

"How did my father react to your coming into his store?"

"He gave me a new behind for getting suspended." Alex took off his hat and readjusted the Stetson on his head. "He can take the hide off a bear when he gets started."

That made her laugh, and he drank in the sound. "Yes, he can."

"He'll make it hard for his son-in-law to call him Father."

Alex didn't know why he'd said that. He wasn't the husband for Camille, and he didn't want to think about some other man standing beside her at the altar. The image of her wearing a white gown, with a veil over her face, made him think about honeymoon trips—kissing, bedrooms, sex, eternity.

Longing set into Alex and he had to force it away.

Captain came up the steps and greeted them with a question. "Alex, what does *revival* mean?" He pointed to the paint card and the square of Colonial Revival Blue.

Alex shoved one hand in his pocket and leaned back against the porch post. "In this case it's a restoration color."

"Restoration?"

"A color of paint that brings back the way a house used to look."

"Oh." Captain clearly wasn't thinking along those lines. His face was a cloud of confusion as he looked at the paint square once more, then at Alex with a puzzled gaze. "I was wondering if it could mean something about a tent, too."

"No. It doesn't mean tent. A tent is a canvas shelter you put up with poles."

"I know that," Captain said with some impatience.

"Do you mean a tent revival, Captain?" Camille asked gently. "Where people meet and there's a man of the cloth—"

"—who wears a thin black tie and he's got liquor in his coat pocket and he asks people for money," Captain finished in a rush, his cheeks flushing in an animated way. "He stands there with a Bible in his hand, and we know he's got booze in that coat pocket because we saw him take a swig when he was behind the curtain, and he yells we're all going to hell if we don't do like he and his Good Book says. And then me and Frankie Munson throw bottle caps at him and tell him he's a worm and a fraud. We had to run from the coppers . . . back over to Frankie's house. He lived at 240th Avenue and his father was a dumb ass just like . . . just like . . ." His words trailed, the look in his eyes distant, as if he were grasping for a thimbleful of information but couldn't quite reach it. "I think I know somebody else who is a dumb ass."

Alex had followed the story with his heart lurching and burning in his chest. He'd listened, his breath trapped in his throat and the muscles in his arms hard beneath his sleeves. Each word of Cap's reflection hit him with the force of a blow. Alex had been waiting for this moment, had told himself he was prepared for it. But now that it had come to pass, it was far harder handle than he could have foreseen.

The memory of a tent revival with a childhood friend was the first to make it out of the storeroom.

Alex almost didn't trust himself to speak. His emotions welded together in a knot that was hard to untie. When he found his voice, it was shakier than he would have liked. "Cap, you shouldn't say *ass* in front of a lady."

"Oh." Cap reached into his back pocket, took out his tablet and pencil, and said as he wrote, "Don't say *ass* to ladies. Or Hildegarde." Then he put the tiny notepad away.

"Are we going to start slapping up paint?" Cub shouted toward the porch. "Or are we going to stand around and scratch ourselves all morning?"

Specs added with a croak, "I don't scratch myself. How many times do I have to say it? I do *not* scratch myself."

"No," Deacon said with a good-humored quirk to his mouth, "you just couldn't catch a bird dropping if the bird crapped in your glove."

And that's how the painting party began.

Half-naked baseball players painted Camille Kennison's house.

It was a good thing she lived at the end of town. The spectacle going on was nothing short of scandalous.

Jimmy had asked her pardon, but he had had to take his shirt off. This being a hot day, he wore no undershirt, and his chest was as bare as when he'd been born. Soon Duke and Doc followed suit. Then Bones and Yank. And finally the rest—until fourteen shirtless men stood on ladders, porches, the roof, and the loggia, painting her house. To Camille, the lack of clothing didn't much matter. What harm did it do for a man to paint with his shirt off?

Besides, she was already on the outs with the Garden Club for managing the Keystones, so what difference did one more infraction make? None, to her mind. Well, none that she cared to examine. She talked herself into thinking this was just fine—they were working without shirts only because the sun was baking them. And another thing . . . at least the players were in good shape and they were something to look at.

But Camille had eyes only for Alex.

She watched the way his muscles moved as his arm stroked up and down the side of the house. His tattoo moved fiercely with each rippling muscle as he leaned left or right. He wore nankeen pants, the cotton a faded buff color, with a hint of the ribbed drawers beneath showing where the waistband dipped at his navel. The hat on his head was the same she'd seen him with when he'd come down the boardwalk that first day she'd been with Captain outside the hardware store. She'd thought it looked very appealing on him then, and now was no different.

In fact, everything about him appealed to her.

His body, his face, the way he moved. The outline of his buttocks in his tight pants. Powerfully muscled biceps that glistened bronze beneath the simmering rays of sun. The way that grizzly bear tattoo seemed to come alive with each motion of his arm, his shoulder moving with each stroke of the brush. The shape of his nose and jaw. The way his lips caught condensation from the outside of his lemonade glass. How he would wipe his forehead with a bandanna and eventually tie the red patterned scarf around his brow and fit his hat back on.

"It sure is hot," Hildegarde commented, sipping on a glass of lemonade.

"It's very hot," Camille replied, wishing she could take off her stockings and shoes and cool her feet with water from the garden hose ... cool her lips with the taste of Alex's.

Sitting opposite Hildegarde on the horsehair cushion of the lawn swing, she watched the men paint her house. The green-and-white canopy above kept the sun from glaring directly on them. The temperature registered a scorching ninety-six degrees on the storm thermometer nailed to a ledge outside her kitchen window.

"I think this is the hottest August I can remember," Hildegarde went on, her hat brim making an oblong shadow over her eyebrows. "It makes me think of those times Meg and Ruth and I jumped into Evergreen Creek in our shimmies. We'd get mud between our toes, but it was fun. You should have joined us." She lowered her glass. "It was a lot of fun. Then again, I think you were too worried about what the boys would say."

"I wasn't," Camille said in self-defense. But maybe she had been. "I was afraid to get wet." Her admission came from a place that she never thought she'd admit to—fear of doing something unflattering.

"Afraid? Honest? We always thought—" Hildegarde said softly, "and I don't mean this to sound awful because I don't think you're awful, but those of us in Mrs. Wolcott's class who talked—we thought you didn't want to come with us because you were stuck up."

Camille could see now how they'd gotten that idea. "I would have liked to come."

"Well, we asked you once and you said no."

"I remember." She'd always regretted that. "If you ever ask me again, I'll come."

"But now we don't do things like that anymore," Hildegarde said as she lowered her glass. "It isn't ladylike. Meg can get away with it, though. She has a husband who doesn't mind her outlandish ways. I wonder if Captain would . . . that is . . ."

Camille watched the young woman's cheeks color. *Hildegarde and Captain.* The thought of them as a couple came as no surprise. And on the heels of that came approval. They would be perfect together.

After a long pause, Hildegarde continued. "What do you think of Captain without his beard and with his hair cut?" she asked, giving the tall man a sheepish glance.

Camille had been startled by his transformation, but pleasantly so. "I think he's handsome."

A little breathless, Hildegarde blurted, "I think so, too. I never would have imagined . . . but he makes me . . ." She blushed and paused. "Well, you know. You have more experience than I do with men. I mean, I was almost engaged to Meg when she was masquerading as Arliss Bascomb. So what do I know about true romance?"

Looking at the other woman, Camille gave her a thoughtful study. She wore the latest in fashion, a full blouse and circular skirt that was pieced out of old gores and flounces. This had recently come in, and not everyone's figure could support it. But with Hildegarde's curves and ample proportions, she wore the new style well.

"I think you don't give yourself enough credit, Hildegarde. I always thought you were pretty."

She squeaked, "Me?" Resting a hand over her heart, she gasped. "I've never had a beau in my life. Men flock to you, but you never go after any of them. Why not? Don't you want to get married?"

Camille shrugged. "Maybe I just haven't found a man who likes me for me." But that wasn't wholly the truth. She'd just been very picky—like her father said. Her reluctance had more to do with men not wanting to know if she had an idea in her head. They liked to make all her choices for her. She didn't want that. She'd given up on a man until . . .

Well . . . until Alex.

Her gaze strayed to him where he stood on the loggia and painted the trim around the windows Indian red. He'd told her she wasn't supposed to lift a finger because this was the team's gift to her for managing them. She didn't think it the team's idea—it was Alex's doing. She loved the thought. She loved . . .

She was afraid to go further with the thought. Love and commitment had never been spoken about between them. She'd feel awkward talking about it. He was everything she'd ever wanted romantically. But to tell him would only put a strain on the relationship. Because they couldn't go public with any feelings while she managed the team. It would be inappropriate.

As the swing slowly rocked, she looked at the men brandishing brushes and swinging paint buckets. She would have painted her house on her own. Her plans had included a full-length cotton duster, gloves, and rubber boots. Neatness. And long, long hours of effort. Thanks to Alex, she would have the entire place done today.

For lunch, she'd set out sandwiches—Hildegarde had brought over the items needed for ham and Swiss cheese—wedges of watermelon, pitchers of lemonade, and a succulent cherry pie that Hildegarde had made that had to be divided in careful slivers so everyone got a piece.

Camille's gaze followed Hildegarde's to where Captain worked on a section of porch spindle. The young woman said, "He's different now. And I don't mean," she continued in a rush, "that he wasn't fine before to me. I just mean that . . . I like him. I like him an awful lot." She fanned her face with the flat of her hand. "It is very hot. We should put out the root beer so we don't have to make up more lemonade."

The afternoon wound down. Tomorrow they were catching a morning train to Philadelphia.

The painting sheets were rolled up, paint buckets

were thrown in the refuse pile, and brushes were laid out on the grass by the back door to be soaked in turpentine. Camille watched the players go and waved as they filed out the gate, some with a jovial laugh, some with a smile, some sauntering, some striding slowly. She missed seeing Alex leave. She'd hoped . . . wanted to give him a special word of thanks.

Hildegarde packed up her belongings and empty baskets and said her good-byes to Camille. Just as Hildegarde was going through the front door, Captain came up the porch steps and offered to help her carry some of the hampers.

"I can get that for you." He took everything she held and made it seem like effortless work. He'd put his shirt back on and wore a new hat that was a fine shade of honey.

"Thank you," she said demurely as they took the walkway, side by side.

"I liked your cherry pie, Hildegarde," he said, complimenting her. "It was good. I could have eaten the whole thing. Could you bake another one?"

"Yes."

"You and I could eat it ourselves."

She nervously laughed. "Oh, I shouldn't eat half a pie."

"Why not?"

"Because I'm . . ."

Captain persisted. "Because why?"

"Well, because my mother says that a lady shouldn't—"

"You know, I've noticed that about your mother," Captain cut in. "She always has something to say about everything. And when you talk, you say 'My mother says' a lot. Don't you ever make up your own mind?"

Hildegarde's face went pale as she faced him.

"I think a mind is something a person needs to keep track of," he said quietly. "Even if he can't always help the way it goes. Sooner or later, if he waits long enough, he'll figure things out. It's time you started figuring out things for yourself, Hildegarde."

As Camille listened to them, she wondered if Captain knew how poignant—and true—his words were.

They approached the gate and Cap said, "So let's eat a whole cherry pie together."

They strolled down the street, their voices fading just after Hildegarde said, "All right, Captain. Let's eat a whole cherry pie together. I'll make one tomorrow."

Their shoulders met and a pang of envy held Camille in the doorway, where she looked out the screen mesh, watching the couple disappear around the corner. She wished she could be so open with her affections, could have that feeling of pure bliss. She wanted to know the discovery of love and its promises, of being courted and returning shy glances and gentle touches. If only she and Alex had met under different circumstances. If only they could openly be sweethearts.

If only . . .

Closing the door, she moved through the house and into the kitchen to clean up. She checked the temperature in the hope that it had gone down a few degrees. It had actually gone up three. An oscillating fan rested on the countertop and she turned up the speed with the intention of staying cool while doing the dishes. But the only breeze that reached her was warm, dry air.

As she looked out the window into the backyard, a figure caught her gaze.

Alex hadn't left.

He crouched by the paintbrushes and was soaking

several in a can of thinner. His wrist moved as he worked the paint out of them. Camille took two Virgil's root beers from the icebox, then went through the back door and outside. She watched him for a moment from the porch. The color of his skin had deepened to a rich brown from having been without his shirt all day. He still hadn't put it back on, and a tiny circle of light gleamed from the chain around his neck. The St. Christopher medal.

His head was down, spilling black hair over the bridge of his nose as he worked the bristles between his fingers. Well-defined forearms and biceps moved with a quiet strength that came from hitting baseballs out of the park.

"I thought you'd gone home," she said, walking over the grass to meet him.

He lifted his chin and looked through the wet hair that had fallen in his eyes. When he saw her, he raked it back, muscles rippling, showing a flash of dark underarm hair. He'd removed his hat and red bandana and it appeared as if he'd drenched his head with water from the garden hose. A burning cigarette was clamped between his lips and he talked around it. "Did you want to get rid of me?"

"I—no. I brought root beer." She wanted him to stay.

With his chin, he motioned to the pile of brushes closest to her. Then he gazed back down and continued working on the few he had in the thinner can. "Hand me those, would you, honey?"

When he called her that . . . *honey* . . . the word evoked a rush of heat through her body. Nobody said it like he did. Nobody meant it like he did.

Camille gave Alex his root beer, then set her own bottle down on an iron garden table. She got the brushes and came back.

"Put them in."

She arched a brow. "In the can?"

"Where else?"

"It's dirty in there." She peered inside where swirls of green and red and russet had made a murky pool of what looked like syrup.

Alex's mouth carried a hint of a smile as he gazed at her. Sweat trickled down his unshaven cheek, and he blew a stream of smoke through his lips. "That's the way this works, honey. To get the paint off the brushes, you clean them in the turpentine. Then the turpentine gets dirty."

"I know that."

"So put the brushes in."

She hesitated. Alex leaned back on his heels and flicked the butt of his cigarette into the hedges. He pulled the porcelain swing-top stopper off the root beer and took long swallows until he'd emptied the bottle on one breath. Her gaze was drawn to his mouth, the glistening sweat above his lip and the dewy droplets of root beer that he licked off with his tongue. She thought about how it had felt to have his tongue in her mouth, sensuously dancing with her. How good it felt with his lips on her skin, sucking her nipples. Her mouth went dry as she remembered the sensations he'd given her that night in the hotel room. She shivered, pure fire shooting through her body. If he kissed her right now, in plain sight, she wouldn't care. She'd—

"Have you had enough time to think it over?"

"What?" she blurted, brought out of her erotic thoughts.

He tilted his head, an unspoken question reflected in his brown eyes.

She didn't want him asking her anything else, so she quickly said, "I was going to." Then she knelt down across from him and plunged the two brushes she held into the turpentine.

"Go ahead. Clean some of them. If I do them all, I might be here until morning." He presented her with a deliberate smile. "Then again, staying until morning would be nice."

The suggestion nearly knocked her over. Every bit of common sense she had told her to run in the opposite direction. And suddenly, she saw him lying on her bed with her, and them both—

"But if I spent the night," he said, intruding on her imagination, "I'd miss the train tomorrow and then my manager would fine me even though I'm suspended. I have rules to follow."

She knew he was teasing her, but her mind was still someplace else. She had to pull it to what he was saying now. "You won't be suspended the entire seventeen days on the road." She pressed the brush to the bottom of the can, careful not to dip it so far she'd get oily paint on her fingers. "I'll put you in on the eighth against Boston."

"I always look forward to seeing Cy."

She knew he didn't mean that.

Their knuckles met in the narrow opening and Camille refused to let the touch affect her. It didn't, not really. Or so she told herself. It was his voice, low and husky, that warmed her skin through the thin sleeves of her dress. "You really want the pennant, don't you?"

She let out a slow breath. "I really do."

"How come?"

Pressing the bristles against the edge of the can, she deliberated giving him the real answer. To pull her father into the conversation would bring up an embarrassing subject for Camille. She didn't want to look like she was in this just to get his approval. Her reasons for wanting the win had less and less to do with Daddy.

After a long pause, she dared to confess, "Because I'm twenty-two and I've never been good at anything that's really mattered."

His head bent low over hers, the fringe of his hair teasing her forehead. The near touch caught a droplet of water against her skin and it rolled in a slow path down the hollow of her cheek. She stilled, feeling the heat cling to her.

"From what I know about you, I'll bet you made good grades in school," he said.

She managed to speak. "I did, and that's the whole point. That was expected of me. I want to do something *un*expected." The thickness of her braid lay heavily on her neck; her chemise felt as if it had been plastered on. The afternoon sun was unkind, bringing beads of perspiration to her brows.

"And baseball defines *unexpected?*"

Her skin burned like the smoldering end of one of his cigarettes; the trickle of perspiration rolling between her breasts felt annoying and almost unbearable. *Is he as aware of my presence as I am of his?* "If I bring the Keystones to the pennant and we win, I'll prove to myself, my family, and my friends that I can succeed at something that depended on my decisions." She was acutely conscious of the way he watched her, looked into her eyes. "My father started his own store from nothing and made it successful. Edwina Wolcott opened her own finishing school for young ladies and gained the respect of every lady in town. And what about Meg's grandmother, Mrs. Rothman? She fights for women's rights. You can't do anything of more value."

"Sewing a straight stitch doesn't matter?"

That he would even offer such an obtuse statement

made her jaw drop open. "Well, I like that. What a thing to say."

"I'm saying it because you shouldn't have to put aside other things just to prove yourself in another direction. I saw those little wall-hanging goodies in your house. I like the one with the bluebirds on it."

"That bellpull?"

"I don't know what it's called."

"It's a bellpull and I could make one in my sleep. Who cares? There is no effort required," she responded sharply, using more vigor than necessary to clean the brush. "The year you left baseball, you were batting two-twenty-one. That's the kind of success I'm looking for. You know what it's like."

"Hand me that other brush," he said, seemingly ignoring her comment.

Absently, she reached for it and smacked the handle into his open palm. She didn't move away in time; a smear of Indian red paint marked the backside of her hand. They looked at the spot together. Her skin seemed so pale next to his, appear even lighter by the luminous white sun above their heads. The sunshine scent of him was like an intoxicant through her blood. Crazy thoughts scudded through her mind as he put his fingertip into the blotch and made a small pattern. A heart.

"Sometimes," he said, her own heart jumping in her chest, "things that seem so great really aren't. Sometimes just being with somebody you care about is the only thing that matters."

His words snatched her breath away.

How had the conversation about baseball turned into this? The hot air surrounding them seemed to be combustible.

"I . . ." She gazed about, then locked onto a distraction. "Somebody took the cushions off the lawn swing."

She rose to her feet, nearly stumbling in the process, and quickly went to the swing. Her breath came in short choking gasps and she told herself to quit acting so ridiculous. So . . . in lust with the man. It was shameless. Her *thoughts* about him were shameless.

Picking up one of the cushions, she leaned into the framework to deposit the molded horsehair back in place. As she turned for the other one, she stopped. White paint made a crisscross pattern down the front of her lavender dress—an imprint from the wooden slats of the swing.

"When did somebody paint the swing?" she blurted in Alex's direction.

A smile caught the corners of Alex's mouth. "Doc and Specs slapped a quick coat of whitewash over it when you and Hildegarde were in the house."

"You could have warned me."

"Yeah." He straightened. "I could have. But I liked you with that dirt smudge you had on the tip of your nose, and I liked you with the plumber's grease smeared under it. I wanted to see what you'd look like really messy. Because I knew I'd love it."

Love? Even though he hadn't said the word as an endearment, as a promise, it settled into her heart, bringing with it a pang of longing. She blinked, unwilling to think of the reference as anything more than casual.

She held her arms out, careful not to get any more on herself than she already had, noting the white stripes on her sleeves and on her wrists. There was even a thick line across her breasts over two of the pearl bodice buttons. "Get the turpentine. Quick."

"Whitewash is harmless. It'll come off with water."

"Get the hose. Quick."

Alex's amused laughter didn't help matters; it only

served to prickle her. He moved—*slowly*—to the spigot and the coil of garden hose by the side of the house. He took his own sweet time about it, as if he wanted her to stand there as long as possible and feel sticky.

The spray nozzle must have gotten knocked into the bushes, because he moved the edge of her box-wood to the left, then right. She called out to him.

"Forget about the nozzle."

"I have to put the nozzle on."

"You don't need it."

"I need it."

He continued his search, wearing an easy smile on his mouth that she wanted to cover with paint.

Beside the porch, on the pile of pebbles she put in the bottoms of her houseplant containers, she spied the paintbrushes that had been used on the swing. Walking with care, she went over to them and grasped the handle of one.

"You don't need the nozzle," she said one more time.

"I need the nozzle." His voice held a hint of mischief, as if he planned on hosing her down like one of the firehouse horses.

On second thought, she didn't want him coming anywhere near her with the garden hose. As he scrounged around in the hedges, she crept toward him, determined. With a bite of her lower lip, she aimed the paint-coated bristles at Alex, flicked her wrist, and let the spatters fly in his direction.

"What the hell?" Fast on his feet, he faced her, hose in his grasp.

He'd found the nozzle.

The paint splashes caught him on the side of the arm, down his torso and one thigh of his pants. His gaze lowered, and he gave himself a perusal that seemed to drag on forever. Then he surveyed her from head to toe, his eyes looking lazily seductive. His broad shoulder dipped right as he leaned to the house.

"Don't you turn on that hose," she cautioned.

His large hand came down on the spigot and gave it a blatant twist.

Camille bolted. Water sprayed the small of her back, causing her to shriek. As hot as her skin was from the sun, the water felt like just-melted ice as it hit her. She screamed as a fresh assault doused her neck and the backs of her arms. Running in a circle around the old elm, she yelled. But even she had to admit there wasn't much terror to the sounds coming out of her throat. They were more akin to giggles.

"Turn it off!" she begged. "Turn it off!"

"I don't think so."

She caught a glimpse of him as she ran through her graveyard of a garden. Paint speckled the hair on his chest, dotted his skin, and was smeared over his flat nipples. Black hair framed his face in a wild, untamed way that was both wicked and alluring. She hid behind the tree, its rough bark next to her cheek. But the sound of the water hissing over the grass reached her ears as he approached. She made no effort to dodge him. She was trapped.

His voice came to her in a low rasp. "I think you need to cool off."

Looking into his eyes, she said, "I am cooled off."

"I'm not."

Then the water showered over them both as he kissed her beneath the sweet rain. His mouth covered hers with a passion she had felt only a few times in her life—all with Alex. Her neck arched to meet his lips more firmly. She would have clung to him if she could have moved. The hose was slowly lowered, her skirts and his pants legs drenched from the stream as he ignored it. He forced her mouth open with his tongue, sliding it between her lips and deepening the kiss. He tasted of root beer.

She groaned into his mouth. She was incapable of thinking clearly. She stood there like a statue, her body hot and blood flowing. The scent of his skin filled her nostrils. They touched only at the lips, which made her grow restless. Yearning ran deep inside her. She wanted him—wanted more than his kiss. She wanted him as she'd wanted him in Boston—and more. This time, she wanted him to feel the way she had.

If he hadn't broken the kiss, she would have let him kiss her forever, outside, with no regard to consequence. His eyes bore into hers with dark desire that made her pulse skip. He had to be used to women swooning in his arms; she was no different. Why couldn't she resist him?

Water dripped off the tendrils of her hair that had come undone from her braid. She stood before him, her breasts rising and falling.

Seconds ticked by before she felt she could trust her voice.

"You get to me, Alex . . ." She still held the whitewash paintbrush, she painted an X on his chest. "Right here."

She didn't want him to say anything. She was afraid he might not feel the same way. So she quickly went on, "I have a cake of scouring soap in the house. Come in and clean up."

Walking swiftly, she left him and climbed the porch steps. She shouldn't have invited him in. She was courting danger. But it was the very danger that lured her to him, that made her crave him.

Would he follow her?

Chapter
❦ 21 ❧

Camille took her shoes and stockings off outside the door so she wouldn't track paint inside. She went to the sink but didn't touch it. Murky drops of diluted whitewash trickled off her hair and dripped over her collarbone and edge of her neckline. She should have gone to the pantry first and found a towel to dry her face. Instead, she stood still, liking the feeling of cool water on her bare toes as it ran off her skirt hem.

The blades of the fan stirred the thick kitchen air as the oscillator turned the grill first toward her, then away. The soap was beneath her in the cupboard, but she didn't go for it. Never mind the fact that she was making a mess on the floor. She wanted to be messy. She wanted ...

She heard the back door open and close. On a shaky sigh, she reached out to hold on to the edge of the sink. Her breath held in her throat as Alex's footsteps sounded on the floor. Closer. Closer.

Closing her eyes, she lowered her head. Waiting.

She felt him behind her and she fought against

turning around to take him into her arms. Could he tell her world was turning upside down? From the day she'd first spoken to him, he'd worked his magic on her until all the barriers she'd tried to put up against him had been dissolved. He aroused in her a need nobody else ever had. She was a hopeless case.

She was in love with him.

He slid his fingers over her shoulders, up her neck, and to the sides of her face, where he caressed her cheeks. The quiet and unassuming power of his fingers was gentle as he cradled her face in his hands. Tenderly, he brought his mouth to the column of her neck and kissed her, his hair tickling her ear. Expelling a breath, she leaned into his chest, the warmth of his body seeping through to her back and the damp fabric that clung to her. She could feel the hard length of him pressed against the fly of his pants. Against her.

Without turning her body, she lifted her face to his for a kiss. Their mouths came together. His tongue glided over the seam of her lips, tasting and teasing. He taught her things she had never imagined. His slow and silken strokes swept through her mouth and she kissed him back in the same way. Erotic. Intimate. She loved the hard feel of his chest next to her.

A quickening deep in her stomach made her knees grow weak. His hands skimmed over her shoulders, and down her arms and locked around her waist. She felt the strong arms that held her, the light sprinkling of dark hair that roughened them. She ran her palms up his biceps, up the smooth and warm skin, feeling every contour.

With her head tilted toward his, their mouths joined in hot fusion, he slid his hands up to cup the sodden fabric covering her breasts. She leaned her back tightly into his chest, her hands over his, wanting him to bring her to his mouth like he had done once before. She wanted to do these things to him. To make him feel the way he made her feel.

In the hotel, it had been about her. Now, she wanted this to be about him, giving to him that feeling of completeness. An utter and total release that brought with it shock waves.

The breeze from the fan flirted with them, touching, retreating, then caressing. Warmth and stillness. A fluttering, then nothing. It was like a sensual dance that passed over them, catching them in its wake, then receding.

Alex's fingertips teased her nipples as they grazed across the thin wet covering over her breasts. He brought an exquisite pleasure through her and a muted cry rose from her throat, lost on his lips. She gripped his hands, keeping them over her breasts, and kissed him. He used tiny soft pulls to peak her nipples into hard tight buds. Her skin prickled and she could barely stand. She pulled back, turning in his arms to face him. Wanting to feel his body beneath her exploring palms. She stared at him, watching his face.

His brown eyes seemed to grow richer, darker, more intense as she looked into them. The shadow of his beard gave him rugged appeal. She touched him with her gaze, then touched him with her hands. He let her explore him in a timeless way.

She skimmed her fingers across his deep-bronzed skin, warm and hard to her touch. She savored the feel of sinewy muscle that defined his broad chest, his wide shoulders, his granite biceps. The white X she'd painted on him had blurred and she rested the flat of her hand over the smudge of paint. She felt his heart beating strongly. It seemed to leap and join the painted red heart on the back of her hand.

Two hearts.

Together.

She trailed her fingers into the dark hair that lightly covered his chest. He sucked in his breath with a low moan as she traced a path between his flat nipples, around each one, then down, to the corrugated plane of his hard stomach. She dragged her fingertips across the top of his waistband, then a fraction lower, to touch his navel.

He groaned. He caught her by the shoulders, brought his mouth to hers and kissed her until she thought she'd go limp in his arms. She wanted him to show her what sex was like—for two people, not just her. But she didn't know how to ask. She couldn't make him love her, but she couldn't let him leave her again without knowing what lovemaking was like, in every way—for her, for him. Her body tingled in every sensitive place.

Her hands slid down his chest once more. She molded her palms over every contour the white paint touched, and in turn, her fingers went white. In her mind, this was an intimacy in itself. Taking paint from him and bringing it to her. It was like being inside each other without doing so physically. The thought was shocking, exciting and wanton. Her desire for him staggered every sense she had.

"I don't want you to leave," was the only way she could voice her true feelings. She looked up at his face for a sign that said he understood what she meant.

The line of his jaw seemed set, his brows black lines of thought. Or was that consideration? She dared not answer. Anticipation, fear, and dread—they held her in their clutches until she had to remind herself to breathe.

He tipped his head to hers; their foreheads met. "Jesus," he whispered against her skin, his hand trailing down the curve of her back, pressing her against his desire. "I want you."

"And I want you." She kissed the bristly line of his jaw; his skin was warm and wet and tasted faintly of salt.

His body stilled and he drew a deep breath, then carefully set her at arm's length. "No, honey. We can't. I can't let you do this."

Alarm mixed with desire. "Why not?"

He ran his finger gently over her cheekbone. "Because." His strong fingers caught her chin as he looked directly into her eyes. "I'm not in a position to make promises. Promises you deserve."

The actual reality of the world beyond this room threatened to press in on her. "What do you mean?"

"I mean that I can't make promises to you. This is now and it's the moment . . . but beyond . . ." He said nothing further. He didn't have to.

"I understand." She wet her lips, tasting him on her tongue, then made a decision. "I'm not asking for a lifetime, Alex. I know exactly what this is. And if you walked out the door right now, I'd always wonder. I don't want to wonder. I want to feel." She brought her hand to the low-riding waistband of his nankeen pants. To the buttons that rode up his fly. "I want *you.*" Her lips parted, and her eyes held his. "I want the moment."

The fanned air caught them in its web, suspending time with each slow pulse of warm air over their bodies.

"Are you sure?"

With those few words, she almost grew weak. "Yes."

The color of his eyes deepened and she knew he wanted her but wasn't convinced.

Only when her fingers slowly worked each closure free did his hands rise to her bodice. He began to flip open the row of pearl buttons. Untried emotions rushed through her. Her rapid heartbeat slammed into her ribs; she had no doubts. Excitement flooded her senses. She couldn't slip the heavy, wet cotton down his thighs over his underwear and she wasn't sure what to do next. That she had taken such bold initiative as to unbutton him, and now to ask for his help with it—

But that thought dissolved as he opened her bodice, separating the gathers of lavender. He slid the sleeves down her arms and pulled her free of the fabric. The dress slipped off her waist and hips, pooling around her bare feet in a wet circle.

As she looked down at herself, the airy linen of her chemise appeared paper thin against her skin. With an agile motion of his wrists, Alex removed her corset and flung it on the counter. Her petticoat followed. She wore only her shimmy and knee-high drawers. Both did nothing to hide the rosy tips of her nipples or the pale blond curls at the juncture of her legs.

She didn't shy away from him but boldly stood before him so that he could see her. She *wanted* him to see. Just as she wanted to see him. Her hand rose to his fly once more and she slipped her hands inside the elastic edge of cotton drawers. He kissed her before putting a hand on the table so he could kick off his shoes. She put her hands at his belt loops and tried to slide his pants down his legs. But he gently moved her hands away and, in an efficient tug, removed them himself. He wore nothing but drawers that hugged and cupped every part of him . . . and a disarmingly slow smile that held her captive.

Her arms slipped about his neck; hands rising to the nape of his neck; his hands closed in around her waist. They kissed once more, this time with a fire and intensity, an urgency that had her frantically seeking. Her fingers tangled in his hair, brought his head closer to hers. She felt herself moving, being walked toward the center of the kitchen ... out ... away ... to the dining room.

"No ..." she mouthed against him. "We'll get paint on the rugs." *And if I have to walk through my house, up the stairs to my bedroom, my courage may falter with each step I take.* "Stay here. Stay with me here."

"Do you want to change your mind?" he asked on her lips. "You can change your mind."

"I don't want to."

Alex backed her into the edge of the kitchen table. The smooth rim of wood pressed against her buttocks. His hand reached between them to touch her breast, to coax her nipple to a hard point. She felt herself tighten, tingle. A shaft of pure fire went straight to the place between her legs. As he gently pulled and fondled, her fingertips curled into the flesh of his bare shoulders.

With an easy glide of his hand, he had her drawers freed of her legs so that only the hip-length shimmy with its thin ribbon straps remained on her body, a body that was straining and pulsing with need, that had paint smeared here and there. It was nothing short of wicked to see that paint contrasting with the rich color of Alex's skin.

She reached out to him, brushing her fingers against the hot, straining bulge behind the soft cotton he wore. He moaned in the back of his throat as she stroked him, gently, curious. She liked that she could make him feel this way.

Alex took her hands, lifted them over her head, and bent her backward over the kitchen table. She lay on its flat surface, staring up into his face. The tablecloth of appliqué apples and cloves cushioned her as she pressed her shoulder blades and the bottom of her spine into the top. My God ...

She should have been mortified and at least ... for her fall from grace ... considered her bedroom.

But there was something about the table that got her pulse to trip and flow through her like an electrical current. They collided, warm and cool and fully alive. And she liked the feeling—liked it so much she was anxious and almost writhing, waiting for him, anticipating and breathless.

Alex's hand rode her thigh, higher, bunching her shimmy in his hand until her woman's place was exposed to him. The heel of his palm brought a friction that had her parting her legs. The sound of her heart seemed to fill the kitchen, flowing with the low hum of the fan and the soft-sounding ripple of the tablecloth as it swayed on the current.

His finger slid inside her, and she whimpered, unsure of what she should do. But those fears and uncertainties vanished. With light rubbing motions, he controlled her. Everything there felt swollen and wanting. She wanted too much to—

He leaned forward and gave her breasts soft and tormenting kisses that rocked her to her toes. His tongue circled each nipple, sucking, licking. She squirmed beneath him, her neck arching. Once more, her fingertips reached out to touch the length of him behind the soft cotton. He jolted, his legs tensing as they crushed into her inner thighs. She was able to slip one hand inside the cotton and touch. Feel the hard and marble-smooth length of him that seemed to pulse, strain, grow even thicker.

Then he lifted his head and stood before her, his feet planted apart on the floor . . . and he slipped his ribbed drawers from his legs. She looked at him without flinching, without worry.

He was beautiful to her. Large and full and hard. She didn't know what to expect, what to feel, when she saw him. But she knew she wasn't making a mistake. She wasn't afraid.

The very sight of him made her need rise another notch. This was a place that she hadn't gone before. A joining of need that put them both in the same place and same moment together.

Alex braced his arms on either side of her, his hair falling away from his brows. The strands had dried to a glossy block that ruffled as the air stream passed over them. He gave her a kiss that was surprisingly tender.

The low rasp in his voice brought out her goose-flesh as he spoke. "If we . . ." He cleared his throat. "Tomorrow, you can't go back to today and wish this away."

That he would give her every opportunity to change her mind made her love him all the more. She shook her head. Tomorrow didn't matter to her. "I want to go with you . . . right now."

Moving his mouth to her ear, he teased its outline with the moist tip of his tongue. "Then let yourself come, honey. Don't hold back."

Then he was against her, the long smooth length of himself that was hot at her entry, probing and so full she thought she might have to say she couldn't. Her hands lifted to hold him by his shoulders; she needed to feel him, connect to him. Her legs came up to lock around his hips. Gradually he slid inside her. Slowly. The pain was sharp and she flinched, her breath a wounded cry.

Disoriented, she felt tears threaten.

"That's the worst, honey." He kissed her lips, pulling her back to his world where kisses and mouths and hands on her body were the things she longed for, desired.

He pushed into her tender skin until she thought she'd taken him. But he pulled back, not all the way, then pushed in. He continued this slow way of entry, in and out, until the apex between her legs felt thick and warm and beyond the initial pain she'd experienced.

When at last he pushed into her all the way, she was ready. A strange thrill consumed her. Her fingers bit into his skin, her hands grasped his biceps tightly. She was intimidated to look at him as he looked at her. She didn't want to imagine what she looked like with her braid over her shoulder, her breasts jiggling. She didn't want to confront the wanton in herself. So she watched where they joined. How he fit into her so perfectly. How this dance between man and woman was joy on earth. A lovely torment made more lovely when they reached that edge of the plateau and their bodies sang.

With each slick stroke that moved within her, he kindled flames in her, a hot ember that built and grew. Hotter. To a field of wildfire that nothing could put out other than Alex himself as he brought her to a new crescendo of fiery explosions. They began small—first a spark, tiny embers that grew. Then rolling heat that covered her skin, made her damp with perspiration. The wiry feel of the hair on Alex's legs abraded the sensitive skin of her thighs, stimulating her more than she thought possible.

Sounds vibrated in her throat, nothing coherent—a lingering moan, a whimper, the soft utterance of his name.

"Come with me, Camille." His whisper was like kerosene on a matchstick. An instant torch of fire. He moved harder and faster, his arms on either side of her shoulders, his head down. A droplet of water rolled off his nose and onto her lips. She licked it, as if she had kissed him.

In those seconds of floating time, she knew she'd been fooling herself. She would never be satisfied with just this one time. Heaven help her, she wanted him forever.

Then he took her with him, in one deep thrust, and she shattered. He filled her, made her drift on a cloud in heaven. The intense heat cooled to a rush of liquid warmth that she could feel quivering and pulsing. Was that her or him? Or both? His rapid motions slowed to a final strain as he swelled inside her and a low moan of ecstacy escaped his throat.

She held onto him as he collapsed over her. His chin burrowed in the moist hollow of her neck, his nostrils next to her skin. Their breath came together in ragged pants, mingling like mists on morning roses.

There were a great many things she wanted to say, but they would have been too poetic, and in her present state, she probably would botch all the words anyway. So she simply said the one thing that she knew would matter to him.

"I'm not sorry," she said, her hands cupping his head, fingers sinking into his hair. "I'm not sorry."

He held her close, so close that she could feel the pounding of his heart. "I only hope you still feel the same way tomorrow."

Chapter

❧ 22 ❧

Somebody sabotaged the jockstraps with Doctor Schmaenkmen's Gold Seal itching powder.

It hit Specs first. One minute he was joking with the guys; the next, horror flashed across his face and his hand inched its way to his cup. The maneuver was subtle; he appeared only to be engineering a minor adjustment, but in reality, it was a scratch. Specs, who had devoutly avoided scratching that particular location on his body, looked left and right to see if he was being observed doing the unthinkable.

"Uh-oh," Specs mouthed as the men around him fit pants up their legs and jerseys over their heads. He gave himself another scratch, a vigorous scratch. Then some more scratches, and still some more.

Alex narrowed his eyes and gave Specs a hard stare, a niggling sense of foul play at the back of his mind. Having been in a professional league before, he never took anything for granted and supplied his own jockey. Always had. Always would. And a time like this proved him right in his distrust of how low one team would go to disable another.

"Everyone stop dressing!" Alex yelled just as Specs moaned.

"Did the regular laundry do the uniforms and jockeys?" Specs's tone was high-pitched as he sat on his locker trunk; he crossed his legs so tightly, he looked like he was going to crack his kneecaps. His cheeks colored pink as he tried desperately to refrain from scratching.

"What's going on?" Duke asked, absently scratching his parts.

"Something's wrong," Specs snapped, "that's what!"

"The jockstraps aren't pure cotton," Alex said, stepping into his pants.

Specs wailed, "Itching powder?"

"Charlie." Noodles motioned to the centerfielder with his chin. "You were the first one in here—anything different about the laundry?"

Charlie paused in putting on his pants. "The uniforms were on the desk, paper-wrapped like they always are. Along with a new box of Spalding jockstraps. I figured Kennison sprang for them, so I doled them out."

"Well, whoever sprang for them sprinkled itching powder in the cups!" Specs shot up as if somebody had given him a hotfoot. "These jockstraps," he said while scratching, "have been sabotaged!"

The players stared at one other. Some of them had been in midscratch. Because they'd always had relaxed manners in that department, it had gone without saying that scratching was regular part of getting dressed. But now that Specs had brought it to their attention, their hands suddenly became restrained—as if they were testing Spec's theory. But the no-scratch concept didn't last long. Soon, the Keystones were scratching en masse.

Everyone except Alex.

And that's how Camille came into the clubhouse and discovered them. At first, she didn't see anything out of the ordinary—she'd been looking right at him as she walked to her desk.

Their eyes met, then her gold-tipped lashes cast shadows on her cheeks as she looked down. Her face turned as pale as the ivory shirtwaist she wore and he thought she might cry. It stabbed at him to be the cause of her tears.

Since the afternoon they spent together a week ago, he hadn't been alone with her. He wanted to talk to her, badly. Because in spite of what he'd told her, he had found himself going to her house the next night. The night after. And the following night. But he'd made it only as far as her gate before he stopped himself. He stood there, in the darkness of the sidewalk, and stared at the house. He watched lights turn on and wondered what she was doing, what she was thinking. Sometimes he'd catch a glimpse of her moving in the front room, then into the dining room. Then later, the lights would dim, and like a slow-fading haze, they would diminish from one riser to the next on the stairwell as she climbed the stairs to her bedroom. Alone.

Each time he put his hand on the latch of that gate so he could follow her, the realities of his life prevented him from opening it, from walking up the path to her door, taking her into his arms, and telling her that he—

But there was no point to buying into the dream that he could have a life with this woman. That he could live in a house with her, be her husband, be the father of her children. That he could have a family of his own and live happily ever after. He'd only be pretending, deluding himself and Camille.

Because his obligation was to Captain. Always. Or until Captain was well, which could take months, years. He had no right to ask Camille to wait.

There were days when he believed Cap was getting better, days when hope wound through his soul. But last night hope had been snatched away so quickly, and so cruelly, that he wished he had never felt hope at all.

He'd gone to her house, and this time, his fingers had snagged the lock on the gate and flicked it open. He hadn't thought about it; he'd just done it. He had gone halfway up the walkway when Captain's voice called out to him.

"Alex . . ." His tone was shaky, giving Alex pause. He looked up at the house, and as much as he wanted to keep walking to those steps, he couldn't. He knew that tone in Cap's voice.

He turned away and went out the gate. It quietly fell back into place, the way it had been—the way he should have left it to begin with.

"I've been looking for you, Alex." The dark night washed over Captain. All but a quarter moon was in the sky—but it was enough for Alex to see his face just as Cap said the obvious. "A guy hit me in the mouth."

Alex's muscles went taut. Shock quickly yielded to anger as Alex viewed the blood smeared on Cap's swollen lips. Cap had tried to stop the flow; he held onto a bloodied handkerchief and raised the cloth to his mouth once more to press at the cut in his swollen lower lip. The offender's fist had really packed a wallop.

Alex's nostrils flared with fury. "Who hit you?"

"I don't know."

"What do you mean you don't know?" He felt his temper rise. "Did he jump you?"

"No . . . we were sitting down. He looked right at me and—*bam!*—gave me one in the chops."

"Have you seen the guy in town? Think hard. Where can I find him?" Violence coiled in Alex, like a deadly snake ready to strike. Whoever had hit Cap was going to be damned sorry.

Captain looked at the blood on the handkerchief. "I know where you can find him, but you're going to be mad at me."

"I won't get mad," Alex assured Cap, his words tightly spoken.

"He's at Dr. Porter's office getting *his* chops sewed up." His eyes rose to meet Alex's. Disquiet marked his brows and the corners of his mouth, as if he were troubled by his actions. "I hit him, Alex. A good one. You know I never hit people, but something got into me tonight and I felt like he had it coming. So after he belted me, I said, 'Damn sorry about this' and sent him some knuckles right back." Moonlight caught in his eyes. "But I lied. I wasn't sorry about it. Are you sure you're not mad?"

Alex wasn't sure what his response was—more like surprise that Cap had slugged a guy. But he wasn't angry with him for doing it. "I'm not mad."

"I worried that you'd be mad at me." Cap lowered his gaze in apparent confusion. "I shouldn't have hit him back. I don't know why I did." Then his voice faded to a hush. "You said that new medicine was supposed to make me feel better. Well, I don't feel like myself anymore. Sometimes I think I'm somebody else thinking things and doing things." His eyes moved upward, glittering with emotion. "It scares me."

Captain stood before him with quiet power in his

body and an innate pride to his stance. *It scares me.* It was a confession Alex had never expected to hear from him. He wished he could give him an answer that would be reassuring. But Alex didn't have answers.

The chirp of crickets played, their songs of summer surrounding the men.

Alex ran his fingertips over his mouth in thought. "What happened to make this guy hit you in the first place?"

Cap's strong white teeth flashed in the darkness, with a vague hint of a smile. And a wince from the cut. "I kicked his ass at poker."

"Poker?" The implication hit Alex with stunning force. "Where were you, Cap?"

"The Blue Flame Saloon."

He tried hard to contain his expression of surprise. "How come?"

"Because I felt like drinking a beer." Cap's reply was matter of fact.

Before he thought, Alex said, "But you don't drink beer."

"I know that." Captain's features grew set. "But something in my mind said a cold one would hit the spot."

"So you went into the saloon."

"I did. I ordered a beer and I played some poker. All I had to do was see those cards in my hand and I knew how you arranged them to win. I didn't lose a single game. That's how come that guy hit me. He accused me of cheating." Cap shoved his handkerchief into his pants pocket. "Have you ever thought about the nice sound cards make when they're being dealt?"

"No, Cap, I haven't." But he remembered hearing about somebody else who always said that very same thing many years ago. He pointedly looked away from Cap, unable to meet him fully in the eyes.

"Well, they do. I could sit and listen to the sound of shuffling cards all night. And I would have if that guy hadn't hit me."

Keeping still, Alex said, "I don't know why you'd ask to play, Cap."

"I wanted to win all that money."

Alex's chin lifted. "Why? I would have given you some."

"I couldn't have taken your money, Alex. When a man wants to buy a woman a present, he doesn't go borrowing the money from somebody else."

"What woman?"

"I noticed Hildegarde fancies the bottle of that Violette France perfume they sell at the mercantile. It's from Paris." An expression of wonder appeared on Cap's face. "Do you think it's really from Paris?"

Without weighing the question, Alex replied, "I don't know."

Thoughts flashed through Alex's mind. He wanted Captain to get well, and tonight was another step toward his reawakening. Beer and cards and a fight. This was all Alex should have desired—Cap returning to his former self. It should have been all he needed. But he wanted to reach out and grasp Camille and her love as well.

Hell. Alex wanted too much. He wanted everything.

He was dreaming. It wasn't going to happen. He couldn't get around the fact that Captain was his first responsibility, and Captain needed to go to Silas Denton to fully recover.

"Hey, Alex?"

"Yeah, Cap?"

"I won six dollars and some change."

"That's good." Alex fingered the matches in his pocket, the pack of smokes he couldn't go for with Captain around. "But next time, don't get hit after you win it."

"No, I don't think I'll be playing poker anymore. It's dangerous."

As they walked away, Alex couldn't help looking over his shoulder for a parting glimpse of the house. The bedroom light had been turned down and the inside grew dark and quiet. Camille remained hidden to him, much like the feelings for her in his heart.

But as Alex's thoughts returned to the present and his gaze followed Camille as she walked to her desk in the clubhouse, he wondered just how much a heart could betray before it was found out. Would there come a time when she'd look at him and know he was lying about his feelings for her?

She slid her chair out, but she didn't sit in it right away. She looked at the men who should have scattered behind the dressing curtain as soon as she'd come in. Her frown wasn't for their lack of modesty. It was the fact they'd been scratching it up— trying to be discreet about it, but failing for the most part.

"I thought we've had this discussion before." She stared at Specs with disappointment. "I see they've finally corrupted you."

Specs firmly shook his head. "No, ma'am. Somebody has corrupted the jockstraps."

"What?"

"Somebody sprinkled itching powder on them," Alex explained, bringing Camille's head around. He liked her eyes on him, even if they weren't filled with shy invitation. "Charlie found a new box on

351

your desk. The White Stockings must have put them there knowing we wouldn't question using them."

"Those White Stockings are some dirty bas—" Mox started to say one word and sliced it short, rephrasing. "—dirty-dealing dogs. We have to go get them."

Immediately, every player hushed and turned to Camille, certain, no doubt, that she would reprimand them. But their manager surprised them when she raised a brow and said, "Get them. Just don't get caught."

The men broke out in a cheer.

Alex watched as Camille sat back in her chair and studied her notebook. When she looked up, their eyes met, and for a second they seemed to lock together, cocooned by the din of cheers and voices. Alex wanted to touch her, pull her close. But before he could move, she looked away and gained the team's attention.

"Each day, we're improving in the rankings," she said. "The Senators lost yesterday, so we're number sixth in the league now."

Another chorus of cheers rose, in spite of the scratching.

Specs was the one who reminded them, "We can't go out there and get them if we're itching. I won't do it. It's embarrassing." Specs shoved his glasses higher on the bridge of his nose.

"Your bad gloving is embarrassing," Yank mumbled beneath his breath while turning away from Camille.

"Shut up, Yank." Specs sat back down and crossed his legs.

"Let's not argue among ourselves," Camille said calmly, her hand lifting to toy with a honey-blond curl that had slipped from its pin. She wore no hat, which was totally unlike her. No gloves, either. Alex caught the subtle fragrance of her perfume. The sweet smell hit him hard; his chest tightened, as if a physical blow had connected with him. And in truth, his body felt like he'd been knocked around.

He hadn't slept worth a damn for a week. He was smoking too much, and if he thought he could function as a player the morning after, he would have been drinking at night.

"I say we call out the White Stockings," Duke suggested, "and bring the matter to the official in charge of the game. What do you think, Miss Kennison?"

Camille read the face of the tiny watch pinned to her bodice. "I think we have to be on the field, ready to play, in thirty minutes." She tapped her notebook and gazed at the men in contemplation. They stood as still as they were able to, given the problem.

They looked at her, waiting for her to advise them on what to do. Alex was just as curious about the situation as the others, only he thought about what it really meant. It was a revelation—seeing twelve men who had resisted her for months now hanging on her opinions. No longer did the players underestimate her value to the team. She was a viable part of the Keystones, an intelligent woman.

And a woman Alex was in love with.

Camille opened her pocketbook and withdrew a key. "Go over to my house. Use my shower bath, and hurry up about it. There are towels in the cedar chest in the first bedroom. It would seem your uniforms are all right. It's what's underneath that's the problem. So obviously, don't put on the same . . . you know. When you're done, get back to the field and we'll show the White Stockings they can't stop us with itching powder."

Affirming nods went around the room. She handed Specs the key, and the players quickly filed out of the clubhouse, leaving Camille and Alex alone.

Without a look in his direction, she opened the notebook before her and selected a pen from the ink-stand on the desk. She began to write, although he doubted she gave any thought to the strokes of her pen. From where he stood, the slants and crossed let-ters looked like chicken scratches. All she was doing was avoiding him. Knowing her, she'd had the lineup ready last night. There was nothing to do but face him.

And from the way she sat stiffly in her chair, that was the last thing she wanted to do.

He understood her hurt, and he regretted being the cause of it. He'd thought that if he were as honest as he could be about making love to her, there would be no emotional attachment. But he'd been wrong. He felt a connection to her like none he'd ever had with a woman. And walking away from her had to be the most painful thing he could ever think about doing, much less follow through with.

Silence stretched out between them.

With her profile to him, she kept her head bent. And ignored him. Her lashes seemed longer to him. Her pink lips fuller and softer. Her smooth skin turned to a golden hue as the sunlight filtering through the window touched her face, a face that had both delicacy and strength in its structure.

"You think the White Stockings got into the club-house?" was about the only thing he could say with-out breaking down and taking her into his arms and kissing her.

The pen quill stilled. "Actually, I'm not sure."

Her answer surprised him. He would have called the White Stockings bums. "Then who do you think?"

Not turning toward him, she spoke to the open notebook. "I'll let you and the others know when I figure it out for certain."

The curtness in her tone fell over him with the bite of a double-edged razor. He almost wished she'd slap him. He'd taken a slap a time or two, and at least a man knew where he stood with a palm imprint on his cheek.

"Camille, I never meant—"

"I really don't want to talk about personal things between us." She abruptly rose to her feet, grabbing her notebook and pen in the process. For the first time since the players had departed, she looked at him. "You were frank with me last week, and I appreciate your honesty."

Honesty. The way she said it sounded so honorable, like he'd done her a favor, when in reality, he'd cheated her with their casual encounter.

"There's no point in going over what was already made clear," she continued. "We can't let one night interfere with our professional relationship. The season isn't over and we have to move ahead." She looked down a moment, then back at him, her clear blue eyes direct. "I knew what I was doing, and I already said I wasn't sorry. I'm still not." She walked past him, careful not to come close enough to chance brushing against him. "You taught me what I wanted to know about sex. Now there's no more to be said on the subject."

Then she was out the door.

Not long after, the day went from bad to worse.

The team was back from their showers and Alex stood on the pitcher's mound trying to stay focused on the batter's stance. Frank Isbell was up to the plate. He'd been hitting deadly line drives throughout the game, nearly killing Alex with a ball in the eighth as it sizzled its way over the left field markers.

Alex went through the windup in his mind, closing his eyes a moment and seeing himself on the pitcher's box. It was a mental thing he did to work through the motions. *Anticipate* and *think*—two of the greatest words in baseball. When he opened his eyes, his attention was drawn for a brief moment to Captain, who sat in the last row of the bleachers. That was a first. Cap always took a front-row spot. But Hildegarde Plunkett sat beside him, and their smiles at one another had nothing to do with the fact that the Keystones were leading by three.

Alex put every ounce of strength from his body into his arm and lifted one leg high, then released the ball with the speed of a bullet. The umpire called a strike, and Frank would have stayed at the plate if it weren't for the fact that Noodles didn't gulp the ball in his glove. It rolled behind him after short contact with the leather. The catcher struggled after it, but by the time he threw to first, Frank had taken his base on the wild pitch.

Calling time, Alex waved Noodles up to the box. The catcher went to him and shoved the cage up his forehead. Sweat poured into his eyes.

"I know what you're going to say, Alex, but a white butterfly flew right in front of my face just when that ball came over the plate." Wiping his brow with the back of his hand, he gulped. "You know what that means."

The muscles in Alex's neck went taut as he tried to swallow. He wasn't about to be sucked in, despite the fact that old fears pulled at his nerves. "It means bullshit, Noodles. Absolute bullshit."

"Yeah, but—"

"Get back behind the plate so we can win this one and go home."

Noodles slid the cage in place over his cheeks and resumed his crouch. With his right hand up, glove open wide, he nodded at Alex.

The next batter took the first two pitches as strikes. The third he foul-tipped toward the grandstands. Way high and deep. The blur of white sailed back to the top riser.

Alex watched as Captain stood and caught the ball bare-handed. The motion was so automatic, it seemed to have been prearranged. Cap looked at the ball, tested it in his palm by rolling it around, then gazed out at the field.

Remaining motionless, Alex was thankful he could pull down the bill of his cap to conceal his eyes. He turned away, kicked the dirt beneath the toe of his shoe, and acted as if he were waiting for the game to pick back up. The catch Cap had made had been one of instinct. One of memory. The rush of emotions that claimed Alex made his throat ache.

The umpire hollered for the ball to come back in play. Then as if Cap had done it a thousand times, he fired off the ball like a rifle shot directly to Alex. Alex stopped the ball in his glove, the hard impact sizzling through the leather into his hand like an imprint. It was with great effort, that he tipped his cap to Captain and gave him a smile. But Cap didn't smile. His expression was bemused, full of thought and wonder. As if he didn't know quite what to make of his actions.

"Holy cripes," Cupid said from first base.

From behind Alex, Specs spoke from the shortstop position. "Did I see what I think I just saw?"

"We could use a guy who throws like him," Bones called out as he stood on second base.

Shutting out their comments, Alex tunneled his mind in on the game and pitched out the inning. The Keystones went on to win it 7–4. Whether or not the White Stockings were the guilty parties in the itching powder incident, the prank had fueled the home team's aggression. Each man had hit at least a single, Deacon and Duke got three-baggers; Jimmy, Yank, and Cub doubled. Alex powered a home run early on for the Keystones to take the lead. Defense had been the best it had ever been, with a masterful six-four-three play in the bottom of the fifth, thanks to Camille's ragtime tempo influence.

After signing autographs for fans and talking to the ladies who were now a regular part of the crowd, the players returned to the clubhouse with laughter and good cheer. They didn't bother dressing in their regular duds; they were going over to the restaurant for steaks and pie to celebrate. Alex didn't plan to go with them to sit around and rehash the high and low points of the game, as was the habit of players. He wasn't in the mood to relive the throw Cap had made.

As they walked out of the clubhouse, Camille called to Alex.

"Mr. Cordova," she said, causing him to turn at the unfamiliar sound of her voice speaking his proper name. "There's a matter we need to discuss, and it can't wait."

It was just the two of them. The door stood open, and Alex figured that was best. Because he wanted to take her into his arms in the worst way.

"What can I do for you?" he said, knowing full well that he'd done more than he should have last week in her kitchen.

Maybe if there hadn't been that tension between them, she would have made a quip about his comment, an innuendo that would have had them both smiling and melt away some of the friction that charged the air they shared.

But she said nothing to put him at ease. And what she finally did say pressed down on him like a steel weight.

"Captain's Joe McGill, isn't he?"

Chapter

❦ 23 ❦

Time ebbed slowly. As Camille waited for Alex to answer her question, she didn't back away from his stare. She held it, much like she wanted to hold him, for she knew the answer. There could be no denying the truth in Alex's eyes. She had watched his reaction on the mound when Cap caught the fly ball. She'd seen how he'd had to turn away to hide the true depth of his emotions.

At length, Alex said in a low voice that seemed to come from a long way off, "Yes, Captain is Joe McGill."

Her heart pounded.

"Why did you say you ended his life when clearly you didn't?"

"But I did. Joe McGill died on the playing field the minute I swung for that ball and hit him instead. He died as surely as if I put a gun to his head and pulled the trigger." A shudder rocked him. "Captain was born in his place. Same body, sure. But a different man inside."

Tears welled in her eyes. "Oh, Alex." She wanted to hug him, but she couldn't move. She blinked, wishing she could make him feel better. "Why do you call him Captain?"

Alex pulled in a long breath of air. "It was Cap's idea." Alex sank onto the trunk of his locker and rested his elbows on his knees. He took his ball cap off, ran his hands through his hair, and dangled the hat in his fingers by its sweat-stained brim. "The day before the accident, some of the Giants rented a boat and took it out on the Chesapeake for the afternoon. The players who'd been with him said Joe really took to it. He decided then and there that when he retired from the game, he'd buy himself a boat and captain it. They thought he was joking, but that night at the bar, he said everybody should start calling him captain if they wanted a ride on his boat when he got it."

He stared at the laces of his athletic shoes. "When he woke up in the hospital, he couldn't remember what happened to him." Lifting his eyes to hers, he said, "The docs asked him if he knew his name. He said yes. His name was Captain."

She imagined the pain Alex must have felt when he witnessed the man he'd injured declare he was somebody else without any indecision. A somebody else who didn't even exist . . .

"Sandy Beecher, the manager of the Giants, didn't want me anywhere near Joe. But when it became evident Joe wasn't himself and looked like he never would be again, the visitors stopped coming. And with Joe not having any family, there was nobody. So I went. Every day. I wanted to see him. I wanted him to remember. I wanted him to tell me I was a son of a bitch for doing what I did to him." The ball cap in Alex's grasp went still as his eyes locked on the felt *K* emblazoned at its center. "But he never told me to go to hell. Never mentioned the game. Never talked about anything that had mattered to him. Because he didn't remember."

Camille listened as Alex told her about the two hospitals Cap had been in, the horrific treatments he'd received—the foot bleeding and probing. The restraints tied to his body. Daily routines that made him less and less the person he'd been. The medicine with arsenic.

Her pulse stilled. "Arsenic?"

"I found out the day we got back from Dorothy. The medicine Cap had been on since he was admitted to the hospital had small amounts of arsenic in it. If it hadn't been for Dr. Porter, Cap might have—"

She went toward him, but he shook his head.

"I don't want you to feel sorry for the way of things."

"Alex, you could have told me."

"It's hard for me to talk about it. I don't like to think about what Cap's been through. He was dying in that hospital." Averting his eyes from her gaze, he exhaled quickly. His brow had beaded with sweat. "In Montana, I was hoping Captain would come around without more doctors. But he's not going to. I'll do whatever it takes to make Cap get well." Then he looked at her with directness. "And I'll do whatever it takes to make that happen."

"Of course you will." She desperately wanted to touch his cheek, to reassure him. But he wouldn't have let her, so she tucked those thoughts away— right beside the afternoon they'd spent in each other's arms.

She'd been devastated when he hadn't come back to her house the next day, even though he'd told her he wouldn't. She'd hoped, wanted him so badly to care for her in a way that went beyond a physical sharing. She wanted his love, his heart. But he'd made it clear that he wasn't offering any commitments or bonds beyond the moment. She'd accepted that. But it was so hard to let go of the wanting anyway.

In the darkest hours of the night, she tried to convince herself it was for the best. Although she hadn't been thinking of repercussions, she didn't regret losing her virginity to Alex—not then, and not now. She just wished she didn't hurt so much inside and feel so lonely without him.

She thought she'd feel relief that she'd been right. That she'd put the pieces together about Joe and Captain. Instead, her heart broke for Alex, who had carried the real truth with him and lived with it daily, but for reasons she didn't understand. Nobody would have blamed him. It had been an accident. She sympathized with Alex and yet she felt hurt that he hadn't confided in her.

She masked the letdown she felt. She wouldn't bring it into the conversation. This wasn't about her. It was about Alex.

"I'm glad you told me, Alex," Camille managed to say with only a slight waver to her voice. She wouldn't let him see her cry; he'd think she felt sorry for him. "If there is anything I can do to help . . ."

"Ah, Camille . . . honey." He stood from the trunk and came to her.

She swallowed the thickness in her throat and kept her chin high. She didn't move, even when he was within inches of her. She could smell the sawdust and sunshine and the unique masculine scent that was his alone. When she looked into his eyes, she could see the various colors of brown, the thickness of his dark lashes. His jaw was shadowed by stubble, his mouth gentle. She thought of the times his lips had been on hers, and a bittersweet ache settled in her breast.

She felt hot tears in her eyes.

His hand lifted to her face. He was close to touching her when her father came into the clubhouse, his voice raised with animation.

"I got him! I got Nops on a vandalism charge!"

The intrusion put an immediate space between Alex and Camille that had her pulse dancing at her wrists. Taking quick hold of her composure, she absently smoothed the cuffs on her sleeves.

"Daddy, what about Mr. Nops?" She said the words, but she didn't hear them above the pounding of her heartbeat.

"I sicced Hogwood on *him,* since that Will White business was a bust." His expression was one big happy grin. "I've had Hogwood tailing Nops for a month, and the things my investigator uncovered about him," he said with glee, "are as solid as a padlock. Nops put pine tar on the bats, flooded the outfield, switched the uniforms, and was the one behind the itching powder. Hogwood has concrete evidence on all of it, from mail receipts from Doctor Schmaenkmen's company to empty tar cans. Nops manipulated things to foil the team's potential because he couldn't be manager." He gave a big huff of excitement. "And wait until you hear this—as of nine o'clock this morning, I now own the entire caboodle once again!"

Camille had followed his fast words with dizzily, but the focal point of her feelings were for Alex. "What are you talking about? Entire caboodle?"

"I've got Nops on vandalism." The mustache on his lip curved. "The police have been brought in, and since it was up to me to press charges, I cut a deal with that lug nut. I don't send him to jail if he relinquishes his share of the team. He agreed. He loses his money and I get everything. It's been signed, sealed, and made a done deal this morning in Stykem's office." He gave Camille a hard hug that she was too stunned to return. "The Harmony Honeybees are the Kennison family. Father and daughter. Together."

"You just said Honeybees," she pointed out as she looked at Alex, "not the Keystones."

His brows lifted. "So I did . . . so I did." Then he laughed. "I don't care what the rags call us. We're a winning team! The Washington Senators lost again today and so did the Baltimore Orioles. Our club has just moved up to fifth place!"

Her father moved away and looked at Alex as if he'd just noticed him in the room. "Cordova! Great job. You've been pitching some fine innings. Keep up the good work!" Then to her, "Now, come on, Camille sugar, I want to show you the Spalding mitts that came in. They're top of the line and cut from the best leather. I've got them in the dugout."

And her father steered her out of the clubhouse before she could say another word to Alex.

"A glass of sangaree for the lady," Alex ordered, bending his elbow at the counter alongside men lifting their voices in laughter and tipping back drinks.

"Coming up." While the barkeeper opened a bottle, Alex turned to lean on the bar and hooked his foot over the brass rail. His gaze scanned the crowd in the Firedog Tavern. Nearly all men, except for the women moving from table to table, serving drinks. The Firedog was a respected pouring spot, its waitresses a virtuous link to the nonvirtuous dance hall and cathouse women who plied their wares up on 66th Avenue— the seamier side of Cleveland.

At one of the felt-covered tables along the back wall, Camille sat with the Keystones. Peanut shells scattered on the tabletop and pitchers of beer made for table ornamentation. A man couldn't miss her in the sea of dark-colored suits. She stood out in her apricot-colored dress. Her blond hair was curled and pinned in the right places to softly frame her face. The hat on her head was decorated with frosted fruits, peaches, and blushing cherries. Her cheeks flushed a pretty pink as she laughed at a joke Yank must have told.

As her mouth widened, her lips curving into a smile that could melt a man, Alex thought back on the past weeks. August had been left behind and September heralded in opportunities. The Harmony Keystones played nine home games, and fifteen games on the road, losing six and winning eighteen. The latest win this afternoon capped off a four-game stand with the Cleveland Blues. And the victory moved the Keystones up in the ranks to third.

After today's game, the players called for a hurrah at the tavern next to the hotel and invited Camille along. He hadn't thought she'd agree, but she had. She added to everyone's enjoyment, making the Keystones envied as they kept her company. Alex hadn't failed to miss the stares in her direction and the gestures of respect as the men tipped their hats.

Camille Kennison had developed a reputation for delivering a baseball team who could go nine innings and come out on top. It was no small feat for a man, much less a woman.

Alex paid the barkeep and took the fruity drink to the table. "Here."

Cautiously, she studied the rose-hued liquid inside. "What is it?"

"It's the closest thing they have to punch. A sangaree is pretty tame." He extended his arm and she reached out to take the drink. Their fingers brushed as she connected with the glass, and she jumped.

"Sangaree doesn't give the same glow as sipping whiskey."

"Sangaree," Cupid said as if it were a mouthful. "Isn't there rum in that?"

"No rum." Alex dragged out a chair and straddled it. "Wine. And fruit juice. Nutmeg on the top."

Noodles took a sip of beer. "I once knew a woman named Nutmeg."

"Why'd they call her Nutmeg?" Jimmy's grin was one big wide-gapped mouthful of teeth.

"On account of her—" Alex slammed his elbow into Noodles, knocking the wind from his story.

He archly reminded Noodles, "There's a lady sitting at our table."

When Alex looked at her, his brows rose in surprise. She'd drunk half the sangaree already and was gazing at him as if he'd brought her a lemonade rather than alcohol. The wine wasn't strong, but a woman who got a glow off of a thimble's worth of sipping whiskey had better take it easy on all kinds of liquor. But he wasn't about to point that out to her with the players sitting around. She'd take his hide off him for putting her on public notice.

Specs, who was short on eyesight and long on inexperience, pressed the subject. "On account of her what?"

Noodles scooted away from Alex before replying with a cleaner version. "Well, shall we say a certain part of her was the color of nutmeg?"

"I can guess that one. Something below the neck and above the navel."

All heads shot toward Camille's voice. She smiled at them. The glass in front of her was as empty as a burned out lantern. "I'll have another, Mr. Cordova, thank you."

Alex narrowed his eyes. "I don't think so."

"I don't feel a thing. The barkeep must water the drinks down." She straightened the angle of her fruity hat and raised a brow. "If you won't get one for me, one of these gentlemen will."

"What gentlemen?" Mox asked, looking left and right.

"Us, you numbskull." Cub rolled his eyes. "Mox, you have less smarts than a mule."

"I don't see us wearing suits," Mox explained, "like these other fine swells in the establishment."

Duke took issue and lifted his mug of beer. "We're fine swells, too. We may not wear the fanciest duds, but we're a winning ball team."

"That we are," Charlie said around the cigarette between his lips.

"Gentlemen, I . . ." Camille licked her lips as if gathering her thoughts; she ran a casual fingertip down the beads of water on the sangaree glass. The move jabbed Alex in the pit of his stomach. He barely heard her next words. "I wanted to say that regardless of what happens this week, each and every one of you should be proud of what the team has achieved."

A solemn silence momentarily held the table.

Then Bones assured her, "We'll make it, Miss Kennison."

"I'd like to think so, but if we don't . . ."—her gaze went in turn to each player, not lingering on Alex, an intimacy he missed—"we'll come back next year and grab it."

Duke's crooked nose made his face seem lopsided, yet not unkindly so. He spoke in a soft tone. "You're going to continue to manage us?"

The clarity in her eyes didn't fade when she replied with unflinching firmness. "Nothing could make me quit."

"I speak for all of us, Miss Kennison, when I say we don't want you to quit." Yank's words were met with nods. "We've talked about it, and we like having you as our manager."

She smiled, her lips full and soft, yet delicate. Alex struggled to control the emotions running rampant inside him. With her white teeth teasing the curve of her lower lip and her eyes a dazzling blue, she seemed ethereal.

"Now, if you'll excuse me, Mr. Cordova is right. I shouldn't have another." She rose and promptly wobbled on her legs. She quickly reached out to hold on to the back of her chair for support. "I'm going back to the hotel."

"You're not walking alone." Alex shoved out of his seat and went to her side. He thought she might argue with him, but she didn't.

The players said their good nights and Alex guided Camille outside to the warmth of the evening. He tucked her hand into the crook of his arm as he turned onto the sidewalk. She didn't object. She was too busy taking in deep breaths in an effort at unclouding her head.

The Lexington Hotel was around the corner, so they didn't have far to go. Buggy traffic had thinned to near nothing; there was only the occasional slow clop of shod hooves as a horse and dray rolled passed them. Darkness clung to the storefronts, the window displays in shadows. A lone cigar-store Indian stood on the corner in front of the tobacconist's shop.

Alex was keenly aware of the way the side of Camille's breast brushed his arm as they strolled. He could have walked around the block a hundred times just to keep her beside him.

"Did you get cut?" she asked, the question throwing him.

Thinking a moment, he finally shook his head. "Nope."

The game had been a close one. Cub had given one of the hecklers an old-fashioned nose thumbing that caused all the pop bottles and trash of any kind to come flying onto the field in the Keystones' general direction. Alex had been hit in the back of the leg with a bottle. But he'd gotten a fair shake when he'd hit a grand slam in the ninth to win the game.

He added, "Thanks for asking."

"Don't be so polite with me, Alex." Exasperation showed through her tone. "I like you better when you're not on your best behavior."

She let him mull that over, keeping her profile to him and slipping out of his arm. They reached the double doors of the hotel; he wasn't fast enough to hold one open for her. Making a point to let herself inside on her own, she strode over the lobby tiles and directly took the stairs to the floor of rooms. Down the hallway she went, with Alex at her side. Once at her door, she unlocked it, turned, and looked him fully in the eyes.

The pace she'd set had been so swift, he expected her to slam the door in his face. But she didn't. She did something totally unexpected.

She kissed him. Soundly on the mouth. Long enough to arouse him, short enough not to bring her arms around his neck and press her body next to his. Almost immediately, she stepped back as if she had to run from him.

He searched her face, looking for a reason why. These past few weeks he had battled to stay away from her. With this one kiss, he was losing.

"Don't ask me why." The words were a whisper. "I just wanted to."

She went to move away from him, but he shoved

his knee in the door's path and prevented it from being closed. He entered the room and shut the door with a kick of his foot. She gasped as he caught her in his arms, jerked her to his chest, and held her tightly.

Then he was kissing her until he heard her breath catch; opening her mouth with his tongue and sliding between her startled, wet lips. He felt a thickening deep in his groin. She clung to him, a whimper sounding from her throat as slender fingers slipped into his hair and his Stetson fell to the floor. Without backing out of the kiss, he raised his hands to the buttons at her collar. He loved the taste of her, could feel the blood pulsing beneath her skin.

The fullness of soft, round breasts filled his hands, the nipples peaking as his fingers teased them through the thin chemise covering her silky skin. He inhaled her scent, the lavender that was uniquely hers when the perfume veiled her body. Heat rippled under his skin wherever they touched. Shivers ran through her in all directions when he pressed tiny kisses along her jaw, down her throat, and along her shoulder.

She tugged at the buttons on his shirt and softly worn pants, sliding her fingers beneath his clothes and caressing his chest. Stroking him, her hands blazed a hot trail across his skin. The kiss broke, then began anew, then broke again as slowly, piece by piece, items of clothing were shed.

With exploring fingers, he found the long pin that kept her silly hat on. He took it off. Then he gently pulled the pins from her hair, capturing the thick mane in his hands as it fell to her waist. Naked, she arched her back as he massaged one breast, the bud swollen beneath his touch. In a torturously light way, she skimmed the side of his ribs, then lower to the part of him that ached with wanting her. She encircled him. His body tensed, then reacted with a shuddering ecstacy when she explored, and touched him in the ways he had done to her.

His mouth left hers with a groan, and he stilled the kiss long enough to take her to the bed, where they fell into the downy coverlet. Taking her open mouth, he kissed her once more as he moved over her parted legs. She lifted herself to him but stilled before he touched her.

"Alex . . ." she said against his lips, but she said nothing more.

He knew what she was going to say because he had thought it himself.

The beat of his heart raged in his ears and he wanted her more at this moment than he ever had another woman in his life. But to take the same risks as last time would be tempting fate. He murmured next to the corner of her mouth, "I know what to do. You don't have to worry, honey."

That was what she needed to hear because she held onto his shoulders and moved beneath him in abandonment and surrender, taking him into her and moving in a rhythm with him. He pulled her against him, holding her close so that he could feel every trembling emotion beating through her. She clasped her arms around his back and met each thrust as he brought her to a climax that made her cry out against his lips.

As the last quake of her body enveloped him, he withdrew and spent himself, kissing her, holding her, feeling utterly complete.

Alex spent the night in Camille's hotel room. They lay in each other's arms, making love until the sun began to shimmer through the curtains. As they talked, one subject was never touched upon—the future.

They traveled to Boston to play the Somersets, who

were in the lead for the pennant. After the team won an early afternoon game against the team, Alex took Camille to the public gardens.

The sky was laced with gray clouds, but the air was warm and muggy. Alex held her hand while they walked down a path through the waist-high wrought-iron fence surrounding the garden. Moored at the banks of a lagoon were swan boats with gondoliers waiting to take couples on a ride over the water.

"Which one?" Alex asked, referring to the white swans with their painted black beaks and yellow eyes.

"Hmm. Let me see." She shrugged with a smile. "They all look the same."

"I think we should ride in that one. It looks like a bird from your hat."

Her mouth fell open in mock offense. "I've never worn a swan on my hat."

"A duck, then."

"Duck *feathers.*"

"Same thing. But I like your hats, so I don't care if it's swans or ducks that decorate them."

He took her toward the boat on the end. The gondolier doffed his beret and welcomed them.

Camille stepped into the gently bobbing boat with Alex's help. He sat beside her, their backs cushioned by red-and-white-striped pillows. Their fingers entwined. With the smooth strokes of the gondolier's pole, the swan was propelled out to the middle of the lake. Water softly lapped against the hull and made a quiet trickling sound as it ran down the pole with each stroke.

Tipping her face toward the sky, Camille closed her eyes and let the warmth of the sun, peeking out from behind clouds, fall over her face.

"This is better than a flatboat ride," she said with a dreamy sigh. "My Uncle Grant worked for the

Shreveport Boat and Boiler Company, and when I was a little girl, he'd let me ride the flatboat with him. I thought nothing could be better than floating down the Mississippi. But this is." She looked at Alex. "Because you're with me."

He lowered his head over hers, his eyes a rich brown that could make her lose every conscious thought in her head. "I don't want to be anyplace else." Then he kissed her.

It didn't matter that they weren't alone. The kiss was soft and special, making her heartbeat thud.

She smiled with Alex as they admired at the lush weeping willows and beautifully kept garden paths leaving the banks. Halfway to the other side of the lagoon, a fat raindrop fell. Then another. And another one—until the sky unleashed a downpour.

The gondolier propelled them faster to the shelter of trees. Once at the sandy shore, Camille and Alex stepped out of the boat and ran beneath the canopy of willow branches.

With her back against the trunk and Alex's arms braced on both sides of her, she breathlessly asked, "Now what shall we do?"

"This."

And he kissed her once more, his tongue entering her mouth. She clung to his shoulders, kissing him back. The taste of him melted against her lips. She didn't want the kiss to end.

She didn't want this day to end.

She made a conscious effort to keep her mind focused on Alex, the way he made her feel in this fragment of time. She'd remember it, always.

"We're getting wet," Alex murmured next to her mouth.

"I don't want to go back to the hotel yet."

"No?"

"No. I want to go window shopping."

With a soft smile, he nodded. "All right."

They held hands, laughing and running through the downpour to the end of the gardens and onto the streets, which were all but empty. Most of the pedestrians had gone inside to wait for the skies to clear from the late summer shower.

Camille and Alex walked down the sidewalk, hand in hand, stopping every now and then to look at a display, to admire this or that.

Every block or so, they held back beneath an awning to share a stolen kiss, then moved on without any hurry at all in spite of the fact they were soaked through.

Once at the hotel, they went through the lobby and up the stairs with a respectable distance between them. At Camille's door, they entered the room together, walking across the floor and kissing at the same time, stripping away wet clothes that fell in sodden piles about them. And on the bed, they lay naked in each other's arms, caressing, touching, marveling.

Making love.

Alex didn't leave until the first rays of light filtered through the room.

The next day, they left for Chicago. And each night when the hallways grew quiet and guests had extinguished the lights in their hotel rooms, Alex and Camille found their way to one another, sharing a bed and the needs that had been building during the day through brushes of their hands, caressing gazes, and conversations that held a more intimate meaning than was apparent on the surface.

Discussing promises that hadn't—and wouldn't—be made would only make Camille long for something she couldn't have—his love, the gift of his name, a wedding ring, and a walk down the aisle to be his bride. Alex had been perfectly honest from the beginning. She'd take what she could of their time together, and perhaps along the way, something would change.

The word *affair* didn't linger in her mind. To confront it would mean she'd have to admit she wanted to make love with Alex Cordova without any promises. What did that say about her?

For now, she didn't give herself a chance to think about it.

Because the Keystones had defied every odd against them and, this afternoon, had beaten the Chicago White Stockings.

Harmony's Honeybees were going home to play for the pennant.

Alex tucked the newly arrived letter behind the boxes of cut nails and cans of varnish. There was no question now. No more wondering what if. Captain had been accepted by Silas Denton as a patient. They were to be in Buffalo next week.

Sunshine splashed through the open doors of the wood shop as Alex sanded the long piece of ash he'd made into a bat. The wood was finely grained, perfect for hitting balls out of the park if a batter knew how to wield it with just the right pull in his swing. He took a cloth and wiped the bat clean, ridding it of all dust. Then he reached for the red-hot iron bit and started to draw the face of a bear on the wide end of the bat. Tight and controlled strokes, he drew the nose and hair, the eyes, the muzzle, the teeth.

For his last game with the Keystones, Alex was going to play as "the Grizz." In a few hours at Municipal Field, either the Boston Somersets or the Harmony Keystones were going to win the pennant. The series was tied three apiece. Camille had done it. She'd brought them this close.

When he finished with the bat, he went outside to let the heat pour over his face. He walked to the back of the property, to the square pitching zone he'd made from timbers. Staring at it, he looked at the bucket of baseballs, his thoughts going to Camille. To the day she'd found him throwing balls. He couldn't imagine not staying with her. He couldn't imagine not taking Cap to New York.

Cap appeared from behind the building's corner. Confusion marked his expression as he frowned at Alex.

"Alex, I have to ask you something."

"Yeah, Cap?" he replied, absently picking up one of the baseballs and throwing it into the mound of dirt. He grabbed another ball. "What it is?"

"Do I know a guy named Joe?"

Alex froze. He looked at the baseball in his hand, then at Cap, who waited with quiet expectation in his eyes. As if he already knew the answer. "Yeah, you do."

"I thought so. He plays baseball, doesn't he?"

No shock or surprise registered in Alex. Deep down, from the progress Cap had been making, he knew this would come out. "He did."

Captain nodded, then ran his hand through his clipped black hair. His eyes lowered to the baseballs in the bucket, then at the one in Alex's hand. "I think I want to try to see if I can play baseball. Would you throw me some balls, Alex?"

"Yeah, sure, Cap."

Cap stood a fair distance apart and Alex tossed him a soft one.

"Not like that," Cap directed him. "Throw me one like you'd throw to the Keystones."

Alex wound up and threw a hard pitch. Cap

reached out for it without flinching. Then he hurled it back to Alex. They shot the ball back and forth to each other for a while, then Alex quietly asked, "Cap, do you want to meet Joe?"

Captain nodded. "I think I'd like to."

"I'm glad to hear that, because we're going to go to a doctor in Buffalo, New York." For the first time, he said the plans out loud; it gave him resolution—no backing away or changing his mind. "Not like those docs you saw before. This doctor is the best. He said you can come see him. It's all set. We'll leave next week."

Captain lowered his arm. "You say he's not like the other docs?"

"No. He's a good one. He can help you get to know Joe."

Regarding him with undiluted trust, Cap said, "Okay. I'll go to Buffalo as long as we'll come back to Harmony—all right? I have my job and Hildegarde is here. I don't want to leave Hildegarde forever."

Alex didn't know how to reply. It all depended on so much. In the end, all he could offer was, "It'll all work out, Cap."

"This could be it," her father said with unbridled euphoria. "The last game of the pennant is only hours away and we could win. Camille sugar, are you sure you have everything ready? The lineup, the equipment? You should have plenty of drinking water in the barrel, towels, bandages—but we won't think along those lines." He stood in his store wearing his best suit and black string tie. Pacing in front of the counter, he continued to question her without giving her a chance to reply. "Do you have plenty of new balls? Glove leather oil? Is the lineup made out? Oh,

I asked that already. What did you say? All right, it should be good weather for today's game. Sunny. Not overly hot. But then again, I saw clouds on the horizon. White, though."

Camille reached out and touched him on the arm. "Daddy, if we win, it's not going to have anything to do with having bandages on hand and the water barrel in order. We'll win because the players have played the best game they can."

"I know that." His eyes searched hers and he smiled. "But this could be the biggest day of my life. If we win this one, we win the pennant. It all rides on these nine innings. Do you think the Keystones can do it?"

"Yes, I do."

Unexpectedly, he engulfed her in a bear hug. "Camille sugar, however it goes, I'm so proud of you."

Her heart sang with his love and appreciation.

He patted her back, then awkwardly pulled away, and, to her surprise, took the handkerchief from his coat pocket and loudly blew his nose. "You'd better get over to the ball field if you're going to make it on time."

She grinned, feeling tears fill her eyes. "I'm never late."

She left the store with mixed feelings. The Keystones had come so far. So had she. But her steps lacked the lightness they should have as she walked to Municipal Field.

Today Camille was going to tell Alex she loved him.

She couldn't pretend that stolen moments were enough anymore. They weren't. The baseball season had come to an end. She'd give it up for him, if that meant they could be a couple. She knew she'd told the players nothing would make her quit; she'd do everything possible to keep her relationship with Alex and manage them. If they were married, she didn't see how there could be a problem.

Either they'd commit to spending the rest of their lives together or she'd tell him she couldn't see him anymore. It was too painful to go on wishing for things that might or might not ever happen.

She thought she'd be happy going to the pennant, having that chance to prove to her father that she'd done the job well, but she realized now that it meant nothing. Not without knowing that Alex would be there for her for all the days to come—that win or lose, they'd have each other.

She was about to step off the corner when Hildegarde hurried up the boardwalk. She was crying. She had both hands on her round cheeks as she moved swiftly toward Camille.

"Hildegarde," Camille called to her friend, going to her side to stop her. "What's happened?"

Hildegarde's face flushed with bright color. "I have to go home and tell my mother." Her eyes glittered as she stared at Camille. "Captain told me he's leaving town next week. He and Alex are going to New York."

"New York?" A soft gasp escaped her. She stared at Hildegarde, her insides quaking. "But they'll be back . . ."

"I don't think so. I couldn't listen to any more. I just kept thinking that he gave me Violette France perfume. And that I love him with all my heart." Fresh tears caught on the young woman's thick lashes. "Captain said he's going to be seeing a new doctor. I want him to, but I want him to be with me, too."

"New doctor?" Camille heard herself speaking, but it didn't seem to be her voice. *Leaving for New York next week.*

Hildegarde's tears came anew. "I need to go home. I . . . can't believe he's leaving."

Then she was gone.

The shock of the discovery hit Camille full force, holding her to the spot, with only a fragile control keeping her from crying herself. But there was no time to do anything, to say anything.

Less than fifteen minutes later, she was in the Keystones clubhouse, reciting the most important lineup in her career as a manager and giving Alex glances that were so unsteady, she could hardly breathe, much less think.

As the game began, Camille sat on the bench, numbness seeping into her bones. She could barely keep her mind on the activity in front of her. A brittleness edged her normally calm demeanor. Her temper rose to a degree where it boiled, something she rarely experienced, much less showed. She was angry and hurt, wanting to say nothing to Alex other than tell him he was unkind.

Once, their eyes met, and she sensed he knew what had gotten her so upset. Clearly, her dark mood was evidence enough that she wasn't herself. But the fact that she couldn't look at him without her pulse tripping, without wanting to ask him why he'd not told her his plans, had her snapping at him in front of the players rather than questioning him. And even if he did have an explanation to offer her, he couldn't exactly talk about it in the middle of a pennant game, in the middle of a dozen players watching and listening on the bench.

Fly-off-the-handle comments came out of her mouth at the umpire; as luck would have it, Mr. Carpio, the man she had to remind herself not to call something else, bore the brunt of her raised voice.

In the bottom of the ninth, the score tied, with

Boston turning on every bit of power they had. Bones smacked one into right field and dashed to first. Seeing he had to hustle to make the base, Bones slid into the bag, only to be called out by Mr. Carpio when the first baseman tagged Bones on the leg.

Camille hopped to her feet and rushed the field. "What's the matter with you? Do you need spectacles or something? The first baseman wasn't even on the bag. He's safe!"

Mr. Carpio pursed his fleshy lips, spit spraying from his mouth as he spoke. "I've had about all I can take from you. Lady or no lady, you've come out here one too many times to question my calls. You're fined two hundred big ones."

Her mouth dropped open; her lungs fought for air. As soon as she started giving him a piece of her mind, she couldn't hold back. "Why don't you make it three hundred? You don't know the difference between a ball and a strike. You've been miscalling them all day. You couldn't flag down a wagon if it ran over you, much less make a judgment on a small white ball flying in the air. You don't know what you're doing you . . . you catfish-faced sourpuss."

"You're *out* of the game!" His fist came down in one big swoop through the air, a sign of ejection.

"You can't do that to me!" she cried. She was beyond being reasoned with. Tears had begun to roll down her cheeks and she dashed them away with the back of her hand. "It's not my fault you're blind."

Mr. Carpio pushed his face up close to hers and yelled so loudly, her eardrums rang. "Get out of my ballpark, lady!"

Completely losing her composure, she hollered back, "You can't make me!"

"I'll have the coppers take you out by force," he

shot back, spittle on his lips. "I can and I do have the authority to get my demands met!"

Before she knew what was happening, strong hands held her beneath the arms and lifted her off her feet. Startled, she jerked her head to the side to see Alex, who was in the process of hauling her from the field.

As she protested and tried to wiggle free, he only gripped her tighter. Several more attempts to rid herself of him got her as far as littering the grass with fruits that had flown off her hat. It was useless to fight him. He had the unbending strength of an iron fence.

Once in the clubhouse, he set her on her feet. She scrambled away from him to catch her breath. She would have put the desk between them if it had been in the middle of the room. As it was, it sat in the middle of wide open space she didn't want to venture into. And when he took a step toward her, she halted him with a raised hand.

"Don't come near me, Alex."

"Camille—"

"I don't want to talk to you. I'm upset about the game. I never lose my temper." Devastation spun inside her. "I got thrown out by the umpire."

"You're not upset about the game." He moved toward her and she took a step back. "It's more than that, and we both know it."

"Then there's no point in saying anything."

The words hung between them.

On a shuddering breath, she blurted, "You're leaving me." A stabbing hurt settled in her heart and she almost laughed at the revelation. "Is that what 'no promises' meant? You've known all along."

His jaw visibly tensed. "Yes."

"I never thought you'd walk out on your contract and . . . leave me." She couldn't face him any longer. She had to turn away so he couldn't see the fresh tears in her eyes she tried desperately to keep from falling.

"I'm taking Captain to a special doctor in Buffalo, it's true." Alex's tone was low and pained. "Silas Denton is the best in his field. He can help Captain remember Joe."

"Well, good then. I think you should go," she said with some bitterness in spite of the fact that Alex had Captain's best interests at heart. They came at the expense of breaking hers.

She felt Alex draw up to her back. He stood so close to her, his breath touched the side of her neck and brought shivers across her skin. Thank goodness, he didn't touch her. She would have broken down if he did. "Camille, I don't want to leave you—"

A burst of noise intruded on the clubhouse as Cub and Yank came rushing in. "Cordova! Come on!" Cub shouted.

Yank hollered, "You're up to bat!"

Alex looked at them, then at her.

She fought hard not to start crying again. "Get out there," was all she managed.

Then after a glance at her, he left.

Chapter
❧ 24 ❧

It was up to Alex.

All of a sudden everything had come down to this. A 1–1 score. The Keystones up at bat with two outs. Jimmy Shugart on second and Duke Boyle on third.

Alex stepped into the batter's box, but his gaze wasn't on the men waiting in their places for him to hit a ball that would either end this game or bring it to extra innings.

Indecision sliced through Alex. Everything about the situation told him he should have stayed with Camille. She was more important to him than winning. But he knew what was important to her—proving to her father that she could manage a bunch of ballplayers and make them into a winning team. So he had to do everything he could to help her with what she wanted.

Giving the Keystones the pennant.

"Are you going to take a pitch, Cordova," came the needling voice of the catcher, Lou Criger, "or are you going to stand around all day, *honeybee?*"

Alex shot his gaze over his shoulder, looking into the face behind the wire mask. The Somerset catcher crouched low, knees ups and legs wide. He popped his fist into his glove and gave Alex a sneer.

"What are you waiting for, honeybee? An invitation?"

The noise of the cheering fans amplified, rushing in on Alex. He could barely think above the screams and shouts that roared onto the field.

In a quick glance at the soaring stands, he saw Captain in the first row amid the sea of hats and parasols. Though sitting, Cap stood out. Tall, wide-shouldered, with gleaming black hair and a body that emphasized his strength. Sunlight glimmered in Cap's gaze. He stared at Alex with an undefinable emotion in his eyes. The way he held himself was so much like Joe.

Alex's heart hammered in his chest. He looked away, struggling with keeping his head clear. His grip on the bat slipped and a heavy feeling settled in his stomach. He needed more time. He had to talk with Camille.

Turning once more, he continued to search the crowd in the hope she'd taken a place among them. He sought a fruited hat and a dress that was as white as snowy clouds.

He found neither.

"Cordova, I'm going to call a strike on you if you don't get into the box and take a pitch," Carpio warned Alex from his position behind the catcher.

Alex stepped back up to the plate, stared beyond Cy on the pitching mound, and narrowed his gaze down the diamond to the runners. Jimmy and Duke were counting on him. The Keystones were counting on him.

Camille was counting on him.

Lifting the bat in his grasp and digging his feet in,

Alex nodded to Cy. Cy came after him with a fastball, waist high, right over the plate. Alex took a swing. And missed. The ball thudded into the catcher's glove.

"Sttttttttttrike one!"

Swallowing, he took his stance once more, the catcher riding up to his leg, bumping next to him, talking to Alex beneath his breath.

"That was as dim as a headlamp, Cordova." Lou's laughter floated to Alex. "You took a strike on a ball that should have ripped Cy's head off and gone out into right center field."

The truthful commentary had Alex gritting his teeth. He inched up on the plate so the catcher would give him some room. But the Somerset player crept forward with him, nudging his right leg with his shoulder.

Undulating waves of heat radiated off the field, popping beads of sweat on Alex's brow. The dampness of his skin made his uniform stick to him. The underarms of his jersey were wet with perspiration. He tried to focus on the images in front of him, but he couldn't see clearly.

And that's when he felt her as sure as if she'd touched him. Releasing his position, he took a step toward the stands and shielded his gaze with his hand. He raised his eyes, searching, wanting to find Camille.

And there she was.

Watching. Waiting with an expression that spoke every hurt she must feel.

"Play ball, Cordova!" Carpio shouted, drawing Alex back toward home plate. The umpire stood with his knees bent, hands clasped behind his back, peering at the batter's box. Reluctantly, Alex stepped into it, shifted his feet, and lifted his arms with a grim grip on the handle of his lumber.

The catcher butted up against him, glove out wide, waiting to catch the next strike.

Alex choked up on the bat, his nerves stretching thin. "Get back, you son of a bitch," he cautioned in a low tone. "I'm liable to rip your head off when I swing."

"Fat chance, honeybee. I'm a lot faster than you."

Alex's arms crooked, his shoulders swung forward. In that fraction of a second it took him to get ready, Cy had already released the ball. Caught off guard, Alex took a slice at it, drawing the bat too far back. The tip connected with the catcher's shoulder, the jolt his body received knocking his mask off his face. Lou went down in the dirt, a spurt of dust coming up as his steel muscles collapsed. Laying beside him was the iron cage that was supposed to protect his head, banged up—useless.

Oh Jesus. No!

Tossing his bat, Alex was on his knees before he thought, leaning over Lou with a chill in his blood. Fright held him in it clutches, cold and icy. He began to shake as old memories came at him with a speed he couldn't shake. Captain out cold on the plate. Blood spilling from the side of his head. The umpires closing in. Sandy Beecher hollering for help. Chaos.

Oh sweet Jesus.

Seconds ticked by that seemed like minutes.

Motionless, Lou lay there, his eyes closed. Alex gently laid a palm on Lou's shoulder, turned, and opened his mouth to call for a doctor.

"Get away from me, Cordova."

Alex jerked his face back to the catcher.

Lou's eyelids had snapped open, and he struggled to sit. "I can get up myself, you damn honeybee."

As the catcher went to his feet and dusted himself off, Alex stumbled to his feet. He took a deep breath and tried to relax; it was hard not to be caught in the cobwebs of the nightmare. He heard sounds around him—the jeers from the Somersets, the return taunts from the Keystones.

The specifics of the taunts didn't register in Alex's head, but their meanings were clear in the tones of the voices. Alex's troubled spirit wouldn't quiet. He retreated a step, then another. He began to walk—to walk to the dugout, walk out of the game. He couldn't do this. He couldn't play.

Everything around him had fallen apart.

Reaching the bench, he threw his cap into the dirt and didn't meet the gazes of the Keystones who had stood and pelted him with their disbelief. They tried to shout over one another.

"What's the matter?"

"Go hit the ball!"

"Are you crazy?"

"You can't quit!"

"Get your bat!"

Crowding him and hollering over each other, they told him to get back out there. Amid all the uproar, only one voice got through to Alex.

"It wasn't your fault."

Alex spun around to find Captain standing in a slash of sunlight that tipped the edge of the dugout. His expression was sober, his eyes filled with depth. And understanding.

"It wasn't your fault."

Alex couldn't have heard him correctly. He thought Cap said . . .

"Shut up!" Alex yelled at the Keystones harshly in a voice sharp with warning. "What did you say, Cap?"

The discord in the dugout faded to mumbles.

Captain continued with quiet emphasis. "Lou was leaning into you." He lowered his chin, shuddered, then raised his head—and Alex stared directly into the eyes of Joe McGill. "Just like I did."

Alex stared at Joe; his thoughts spun in a hundred different directions. *Joe knows me. He knows what I did. He has to know who he is. And he's not telling me I ruined his life.*

"I remember," Joe said.

Clamping his lips together, Alex shook his head. He couldn't trust his voice.

"It's okay, Alex." Joe went to him and comforted him with a pat on his arm. "I'm not mad."

Hot moisture in Alex's eyes blurred his vision as he studied Joe's face. "But you should be."

"I can't get mad at things I did to myself. And I don't think you should be mad at yourself."

Joe bent down, picked up Alex's baseball cap and handed it to him.

Alex took it but didn't put the cap on.

"Go out there and play baseball." He turned to go back to the stands, pausing a moment to add, "Go kick some ass . . . busher."

Alex stood there, shaken, knowing he'd cheated Joe—but Joe forgave him anyway. He'd even given him an out. He took the blame himself. The act was selfless, which disquieted Alex. Joe hadn't seized on the moment to take a piece out of him, to make him pay for a life left overturned these past three years.

It had always been Captain who'd needed to be freed, but it was Alex who had been released by the man he'd hurt. The guilt and regret lessened, though lingered at the edges of Alex's mind. He would never fully let go. But Joe had said it was all right to move on.

Lowering his head, Alex made his way back to the batter's box, picked up his bat, and took his batting stance.

The crowd began to chant. Cheers of encouragement rose up to the skies, along with whistles and calls and the sound of clapping hands and stamping feet.

Alex was behind by two strikes. This was it. Everything or nothing.

Cy's tall form made an imposing picture on the mound. The red-gold of a sunset cast its colors over his dingy uniform. He clenched his teeth in resolution as he wound up.

Kick some ass . . . busher.

From the plate, Alex could hear the ball snapping off Cy's fingers as it left his hand and headed like a dart straight for him. Bulking every ounce of strength in his body, Alex hit the ball with a solid smack, driving it over the right fielder's head—over the wall and out of the park.

Home run.

The pennant belonged to the Harmony Keystones.

The hometown crowd went wild as Alex tagged the bases. People rushed out of the stands and onto the grass, disregarding the ropes the Harmony police department had put up to keep fans from interfering with the plays.

A commotion of goodwill ensued, but Alex crept away from it, away from the tight knot of fans and well-wishers, away from those who surrounded him, who touched him. He smiled; with each smile, he backed away from the press of people. As he walked, he searched.

For the woman he loved.

Camille saw Alex, watched him over the shoulders of the many who'd gathered around her to offer compliments and congratulations. Her father had given her a crushing hug, and her mother, a kiss on the cheek. And the players had shouted, "Three cheers for Miss Kennison," and would have hoisted her in the air if she'd let them. But her heart wasn't with the chants. Everything in her was focused on Alex.

She excused herself from those around her and ran after him.

"Alex," she called.

He stopped and inclined his head in her direction. Meeting him, she stood close, searching his face— hoping to find a message from his heart written in his eyes. She saw a sadness that seemed impossible to touch.

The moment stretched taut between them.

She could stand the silence no longer. "Why are you doing this, Alex? I know that you care." A sob broke free from her throat. "But you're going to walk away from me."

Conflict raged in his brown eyes as he took her chin in his fingers. The touch was soft and gentle. "I love you, Camille."

The avowal wrapped her in velvet warmth. They were the words she'd dreamed of hearing these past weeks, but he didn't say them with a promise of happily ever after. "I know where you're going and why you have to go. I don't understand why you aren't coming back. Harmony's your home. If the doctor can make Joe better, you don't have to stay in New York. And if you love me, you should have asked me to go with you. I would . . . I will. I love you, too, Alex."

He brushed his knuckles alongside her jaw before lowering his hand. His handsome features softened with the light that kindled in his eyes. She took small satisfaction that she had affected him; that she could break his resolve a little—if not crumble it altogether. He had difficulty swallowing, keeping his gaze level as he struggled for his next words.

"God, how I love you. But what you don't understand is the reality of a life spent in hospital hallways.

A life of treatments and medication. A life with no guarantee that Captain will get better."

"But Captain *is* better."

"Yeah, he's better. But I still have to take him. To make sure he has every chance to fully recover."

"Alex, I mean it. I'll go with you."

"I can't ask you to sacrifice your dreams."

"Sacrifice? It's not a sacrifice to be with the person you love." She put her fingertips on his lips; her hand trembled. Her eyes filled with tears. "My life is with you."

He took her wrist in his fingers, stilling her caress. "Your life is here, Camille. In Harmony. Where you've achieved what you set out to."

Desolation claimed her as he released her. She lowered her arm and clenched her fists in frustration. Bringing her arms to her sides, she gazed hotly into Alex's face. "You're right. I won. I fought to manage this team. I fought to have my father accept me. I fought to be independent and make my own way."

She couldn't check the tears that ran down her cheeks as she reached out and touched his hair with her fingers. In a whisper, she said, "But I never fought for *you*—the one thing that means more to me than anything else in the world. I want to help you. I want to go with you. You never gave me a chance to answer, because you never asked me. You can't decide for me ... unless you really don't want me ..."

"Want you?" His breath shuddered in his chest as his large hands took her face and cradled it. "Camille, from the first time I saw you with the sunlight spilling over you in that pale dress, I've wanted you. Wanted you so badly I could have turned my back on Captain and forgotten the vow I made to myself to see him out of the hell I put him in. It's been torture of the worst kind, holding you at night, kissing you, making love to you, knowing that it wasn't going to last. That I couldn't have you forever."

She choked. "But you can have me forever."

"I don't ever want you to feel like I cheated you out of what you could have had for yourself, like I did Joe." His voice broke, a strangled cry in his voice as he struggled to keep his composure. "I couldn't stand it. I couldn't."

Her hands slipped up his arms. Through the moisture in her eyes, she gave him an exasperated glare. "You hard-headed man. I have *nothing* if I don't have you."

He looked at her and she knew he was looking deep, looking for the truth in her soul. "I love you, Alex Cordova. And if you don't ask me to go to Buffalo with you, I'll just pack my bags and follow you."

His long, drawn-out silence was sweeter than any words he could have given her. Because his mouth held the most beautiful smile she'd ever seen. It was a smile of love. Of hope. Of promise. Of the future.

He swept her into his arms and lifted her off her feet, swinging her in a full circle. When he set her back on the ground, his mouth sought hers in a deep and wondrous kiss that turned her to fire. Her heart pounded; her skin burned. Everything inside her trembled.

"I'm asking," he said huskily. "Will you come to Buffalo with me, honey?"

"Yes," she said against his lips.

"Then we'll have to do something first."

She broke the kiss to look up into his face. "What?"

"Get married."

❦ Epilogue ❦

"You may be disappointed," Alex said, an easy smile on his lips. With his shirt hanging open and nankeen pants hugging his hips, he set a pair of beer bottles on the dresser in their hotel room. "I've built up the whole idea of drinking beer in the bathtub. It may not have the same appeal for you that it does for me."

"If you're in there naked, then it'll appeal to me," Camille assured him, her gaze roaming over her husband as he shrugged out of his shirt to reveal a muscular chest covered with crisp dark hair. She never tired of looking at his body. The way his arm movements were smooth and full of virility, his biceps well defined. His hands were big and square and tanned; he flipped open the buttons on his fly, then stepped free of his pants and drawers at the same time. She studied his long, sturdy legs that were lean and sinewy with a light dusting of hair. Perfect. He was perfect. She moved her eyes upward and froze on the part of anatomy that was nestled in his groin. Big and full.

He stood before her, devilishly handsome. Completely nude. Completely at ease.

She felt her self-control slipping. He was hers now and she could have him whenever she wanted.

Alex's grin was lopsided, as if he could read her thoughts. "Strip down, honey."

Giving him a smile in return, she began to unbutton her shirtwaist and pull her arms free, letting the silk billow to the floor in a cloud of white. She undressed with deliberate slowness, watching his eyes darken as he followed everything her hands did. Unhooking her skirt, the rose-colored voile glided down and over the taffeta of her petticoat. She worked the fasteners of her corset, then tossed the stiff whalebone on top of her shirtwaist. The batiste shimmy, her pantalets and her shoes followed, as did her stockings, but with a long, slow roll down her thighs, knees, and calves. Then she pulled the pins free from her hair, letting them scatter onto the carpet, not caring where they fell. She shook her hair and the curls tumbled over her shoulders.

He held out his hand for her. "Let's see if you like what I have in mind for you."

"I know I'll like what you have in mind." She grasped his hand.

His broad shoulders disappeared around the corner of the connecting bathroom, but she stopped just shy of the frame.

"The beer," she said. "I'll get the bottles. You warm up the water."

"The water will warm up when you sink your luscious body into it."

In spite of the fact they'd touched each other in every way and had kissed countless times, the comment made her blush.

She turned away, went into the suite, and grabbed

the bottles of beer. Then she glanced at the open suitcases on the four-poster bed. They would be leaving tomorrow to go home. Back to Harmony. Where Alex would move his belongings into her house on Elm Street and she would spend her days in her garden while he worked at the wood shop. And come the spring, she'd manage the Keystones for the new season.

They'd been in Buffalo for a month.

Camille and Alex and Hildegarde and Joe were married in a double ceremony two days after winning the pennant. It had been a small service, with only immediate family and friends in attendance at the Harmony General Assembly Church.

It hadn't surprised Camille or Alex that Joe had asked Hildegarde to marry him. The pair had fallen in love, with a deep devotion for one another. Joe hadn't wanted to leave Harmony without Hildegarde by his side. As his wife.

Mrs. Plunkett wailed so loudly in the church when Hildegarde said "I do," she leaned over in a dead faint against Mr. Plunkett. He'd had to use smelling salts to revive her. Camille's parents sat in the front pew, hands clasped together as they watched her pledge her heart, her love, to Alex Cordova from that day forward. The following morning, the couples had left for New York.

Since they'd been in Buffalo, Joe had seen Dr. Denton daily. Joe had stayed in the hospital as a patient for the first week, then he'd moved into a small apartment along the river with Hildegarde when the doctor said his tests were completed. Alex had insisted on paying the rent.

Each day, Joe resumed more of his memory. Enough so that he'd told Alex to get on with his life, that he'd be all right without him. He had plans to return to Harmony as soon as the doctor told him he could.

The emotional steps the two men had taken to forge a bridge, from what had been the past to what was now, had been uncomplicated. Joe looked at life with the eyes of a man ready to get on living. Alex at long last tucked his memories away and let himself move on.

And Camille was the woman he'd chosen to be with.

The thought brought tingles over her arms. She was more in love with Alex today than she had ever been.

The beer bottles clinking in her hand, she joined her husband in the bathroom.

Alex lounged in a claw-footed enamel bathtub filled to the brim with a flurry of bubbles. His feet were propped up on the edge of the tub. When she quirked her brow at the foaming white suds, he simply said, "For you."

She smiled. "I think more for you." A hint of dubiousness played in her tone. "You're always telling me to put on my lavender perfume." She spied the empty bottle of bath soap. "You used the whole thing."

"Accident."

"Hardly," she said, laughing as she stepped one foot into the warm water.

"Now if you want to discuss something hard—"

She cut him off with a kick of her toe, splashing him in the chest. "You are horrible, Alex."

"And I'm all yours." Sudsy water dripped down his chest in tiny rivers; bubbles caught on his sunbrowned skin.

The warm water eased her muscles as she sank down on the opposite end of the tub as Alex and entwined her legs with his. She settled in and all but purred her contentment as she stared across at her husband. Stretching out her arm, she gave him a beer.

"So now what?" she murmured.

He gave her a disarming grin. "A gentleman always opens a lady's beer bottle."

Camille was certain that wasn't in her deportment book, but she didn't beg to differ.

He took the amber bottle from her, settled an opener on the crown cap, and popped the top. A spurt of fizz shot over the rim. He handed the beer back to her. She lifted it to her mouth and took a sip. The taste was cool and mellow against her tongue.

"Now," he said, sitting taller and reaching over the side of the bathtub, "we read." He gave her a copy of the December *Good Housekeeping* while he picked up a different issue for himself. They set their beers aside.

She took her magazine and opened the pages. Her gaze skimmed over the pictures and words, but she didn't take a good look at them. She looked over at Alex. "You never told me why you read *Good House-keeping*."

"I like to keep a clean house."

She couldn't help bursting out laughing, a spray of bubbles rising over the tub's porcelain rim. "I don't believe you."

"You think because I play baseball I have no other interests?"

"No. I just don't think a man of your masculinity would find recipes for furniture polish interesting." She turned the page of her magazine but kept her eyes on Alex. The water's edge came to his flat nipples.

"I find anything written about making a woman happy interesting." A trail of water soaked the corners of his *Good Housekeeping* as he flipped to the next page. "Even something as simple as the right furniture polish."

Camille wasn't able to keep her thoughts from straying off the pages. She moved her foot a little, skimming her toes along Alex's outer thigh. The crisp hairs on his calf rubbed the side of her arm as he inched his leg inward. She shifted, her toes sliding between his legs; his foot rose slowly to the side of her breast. A shiver worked through her. She snuck a slow peek at him. Either he was engrossed beyond belief, or he was pretending.

She frowned, gazed back at the article on milkweed cream. Then a big *thwack* sounded in the tiny room. Looking over the top of her magazine, she saw Alex had thrown his on the floor. "Something wrong?" she asked, feeling a smile pull the corners of her mouth.

The heat in his stare melted her and made warmth pool between her legs. Alex said, "I'm having a real hard time concentrating on 'How to Arrange an Attractive Table.' "

"But maybe an attractive table would make me happy."

"Honey, I think arranging ourselves on the table would make you happier than a vase of flowers and the right placement of silverware."

As he leaned forward, she tossed her magazine with a plop on the floor. "Alex, you make me happy. No matter where I am."

He moved his face over hers. Slowly, downward, until she closed her eyes and all there was to think about was his mouth on her mouth. And the kiss that was in no hurry at all.

Dear Readers:

I've always been a baseball fan. My warmest regards to Sammy Sosa and Mark McGwire for the 1998 major league season. I haven't had that much excitement as a fan since 1988 when the Los Angeles Dodgers played the Oakland Athletics for the World Series title.

It was October 15, 1988, when Kirk Gibson hobbled to the plate in the bottom of the ninth. The Dodgers needed to get one run to score and win the game. Gibson was a major long shot—he could barely walk because of leg injuries. Oakland's Dennis Eckersley pitched the ball and Gibson hit one of the most dramatic home runs in the history of the game. I watched in stunned amazement as Gibson limped around the bases, touching each bag with raw emotion on his face as the crowd cheered. Gibson's spectacular hit gave the Dodgers a 5–4 victory.

Not since that day have I witnessed such courage and determination in the game of baseball. Then came Mark and Sammy, who went at the home run record with unfailing sportsmanship. You three were my inspiration for Alex Cordova. Thank you, fellows. You bring baseball home to us, your fans.

Now, on to *Honey*.

In 1901, the American League was formed. The eight teams in this novel actually existed, as did the ballparks they played in, right down to the descriptions of the grandstands. The Somersets really had a toolshed in the outfield and would use rakes during the game. The manager and player salaries mentioned in this book are also accurate—amazingly low when compared with the figures of today.

Aside from the Harmony Keystones, the names of players on the other teams and the positions they played are authentic. Their personalities, however, have been fictionalized to suit my story. Joe McGill never played for the New York Giants, nor existed outside of my imagination.

Boomer Hurley, the manager of the Boston Somersets, is fictitious, as are all the other team managers. But his attitude was all too real the year Camille took on the position. Sad to say, she probably wouldn't be given any better reception a hundred years later.

The origin of the term *bullpen* is ever being disputed. Some claim it came about because of the advertising Bull Durham on the outfield fences; the pitchers warmed up in the shadows of those big, bull-shaped signs. Others say no manager wanted his pitchers shooting the bull on the bench so he put them in a kind of pen in the outfield to warm up their arms. The first documented use of *bullpen* came in 1915. I'd prefer to think that Camille Kennison came up with the idea some fourteen years prior.

Cy Young is presented in this novel as a competitive fellow. Between 1890 and 1911, he won 511 games. He's probably the most famous player in baseball. He was a tough pitcher to beat. But it wasn't until seven years after Alex Cordova that the Cyclone pitched the first real perfect game—May 5, 1904, Boston versus Philadelphia. Young shut out Philly 3–0. In other words, not one player advanced off a pitch he threw. He retired them in order. The Cy Young Award was first handed out in 1956 and went to the single best pitcher in the major leagues.

Candy-coated Chiclets were conceived of around the turn of the twentieth century, but they were not officially a product of the American Chicle Company until 1914. Still, I couldn't resist fudging a little.

I'd like to thank Rachel Gibson and Linda Francis

Lee for their critique on this novel. Rachel keeps my heroes manly men and Linda makes sure the plot pieces all fit together.

I'm grateful to Gloria Dale Skinner, who read *Honey* chapter by chapter through e-mail because of my tight schedule. Her insight was invaluable. I went from not knowing the answers to the questions she asked me about plot and characters to knowing more than I ever thought I would about the cast in this book and the reasons they did the things they did.

I thank Katharine O'Moore-Klopf, my copy editor, who always takes time out of her busy schedule to answer my questions on grammar and punctuation. She not only is right on when she rearranges my sentences but is also married to a swell guy named Edward, who, as it happens, is a cabinetmaker. Thank you, Edward, for helping me along with some of my wood shop queries.

Well, what's next? The last in the Brides for All Seasons books will be *Hearts*. For generations, the Valentines have married on Valentine's Day—every Valentine except for Truvy, who doesn't have a prospective groom. Although it's disappointing to think that the tradition will stop with her, there's a part of Truvy that's exhilarated and feeling freed. She travels to Harmony to visit her college friend, Edwina Wolcott. Since Truvy is the tennis and basketball coach at St. Francis, the all-girl school where she teaches, she's not interested in big, brawny athletic types. She has her reasons. But who picks her up at the train station when she arrives in town? Tom Wolcott's friend, Jake Brewster, owner of the local gymnasium called Bruiser's. Clearly these two aren't meant for each other. But tell that to Cupid.

I enjoy hearing from my readers. Drop me a note and be sure to include a self-addressed stamped envelope. And when surfing the web, visit my site at:

http://www.paintedrock.com/authors/holm.htm

Best,

Stef Ann Holm

Stef Ann Holm
P.O. Box 5727
Kent, WA 98064-5727

Return to
a time of romance...

SONNET
BOOKS

Where today's

hottest romance authors

bring you vibrant

and vivid love stories

with a dash of history.

PUBLISHED BY POCKET BOOKS

For generations, the Valentines married on Valentine's Day—every Valentine except for Truvy, who didn't have a beau, much less a prospective groom. With February the fourteenth mere months away, she resigned herself to the fact that Cupid's arrow would be passing her by. Yet again. And while it was disappointing to think that the tradition would stop with her, there was a part of her that was exhilarated and feeling . . . freed.

The train began to slow into the Harmony depot, and Truvy couldn't quell the wild trip of anticipation in her heartbeat. This was the first time she'd been out on her own, completely dependent on herself. She'd always longed for adventure. But in college, it had been Edwina who danced ragtime and smoked cigars. Not Truvy. She'd kept her nose stuck in her books, the aunts' words always in the back of her mind.

"You're the first lady Valentine to go to college, Truvy."

"Yes, the wonderful first. Do make us proud."

So she had. She'd become a teacher. And a sports coach. Not exactly what the aunts had had in mind with their tuition money. But for Truvy, she had found joy on the playing field. Quite by accident she'd discovered she had a talent for tennis.

The train's whistle sounded in a blast of steam. Its brakes screeched.

Truvy looked through the soot-covered window at the platform. She couldn't see Edwina. Or her husband, Tom, whom she'd described in her letters. A dozen or so people milled about, their breath creating misty clouds in the cold air. She scanned the group. Men in heavy collared winter coats and women in fur-lined capes, some with children tagging after them. All of the townsfolk were unrecognizable. The thought of getting off the train and knowing no one terrified her to the core.

What was the matter with her?

This trip to Harmony was the means to get every indelicate thing out of her system. Pink satin petticoats, ice-skating in trousers, sips of brandy, and anything else she could think of that she'd wanted to do—but hadn't. Then she could return to St. Francis and settle in as a dignified spinster who had done what she'd wanted to in life.

She should be rejoicing the opportunity to let her hair down.

Instead, she was filled with doubt and worry. The admission came from a place beyond her normal way of thinking. She had such confidence in the classroom. But the only faces she'd faced, were those of young ladies who hung on her every word.

In daily life, Miss Pond said you must show you're invincible. Hold your head high with courage, to everybody you encounter.

And so Truvy would.

Hold herself high, that is. Quite literally.

She'd bought her first pair of high-heeled shoes.

At an early age, she'd been tall. At twenty-five, she was *very* tall. Self-consciously so. As a result, she lived in Spalding athletic shoes, even when she wore the proper skirts and shirtwaists. The soft leather and flat soles were quite comfortable.

But the stiff leather of the ladies welt button high-tops now tight around her feet, had given her pinkie toes blisters. Which made walking difficult without flinching. The black Vici kid didn't massage her soles like the shoe salesman had proclaimed. Instead, her insteps ached from being elevated by the two-inch high heels.

She hadn't stared a single person in the eye from Denver to Montana. She never realized how many bald men there were beneath doffed hats.

"Harmony!" the porter cried as the train came to a stop.

Truvy stood and winced as her shoes pinched. She gathered her handbag and adjusted the angle of her new hat. A hat which was frivolously delicious. Stacked high with blue taffetine rosettes and two quills on either side of the knobby crown. She'd never worn such a concoction. But neither had she worn such scandalous underwear.

Blushing pink.

Everything.

All satin.

Her corset, chemise, petticoats and pantalets. Embroidered in the most risqué little places with white butterflies and ruby-red roses. As soon as she'd put each piece on, her entire body shivered. Wicked.

Truvy moved into the narrow aisle to exit with the others. Each step she took, she could hear the faint rustle of cool fabric gliding between her legs, skimming over her sheer stockings.

Once at the exit, she went to grasp the railing in the narrow space with its even narrower steps. Before she could, the station porter sprinted forward and lifted his hand to offer assistance. A moment passed before her surprise evaporated; then she laid her gloved fingers in his. She smiled as he aided her in disembarking.

A porter had never tripped over himself to help her.

Had a hat and new dress really made the difference? She thought of the reflection that had greeted her in the Pullman's mirror this morning. She had indeed looked quite unlike herself with her thick brown hair piled in glossy curls, a few dangling here and there; with her smart hat and blue velvet cape to match with its black soutache braided and beaded trim.

Her students wouldn't recognize her stylish apparel. And she had them to thank for the change—but they didn't know it. Last week, she'd overheard them discussing her unfortunate encounter with the school's benefactress. Their conversation regarding her romantic affairs had been spoken with fondness, but their words sparked something deep within Truvy.

"I say he won't mind at all."

"That's right. The athletic director at Ward is sweet on Miss Valentine and he doesn't care a whit that she roller skates in hallways in her bloomers."

"Of course not. I'll bet he likes a woman in trousers."

"And who plays basketball."

"Not to mention, can throw a softball harder than a man."

"But what does it matter?"

"That's right. She doesn't want a husband."

"True. Miss Valentine isn't the marrying type and she's proud of it."

That last part had made her think. From now on, she was going to spend more time on her appearance. Yes, she didn't have a husband, but it wasn't her fault. Nor her desire to be married anyway.

She pictured Coach Moose Thompson from Ward's—the boys school adjacent to St. Francis where she taught. He had big hands and strapping arms. If she didn't see a basketball the entire time she was in Harmony, the happier she'd be. She needed no reminder that every disaster she'd ever had with the opposite sex had revolved around a piece of athletic equipment.

The chill of the afternoon swirled around her while she took several steps on the platform. In spite of the nip to the air, she felt beautiful and dainty for the first time in her life. But the lift to her spirits sank when she realized there was nobody here to greet her.

As the crowd thinned, the more dismayed she became. Until nobody was left on the platform but herself. Steam wafted from the bellow of the train's engine as it readied to depart for the next town. And still, nobody came to collect Truvy.

"Where would you like your trunks, ma'am?" the porter asked. Both of her suitcases were stacked on the end of a handcart he pushed in her direction.

"Oh. Well ... hmm ..." She looked once more at the town across from the depot. Dirty snow banked the boardwalk in places where the sun hadn't melted the shoveled piles. The storefronts were decorated in holly garlands and colorful trimmings for Christmas. A town square was occupied by people who belonged. Who strolled in front of businesses, window gazing and conversing. Smiling.

A man striding toward the station caught her attention. For the simple fact that he was quite tall and broad-shouldered. Extremely so. He stood out heads above the gentlemen he passed. His legs were long and lean, propelling him forward with an effortless pace—but one that was clearly marked with hurry—directly to where she stood.

She swallowed.

This couldn't be Tom Wolcott. Edwina said Tom had light brown hair. And was of sound character; respected in the town. A good businessman. An upstanding citizen.

The goliath descending upon her didn't look like any of those things. Namely, because he was drinking a bottle of beer as he walked.

He crossed the street and she fought the urge to turn away. To get back on the train and go home to Denver. Dread inched up her spine and she just *knew*. Knew this ... *man* ... had been sent to greet her.

Climbing up the depot steps, he drew up to her. "Miss Valentine?"

There was no surprise when he spoke her name. But he didn't sound drunk. To her chagrin, she liked the deep richness of his voice. It was warm and liquor smooth.

"Yes." Tilting her chin way up, she met his eyes. They were the color of frosty green leaves. A silvery-olive. She'd never seen such a shade before. He gave her a slow once-over with those eyes of his, brows raising.

"I was expecting a dowdy teacher," he said at length.

Before she thought better of her reply, she caught herself remarking, "I wasn't expecting a man carrying alcoholic refreshment. On a public street."

He lifted the beer and stared at the amber bottle. "I just ordered this at the Blue Flame Saloon when I checked the time. I knew I was late."

"You could have left it behind."

"Could have." And at that, he took a sip. A crescent of foam stayed on his upper lip; he licked it in such a way, she thought that beer had to taste as good as any soda pop—if not better. The notion intrigued her. Made her curious. Maybe she wouldn't sample brandy first. She'd try a beer.

She studied her escort. His hair, a rich dark brown, was clipped short and neat. He didn't wear sideburns, as was the rage with men. Nor had he shaved today, either. Dark stubble shadowed his chiseled jaw, and somewhat square chin. His shoulders were far too wide; his defined biceps straining in the red plaid flannel sleeves of his shirt. A shirt which wasn't tucked into trousers that molded his hips. How could he be out in the raw elements without a coat?

All those muscles must keep him warm.

As he lowered the bottle, she noticed his hand was wide, the fingernails perfectly trimmed.

"Hey, Bruiser," the porter said with a jovial chuckle. "Bust anybody's chops today?"

Bruiser. Naturally.

"Naw." Bruiser's smile was disarming.

"I've been thinking about entering the Mr. Bulldog contest," the porter remarked matter-of-factly. "You think you could teach me how to knock a guy's lights out?"

"The contest isn't about knocking men out, Lou. It's about being the best in boxing. Fast on the feet. Strong on body definition."

"I've got strength." The porter strained and made a fist.

Truvy was certain she had more strength in her left hand than the puny porter. But she wasn't about to debate the fact.

"If you want to enter, Lou," Bruiser said while taking another drink of beer, "come by the gymnasium and I'll sign you up. I'll put you on the rower and that'll beef up your arms. Have you try some ten pound dumbbells—"

"Mr. Bruiser," Truvy interjected. "Where are Mr. and Mrs. Wolcott?"

He looked at her with a slow skim of his gaze. Her heart skipped. She didn't want to think about how odd it was to have a man have to stare *down* at her, rather than up or on eye level.

"I'm doing Tom a favor. He had to stay with Edwina."

Alarm caught in Truvy's pulse. "She's all right?"

"She wasn't feeling that great today."

"I hope it's nothing serious."

"Are you taking Miss Valentine's trunks then, Bruiser?" the porter asked as he removed the first one from the handcart. It held her personal belongings: clothing, unmentionables, toiletries, a reading book or two, and her Spalding shoes. The second suitcase had . . .

Lou went to pull it by the handle and a whosh of air instantly expelled from his mouth. The case didn't budge. Honestly, she could carry it. The contents inside weren't *that* heavy. She supposed she shouldn't have brought them all the way to Harmony. But she couldn't bear the thought of leaving them behind. They were her pride and joy. Her fait accompli.

"I'll take that," she said, nudging Lou's hand aside.

But before she got within inches of the suitcase's handle, Mr. Bruiser gallantly came to her rescue. She didn't need him to tote her cases. Well, maybe the one. She could definitely manage the other. But as she went for her clothing trunk, her hand was met with the circumference of a beer bottle being shoved into her grasp.

"Hold that for me."

She told herself she should disapprove, but she took a quick sniff while he grabbed the other suitcase and wasn't looking. Gripping both leatherbound handles in his strong hands, he lifted them as if there was nothing but air and flimsy underwear—which there was in the one—packed inside.

Truvy was helpless other than to keep his beer for him when he began to walk down the platform steps. She followed, purse in one hand, Heinrich's Lager Beer in the other. Heat stained her cheeks; but not enough to keep her from squinting into the bottle's mouth to see the liquor inside.

As she walked over the frozen ground, the icy road crunching beneath her new shoes, she politely smiled at a pair of ladies who stood in the doorway of Kennison's Hardware store. They tsked and turned their noses up at her. It took her a moment before she realized what was wrong.

"Oh . . . no." She gave them a dismayed shake of her head. Why was it these things always happened to her?

"Mr. Bruiser," she called, increasing her stride to keep up with him, "I'd rather not be responsible for your beer. People will get the wrong idea about me."

"My name's Jake. Jake Brewster."

"Pardon?"

"Bruiser's just a nickname. My old boxing name. I'm Jake. Just Jake. No mister."

"I'd like for you to take this beer back."

He gave her a shrug and an easy smile, his broad shoulders lifting. "I don't have any free hands. You can take a sip if you want to. I won't tell."

Her mouth dropped open. She glared at him. The big oaf. Insinuating that she, a teacher and woman who carried herself with dignity and bearing, wanted to sample a drink . . . it was beyond appalling. Beyond gross offense.

And so close to the truth, she felt herself blushing to her hairline.

"No thank you."

They walked passed Plunkett's mercantile and the Brook's House Hotel on the corner where Jake turned up the street. Edwina had arranged for her to stay with the Plunketts, the family of one of her former students. The Plunketts' daughter, Hildegarde, had recently married and left a bedroom free in their home. Truvy would have stayed with the Wolcott's but their house was under renovation; an addition for the new baby. Truvy hadn't wanted to impose. Two under a roof where things were out of place was inconvenient. Three would have been too much of an imposition.

"Bruiser!" called a male voice. "Is the poker game on for tonight?"

Truvy turned her head. Across the street was Bruiser's Gymnasium, a fellow in athletic togs standing in the front, jumping up and down in the cold.

"Seven o'clock," Jake said, his deep voice carrying over the road.

"See you there."

Beer. Boxing. Poker.

Jake Brewster was the epitome of manhood defined by his male friends and things deemed "manly." If she were looking for a soul mate, it would never be him. Not in a hundred years. Were she so inclined to seek a beau, she desired a gentleman who won his masculinity with honor.

As they passed a granite-faced office building, she thought she heard a soft click ahead of her.

About where her suitcase was in Jake's hand. But as she looked at it, nothing out of the ordinary happened. Toward the end of the block, yet another shuddering noise—more than a click, then suddenly, the clasp on her one trunk sprang free, and Jake stopped to look at the contents which had scattered onto the boardwalk.

Mortification made her stand still. She might very well have been less embarrassed if the items had been her underwear. Instead, they were her trophies. All of them. Heavy, die cast bronze, silver and gold. Shining and glittering beneath the frosty December sunshine. Some of angels with wings, others replicas of softballs and bats. Several basketballs. A torch and ribbon. Every statuette for outstanding sports achievement she'd ever won for St. Francis or while she'd been enrolled at Gillette's. The trophies signified a lot of hard work and years of practice, and they always graced the top of her dressing bureau.

To her horror, Jake Brewster gave her a sideways glance as if he didn't know what to make of her all of a sudden. She didn't like that. Her attempt at pulling off suave and sophisticated wasn't off to a great start. But she veiled her discomfort, shoved the beer into his free hand—the trunk having landed with a hard *thwack* on the boardwalk—and began to gather the variety of statuettes without a word of explanation.

Let him wonder.

When he bent down on one knee to help, she shot him a glance that said she could do it. But he ignored her and picked up her first place trophy for all around girls' tennis, looked at the inscription, then deposited it back into the trunk. With quiet precision, he examined yet another one of her prizes, and then another, until all of them had been safely stored back in her suitcase, the lock firmly in place. She tested it twice.

Jake ran a hand through his hair, his eyes filled with admiration she didn't want—because with it came discussions of jockeys and all those other ridiculous things men thought impressed sportswomen.

With awe in his tone, he said, "The only athletic sport I mastered was belting a guy."

"You don't say." She couldn't keep the sarcasm from her voice as her eyes swept over his physique. Perfectly formed, honed with sinewy muscle and a face that wasn't at all unpleasing to look at. He was brash and flawed in manners. And yet, her pulse raced as she met his eyes. Her breathing hitched in her throat. She never thought her body would react to a man nicknamed Bruiser. She was wiser than that.

Because Truvy Valentine knew a relationship disaster when she was staring at one.